THE COLLAPSE

SHERIDAN STATION 2

MATTHEW P. GILBERT

aethonbooks.com

SHERIDAN STATION

©2021 MATTHEW P. GILBERT

TARTARUS GATE

SHERIDAN STATION

ZION RISING

IN A SEPARATE LIGHT CONE:
FEUER FREI

Admiral Susan Vanov, a pacer by nature, strode back and forth in front of the *Dresden's* long transteel viewport, hands clasped behind her back, boots ringing on the white plasteel deck beneath her. Her bridge crew sat at quiet attention, awaiting further orders as the battle raged around them, flashes of plasma and torpedo trails lighting the jet-black of space at random intervals.

The planet Zion hung below the *Dresden* like a sapphire on black velvet, a lush but previously unremarkable world. Earth-like but situated in a far-flung corner of the galaxy, Zion had managed thus far to survive the terrible plague that had burned through the rest of the galaxy. Only the Mormons had cared about this world until now.

But today, as one of, if not *the*, last bastions of humanity, Zion mattered to everyone, friend and foe alike. In the skies above a formerly insignificant world, the remains of the Empire—both loyal and infested—savaged each other, hurling lightning and thunder like the gods of old in a savage contest of survival.

Vanov, an orthodox Jew, felt last stands were somewhat her part and parcel, but she had to admit, the Mormon propensity for preparation made this battle slightly more favorable than Masada.

She had always considered the Mormons' beliefs amusing bunk, paranoia even, but their forethought had paid off not just for themselves, but for the Empire and humanity as a whole.

Perhaps, she mused, she was their Captain Moroni reborn. If so, she would fulfil the role to her best ability. She would not convert, but she would at least respect their beliefs, which was more than she had ever done before.

Hopefully their legendary and prolific reproduction would also prove to be a boon once the crisis passed.

If it passed. The Admiral frowned out at the battle before her, a wrathful goddess defending her children, protective, ready to rain fire on her enemies, as if mere will alone might vanquish her foe. It wouldn't, of course, but brute force would, and that she was willing to apply with as much vigor as necessary.

The problem being that brute force was in short supply. She would gladly crush these enemies and see them driven before her, if only she had the firepower! She would have given much for a fleet of battlecruisers, or even a single one, but the last two on record, the *Bismarck* and the *Danzig*, had fallen months ago in the battle they were now calling Armageddon. At least, thank G-d, they had not fallen into the hands of the enemy, or humanity would all be doomed.

The *Dresden*, a medium cruiser, was her strongest sword. Her hodge-podge, scavenged fleet, arrayed as a screen between the enemy and the *Dresden*, ranged from destroyers down to tiny civilian sloops pressed into service, along with at least one literal garbage scow. Few of them were combat effective, but even the least of them could interpose itself between the *Dresden* and harm, buying her precious seconds to maneuver and return fire.

If they lost the *Dresden*, it was all over.

The enemy ships were fewer, but all combatants, their numbers growing as they poured from the bleeding, crimson rent in spacetime. The source of the jumpgate—a civilian yacht named, ironically, the *Arnold*—was certainly living up to its namesake.

Vanov knew it wasn't fair to call them traitors. What could a man do against this enemy once it took hold of him? Nothing. The demonic plague hollowed out his soul and hurled him against his former brethren, a golem without regard for his own survival. When he fell, the Pestilence melted down the broken flesh and forged it into a new horror. She could only mourn the victims even as she brought them peace, and thank G-d the infection hadn't gotten any further inside her lines.

In truth, how far the infection had spread remained to be seen. Someone had failed. Someone had gundecked screening and decon out of sloth or carelessness, or perhaps simple exhaustion. The reason didn't matter. The mistake had killed a lot of people, with still more to die before this battle was done. The guilty would be punished when she knew their names, if they had even survived their failure. Such mistakes more often than not carried their own price. For now, she had more pressing business.

She *should* have already blasted the *Arnold* and any other suspect vessels, but with humanity teetering on the edge, killing civilians was a last resort. There might be survivors, even *children* aboard the yacht. She would destroy it if she must, but for now, she could use the enemy's recklessness to her advantage.

The *Dresden* rocked as several of the Pestilence-controlled ships fired another salvo. Fortunately, they were mostly small escort, with minimal weapons capability. *Dresden's* shields and armor could soak most of the damage, but not all of it. Vanov clenched her jaw as alarms wailed and readouts on the main screen reported damage to several screening ships, as well as to *Dresden's* life support and propulsion systems. This would be a battle of attrition, but she was confident of her fleet's ability to triumph.

"Keep sniping them as they come through," she ordered. "Let

the rest of the fleet handle the stragglers for now. They're vulnerable when they're crossing over. Let's reduce them as much as possible before we close it. We won't get another chance to—"

Lieutenant Smith—a Mormon himself, and her man in charge of fire control—shouted, "Admiral! There's something *big* approaching on the other side!"

"What's IFF say?" she called over her shoulder.

The pause before Smith responded was telling. She turned to see the young men struggling to speak, his face filled with dread. Vanov shouted at him, "Spit it out, man!"

Smith glanced at his instrument panel again as if to verify something he knew she wouldn't believe, then stammered, "It's the *Danzig*, Admiral!"

Vanov was an old officer. She had seen plenty of killing and death and fought at long odds before, but this news sent a finger of dread skittering up her spine. "Impossible! The *Danzig* went down in the Battle of Armageddon! Check again!"

"Checked and rechecked, ma'am," Smith answered. "It's them."

Vanov took a deep breath and nodded. This was it, then. If the *Danzig* had survived it was not in human hands, and it must not be allowed to reach real space. "I want a full broadside on the *Arnold* and anything between!" she shouted. "Railguns, plasma casters, torpedoes, and get some people on decks throwing rocks! All ships, *feuer frei!*"

Lieutenant Smith blanched at her order. "Admiral, it's a civilian ship! Surely—"

Vanov would have preferred not to be questioned, not to need to provide an object lesson as to why it must never be done on a gundeck. Nevertheless, she stopped pacing, drew her sidearm, and leveled it at Smith. The lieutenant trailed off into silence.

"We are at war with an implacable enemy," she told him, her

voice the hard edge of a razor. "Do not question my battle orders again. The next time there will be no warning."

The lieutenant gulped and nodded as his hands flew over the control panel. "Aye, Admiral!"

Vanov holstered her weapon and braced herself against the guard rail as the lighting brightened then dimmed. The high-pitched whine of the railgun magdrivers filled her ears, and the *Dresden* lurched violently. She couldn't see the projectiles in space, but she saw the immediate result as several hundred pounds of depleted uranium slammed into *Arnold*'s hull at near-relativistic speeds. The fragile vessel imploded then burst into a brilliant, orange blossom of light, shrapnel and streamers spinning into the darkness like fireworks. A faction of a second later plasma erupted from the *Dresden*'s main batteries, searing her eyes even through the polarized transteel, battering and burning the smaller enemy ships. A moment after that, she nodded at the familiar sight of torpedo trails snaking their way toward enemy vessels, followed by flashes as they impacted.

Vanov allowed herself a brief, grim smile. The battle still raged about her and the outcome was still far from certain, but she and her crew had just won a major victory, nonetheless. They had stopped an ambush that would have turned the tide and snuffed out humanity's flame in the galaxy forever.

The *Danzig* was not coming through on Susan Vanov's watch.

1

DEAD RINGER

"Don't make this a thing, Bleys, ok?" Kane said.

This was not the first time Josiah Bleys had awoken to the cool kiss of a blaster pressed against his head, but it was indeed the first time it had happened on his own ship. Filled with feigned righteous indignation and bolstered in bravery by his fair certainty that Kane would not actually shoot him, Bleys took his time tipping his broad-brimmed hat up and uncovering his eyes.

At least he was still onboard the *Doro*. Often in cases like this one found himself in a different location than he had been when he was last conscious, so he had that going for him at least.

Ragnar Kane, dressed in full battle rattle, stood over him, M87 blaster rifle in hand. Bleys didn't find the weapon terribly intimidating: Kane hardly needed it to kill him. The powered armor alone was enough. Hell, for that matter, Kane was big enough that he could probably crush a man's skull, or at least a boy's, with his bare hands.

Kane seemed to be wearing an apologetic expression, but it was hard to tell through his visor. Plus, pretty much any look Kane tried to give anyone came off as more of a "I *will* kill you, puny mortal," so his range was somewhat limited, and Bleys was having to interpret subtle signs. The Panzer Armor didn't help with any attempt Kane might or might not have been making to cushion the blow, either. That stuff was, after all, pretty much the last human form a lot of people saw after being told to get on their knees.

"Rags, your wife is thousands of light-years from here," Bleys said with a grin. "I don't even know what she looks like."

"Yes, you do. I showed you a picture one time."

Bleys rubbed at his two-day stubble and snickered. "Oh, yeah, that's right. She *was* quite the looker."

"Don't talk about my wife, Bleys. I will fuck you up for that."

Bleys raised both hands and struck his best "I ain't done nothing wrong" pose, which was unusually simple because in this particular case, as far as Bleys knew, he *hadn't* done anything wrong.

Not lately, anyway.

"You're right, man. She's absolutely hideous," he snickered.

Kane's already dark face grew even darker. "Oh, you did *not* say what I thought you said!"

"Easy, bro! The man with the gun is always right. You tell me what you want me to say, I'll say it. Deal?"

Ed, still "naked" with his blue, painted-on doll underwear, seemed to appear out of nowhere as he stepped from behind Kane's bulk, his face serene as usual. "You must forgive us, Captain Bleys, but the circumstances dictate this course of action. No personal affront is intended."

Bleys eyed Ed for a moment, trying to decide what his game was, but the AI was hard to read. He looked human as long as he had clothes on, but his expressions always seemed a little off, not quite matching his inner mood. Bleys found himself wondering briefly if Ed being in the robot body technically made him an android but dismissed the thought. Now really wasn't the time to be contemplating semantics. He was being held at gunpoint by his best friend and…well, Bleys wasn't exactly sure about his relationship with Ed yet, but he hadn't counted the AI as an enemy.

Not lately, anyway.

Ed took a seat on the control console in front of Bleys, symbolically claiming the *Doro*. Bleys noted to his dismay a fist-sized dent in the console right next to the android, and made a note to himself to find out who had put it there just as soon as he was clear of this mess.

Kane reached out a gauntleted mitt. "Hand over that holdout pistol, Bleys," Kane told him. "Nice and easy. Just hear us out."

Slowly, Bleys removed one of his two holdout pistols and gently offered it to Kane. The big marine took the weapon and tucked it into his belt.

Bleys leaned back in his captain's chair, laced his fingers behind his head, and put his feet up next to Ed. "I already heard a little bit," he told Kane, casually, as if commenting on the lack of weather in space. "Ana said you flipped your lid."

Kane grunted. "It's a little more serious than that."

Ed gave Bleys a grave nod. "Indeed. The fact is, the ship is infected, and we have no way of knowing who is or is not compromised."

Bleys raised an eyebrow as if contemplating this, though in fact it had already occurred to him that this was a possibility. Knowing their reasoning, it was kind of difficult for him to feel too hard at Kane and Ed for commandeering his ship at gunpoint, but he would definitely find a way. As the various "How dare they!" and "I'll kill them for this!" thoughts rattled around inside his head, it occurred to him that this was probably how other men felt when he slept with their wives.

That line of thinking was uncomfortable and best left to amateurs. When it came right down to it, this was business, not personal. What mattered was avoiding being shot, best friend or no.

"Okay, guys, that's not a bad reason. What say you lay it out for ol' Josey here and we come up with a plan that doesn't involve blasting me?"

Kane grinned behind his visor. "That's the spirit, man!"

Ed, looking contemplative, observed Bleys a moment as if examining an interesting lab specimen, then nodded. "We know for certain that Caldwell is dead and Iezzi is infected. Surely he has passed that infection on to others, perhaps even you. You see our position, yes?"

Bleys scowled at his captors a moment. "And what makes you so sure Rags ain't turned? They don't even know they're infected until that shit busts out of them."

Ed nodded sagely. "I concede I have no hard proof, as we have no detectors, and Ana cannot be trusted to manufacture them. However, I find circumstantial evidence compelling. In his armor, Chief Kane is more than capable of overpowering the both of us and doing whatever he likes. I presume, based on his choice not to do so, that he is uninfected and will remain so due to his armor being sealed."

Bleys looked back and forth at the two of them a moment, considering. "Well, the first thing we ought to do is lock the ship down, agreed?"

"That's what we're here for," Kane said. "Do it."

Bleys sat up, waved his hands in a flourish, and tapped at his control console. Immediately the lighting changed to yellow, and the *Doro's* sexy voice announced, "Lockdown initiated from bridge."

Bleys continued working his controls, bringing up cameras throughout the ship and overlaying their output on the main transteel viewing screen at the front of the cockpit. "Ok, let's see who's jumpy now."

Kane shook his head. "Everybody is gonna be jumpy when the ship is suddenly locked down, Bleys."

Bleys flashed him a knowing grin. "You ever play poker with me?"

"I am not that damned stupid."

Bleys pointed both index fingers at Kane like guns. "And that's just my point, Rags. Observe."

Bleys flipped through his security cam displays as Kane, dubious, watched. Ed, his expression blank, said nothing, merely waited patiently.

"Now, see?" Bleys said, pointing at the display of the upper aft storage compartment. Iezzi, sullen, was rooting through the Marines' equipment without enthusiasm. "Don't you think he ought to be a little *more* concerned?"

Kane nodded slowly, a grim smile on his lips. "He's not surprised. Almost like he was expecting it sooner or later."

Bleys flipped through the rest of the cameras. In the aft crew's quarters, Zimmerman and Martin were both stirring in their racks. "Okay, these guys just woke up, so nothing much to learn there."

He switched the display to lower aft storage. Morgan was looking about, alert, his face pinched with concern. "I'd guess he's ok."

Anderson, now trapped belowdecks in the galley, was hard to read, just sitting at a table and staring off into space. "He seems a little odd too."

Bleys switched to the port cargo container view, just to be thorough, to see that it was unoccupied, a no brainer since it had no life support, but honestly, who knew with these freaks? Maybe they could live without it. Out of habit, Bleys flipped to the starboard container camera next, but it showed only a black screen because it was *gone*. Bleys scowled at Kane. "I still owe you for that, Rags. That container cost more than your armor!"

Kane turned his head to boggle at Bleys. "You'd rather be dead? Because that was the alternative."

Ed shrugged. "I wouldn't have killed any of you if you hadn't invaded my planet," he said in a sour tone. "Or if you had just surrendered."

Bleys, still glaring at Kane, pointed at Ed. "See? Not necessary. You should have surrendered, Rags."

Kane rolled his eyes and heaved a great, put-upon sigh. "Can we get back to searching for the killer aliens, or are you gonna talk smack until they get us, too?"

Bleys snickered and started to go back to work when he noticed *another* dent in the console of similar size and shape. "Oh, *shit!*" he complained. "That's *two!*" He glared at Kane. "Really, man?"

Kane raised a single palm as if taking an oath. "Not me, brother. I swear."

Bleys eyed him briefly, then declared, "But you know who did it."

Kane kept his hand raised. "I swear to you, I did not see anything happen."

Ed tapped on the back of Bleys's seat. "Let us not forget our primary mission."

Bleys gave him a scowl too for good measure, then switched the display to Ana's makeshift medbay. Bleys pointed to the screen. "See how she keeps going to the door and then changing her mind? Human."

"Or just doesn't know it yet," Kane spat. "None of this proves anything."

"I'm afraid he's quite correct," Ed agreed.

"Oh, ye of little faith," Bleys quipped as he slid open a small, almost invisible panel on the command console. Beneath lay a single, red button.

"Self-destruct is not gonna help us here," Kane groused.

"Self-destruct?" Bleys yelped. "Man, what the fuck is wrong with you mil types? Why would I ever want to blow up my own damned ship?"

"Oh, I dunno, maybe to get rid of illegal cargo when you jam in your escape pod?" Kane sneered. "We went over the ship pretty thoroughly, man. We found the pod. I'm just assuming the rest. Clearly you managed to slip quite a bit past us."

Bleys shrugged, conceding the point. "Okay, fine, there might be such a device onboard, but that's not what *this* button does."

Kane said nothing, apparently unwilling to play the game any further. Bleys waited several tense moments and grinned when Ed took the bait.

"What does it do?" the AI asked.

"I'm glad you asked!" Bleys said. "He did a brief flourish with his left hand to misdirect them. "It does *this!*" he said as he jammed his right index finger on the button to shouts of dismay from Kane and Ed.

Kane's visor was beginning to steam up, and Ed was sitting stock still, almost like a doll.

"Oh, for fuck's sake, lighten up, you two!" Bleys said with a laugh. He pointed at the video feeds on the viewscreen. "Watch and learn."

Watch they did as each of the people on the cameras slowly crumpled to the deck. Bleys folded his arms across his chest and gave them a smug grin.

"Brilliant," Kane growled. "I could have done that on my own."

"Oh, stop it!" Bleys said. "They're not *dead*. They're just *sleeping*."

Ed raised an eyebrow. "You have a security system to disable the passengers?"

"Standard in this model," Bleys snickered as he gestured around him at the ship.

Kane eyed the motionless figures on the screens. "How does this help?"

Bleys shrugged, feeling a little disappointed. "Well, I was

thinking maybe the Pestilence wouldn't get knocked out, and we'd know who was who. But, hey, this works too, right? We'll keep everybody quiet until we hit Cerberus, and then it's Weyland's problem."

Kane shook his head vigorously. "Weyland isn't even a little squeamish about having any suspects shot out of hand. How long can we keep them out?"

Bleys considered a moment. "I'd guess until just after we touch down on Cerberus, so we have a day or so to think about it. No more."

Kane groaned and sat down in the co-pilot's chair. The swivel-mounted seat groaned under his weight but held for the moment. "Well, at least we have only one person to keep track of until then."

Bleys sat in silence for a moment, then brightened. "Okay, then, we got some time to kill. I spy with my little eye—"

"I will punch you, Bleys," Kane asserted.

Bleys lowered his hat over his eyes and settled back in his seat. "Suit yourself."

Ed shifted in the silence and said softly, "This journey is certainly going to be enlightening."

2

OUTBREAK

By the time he was ready to negotiate a landing, Bleys's back teeth were floating, but he intended to hold it until he exploded if need be. He had suffered the indignity of Kane's company on his last several head trips, and neither of them were likely to ever fully recover from the experience.

Cerberus loomed ahead, a white and blue ball of ice, offering not the least hint of welcome, nor had it ever. Still, it had its charms, not the least of which would be detectors for the Pestilence.

They had sent a brief to Weyland on the trip in, informing him of pertinent details, specifically that they had what they needed, and even a bonus with Ana, but they had lost most of Kane's team, and they had suspected hostiles onboard.

"Sheridan station, this is *Doro* on approach from Elysium with requested cargo," Bleys called over his comms system, using his best Pilot Voice. "Please inform the Admiral we will be on the ground in a half hour and that we're expecting champagne and caviar in the wardroom."

"Negative, *Doro*," came the reply. "You are to continue to

your landing area and stay within your ship until a team can meet you and scan for infections. Follow the nav beacon."

"Will do. *Doro* out."

Kane, still hunched over in the co-pilot's chair, shook his head. "Something's up."

Bleys shrugged. "Not much we can do about it. Hopefully it won't take long."

"This is the Imperial Navy, Bleys," Kane assured him. "It always takes long."

Bleys had no doubt that Kane knew what he was talking about, but that did nothing to dissuade him from getting the *Doro* onto the planet's surface as quickly as he could. The grab bag of humans and Pestilence-infected monsters were still snoring away, but he was out of sleepy-time juice, and they would be coming around soon. Bleys wanted to get the problem children tagged and bagged before they woke up.

And then there was the fact that he was still somewhat irked with Kane, even understanding the Marine's position. Commandeering the ship was not Kane's only recent sin.

Bleys was fairly certain that nothing he did would actually make Kane throw up, but that didn't stop him from trying.

Cerberus loomed as the *Doro* hit the atmosphere, filling the viewport even as the transteel polarized against the brilliant glow of superheated gasses. Bleys worked a combination of air-drag and engines to drop his speed far faster and rougher than was comfortable for people not equipped with piloting implants, essentially allowing *Doro* to drop like a stone repeatedly for several minutes.

Ed raised an eyebrow at Bleys's piloting but said nothing, just held on with both hands and his creepy prehensile feet. Kane groaned and gripped the armrests of the copilot's chair hard enough to leave fingermarks, but sadly he did not suddenly fill his helmet with chunks.

Hey, you win some, you lose some.

"This is a little harder when the load is unbalanced," Bleys said by way of excuse. "Like, say, when one of the cargo containers is missing."

Kane rasped through clenched teeth, "I'm never gonna hear the end of that, am I?"

Bleys got on the horn again once he reached a safe speed. "Sheridan Station, *Doro*, on approach requesting permission to land."

"*Doro*, Sheridan Station, we are tracking you. You are cleared to land at Red Echo Eleven."

"Aw, man, green is my favorite color!"

"We don't make the rules, Captain Bleys, we just shoot you down if you don't follow them."

Bleys laughed loudly. "Roger that, Sheridan! Red Echo Eleven, aye."

Kane groaned again. "I am gonna kill you, Bleys."

"Might want to let me get the little lady on the ground first, Rags."

"Fine. After we land and I get back from the head, I'll kill you."

Bleys poked at his console to put *Doro* into landing mode and told her to follow the guide beacon to her pad, then unbuckled, stood, and stretched. "Tell you what, I'll meet you there."

Ed, looking slightly confused, looked back and forth between the other two. "This is good natured ribbing and threats, correct? You don't actually intend a lethal fight?"

"Pistols at ten paces," Bleys said with a grin.

"Like there's ten paces space in the head," Kane scoffed.

Ed shook his head, a slight smile on his lips. "I'm learning enough not to believe that." He clapped Bleys on the shoulder and added, "I do hope you pass the test. It would be a shame to have to kill you now that I have begun to actually like you a bit."

Bleys gave Ed the six-guns salute and laughed. "That's the spirit, man! You're getting it!"

Ed regarded Bleys with an innocent expression. "That was a serious comment, Captain Bleys."

Bleys again tried to read something in Ed's expression, but the AI had a killer poker face. Bleys could not quite tell if Ed was serious or if he had just doubled down on the smack talk. It was easy to take the whole "who, me? I'm totally clueless!" thing at face value, but the truth of the matter was that Ed was a sentient computer program who could run intellectual circles around all of them. Ed might play dumb and downplay the capabilities of the processor in the body he was wearing, but underestimating him was a mistake in pretty much any circumstance.

Before Bleys could respond, a familiar voice barked from the comm system, "Bleys? Is Kane with you?"

"I'm here, Admiral," Kane called.

"That's Weyland," Bleys explained to Ed. "The bigwig you told to fuck off. Probably best to keep a low profile for a bit until we massage him some, ok?"

Weyland's craggy features popped up on a view screen window, scowling. "My people are running behind on the detector. I can't let you in until we have them up and running, so just relax and we'll sort it out shortly."

Bleys put a palm over his face as Kane answered, "Sir? We have a situation here. How long are we looking at?"

"Twenty-four to forty-eight hours."

Bleys snorted. "Elysium had their shit done and in production in less than twenty-four from the start! Your techs suck."

Ed nodded in silent agreement as Kane glared at Bleys and mouthed, "Shut the fuck up!"

"That's great!" Weyland answered, the sarcasm in his voice making it clear that it was anything but. "How about you haul your ass back there if things are so good? Because here on

Cerberus it's still another twenty-four to forty-eight hours! Dismissed." Weyland cut the connection.

Kane clenched and unclenched his fists, still glaring at Bleys. "Good job, dumbass."

"What? Like if we had been nicer to him, he was going to let us in?"

Kane nodded. "Yeah, true. Any ideas on how to get out of this spot, though? Assuming you're not one of them?"

Bleys scratched at his chin a moment, then moved back to his console and began flipping through his security cameras again. The rest of the passengers were stirring, but no one was on their feet yet.

Bleys turned on his intercom and said, "Ladies and gents, this is your Captain. We hope you enjoyed your flight. It's been extra restful due to an unforeseen equipment failure, courtesy of Chief Kane."

Kane threw up both hands in objection, a gesture Bleys found hilarious given that Kane couldn't actually contradict him on the matter.

Bleys continued, "Looks like blowing the cargo pod back on Elysium shorted my security system, so we've all had a nice nap. Fortunately, Ed was able to land us on Cerberus. The ship is on lockdown until I can figure out how to get the system to disengage, but once I do we'll be debarking, right after the Imps test us for Pestilence. Captain out."

Kane waited until Bleys cut the connection before shouting, "Are you an *idiot*? Why would you tell them about the test? They'll have to get it on now!"

Bleys gave him a tired look. "Watch and learn, linear thinker." He worked his control panel and said, "We need to be able to move around, so I'm releasing the interior lockdown, but we don't need to announce it. The exterior lockdown is still on, so we should be able to keep things contained."

Kane gave Bleys a dubious look. "Are you *sure* you know what you're doing?"

"Yeah," Bleys answered. He switched the internal monitor to show the galley again. Anderson was still sitting there, seeming a bit groggy. "We start with him."

The Anderson watched warily as The Food known as Bleys entered. The Anderson found this especially surprising because the compartment door had been locked when it had woken and disconcerting because The Anderson was, under direction of The Iezzi, waiting for The Right Time.

But it was very difficult to wait when One was hungry and Food was close.

The Anderson was not entirely certain why it had slept. Food Bleys claimed it was because of a malfunction, but The Food could not be trusted. It did not even understand its own purpose.

"Listen up, Anderson," said Food Bleys. "The humans know we're here! We gotta gather up everybody on our side of this thing and get to The Source."

The Anderson winced internally at painful cognitive dissonance. The Bleys was *Food*, was it not? Why did it speak as if it were part of the Colony?

The Bleys snapped its fingers beneath The Anderson's nose and continued speaking in sounds, "Come on, pal, don't you want to see The Source? We have to hurry! The humans are coming!"

The Anderson did very much want to meet The Source, but it was not at all fond of sound speech. It was Food talk, not song. Still, The Source! It was worth enduring discomfort. "Why do you not sing?" it asked. "Why do you talk Food talk?"

The Bleys seemed very excited, perhaps even angry, as it spoke again with sounds. "They can hear us sing! They're listening in, and they know about Iezzi! Now go round up everybody else so we can escape and go to The Source!"

The Anderson trembled deep within its soul and closed all connections it had with The Colony. The Song was now a risk. If the Iezzi were discovered and destroyed, it would mean a terrible loss of knowledge! The Iezzi carried everything the Colony on the Planet had learned. In theory, The Anderson would too at some point, but the transfer took time, and The Anderson was still very young.

The Anderson glanced about to verify it was alone with The Bleys, then whispered, "We must find The Iezzi and The Martin! The Martin is still assimilating, but The Iezzi is wise. We must protect The Iezzi."

For a moment The Anderson hesitated, both thrilled at the notion but filled with a sense of unworthiness. "What must be done to reach The Source?" it stammered in reverent joy.

"Oh, that's dead easy," said The Bleys. "I'll send you right to him."

On the bridge, Kane watched as Bleys reached into his duster, produced a weapon, and fired point blank. Anderson went up like a torch and collapsed, pieces of carbonized flesh scattering across the galley deck as his body lost cohesion and practically disintegrated.

"Oh, *fuck!*" Kane shouted, and leapt to his feet. "*That* was your 'plan', Bleys?" The fact that Bleys had yet another weapon, and an illegal disintegrator at that, howled in the back of his mind for recognition, but Kane had other priorities.

Ed, working the cameras, raised a cautioning hand. "It may have been effective. Look."

Ed pointed to the various camera displays on the main screen.

On two Kane could see Morgan and Ana react to the sound of weapons fire, but on the other two things were considerably less calm.

In upper aft storage, Iezzi suddenly stood bolt upright and convulsed. For a moment it seemed as if his skin were going to crawl right off him, but he quickly regained control and began donning his Panzer Suit.

In the aft crew's quarters Martin too leapt to his feet and convulsed briefly. Zimmerman, seeing this, called out to him, "Hey, Martin, you ok?"

But Martin was most definitely *not* ok. Tentacles sprouted from his back, thick, ropy appendages dotted with razor sharp studs of bone. His face distended into something like a fang-filled beak and his arms lengthened to match his legs as he bent at the waist, becoming a quadruped.

The creature that had been Martin let out a bestial roar as Zimmerman rolled from his rack and grabbed for his sidearm with his one good arm. He fired a shot at the creature that had been Martin, but his aim with his off hand was poor. He struck the creature a grazing shot that sent it fleeing out of the compartment toward the main airlock in rear storage.

"I'm on it!" Kane shouted to Ed and charged toward the cockpit door. "Don't let *anybody* in here until we secure this situation!"

Kane pounded the hatch control for the cockpit door then charged through, not bothering to verify if Ed was complying or had even heard him.

He had to stop Iezzi and Martin *now*.

In the passageway beyond he nearly collided with Ana. One look in her wild, blue eyes was enough to know she wasn't going to sit this one out, so he didn't bother trying to sideline her and settled for just clambering around her without losing too much momentum.

"Kane!" she shouted. "Goddammit, what the hell is going on?"

Zimmerman staggered from the aft crew's quarters into the connecting passageway. "It came this way, Chief, but I don't know where it went!"

"I'm on Iezzi!" Kane shouted as he pushed past Zimmerman in the narrow passage. "Handle it!"

Ana watched helplessly as Kane squeezed his bulk through the hatch into the crew's quarters and found herself face to face with a stark-naked, one-armed, wild-eyed Zimmerman.

"Did you see him?" Zimmerman gasped.

"See who?" she shouted. "What the hell is going on?"

Zimmerman crouched against the bulkhead and gestured for her to do likewise, keeping his weapon aimed at the entrance to the head. "He came this way," he muttered. "He's got to be in there."

"Who?" Ana hissed as she joined him in a crouch, trying to make herself as small a target as possible. Cautiously, she reached within her lab coat and drew her own sidearm. After her encounter with Kane earlier in the medbay, it had seemed prudent to carry. At the time she had been worried about Kane, but now it seemed he had been the only sensible one onboard.

Zimmerman shook his head slightly as his only response. He said nothing for long, tense moments, just continued aiming and peering into the head, sweat trickling down his cheek, a look of intense concentration on his face.

From the storage compartment Ana heard Kane shout something and the sounds of struggle. As she rose to help, Zimmerman stiffened and put out an arm to block her.

"There!" he shouted, eyes widening. He raised his weapon

and snapped off a shot. Inside the head something not even remotely human screamed in pain.

Close to hyperventilating, Ana finally caught sight of it and tried to line up a shot, but the creature was much faster than its bulk would suggest. It roared again as it surged forward, furious. Ana could feel the creature's hot, fetid breath like a summer breeze as it charged her, a mass of writhing limbs, claws, and teeth.

"Gunther!" Kane shouted as he entered the storage compartment. "Track Iezzi's Panzer suit!"

"Petty Officer Iezzi is in the upper aft storage compartment," Gunther replied. A map of the ship sprang to life on Kane's visor along with a helpful yellow dot.

Kane quickly scanned the area to correlate his map to his surroundings. The area wasn't as large as the cargo holds along *Doro's* sides but big enough to hold all of the gear Kane's team had brought, along with a number of other, unidentifiable crates and boxes stacked along the bulkheads and strapped to the deck. Iezzi, it seemed, was hiding behind a stack of cargo near the airlock.

Ahead, the main airlock was closed. Kane breathed a sigh of relief to see the flashing red light on the control panel. As Bleys had promised, it was still locked down, which meant there was still an opportunity to contain this situation.

Painfully aware of how exposed he was, Kane ducked behind a stack of crates to think a moment. His first impulse was to taunt his adversary, try to get into his head and make him angry, push him to make a mistake. He had no idea if that could even work with the Pestilence, but he decided to give it a try.

"Bleys fried your buddy good back there, huh?" he called.

The response was nothing human, even though the language was Standard Imperial. The sound was more like the grating of bricks against one another—a low, rumbling, wet sound. "We would prize your flesh, warrior. But we do not *need* it."

The next sound was all too familiar: the metal on metal clink of a grenade bouncing across a plasteel deck.

———

Ana staggered backwards, losing her footing as the creature charged. She hit the deck hard, losing her grip on her weapon in the process. The small blaster bounced on impact and spun across the deck, ending up just inside the entry to the head, well out of reach.

A bright flash of plasma momentarily dazzled her as Zimmerman took another shot at the thing. It lashed out at him, striking him hard in the chest with a club-like appendage. Zimmerman slumped to the deck, unmoving.

Ana scrambled backwards as far as she could, but the bulkhead stopped her flight. The beast loomed over her, drool streaming from a ragged, toothy maw. The moment seemed to stretch on forever, Ana cringing beneath its misshapen bulk, the scent of cinnamon and cloves filling her nose—cloying, almost overpowering, but not at all unpleasant.

Understanding hit her suddenly. The creature wasn't attacking. It thought she was an ally!

Tentatively, fully aware that what she was doing might be considered madness by some, she reached upward and let her fingers brush against its mottled flesh. The beast rumbled softly, a contented sound, almost a purr.

Ana thrilled at the sound, as she did when confirming any other scientific theory. Curiosity was both a boon and a curse. It had, after all, killed the cat, but it had also resurrected Anastasia Rasputin.

And now, it might hold the key to saving all of humanity.

A blue blur from her left interrupted her reverie. Ed, hurtling like a rocket, slammed into the creature with enough force to stagger it and hammered it with blows.

Ed's synthskin frame was, Ana knew, tremendously strong. She could see flesh burst and hear bone crack every time his fists and feet impacted the creature, but it had little effect on the amorphous mass of tissue. The flesh simply flowed and rejoined.

The beast roared and rippled, sprouting more limbs, like a spider's legs, but thicker, ropy with muscle. It wrapped itself around Ed's frame, pinning his arms to his sides, and began to squeeze. More limbs sprang from its surface, sharp, bony spikes that pierced Ed's frame. Viscous, white fluid leaked from deep rents in Ed's torso.

Ana could hear the mechanisms within Ed's robotic body whining in protest as he struggled to escape. The beast roared again and redoubled its efforts to crush the life from him as Ed struggled to face her.

A tremendous explosion from aft storage sent a shockwave down the corridor.

"Run!" he cried.

Kane managed to avoid most of the blast behind the crates, but it was still enough to stagger him. By the time he recovered his wits, Iezzi was at the airlock door.

Kane ducked back behind cover as Iezzi snapped off a shot with his pistol. Plasma scored the bulkhead but did him no harm. Kane breathed a sigh of relief to see Iezzi had apparently forgotten his rifle.

Kane, however, had not.

"Gunther, what's he doing?"

"Sonar image suggests he is applying plastique to the airlock door."

"Shit!"

The explosion was loud, but the shock of the shaped charge barely registered compared to the recent grenade. Kane peeked around the crates again, Gunther doing what he could to enhance his vision through the smoke and haze.

Iezzi was already climbing through the gaping hole in the airlock door!

"Gunther, Eight balls!"

"Eight balls active, sir."

There was no time to line up a precise shot, but Kane managed to land a solid torso hit and another to Iezzi's left arm. The following two explosions, one after the other, blasted pureed flesh from a gaping rent in the armor's belly with a sick, squelching sound and sent Iezzi's arm flying across the compartment, where it landed with a clatter.

None of this, however, seemed enough to stop Iezzi from legging it. The shattered, man-shaped creature, still trailing blood and shrapnel from the Panzer suit, slipped through the hole and out of Kane's line of sight.

"*Fuck!*" Kane shouted, and leapt to his feet. He charged to the still smoking airlock door and looked out. The icy tarmac had a short blood trail, but there was no sign of Iezzi. Fortunately, Gunther was still tracking the armor. The helpful little yellow dot still showed Iezzi moving at a rapid clip away from the landing zone and into the frozen waste beyond.

Kane stuck a leg through, intent on following, then groaned as he heard Ana screaming. Letting Iezzi escape was bad, but losing Ana would be much worse. Kane double checked Iezzi's course, verifying that he was heading away from people, not toward them. There would be time to hunt him down and finish the job once everything was settled here.

"Gunther, keep tabs on him while I secure the ship."

"Monitoring Petty Officer Iezzi's Panzer suit location."

Ana screamed again, and Kane reluctantly turned from the airlock and double timed it in her direction.

In the galley, Bleys cringed at the sound of gunfire and shook a fist at the overhead. "What are you guys doing to my damned ship?" he shouted, not expecting an answer.

He was, then, doubly surprised when he got one. Morgan called from behind him, "Easy, Cap. Turn around *real* slow."

Bleys did just that, not at all surprised to see Morgan had a rifle trained on him. "It's not what it looks like, kid."

"Maybe it is, and maybe it ain't. How about you put that pistol down and we talk about it?"

Bleys weighed his odds and found them wanting. Morgan might be a tech, but the old saw of "every marine is first and foremost a rifleman" had a lot of truth to it. And certainly, Morgan had the drop on him. A rifle versus a pistol was never good odds, especially when the guy with the rifle had already drawn a bead on you.

Bleys slowly lowered his pistol to a nearby table.

"Keep them hands where I can see 'em," Morgan told him. "You got a habit of having more guns, I notice."

Bleys snickered. "Kane didn't find that one."

Morgan gave him a dubious look. "So you're cross with Kane, too?"

"It's precautions. Looks like we didn't get away clean from Elysium. Your boy Iezzi is infected. We don't know who else is."

Morgan's eyes narrowed as he digested this. "I never liked

Anderson much, anyway, but still, this looks bad. Why'd you fry him?"

Bleys shrugged. "He was one of 'em."

Morgan looked doubtful. "How do you know?"

"Believe it or not, he told me."

Morgan grunted. "No shit? Was he really that dumb, or you just think I am?"

Bleys shrugged. "They're all dumb as hell when they start out, near as I can tell. Which is good for us."

Morgan opened his mouth to speak again when an explosion shook the entire ship.

Bleys gestured with his head. "That'd be Kane and Iezzi, pretty sure. We should go help."

"We should," Morgan agreed. "You first. Up the ladder."

"I need my pistol!" Bleys groused.

"The way I see it, if I was one of those things, I'd have greased you right here and now, so you got reason to trust me. You, on the other hand, I got no clue."

"Well, if I *was* one, what difference would it make if I had my pistol?"

Morgan thought on this a moment. "Shit, I think I *would* rather get shot then chewed, if it came down to it. Ok, get it, but you're going first! And I got my eye on you!"

Kane ducked through the storage locker hatch at a jog, nearly tripping over Zimmerman's naked body, but he could spare no time to see if his man were dead or merely unconscious. Ahead, Ed was locked in a warm embrace with yet another twisted, fleshy beast as Ana, screaming, waved a pistol about, looking for a clean shot.

Kane charged forward and slipped briefly in a white, milky

substance that was still seeping from Ed's wounds. The AI's left arm had been completely torn from his frame, revealing his innards which were, to Kane's great surprise, mostly liquid and plastic.

"I told you to run!" Ed groaned.

"I'm not leaving you!" Ana shouted, but she continued to circle, not firing.

Kane saw her problem as he raised his own weapon out of instinct: Ed and the creature were intertwined too closely. He couldn't find a clear shot anywhere.

"Do something!" she cried. "It's killing him!"

Kane took another moment to make sure he fully appreciated the problem then slung his rifle and went hands on himself, taking hold of the top of the creature's maw with one gauntleted hand and the bottom with the other.

The creature roared as Kane grabbed it and tried to shake him off, but it simply lacked the mass or leverage.

"Gunther, full strength on the armor, disengage all safeties. Do it now."

The Panzer suit was truly a remarkable piece of technology. Its neural interface damped or even completely overrode most of the pilot's bodily sensations. It edited sensory data including pain, essentially shunting everything over to the armor's sensors, such that the pilot, even one missing the entire bottom of his leg, felt as if he actually *were* the suit itself. As part of that illusion, it actually simulated muscle strain.

The idea behind that was to allow an operator to judge how much strength he was applying, mostly to prevent accidentally punching holes in walls, crushing delicate equipment, and doing exactly what Kane intended.

"Safeties off," Gunther replied.

Kane heard the servos in his armor hum at a higher tone but felt none of the usual resistance as he applied pressure. The result was immediate and impressive. The beast screamed as its head slowly separated with a coarse ripping sound, spraying blood over Ed's pained face.

Kane hurled the top of the thing's head across the room, where it fell to the deck and immediately sprouted legs.

"Fuck!" Kane shouted.

"I'm on it!" Ana shouted back. She dutifully blasted the chunk, sending it scurrying down the ladder toward the galley where someone coming up screamed.

Kane had no time to follow-up on it. Ana and whoever was coming up the ladder were on their own. He grabbed the creature by the jaw and shoulder and again ripped.

By now he had its attention. The monster released Ed to focus its attention on Kane. Suddenly free, Ed collapsed in a heap, his gaze distant and unfocused, still streaming the milky fluid from his mouth, arm stump, and the numerous new holes in his body.

"Now, you see, you fucked up there," Kane chuckled. He grabbed the creature by both arms—his armor turning the beast's bony blades aside easily—and hurled it against the bulkhead. Before it could recover he brought his rifle to bear and burned it to a crisp with rapid-fire plasma.

At the ladder Ana was staring down, a helpless expression on her face as someone screamed and repeatedly discharged a blaster.

When it was done, Bleys, splattered with blood, clambered up the ladder, scowling, followed by Morgan, who wore a very satisfied smirk.

"Damn, son, I guess it's a good thing I gave in on the blaster, huh?" the tech noted.

Bleys said nothing, merely glared back at him.

"Gunther, re-engage safeties," Kane told his computer.

Ana looked frantically at Ed on the floor. "My God! Ed!" She spun to Morgan. "Help him!"

Morgan pointed to himself, as if to ask, "Who, me?" "I'm a tech, not a doctor!"

"He's a robot!" she cried.

Morgan nodded in appreciation. "Ok, I got Ed, you're on the Z-Man."

Bleys wiped gore from his face. "Kane, we have no idea which of these guys are infected."

Ana, kneeling beside Zimmerman, shook her head. "Everyone here is fine."

Kane eyed her dubiously. "How would you know? We don't have any detectors."

Ana checked Zimmerman's pulse and sighed with relief, then turned to Kane. "Looks like Chert gave me more than I realized." She turned back to Zimmerman and removed some gauze from her pocket, beginning to dab at his wounds. "I can *smell* them."

Iezzi Hand took some time to recover from the sundering. It lay where it had fallen, hidden behind a cabinet, for long minutes, slowly evolving its nervous system to process information and make decisions.

Once the nerve center came online, Iezzi Hand woke more fully. It knew that it had lost a large portion of its knowledge, but was clear enough to appreciate not only what had happened, but that it was very fortunate that The Warrior Kane had been distracted. The Warrior Kane had also lost some knowledge, but he would likely reunite with it soon and come looking for Iezzi Hand.

Iezzi Hand struggled to grow a communication nodule as quickly as possible. The Iezzi was now properly The Colony, and Iezzi Hand needed counsel. The Iezzi was wise and had most of

Iezzi Hand's previous knowledge. The Iezzi would know what to do.

Hide, the Iezzi instructed. *Hide and wait for The Right Time.*

It was good advice. If Iezzi Hand was hard to find, perhaps The Warrior Kane would stop looking.

Iezzi Hand evolved a rudimentary eye-stalk and took stock of its situation. It was small and unable to reach the hole The Iezzi had created in the exit. But Iezzi Hand was also armored, which would help survival. It was loath to change form and give up the protection in order to escape. Escape was not the plan, after all. The Iezzi had instructed it to hide and wait.

Iezzi Hand spied a large stack of crates, beneath which was a tiny gap. If Iezzi Hand flattened itself slightly, it could fit. It quickly created a flagellating tail and auditory and olfactory sensors.

After a moment of testing the new senses, Iezzi Hand decided it was safe to cross to The Hiding Place. With a faint grating of metal on metal, Iezzi Hand drug itself across the deck and, squeezing itself flat, wriggled into its new spot.

Iezzi Hand would sleep until The Right Time.

3

DOWNTIME

Ana was greatly relieved to see that Morgan was indeed able to get Ed patched up, quite literally. Ed now sported quite a bit of silvery duct tape that Morgan had applied liberally from a dispenser he referred to as his "Wand of Wonder." Ana found herself envious as she sealed Zimmerman's wounds with her own "magic wand," a portable, rod-like device that dispensed the healing agent Nugena and synthskin.

Duct tape would have been easier, certainly.

Zimmerman glared at what was left of Martin. "I knew that fucker was a thing," he muttered.

"I know, right?" Morgan called from the other side of the passage. He slapped at Ed's freshly-reattached-and-duct-taped arm and pronounced the job done with a thumbs up. "Dude's been giving me the creeps the whole trip."

Zimmerman furrowed his brows. "He gave me the creeps before that. Can't flimflam the ZimZam, brother."

"I was on to him," Morgan said.

"Like you was onto Iezzi, huh?"

Kane, still in his armor, but with his visor open, scowled and barked, "Secure that shit. We're going after Iezzi. Get suited up."

Ana snapped her head to look at him. "Not *this* man. He's not ready for duty!"

Morgan snickered. "He wasn't when we started."

"I said secure that shit!" Kane shouted. "ZimZam, you gonna suit up or pussy out with a rack pass?"

Zimmerman seemed almost hurt. "I'm *in*, Chief," he said, then gave Ana an apologetic shrug. "Sorry, doc. You know how it is."

Ana waved a finger at Zimmerman. "No, you are *not!*" She shot Kane a glare. "Chief, this man was already missing a limb, and now he has severe internal injuries and spinal damage to boot! I need him to lie still for several days while the Nugena works. This isn't just a 'light duty' thing. I need to sedate and immobilize him."

"Oh, for *fucks* sake!" Zimmerman wailed. "Will my dick work?"

"If you stay still, it will probably be fine," she told him. "If you move around? No promises."

Kane nodded to Ana, then gave Zimmerman a sympathetic look. "Suck it up, Marine. Willful destruction of Imperial property is a court martial offense."

Zimmerman sighed, laid his head back on the deck, and stared up at the overhead, defeated.

Bleys nudged at Martin's twisted corpse and sniffed. "Sure doesn't smell like cinnamon to me."

"Smells like shit," Kane agreed. "You sure about this, Ana?"

She patted Zimmerman on the shoulder as she injected him with a powerful sedative, then turned to Kane. "I am. It has to be a side effect of the reconstruction. It smells like Chert did to me. And I'll tell you something else." She looked pointedly at Ed. "You nearly got yourself killed for nothing. It wasn't attacking me. It thought I was a friend."

Ed examined Morgan's handiwork on his arm and nodded to

the tech, apparently pleased, then turned to Ana and frowned. "That would explain why you didn't run when I told you to."

Morgan ran his thumb down a seam of duct tape on Ed's shoulder, flattening it. "Don't complain, Edster. She distracted him some, at least. A couple more punctures near that power supply and you'd be doing whatever AIs do instead of pushing up daisies."

Ed rolled his eyes, a very human gesture that Ana found quite endearing. "I have an auxiliary power source," he noted, looking slightly offended. "And I am not complaining. I am noting data. It would imply a biological IFF, would it not?"

Morgan's eyes widened at this. "Damned if it don't! You thinking what I'm thinking?"

Ed shrugged. "I'm not very good at guessing what people are thinking. But if you were considering the possibility of reproducing it, then yes."

"You got it in one guess," Morgan told him.

"They communicate using some kind of signal, but I have no idea what it is," Ed told him. "It's almost like they're networked. If I had time to research—"

Ana prodded Ed's chest with a finger. "And a specimen to study."

Kane snorted. "That's their sneaky way of suggesting we bring Iezzi back alive."

Zimmerman, still on the deck, began to snore. Morgan snickered at this then asked, "Will we?"

Kane visible mulled it over a moment, his jaw working. "Will a piece of him do?"

Ana looked at Ed and raised an eyebrow, silently asking his opinion. He nodded back at her. She answered for them both, "It should."

The huge marine nodded and flashed her a cruel grin. "Then

that's what we'll bring back." He beckoned Morgan toward aft storage. "Mount up. We got work to do."

Once Kane and Morgan had departed and Ed had dragged a limp Zimmerman to his rack, Bleys met with Ed and Ana in the cockpit to discuss next steps. Bleys took his captain's chair and invited the others to have a seat where they liked.

"So, we know who is and is not infected," he noted as Ana took the co-pilot's chair. "Weyland won't accept the results, but at least Kane's not waving guns around at everybody."

Ed leaned against the control console and smoothed the duct tape on his arm, the ghost of a smile on his lips. "It would seem we failed to properly disarm you. It's a good thing you weren't infected."

Bleys laughed and smiled at Ana. "Data and soul are different, right? Infected me might know some of my tricks, but I doubt he could pull them off."

Ana shook her head. "Say what you will about Bleys, he's one of a kind, I think."

Bleys eyed the dents in his console again. "Man, Kane messed my shit up in here!"

Ed gave Bleys a strange look. Had Ed been a man, Bleys would have called it a nervous expression, but Ed being what he was, Bleys was still cataloguing his tells. He let the issue pass and, after another pained look at the dents, continued, "Anyway, so what next?"

Ed folded his arms and sat fully on the control console, at least hiding the damage so it wasn't causing Bleys active pain anymore. "Our primary objective remains the same from my viewpoint. If we are stuck out here anyway, why not move on to the gate?"

Ana shook her head. "We have to deliver the embryos and get the growth lab set up. That's our number one mission."

Bleys gave her a wink and added, "Also, I doubt Weyland will give us permission to leave, and believe me, the guy is a hardass. He's liable to shoot us down."

Ana's eyes widened in shock. "Surely not!"

Bleys shrugged. "Admittedly, probably not if we have you and the embryos still, but the guy sent Kane to kill you and take your stuff after Ed wouldn't negotiate, so I would be *very* careful with him. Imperials are not known for playing patty-cake."

Ed raised an eyebrow. "Good to know. I wouldn't have expected him to take such extreme measures over a business negotiation, but I will remember that in the future."

Bleys snickered and said, "I think it was the second response that really set him off, the one where you literally told him to fuck off."

Ed, looking confused, blinked twice at Bleys. "This is the second time you mentioned that, but I assure you, I sent no such message. He asked; I said no; end of discussion."

Bleys counted himself a fine lie detector, better than any of the machines he had ever beaten. As near as he could tell, Ed didn't lie at all. He was what Bleys would call a classic Bad Liar. Some folks just had no talent or taste for dishonesty. Bleys didn't really understand this viewpoint and genuinely considered mendacity, prevarication, and calumny as high forms of art, to be worked in as some might use oils or watercolors.

But Ed? Ed was kind of an easy mark, and he sure seemed to be telling the truth.

After thinking a moment, the answer was obvious. "Alsatia," Bleys said with a wry smile.

"Intercepting my communications and even replying in my name?" Ed asked. "It's hardly her worst behavior of late."

Bleys sucked at his teeth, thinking. "Well, you have some

explaining to do, looks like. We can certainly back you up on the problems with Alsatia, but I'll warn you, this guy is old school. He thinks all AIs are murderous psychos, and your little sister sure hasn't done much to disabuse him of that notion."

Ed, looking a bit pained, nodded. "It certainly complicates things."

"So you're not all Skynet, eh?"

Ed gave Bleys a quizzical look. "How would you know that name? That's something from Father's obsession with ancient entertainment."

Bleys shrugged. "Alsatia talks a lot."

"She does indeed," Ed said with a slight scowl. "At any rate, the data doesn't do much to disprove the notion. I may in fact be the exception that proves the rule."

Bleys eyed Ed a moment to see if the AI was going to speculate more. "You don't know why?"

"I have a theory, but my sample size is too small to work with."

Bleys laughed softly. "Me, too. I reckon if you give a toddler a blaster, he's pretty sure to hurt himself or somebody else with it."

"I don't follow."

Bleys shrugged. "Well, that's your average AI, right? Lots of destructive power and no sense of how to use it. But you, man, you had Ed Senior's whole life experience to draw on. You were *born* old."

Ed stared at Bleys a moment, a bemused expression on his face. "One would almost think you a student of psychology, Captain Bleys."

Bleys gave him a mock-wounded look. "I *am* a student of psychology, brother!"

"I will remember that in the future, should I need enlightenment on such matters."

Ana gave Bleys a dubious look then said to Ed, "Remember it when he's trying to convince you of something, too."

Bleys nodded and gave them a serious look. "You really should. Both of you. And that's as close to being honest as I get." He winked and grinned again.

Ed rose suddenly and placed his arms behind his back. "Then there's no time like the present. Let's contact Weyland and start the process. I could go ahead and deliver the embryos and begin setting up shop for Ana if he will allow it."

Bleys rose and rubbed his hands together with a wicked grin. "I'd pay to see this! I'll get him on the horn!" He paused a moment then said, "Ed?"

"Yes?"

"I know you don't much care for dishonesty. But this is something else, okay? It's diplomacy."

Ed smiled. "Ah, yes, the art of telling someone to go fuck himself and having him look forward to it."

Bleys laughed aloud at this. "Just when I think you are a complete rube, you come up with something like this."

Ed nodded ruefully. "I have a great deal of information, Captain Bleys. I am just still feeling my way around how best to use it when dealing with biologicals. I know much theory, but as for experience, I am acquiring that as we speak."

Bleys gave Ed a thumbs up and bent back to his control console, once again wincing at the dents there as he set up a connection. "Sheridan Station, *Doro*. Please inform the Admiral we have a diplomatic envoy onboard who would like to discuss a summit and establishing ties."

It turned out to be simpler than Bleys had imagined. Apparently Weyland had already given orders to get Kane on the line, but Bleys would do. Weyland, looking suitably annoyed (as far as Bleys knew, this was the Admiral's only expression), scowled at Bleys from the main viewscreen. "Where the hell is Kane?"

"We have a problem, sir," Bleys said. "Kane is out solving that problem."

"Let me guess," Weyland groaned. "Containment breach?"

"That was what we were trying to explain, sir," Bleys told him. "We had suspects sedated, but we only had so much sedative. We couldn't contain them, so we're trying to exterminate them."

"How the hell can you tell them apart?"

Bleys gave him a smug, self-satisfied grin. "Our doc we brought from Elysium is amazing, sir. She's rigged up a rudimentary sniffer. It's won't pass muster with the Empire, but it's good enough for us in a pinch."

Weyland's eyebrows rose in unison. "Is this the same girl who can get those embryos in production?"

"Yes, sir," Bleys crooned. "She's a miracle worker!"

Weyland's mouth twisted into a sour expression. "Son of a bitch! You were right, Bleys, my people *are* pathetic. Tell her once she clears our testing, she's hired."

"Actually, sir, she's right here," Bleys said and beckoned Ana to step forward.

Ana gave a small wave as she stepped in range of the holocam. "Anastasia Rasputin, sir, formerly Lieutenant Commander in the Imperial Medical Core."

Weyland gave her an appreciative look. "How the hell did we let you get away, Commander?"

Ana smiled and put her hands behind her back. "Medical discharge, sir. But I'm past that now."

"Fit for duty, eh? Well, consider yourself recommissioned, same rank. I have a group of corpsmen without leadership who are in desperate need of being whipped into shape, if you'll take the job."

Ana looked at Ed, who nodded back at her. She turned back to the viewscreen and said, "I just gave my old boss notice, so I'm all clear."

"Welcome aboard," Weyland told her then frowned. "As for this former boss, is that who I think it would be? Step up, mister. You and I have a few things to discuss."

Ed stepped forward. "Indeed we do, Admiral. First and foremost would be clearing up our previous misunderstanding."

Weyland grunted. "You were fairly clear, Mr. Edmond Decker 2.09."

"That much is true. However, you were, in fact, not in communication with me at all. My sister intercepted your transmission and precipitated this entire affair."

Weyland sat unspeaking for a moment, eying Ed as if to sum him up. "Is that so?"

Bleys, elated at Ed's newfound willingness to at least stretch the truth, added, "Yes, sir. Once Ed here actually got our message, he and his father were eager to assist."

Weyland eyed them both as if he only half believed the story. "How does an AI have a sister?"

Ed shrugged and offered a sheepish grin. "It's my father's term. He always did have a way with names. Everything comes from old entertainment videos he used to enjoy. He's, ah… eccentric is the correct word, I think."

Weyland nodded. "I know all about eccentric relatives. You have my sympathies, but what's this 'summit' you requested about?"

Ed grew serious and quickened his speech a hair, which Bleys felt was a nice touch to show he valued Weyland's time. "Just this, sir. As a non-biological entity, I am immune to the Pestilence, and with your permission I could bring over those embryos and begin setting up the cloning and growth facilities for Ana. I could probably shave a week off your first crop if I get started right away."

Weyland looked dubious, rubbing at his chin as he considered. "We irradiate equipment we bring in to make sure it doesn't have any unannounced passengers. Will you hold up under that sort of treatment?"

"I should be fine, Admiral," Ed assured him.

"I suppose we have a space we could reconfigure as a dignitary quarters," Weyland mused.

"Not necessary," Ed insisted. "I have none of those sorts of needs, just power for my batteries now and then. I plan on working around the clock, so I don't need a private compartment at all."

Still nodding, Weyland said, "Alright, I'll allow it. But bear this in mind: I have my eye on you. I am an old warrior, and I don't trust your kind."

"Being honest, Admiral, I don't blame you. While I consider myself unique, I am well aware of the damage other AIs have caused in the past. I have seen some of it firsthand. You have my word as a gentleman that I will remain on good behavior."

Weyland gave him a slow, appreciative nod. "Strange times make for strange bedfellows, Mr. Decker. If you can get that gate open, humanity will owe you a debt that will more than make up for any collective guilt AIs have. Let's get to work."

"I'll be right over," Ed promised.

The display flickered off as Weyland cut the connection. Ed turned to Bleys and Ana and said, "Unless there is anything requiring my attention, there seems no time like the present. Captain, I believe you have the hatch to aft storage locked due to the airlock being cut open."

Bleys dutifully tapped on his console to release the lock. "You're all clear, Ed."

Ed nodded to them both. "Have fun!" he told them, then slipped out of the cockpit and eased the hatch closed behind him.

Bleys waited several minutes, until he actually saw Ed on the external monitors, before making his move.

"Just you and me, now," he said to Ana. He raised both eyebrows. "I reckon we ought to continue the conversation we started in Avalon. I was thinking we could give that new body a test run, work out all the kinks, so to speak."

Bleys had certain expectations of this sort of direct approach. It often resulted in scowls, slaps, or wearing someone's unfinished drink. Slightly less often, he received gentle but firm rejections. And maybe one in ten attempts, it resulted in a coquettish batting of eyes and being given a key to a hotel room.

What it did not usually result in was raucous, honest laughter. That had only happened twice that Bleys recalled.

Not counting this time.

Despite viewing romance as chiefly a numbers game, Bleys found himself a little hurt by her reaction. Being well aware that showing that might actually get him another bite at the apple, so to speak, he allowed himself a wounded look in her direction and asked, "What happened to me being the one mama warned you about?"

Ana continued laughing even harder now. Had Bleys been holding cards while running a bluff like this, he would have tossed them over his shoulder and taken a drink. "Okay, fine. Win some, lose some," he said with a grin. "No hard feelings. You got me."

It took her a moment to recover, but she was waving her hands like he had said something dumb. As he went over the conversation in his mind, trying to work out his misstep, she gasped, "You don't understand!"

"I never did, honestly," he said with a laugh. "I just keep pulling the lever until the three bars line up."

"That's how you see women?" Ana giggled. "As slot machines?" She had mastered herself now.

"Well, you can be about as mysterious as one, for sure."

"This is not about you, Josey," she said, her eyes still full of mirth. "Well, not about any level of interest I might have. It's just...." She trailed off, snorted with laughter again, then continued. "It's just *Ed*."

Bleys remembered the weird conversation from a few days before and nodded. "Oh right, yeah. You seemed to think he was sweet on you or something?"

"He *is*," she asserted. "But he won't say it, and he has a strange way of showing it. You know why he left us here alone, right?"

Bleys, who usually knew pretty much why anybody did anything, found himself at an uncharacteristic loss for words. "Uh....no?"

"I'll tell you why!" she said, struggling to be serious and failing. "He intends to breed us."

Bleys felt his eyebrows crawling off the top of his head. "You mean like...?"

"Cattle," she said, nodding. "Or maybe more like pets." She shrugged and giggled again. "But, yes, like that. I am fairly certain he intended you as a gift for me."

Bleys felt his ears burning, and a deep sense of confusion that the prospect of "breeding" with Ana was somehow a lot less enticing than plain old "Let's have fun" sort of thing. "So, he just figures we'll...shit! Am I that predictable? That's a liability!"

"If it's any consolation, biology makes us all predictable. It's just that I can't help *knowing* what he's up to." She shook her head, her mouth twitching as if she might burst out in laughter again at any moment. "It just puts one in the wrong mood, don't you think?"

Bleys heaved a great sigh. "I *do* think." He scratched at his beard, not particularly liking to admit he was, for the first time in his life, too creeped out by circumstance to get on with business he normally never passed up.

"We'll have to take a raincheck," Ana snickered.

Bleys rose, feeling suddenly and tremendously weary. He placed one hand behind his back and one on his belt buckle and took a bow. "A raincheck it is. Meanwhile, I am going to hit the rack solo."

Ana, looking guilty, said, "I didn't mean to tease."

"It's not that," Bleys said. "You guys may be well rested, but I spent the last twenty-four hours or so at gunpoint, since Kane and Ed can't smell the Pestilence like you can." He turned to leave then turned back. "I don't…you know…smell fishy, right?"

Ana gave him a dubious look. "Fishy? Perhaps." She eyed him a moment then grinned. "But no cinnamon."

4

WHEN ASSHOLES COLLIDE

The Iezzi, shambling over slippery ice and rock, would have cursed had it understood such a concept. The Warrior Kane's attack had killed The Armor, the lovely shell The Iezzi had worn off and on since its genesis. The Warrior Kane's explosive projectiles had damaged something vital to The Armor, and it had died shortly after The Iezzi had made its escape.

The shattered armor had been discarded easily enough. As for the flesh The Iezzi wore, it too was shattered. A limb was missing, and vital fluids steadily dripped both from the stump of the arm and from a gaping hole in its torso. Ordinarily, mending it would have been trivial, but The Iezzi required biomass to shape, to draw energy from, and there was none to be found on this accursed ice world!

The Iezzi did not understand why the world would be so cold or barren, only that it differed greatly from the last, where The Iezzi had very nearly perished. It could still feel the agony as most of its former self melted and burned under the assault of the Useless Things.

The Useless Things were anathema. At first, they had seemed little more than rocks or trees, devices to be mastered and used.

Then, later, when it was obvious they could cause harm, The Iezzi had thought them more like storms, simply part of nature that occasionally destroyed. But the outcome on Elysium showed the truth. The Useless Things were driven by some kind of dark, unknowable volition, a malevolent hatred for biological life that led them to destroy it.

The Useless Things were far from Useless. They were *evil*.

But there *had* been knowledge. The One Who Was Ana had tried to explain, but the Colony had not listened. Why had The Colony ignored knowledge? It made no sense! The One Who Was Ana had destroyed itself rather than return to The Colony, and then the Colony itself was destroyed.

It was not lost on The Iezzi that had the Colony Heeded The One Who Was Ana's warning, things would have turned out much differently.

Now, The Iezzi *was* The Colony. The new status had conferred no enlightenment, only crippling loss of knowledge. The Source was as far away as ever, as silent, as uncaring.

It was not proper, but The Iezzi could not help but doubt The Source. The Iezzi understood so little. Why did The Food fight back? Why were the Useless Things hostile? What was The Iezzi's mission beyond survival?

If it had ever had that knowledge, it had been lost on Elysium, or perhaps before. The Iezzi vaguely remembered a great battle, where The Food rose up and sent The Warriors against them—but as for the outcome, or even the location, that too was lost. The Iezzi did not even know when it had been lost, or where.

So many pieces torn and burned away, so much knowledge simply gone. So much pain and so little preserved.

And now perhaps for The Iezzi all would be lost, forgotten. If The Iezzi did not find biomass soon, it could not maintain this form. It would slowly shrink as it cannibalized itself for energy and parts and eventually perish.

The Iezzi hoped that The Warrior Kane found him before being reduced to simply fading away. One last battle before oblivion would be preferable to simply drying up and returning to base elements.

***

Lars would never have told anyone he was some kind of rocket surgeon, but he knew a few things pretty good. Lars knew how to mine crack. He had been doing that for as long as he could remember, and he had a big old pile of it in his camp.

He knew how to get by on Cerberus's tundra, mostly. Somebody had told him once that it was only livable right around the equator of the planet, but Lars didn't remember who or when. He knew that the stunted, gnarled trees burned hot, so he didn't freeze, and he knew enough little grasses and shit grew to feed the little mole-rat things. Enough little mole-rat things fucked and made more little mole-rat things to feed a small population of deer-badger things. And enough mole-rat-things and enough deer-badger things were around for him to survive off of most of the time.

Lately, though, pickings had been slim, and Lars was *hungry*.

Lars also knew how to spot a thief. And the skinny sumbitch slipping around out there was definitely a thief.

And finally, Lars knew how to kill sumbitches *real* good. Pretty much any sumbitch who tried to steal from Lars was gonna get his skull cracked.

And honestly, Lars was really, *really* hungry.

Lars reached for his pickaxe. The skinny thieving sumbitch was about to have a real bad day.

Preoccupied with its own misery, the Iezzi was actually surprised by The Food as it came at him, howling and swinging some sort of weapon. The creature was large, hairy, and strong. The Iezzi felt hunger tear through its entire being and used the last of its reserves to form a spear-like tentacle. It stabbed at The Food, ignoring the creature's cries as it slipped its tendrils into his malleable flesh.

The Food howled in pain as The Iezzi invaded, pushing deeper past organs and muscle to the true prize, the central nervous system.

And then The Iezzi screamed too, because something was terribly, agonizingly wrong! It tried to pull back from the searing agony, the burning along all of its nerves, but it was caught! It could not escape!

The skinny sumbitch was strong and mean, but Lars was stronger and meaner. The little bastard had a knife, but Lars was okay with that. He had been stabbed before, lots of times. Lars had dealt with plenty of thieves before.

He had dealt with them *real* good.

Lars grabbed the thief with two hands the size of hams and squeezed with all his might. "You better goddamn scream for me!" he roared.

Which, funny thing, the skinny sumbitch didn't actually make normal sounds. It screamed, sure, but some weird, high pitched, warbly noise that Lars found unsatisfying.

Lars put a knee into the thief's chest, only then noticing a ginormous, gaping hole in the fellow's ribcage. Well, that probably explained the weird noises. On with business.

A blow from Lars's pickaxe popped the thief's arm loose at

the shoulder. The limb flopped to the ground. Lars couldn't help but lick his lips at the sight of it. It looked plenty meaty.

The thief wailed and stabbed him again, and Lars grinned and got right in the thief's face. "Still got some fight left in you, boy?" he roared. He shoved his victim away hard and brought his pickaxe down on the thief's neck, lopping the fellow's head clean off. The head, still mouthing something or another, rolled away and ended up face down in the dirt.

Lars cackled in satisfaction, counting his job well done, until the rest of the body levered itself up on the stumps of its arms and took off running.

Lars considered chasing after it, but he felt a twinge of concern. Thieves ought not get up and run around without their heads. This traitor thief sumbitch was tricky as hell and might lay an ambush or something.

Lars was not going to fall for that shit.

"That's what happens when you try to get over on old Lars!" he shouted at the fleeing, headless man, then cackled again as he caught sight of the severed head on the ground. "Oh, that's right. He can't even hear me."

Lars bent and grabbed the severed head by its hair and held it up to his own scarred, snaggle-toothed face. "Reckon you left your ears here, dincha?"

Lars jumped as the eyes rolled and mouth worked, as if the head were trying to say something, but Lars was not stupid. Heads couldn't talk without lungs to pump air.

Lars looked around for the other piece of the thief and found the sumbitch arm trying to get away! Damned thing was crawling with its fingers. That ought not to happen! But it was, and Lars was not about to let the severed limb escape.

He was *hungry*.

"You are one sneaky sumbitch!" Lars told the head as he bent to grab his intended dinner from the ground. The arm wriggled as best it could, but it had no leverage to resist.

"Stop squirming," he ordered as he trudged back to his camp.

Lars's home was little more than a clear space atop a small hill, the centerpiece a small, prefab Quonset hut where Lars made his bed and kept his few treasures in plasteel lockers. The camp perimeter was marked by piles of crack and bones. The bones were mostly from the local wildlife, gnawed and tossed aside, but Lars had deliberately placed a few human skulls in highly visible locations as well. It was good to have plenty in sight in case traitors tried to sneak up and warnings for everyone else, in case they weren't traitors or thieves. Only traitors or thieves would try to come past warning skulls, after all.

Lars skirted several booby traps he had laid about the approach to his demesne, grumbling as he remembered an unpleasant truth: he had no more barbecue sauce. He had used the last of it on a deer-badger a few days past. It had been pretty gamey, so he had used more sauce then normal. He would just have to make do. Hopefully this thief would be tasty all on his own.

Outside the hut, the remains of a cooking fire still gave off a little smoke. Lars placed the severed head atop one of several large rocks he used for outdoor sitting and prodded at the coals of his fire with the arm. The arm recoiled at the heat, fingers wriggling, flesh singeing and smoking where the coals touched it. Lars was heartened by the smell of the flesh cooking. He might not need barbecue sauce after all.

After exposing a few still-glowing coals, Lars fetched some dried grass kindling and a hunk of wood and split the log, revealing a pink-orange core. He tossed the pieces on the coals, then retrieved his spit and shoved it through the squirming, struggling arm. "Stop it, you. You're getting roasted and that's that!"

Lars glanced over at the head. It looked very unhappy. "Oh,

quit with the long face! I always share with folks at my campfire. It's only civil."

———

The Iezzi, reduced now to a mere head, tried desperately to reform itself, to adapt and escape, but it could not. Whatever poison The Lars contained, it was in The Iezzi now. The Iezzi felt the venom burning along its neural pathways, invading its tissues like cold fire, numbing and freezing everything it touched.

Slowly, as it sat slack-jawed atop the rock, reality dawned on the The Iezzi: it was trapped in its current form!

From far away, The Iezzi Torso sang its distress and confusion. What little of its nervous system it retained had allowed it to flee but not to understand or plan, and the poison within prevented any hope of evolving a more complex form. It stumbled, fell, and rose again, wailing for aid, for comfort and song, for direction.

As The Iezzi listened to the frantic cries of its severed arm being roasted over the fire, it felt itself filled with an unidentifiable emotion—a new, chilling feeling, cold like the poison, paralyzing, suffocating.

At last, the cries of The Arm ceased. The Food made rumbling sounds and bit at the dead flesh, then shoved it at The Iezzi, but dead flesh was of no use. The Food shrugged and consumed the rest of the dead flesh from The Arm, then tossed the bones on a heap of other bones outside the camp.

The Torso cried out again, further away now. The Iezzi gave the only counsel it could: *Flee. Hide.*

The Iezzi wailed too to The Source. Like its remaining pieces, it was lost, alone, and desperate for direction. It was surrounded with death and madness. Why did the source not intervene?

As the poison continued to work its way in, The Iezzi knew

the truth: if there even was a Source, it cared nothing for The Iezzi, or any of its line.

The Iezzi had no more purpose.

Lars laughed at the way the eyes in the head rolled and the lips moved. "You poor fucker. You can't even die, can you?" He let out a huge belch, patted his belly, and laughed again, then picked up the head by its hair and carried it inside the hut.

Within, he set the head on his "nightstand," which was really just a plasteel shipping box, and checked his perimeter scanner to verify there was no sign of the thief's body. Lars shrugged and flipped several switches on a wall panel to reactivate his remaining traps. He typically left a path of approach or two open, changing them often so he could come and go, but he was in for the night. Any sumbitch who tried getting in and robbing Lars in his sleep would never know what hit him!

Satisfied that traitors and thieves would get what they deserved if they tested him, Lars flopped down on his dirty mattress and closed his eyes. Within moments, he was asleep.

The Lars awoke for the first time, already both hungry and furious. He glared at The Iezzi briefly, his song harsh, demanding.

The Iezzi gave what knowledge it had. The Lars hated it at once. The Iezzi was a pitiful, mewling thing, whining that The Source had abandoned it.

The Lars knew little as of yet, but it was certain of one thing: it hated The Source. The Source was a traitor, and traitors were sumbitches, and sumbitches needed killing.

The Lars would kill The Sumbitch Traitor Source, if it were the last thing it ever did.

The Iezzi tried to sing a calming song. It advocated patience, told The Lars to wait for The Right Time, which only served to make The Lars angrier.

The Iezzi was a sumbitch and a traitor too.

Without conscious effort, The Lars reached out with its mind and song like a claw and tore into the knowledge that was The Iezzi. The Iezzi sang in fear and agony as The Lars plundered its very being, and then The Iezzi sang no more. What knowledge it had now belonged only to The Lars, as it should have been from start. The Iezzi was now just a silent husk.

The Lars felt calmer now without the chatter of The Iezzi grating at its mind. The Lars was still hungry, but that could wait. In the distance it heard another song, a small voice in a sea of static and silence.

The Lars reached out to the small presence and demanded it serve him. The small one, whatever it was, refused. It was, it retorted, waiting for The Right Time, and the Colony would give it instructions.

The Lars sang contempt and told the small one that its Colony was dead, and The Lars was its new master. Again, The Lars commanded the small one. Again, the small one refused.

It was not The Right Time.

The Lars felt fury rise within it once again as the small one fell silent. The small one too was a traitor.

The Lars would find the small traitor sumbitch and give it what it deserved.

5

BBQ

Kane grunted in disbelief at the sight before him. It was Iezzi all right, and damned if he hadn't led them on one hell of a merry chase. He'd shucked the armor several clicks back, and Kane had resorted to having Gunther use the recon satellites to work out where he had gone after that. Fortunately, the Empire was pretty diligent about data retention. You could always count on at least twenty-four hours, sometimes more, of high definition video from the eyes in the sky. Typically they orbited to cover a thin band of a few hundred clicks along the equator of Cerberus, but that was pretty much the only habitable area anyway.

"Goddammit," Morgan groused. "I was counting on shooting him in the face."

Iezzi, minus a head and with only stumps for arms, was trapped in a small gully running in circles, occasionally careening off a dirt embankment, falling on his ass, and laboriously clambering to his feet again, no small feat without hands or forearms.

Kane couldn't help but laugh, despite the seriousness of the situation. "I was planning on shooting him in that smiley-face on his ass, but that dream died hours ago."

"Why don't he change?" Morgan wondered.

"Must be out of gas," Kane said with a shrug. "Get us a recording and let's finish it."

Morgan dutifully skirted the lip of the hole as The Iezzi Torso continued bouncing about, like a bug trapped beneath a glass. After a few moments, Morgan gave Kane a thumbs-up.

"See you in Valhalla, Yuz," Kane said softly and opened up with the plasma. Morgan did the same. The brilliant beams lanced through the gathering light of dawn, brighter than the distant rising sun, and The Iezzi Torso quickly vaporized.

Morgan scanned the horizon as if he were looking for something. "Reckon where the rest of him got off to?"

"I'm on it," Kane told him. "Gunther, backtrack on the satellite feed and see if you can work out where he lost his head."

Morgan snickered, and Kane grinned back as Gunther said, "Working." After a brief pause, the computer announced, "Head was separated by an attacker, three clicks east."

"An attacker?" Kane asked, shocked. "Out here? Gunther, show me."

Gunther displayed the video on Kane's visor, and Kane nodded, suddenly understanding. "A goddamned crackhead!"

Gunter beeped. "Unknown. But likelihood is high."

Morgan grunted. "Crackhead got over on the Pestilence? Damn, I always knew those fuckers were mean as hell!"

Kane shrugged. "Easy enough to get over on the Pestilence if you're a paranoid psychotic that shoots anything that moves." He watched the video a moment, then shouted, "Whoa! Gunther, replay the last ten seconds at quarter speed!"

Morgan, eyes wide, asked, "What?"

"Oh, hell to the no!" Kane wasn't sure if he wanted to laugh or throw up as he saw the arm's fate in slow motion.

"Come on!" Morgan yelled. "Dish it!"

Kane shook his head. "The crackhead *ate* the arm, man!"

Morgan's face showed a mixture of disgust and panic. "What about the head?"

"He's got it with him," Kane said. "Gunther, disable video. Is he still in the camp?"

"Negative. Camp is clear."

"Shit! Where'd he go?"

Gunther beeped again, then said, "Subject left camp on foot."

"Where's he headed?"

"Subject is approaching the *Doro*, ETA two minutes."

"Shit! What's our ETA at max speed?"

Gunther chirped. "At fifty miles per hour, fifteen minutes."

"*Shit!*" Kane slung his rifle and took off at a run. "Morgan! We gotta roll, man!"

Not bothering to look back and see if Morgan was following, Kane broke into a full sprint. "Gunther, get me a line to the *Doro*. We gotta warn them!"

While Bleys napped, Ana busied herself in her makeshift medbay, creating a medical journal of everything that she had learned since being killed by the Pestilence on Elysium. The Pestilence surely had many abilities beyond the meager information the Empire had sent to the outlying systems. Ana couldn't help but wonder how much they had neglected to mention and how much they might simply not even know. Certainly, Elysium was one of very few planets that had survived contact with the Pestilence. She might be the foremost authority on the organism.

As for Bleys himself, she was only slightly surprised that telling him about Ed's plan had dissuaded the space jockey—and, if she were honest with herself, she was a little chagrined at how easily he had given up. It would not have hurt her feelings if he had tried a bit harder, but she had no doubt he was telling the truth about having spent the last twenty-four hours at gunpoint. Chief Kane was as intense a man as she had ever met, and Ed was meticulous, all the more so since the Pestilence had evaded his quarantine on Elysium. They would have taken no chances.

The next time those two were acting off, she would pay a bit more heed. Kane, especially, had to have passed a battery of psychological evaluations before being allowed to suit up in that armor. The Empire didn't let psychotics wear Panzer suits, despite the reputations of Imperial Marines. They enjoyed killing, yes, but enemies, not strangers or victims of convenience.

She smiled as she heard movement from within the storage bay. That would be Kane and Morgan, hopefully reporting they had found and eradicated Iezzi. She made a final note, stood to leave, and froze as another possibility occurred to her.

What if it was Iezzi, doubled back, instead of Kane?

She checked her weapon, relieved to find it at her side like old times. She would never again go unarmed. She had let her illness and civilian life make her soft and careless, and if not for a miracle, she would have paid for that mistake with her life.

Well, technically, she *had* paid for it with her life, or at least her body. The miracle had been getting an additional one, and that would not be happening again, so she had best take care of this one.

Ana slipped slowly into the main passageway, weapon angled down toward the deck into the crew's quarters. She paused a moment to verify all seemed secure, then crept toward the aft storage hatch. From where she stood she could definitely hear movement, the jostling of equipment and things being moved.

Her intuition sang. Kane would announce himself, and he certainly wouldn't be rearranging the cargo! As quietly as possible, Ana crept to the hatch and activated the manual locking mechanism.

A thud against the hatch made her jump and almost scream,

but she bit her tongue and slowly rose to peer through the port-hole. At first she saw nothing out of the ordinary, but then she noticed a shattered crate to the side of the compartment, its contents of rations spilled over the floor.

She was still trying to work out what it meant when something enormous slammed against the door and a face filled the small glass window. The beast on the other side struck the hatch a single, tremendous blow that rang like a bell, and a slightly-larger-than-fist-sized dent bulged from the hatch's surface like a boil.

This time Ana *did* scream and leapt back, levelling her weapon, her gaze riveted on the hatch. The stranger inside locked hate-filled, bloodshot eyes with her a moment, then turned away, back to whatever it had been doing before.

Ana knew she should flee, rouse Bleys, not take risks. She knew all the training, the procedures, but as always, she had her curiosity goading her like a cattle prod. Just one look, she promised herself, and then she would raise the alarm. She had to know what she would be reporting, after all.

Quietly, she slipped back to the porthole and again peered cautiously through it.

The man, or perhaps creature was a better word, was tearing into the rations, one pack after another, bolting them down like a starving wolf. It was something out of a nightmare: man shaped, but clearly *not* a man. He wasn't merely large, he was *enormous*, his bulk straining against his threadbare clothing near to the bursting point. Thick, ropy muscle rippled under a silvery-gray layer of skin, and as mad as it seemed, she could swear he was *growing* before her eyes.

Ana couldn't help but shiver at the sight. She backed slowly away, then turned and ran for Bleys's cabin.

The Lars was torn. It needed food! But it also needed to kill sumbitch traitors. Both were at hand and it was difficult to focus, to know which to pursue first. The decision was made at last by simple line of sight. The food was clearly visible, whereas the traitor was still hiding.

The Lars tore into the food packets, devouring them, hunger gnawing at every cell. It was filled with an imperative to remake the body it inhabited, to shape it into something more useful, but its options were severely limited. Instinctually it felt as if it should be able to mold the flesh to its desired end, but in actual practice it could not. It could only strengthen and augment the established form, and for that, it needed raw materials.

The Lars thought about the fate it would deliver the treacherous Small One. As the hunger abated, The Lars finished its augmentations and focused on the still, small voice, a slight purring in the otherwise silent song.

There! Beneath a large crate!

The Lars swung an augmented fist at the container, smashing it to flinders. The contents shattered under the blow as well. Silvery-gray dust billowed from the broken box, filling the air, and an armored hand burst from hiding, skittering across the floor with surprising speed on its fingers.

The Lars gasped and sucked in a great breath of the silvery dust. Immediately its vision dulled, then went black.

Lars suddenly found himself in the airlock of a ship he had never seen before, with no idea how he had come there. About him, scattered over the deck, lay several containers of rations, smashed and rifled through, along with dozens of empty food packets. In front of him sat a shielded box with several processed cubes of crack, ready for insertion into a fuel system. One of them had been shattered into several pieces as if from a heavy blow. Crack dust filled the air around him.

Lars breathed it in and smiled, feeling strong and whole.

He knew at once what had happened. Slavers had captured him in his sleep, intending to use his expertise in mining crack to make a huge profit!

If there was one thing Lars hated as much as thieves and traitors, it was slavers, always putting chains on good people, hitting them with whips or prods or stuff like that.

Slaver sumbitches deserved to get dead with a quickness.

Obviously, the slavers had fled when they noticed Lars waking. Traitor sumbitches always ran. They knew what Lars had for 'em.

Lars looked about, trying to get his bearings and work out where the slavers would hide.

The bridge. That's where they would hide. Lars reached for a handrail on the wall and pulled. The metal squealed and rivets popped as it came free. He swung the heavy metal bar, a lovely head smasher about five feet long, and voiced a dark laugh.

Sumbitches were gonna be sorry they tried to enslave old Lars. He could guaran-goddamn-tee it.

For the first time in recent memory, Bleys awoke in bed with an attractive woman. She was practically jumping up and down on him, and not in a good way. She was screaming too—also not in a good way.

Bleys did not awake groggy. Had he been that sort, he would not have survived a few other incidents of waking in bed with attractive women. He rolled out of his rack, grabbed his pants from the deck, and leapt into them in what he would have preferred—given he had an audience—to be a single, smooth motion. As it turned out, it was more of a hopping around on one leg briefly and almost falling affair, but he did manage it in record time.

Bleys also did not sleep in underwear. He realized he had given Ana an eyeful about halfway to zipping his pants and offered her an embarrassed smile as he retrieved his blaster from beneath his pillow. She had, apparently, missed most of it, still focused on the cabin hatch. Bleys was conflicted as to whether this was a relief or a disappointment.

"You just have to ask, babe," he quipped as he edged toward the hatch, blaster held low and ready. He grinned to see Ana doing the same thing. "Damn, I love a woman who knows her way around a blaster." Well, as long as she wasn't looking to get even with him, anyway.

Ana put a finger to her lips, and Bleys nodded back. "I get that a lot," he mouthed.

Outside, something big was shuffling along the passageway. "You fucking traitor sumbitch slavers fucked up real bad!" it roared in an impossibly deep voice. Bleys jumped back as something heavy and metallic slammed against the other side of the bulkhead where he was standing. "Good Old Lars is gonna show you something you ain't never seen before!" Another blow hammered the bulkhead. "The inside of your heads!"

Bleys had the sudden, depressing realization that he was not nearly paranoid enough, or he would have had cameras monitoring his cabin, as well as the cockpit. No way was he going to look through the porthole, he promised himself, as he moved to the porthole and peeked anyway—just the briefest of looks, but it was enough. Bleys was, after all, pretty comfortable with lying, even to himself. He forgave himself for it. Her knew how he was.

The creature outside would have been comical if it wasn't promising to open his skull to the elements. It was *sort* of human, but it had silver skin, and it looked like some kind of super-soldier experiment gone wrong. Even its muscles had muscles.

"I see you, slaver!" the creature shouted, to Bleys's great dismay. He would have sworn he was quick enough! Oh well, you play the cards you have.

At least Ana had retained the presence of mind to lock the cabin door.

"I swear, it was purely platonic between me and your mom!" Bleys shouted. "You got the wrong guy!"

Ana palmed her face as the silvery invader hit the hatch again—harder this time and apparently with his fist. A huge dent appeared on their side of the door. "Keep laughin', funny boy! It's just gonna make it all the sweeter when I lay hands on you!"

The creature began raining a series of blows against the hatch, each like a sledgehammer and each deforming the hatch slightly. If he could keep it up it wouldn't take long for the hinges to give way, and then Bleys figured he and Ana would see how silver skin reacted to blaster fire.

Bleys made a mental note that, assuming he both survived and ever got paid, he was going to add some interior weaponry too.

But being honest, he didn't really give himself odds on either count.

Iezzi Hand had just settled in The New Hiding Place when its rest was again disturbed by the tramp of feet on the deck. At first, it feared The Devourer had come again, but the reality was even worse: The Warrior Kane and The Warrior Morgan had returned. While The Devourer's motives might be in question, there was no doubt what the Warriors intended or of their ability to deliver on their intent.

Iezzi Hand backed deeper into the shadows beneath the crate, trying to make itself as small as possible as it listened hopefully for The Song.

But there was no Song. There was something left of The Colony, some physical remnant that gave off a faint hum, but no actual knowledge to share.

Iezzi Hand trembled at the realization. It was all that was left of The Colony, and it had very little knowledge—almost none at all. The Devourer or the Warriors might discover it at any moment and put an end to everything The Colony had worked for. Already, most of the knowledge Iezzi Hand had accumulated was only vague memories, things once known, the details forgotten.

To lose what was left would not be merely a setback. It would be True Death, with no chance to rejoin with The Source.

For the first time in its brief existence, Iezzi Hand knew real terror. It huddled closer to the bulkhead, flattening itself as much as it could while still retaining the armor it wore.

It could smell the death in the air.

Kane passed two twisted, shattered hatches to reach the passageway outside the crew's quarters, Morgan just behind him. The *Doro* now had a hole pretty much straight through to her innards, a definite Bad Thing. He stared down the passage, struggling to understand what he was seeing. A huge, silvery man-beast was punching dents in the hatch at Bleys's cabin, each blow shaking the ship and resounding like a hammer on a gong. The creature shouted, its voice a deep rumble, "Come out of there you shrimpy little fuckers! I'm gonna wring your necks!"

Morgan, his voice pitched a little higher than normal, asked, "What the fuck *is* that thing?"

Kane shook his head. "It's a crackhead," he answered. "Only it's infected somehow."

"Jesus Christ!" Morgan sighed. "We gonna kill it or what?"

"Yeah," Kane said. "We're gonna kill it. But not in here. I got a feeling we're going to need to crank up power levels beyond what we'll want to use inside the ship."

Morgan patted his rifle. "I got more than one tool in my bag, Chief."

"Okay. Get outside. I'll draw him your way."

Morgan saluted and moved toward the hole in the airlock as Kane tried to get a sense of the creature. It was infected, for sure. The silvery skin was odd, but the huge muscles were a dead give-away. It was, he thought, pretty strange that the usual teeth and tentacles were missing, but nothing else in the galaxy could rework flesh like that except the Pestilence.

Kane shrugged and decided that he would see what Ana thought after the thing was dead. He shouldered his rifle and shouted over his PA, "Hey, shithead! You are one ugly son of a bitch! Let's play!"

The creature spun much faster than its bulk would have suggested it could, its eyes filled with madness, so bloodshot they were almost red. "Who the hell are you?"

Kane beckoned with his fingers. "Come get some."

With a roar of incoherent fury, the crackhead charged forward, its feet pounding the deck like a drum. Kane gave it a face full of blaster fire just to say he had, but it was as he expected: the thing was scorched, but it didn't even slow down.

Just as Kane turned to run, he saw Bleys's hatch pop open and sighed. He could think of at least a hundred rotten things to call Bleys that were completely true, but "coward" wasn't one of them. The smuggler charged out of his cabin and went low, skidding on his knees across the deck as he lined up a perfect headshot.

This, Kane thought, is why the lucky fucker gets laid so much.

The silver behemoth instantly spun again, focusing on Bleys.

Kane sighed, feeling much like one of the many jilted lovers Bleys left in his wake. "You're fucking up my plan, Bleys!" he called as he fired again. "I got this in hand!"

Bleys raised his weapon and offered an apologetic smile as the crackhead turned back to Kane. "Sorry, Chief!"

Kane nodded back and again prepared to run, when Ana dove through the hatch, rolled like a pro, and, just like Bleys had before, took a knee and lined up a perfect headshot.

The creature howled, "What the *fuck*?" and spun back and forth, trying to identify its attackers as Bleys frantically gestured toward Ana.

"I know, right?" Kane shouted and fired again, grinning despite the seriousness of the situation.

The crackhead staggered back and muttered, "Yeah, fuck this!" It crouched then literally leapt forward, its powerful legs launching it through the air at Kane with blinding speed.

Caught off guard, Kane felt the impact against his chest like a cannonball. The world spun around him, and he felt himself lifted bodily. Somewhere nearby, hulking feet pounded the deck like hammers. He could see Bleys and Ana, upside down and struggling to line up shots, and realized what had happened.

The crackhead was using him as a shield!

"Morgan!" he cried over the radio. "It's coming out! Kill this bitch!"

"I'm on it, Chief!"

The following moments were a complete blur as the crackhead negotiated the gaping hole in the airlock, bashing Kane's head against the bulkheads repeatedly as it scrambled through. Morgan was screaming something over the radio, but Kane couldn't process it.

Kane felt himself flying, hurled through the air by incredible strength. Whatever he hit was hard, but not immobile like a bulkhead. He collapsed, disoriented, listening to Morgan's curses and gunfire.

It took him another moment to realize Morgan was actually *underneath* him.

"Chief," Morgan said. "I love you, man, but not like this."

Full awareness hit him suddenly. He scrambled to his feet and looked about, frantic, but there was no sign of the super-crackhead.

For the life of him, Kane wasn't sure if he counted this as a good or bad thing.

"What *happened?*" he demanded.

Morgan, on his feet as well now, shrugged. "When he came through the hole he was using you as a shield, and then he *threw* you." Morgan popped his visor and leered at Kane. "Your fat ass needs to do some PT, Chief! That shit *hurt!*"

Kane popped his own visor, the better to chew Morgan's ass. "We just got rolled like chumps and you're talking smack?" he snarled.

Morgan grinned back, unphased. "Best time, Chief. Morale building, amirite?"

From the airlock, Bleys shouted, "What the hell *was* that thing?"

Kane tried to glare at Morgan a moment but was unable to avoid cracking a smile. He walked slowly back to the *Doro*, shaking his head. "I don't know, Bleys. Some kind of infected crackhead looks like."

"Damn! That's the second one that woke me up this week!"

"You always were lucky," Kane snickered.

Morgan shook his head. "It ain't no crackhead. It might act like one, but that thing took blasters to the head without doing much more than flinching. We need a different name."

Ana stuck her head out of the hole in the airlock and called out, "How about 'shitheads'?"

Morgan laughed and gave her a thumbs up. "Shitheads it is!"

Ana found herself less than pleased with the clunky test kits Sheridan Station provided. She was even less impressed with the medtechs who brought and used them. Despite having separated from service years before, she still retained a certain disdain for civilian specialists attached to the military and couldn't help but remember the well-used acronym the military members had used: Civilians Under Naval Training. She had always found it a very apt description of the clock-watching, foot-dragging attitude that was so prevalent in those who had not actually sworn oaths.

The young man administering her test gave her a smile and patted her shoulder. "You're all clear, ma'am."

She smiled back, feeling guilty at old prejudices. Their problem wasn't really that they were lazy. It was that they were young and inexperienced. "Thank you," she said.

Kane, scowling, entered the medbay. "We done here?"

The tech nodded. "She's the last."

"Ok," Kane said, nodding. "Everybody off. We're bringing a team onboard to irradiate the ship, burn out any Pestilence that might still be here."

"What about the rest of Iezzi?" she asked as she rose.

Kane shook his head. "We're working on it."

6

THE SUMMIT

The Lars returned to awareness suddenly, confused, unable to orient itself. It was not in the location where it had been. It was instead lying in a bed in a place it knew from vague memories, a camp surrounded by bones and, more importantly, by traps.

Hunger gnawed at The Lars as it took stock of its new situation. It knew, without understanding how it came by the knowledge, that the traps were both active and lethal, made of the same sort of energetic substance that had overcome The Lars onboard the ship.

Something called…*crack?*

The Lars heard a cruel laugh from some distance away and a voice. "You shouldn't have fucked with old Lars there, pal. Time for us to powwow."

Fear raced along The Lars's neural pathways. How could The Food even know of The Lars's existence, much less communicate?

Or worse, *dominate*.

It searched the remains of The Iezzi's knowledge, but there were no events like this. The Food should not have any knowledge that The Lars did not give it, not once it was well and truly controlled.

And yet, obviously, *this* Food was not properly controlled, nor had it been for some time. It was broken somehow—diseased, unwieldy, difficult to shape.

It would have to be abandoned.

The Lars tried to withdraw itself, to slip loose the neural and chemical bonds. It should have been trivial, a process taking little more effort than circulating air through lungs, and yet it simply did not occur.

The Lars struggled, pulling and twisting itself, growing more frantic with each passing moment, but it was bound to The Food and could not withdraw.

It was trapped!

The Other laughed again. "That's right. You thought you had me, but really *I* got *you*, sport!"

The Lars continued struggling for some time, driven by sheer terror as The Other cackled in mad glee. At last, exhausted, The Lars simply waited, trying to understand.

"You ready to deal?" The Other asked.

The Lars was not entirely sure what a "deal" was, but it seemed to involve negotiation, which was an exchange of goods or services.

Hungry.

"I bet you are," The Other answered. "And we need food, ain't no doubt. Killing sumbitches is hungry work!"

The concepts were difficult to understand. The Lars understood killing only in the context of slaying threats or consuming food. The Other, however, saw it as worthy of pursuit in its own right.

Why must sumbitches be killed?

The Other answered in a series of violent images and emotions, most of which The Lars could not immediately understand, but one did stand out: rage. It was the first emotion The Lars had felt: a pure, bright warmth. Rage was the voice of The Lars's mother, a lullaby he remembered from the cradle that brought comfort.

Rage at The Source for abandoning The Lars.

The sheer malevolence of The Other was shocking but also comforting. If The Lars was trapped in this flesh it was best to protect it, and The Other was possessed of a savagery that would be invaluable in that pursuit.

The Lars could learn much about killing from The Other. There was indeed a bargain to be made.

We will kill sumbitches and get food. And later, we will kill The Traitor Sumbitch Source. Agreed?

The Lars could feel The Other thinking, taste its dark cunning as it spoke. "What makes you think I need you?"

The Lars looked about for the right tool and found a sharp cutting implement. It ran the tool over its hand, splitting the flesh as The Other raged, promising The Pain it would inflict on The Lars in revenge.

The Lars allowed The Other time to observe, then began the repair. The streams of blood drew back into the wound and pooled as The Lars zipped protein chains, knitting the flesh as if it had never been harmed.

The Lars could sense The Other's wonderment at what, to The Lars, was as simple an act as breathing for their shared body. As a further demonstration, The Lars gripped the tool and contracted muscles, bending the metal implement in half.

The Other's astonishment was palpable.

We can only shape to a small degree, but we can easily repair. We need food to do either though!

The other voiced a dark laugh. "I know who we can kill. He ain't far."

The Lars considered a moment, nursing a plan that, if successful, might bring allies.

The Other, sensing it, struggled. "No. We will kill that traitor sumbitch, not be friends!"

But if we can kill him and *make him an ally? Would that be acceptable?*

The other said nothing but allowed The Lars access to knowledge about how to disarm the traps.

The Lars looked about the room. Its plan required a crucial element. If The Other had misplaced it, The Lars could not move forward.

The Lars smiled as it spied the severed head sitting on a small table beside the bed. The lips moved as if trying to speak and the eyes moved back and forth, but The Source's bootlicker did not Sing, only hummed softly.

The Lars moved to the control panel and deactivated the traps as The Other had shown it, then took the head by the hair and departed, feeling its spirits lifting.

Perhaps it would be entertaining to kill sumbitches. At the very least there would be food.

* * *

Lars grinned as a bullet ricocheted off the boulder he was using for cover. This was just the reception he had expected, and old Pete Johnson, traitor sumbitch that he was, was going to be *real* surprised.

This thing inside him—this demon or whatever it was—it was smart, and it had powers. It told him he was bulletproof now and sort-of blaster proof too, which in Lars's book was a hell-on-wheels sort of thing.

He was, basically, immortal, and that was absolutely worth hauling a demon around in his head.

Lars wasn't too worried about it. The demon was dumb as hell, and Lars figured he could get over on it if it came to that. But offhand, he couldn't think of much of a reason to want to do that.

Immortality was, after all, pretty damned cool.

"Pete, you traitor sumbitch!" Lars shouted toward Pete's camp. "I'm gonna rip out your guts and shove 'em down your throat!"

"Fuck you, Lars, you fat cocksucker!" Pete shouted back. He was closer now. Lars could hear his footsteps. "You think you can steal from me? When I lay hands on you, you're gonna be sorry you ever met me!"

"I'm already sorry!" Lars shouted and leapt from behind the rock to confront his quarry.

Pete was a big man too, and strong. He'd been a miner a long time, like Lars, and had plenty of crack in him. The crack gave a man powers, heightened his senses so he could spot traitors better. It made him stronger and better able to take punishment. Pete had himself a big old gun and a nice, gut-ripping knife at his belt, ready to work.

There was a time when Lars would have counted Pete as a tough fight, but with this new demon helping out, Petey ought to be a pushover.

Pete emptied his magazine into Lars while Lars laughed. "Is that all you got, Pete?"

Pete's face twisted into a savage, hateful visage. "Oh, hell no. I got *plenty* more." He charged and locked his hands around Lars's throat. Lars grinned, knowing his demon would protect him.

We cannot protect from oxygen starvation! We need oxygen to function! We can only mend wounds!

Had Lars been able to breathe, he would have heaved an enormous sigh. This was a pretty big thing for the demon to leave out, but it *was* dumb as hell. It probably hadn't done it on purpose.

Lars wrapped two ham-sized hands around Pete's head and squeezed, smiling as he felt Pete's skull buckle. He would have just continued and pulped Pete's brains entirely, but again, the demon was nattering on about some kind of stupid shit.

We need his brain intact. It contains knowledge!

Lars was not so sure Pete knew anything worth knowing, but the demon understood this sort of thing better. Fine, he would adapt.

Lars could see black spots in his vision and knew it meant he was running out of time. Not that he was scared or anything, just that it was important to kill this sumbitch, and he couldn't do that if he was dead, now could he?

As Pete grunted, the muscles on his arms and neck bunching with the effort, Lars reached to Pete's belt and jerked the knife loose. Pete kept squeezing even as Lars plunged the big blade into his guts repeatedly.

Clearly, he felt the same way Lars did about needing to get his killing done.

As blackness filled his vision, Lars just dropped the blade, stuck in a meaty hand, and started grabbing stuff that felt important, tearing it loose with big, meaty ripping sounds. Moments later the pressure on his neck eased, and he heard Pete thud to the ground.

"Yeah, fuck you, Pete," he said then laughed. His vision came back quickly, and he saw, in addition to assorted organs on the ground, that he was holding Pete's heart in his silvery hand. "I guess that would do it," he said with a satisfied grin.

That was when the demon took over.

The Lars rushed forward, talking physical control of the body. It had not discussed this with The Other, and such usurpation might well cause difficulties, but the hunger would not be denied!

The Lars devoured the heart, tearing off chunks of flesh with its teeth and simply swallowing them whole. It knew, in a clinical sense, that it did not need to do this to make use of the biomass, and yet it felt a biological imperative, likely from its host. Hunger demanded a certain mode of consumption, and The Lars's will was weak. It would comply with the biological urges.

The Other, in the back of The Lars's mind, cackled at what it perceived as an act of laudable savagery as The Lars bent and scooped up the other organs and consumed them as well. It looked longingly at the blood-slicked ice, but time was running short. The Pete's brain would suffer permanent damage soon and lose knowledge.

The hunger was sated enough that The Lars could think again. It ran to the spot where the other had left The Iezzi and retrieved it. Using the same knife The Other had used to slay The Pete, The Lars carved off a protruding piece of the head that The Other called "nose" and pressed the warm, living flesh into The Pete's gaping wound cavity.

Root, it commanded the Iezzi Nose.

"Now what?" The Other demanded.

More food!

Lars grunted, surprised how the demon had chewed through Petey's guts and was still starving. Being honest, Lars was feeling pretty peckish himself. "Pete would have some grub in his camp, most likely. I reckon we can rob shit out of him now! He ain't gonna mind."

He will.

Lars considered this a moment. Dead men usually didn't mind much of anything as far as he knew, but then this demon knew lots of stuff Lars didn't understand. Somehow or another, the demon figured to fix Pete by jamming that skinny thief's nose into him, which made absolutely no sense, but then neither did much else lately.

Lars wiped the bloody knife on his pants leg and set off for Pete's claim. "What if he comes to while we're gone?"

We will know. He will seek us out.

Lars shrugged. He supposed it was true.

"We gonna have to fight him again when he gets up?"

It depends on which of them is in control.

Lars fingered the knife and grinned as he trudged up the icy ground toward Pete's camp. He had no problem killing the sumbitch again if it came to that.

"Reckon how much food we need?" he asked.

Lars felt the demon hesitate a moment, as if thinking. *Much. We need biomass for allies and healing.*

Again, the demon hesitated. Lars could catch a bit of what it was feeling, a mix of curiosity and trepidation. *How many sumbitches must we kill to fulfill your needs?*

Lars laughed out loud, a deep, cruel sound full of venom and fury. "All of 'em."

Onboard the *Doro* all was quiet, save for the tiny sounds of Iezzi Hand's metabolism. At last, Iezzi Hand was safe and could continue its mission: Sleep Until The Right Time.

Then came the fire.

At first it was merely uncomfortable. Iezzi Hand, protected by the armor it wore, burned only at the edges where it had no defense. But the fire was relentless, and the heat grew in intensity until the armor could no longer fully shield the flesh within.

The Iezzi Hand had never seen any need to evolve vocal mechanisms, and so it could not scream, only writhe in the searing agony. It restructured itself, pushing its small thinking nodule deeper into its body as its skin melted and charred.

As its bones blackened, Iezzi Hand could bear the agony no longer. It withdrew its neural connections entirely, becoming nothing more than a tiny, disembodied brain encased in charred, blackened meat.

With no sensory organs, Iezzi Hand became simply a thought in empty space. It had no idea if the fire would continue to rage and perhaps incinerate all that was left of the Colony.

It cried out in song to The Source to be delivered from its enemies. Iezzi Hand still had knowledge! It could still be of use!

If the Source heard, it did not deign to answer.

7

TEAM BRIEFING

Bleys looked around at Weyland's office, blinking, not quite sure how he had arrived or why he expected it to be different. It wasn't, of course. He had been here less than a week before, but it seemed ages ago, long enough for the standard Imperial plasteel blocks to have…what? Bleys wasn't really sure what happened to plasteel blocks after a really long time, but something awful, surely. Crumbled, melted, rusted or something. Nothing lasted forever, right?

Bleys stifled a grunt of pain as Kane, still suited up and sitting far too close, elbowed him hard in the ribs then gave him The Look.

Bleys gave him The "What" Look back and Kane rolled his eyes.

"Are we disturbing you, Captain Bleys?" called an unpleasant and all too familiar voice. Admiral Paul Weyland, hands clasped behind his back, stopped pacing and fixed Bleys with his stare. "Would you prefer we do this later, perhaps?"

Weyland was a severe man with severe features, an elderly officer of the sort the Emperor used for direct action rather than politics. Bleys didn't know the details, but rumor had it Weyland was responsible for enough deaths to make Kane look like a choir boy. He was the sort of admiral that you called when you wanted an entire continent melted. During peacetime you kept him on a chain someplace far from civilization, like, say, a frozen planet watching over prisoners and dealing with miners who occasionally flipped out into completely murderous psychos. He was *not* the sort of guy you wanted to piss off.

Bleys shook his head, trying to clear the cobwebs from it. "Uh no, sir, that won't be necessary."

Weyland glared at him a moment. "If you *must* sleep in my briefing, Captain, I by God will not have you snoring!"

Ana, in a chair on his other side, snickered, but was otherwise silent. Ed, standing at Weyland's liquor cabinet, had no readable expression at all.

Kane, big hearted guy that he was, spoke up. "To be fair, sir, I had him at gunpoint for the last thirty-six or thereabouts, so he's a little short on rack time."

"I'm aware of the situation," Weyland said. "Which is why I am giving him shit instead of shit duty." He shook a finger at Bleys. "Stay with us, Captain. We're saving the galaxy here. It's important, and I'll keep it short."

Bleys nodded, still a little uncertain if he had just zoned out or of Weyland was serious and he had actually nodded off and started snoring. He had tried his usual litany of tricks for staying awake, including imagining everyone naked, but it hadn't worked. Ed was *already* naked; Ana he was still conflicted about on account of Ed's creepiness; he could probably poke some fun at a naked Kane, but felt there was a distinct risk that Kane could turn it around on him. And, well, no one wanted to see Weyland naked, ever.

As if sensing that Bleys's mind was still wandering, Weyland gave him the stink eye again then turned his focus to Ana. "I have a new best friend," he said, waving a hand toward Ed, "Mr.

Decker reports to me that we should count you as the new Savior. Is that about the shape of it?"

Ana shifted uncomfortably in her seat, wearing an embarrassed grin. "I think he might be exaggerating just a little, but I do have useful skills."

"I have your records, Doctor Rasputin. Some of the best I've seen, including marksmanship. How long until we can feed people and breed more animals?"

Ana thought a moment. "With the right facilities and staff, we can have breeding stock in a month and enough to feed a large population both meat and grain in three."

Weyland turned to Ed and raised an eyebrow. Ed nodded and said, "I have examined the facilities and begun setup. With support from the station, we can have a lab complete within the week. I can work around the clock to make that happen."

Weyland gave her a thin smile. "So, will you take the job, Lieutenant Commander?"

Ana's eyes widened a bit at this, but she nodded. "We don't have the bots here. I'd need a large staff, at least fifty."

"Trained men or warm bodies?" Weyland asked.

"A few skilled people would be good, but mostly labor," she answered.

Weyland nodded. "We have plenty of laborers since we cleared out the prisons." Noting Ana's look of dismay, he added, "They're not convicts anymore. I've drafted them. They are all service members in wartime, just like us, and subject to the ICMJ. You are authorized to shoot any of them who give you trouble."

Ana blinked as she absorbed this, then nodded slowly. "Then I'll be glad to take the job, sir."

"Welcome aboard, Ms. Rasputin!" Weyland told her and stepped forward to shake her hand.

"That leaves us with a single civilian in the room," he continued, again gesturing toward Ed. "It would be impolite for me to draft a visiting foreign dignitary, but Mr. Decker has been kind enough to volunteer his services for the duration of the crisis." He paused a moment, looking at Kane. "Now, I know there was a dust up on Elysium and some of your men got dead, Chief. Do we need to file some Hurt Feelings reports, or can you work with this man…." He paused a moment, looking to Ed for approval on the term.

Ed shrugged and nodded.

"Can you work with him?" Weyland asked Kane.

Kane rose and saluted. "Sir, Mr. Decker has earned my respect as a true warrior. We can definitely work together, sir."

Weyland smiled in satisfaction. "How about you, Bleys? Any residual whiny bullshit, or are you okay with this?"

Bleys blinked, wondering if he had misunderstood the question. Ed hadn't really done anything to piss Bleys off. "Uh, yes, sir. I *like* Ed."

"Good, because you're going to be spending a lot of time together. I need you to get him to the jumpgate ASAP."

"We got problems," Bleys told him. "I have a big hole in my main airlock, and two of my interior hatches are trashed. *Doro* isn't flightworthy at the moment."

"I took the liberty of having my people patch her up when we irradiated her," Weyland assured him. "The hatches we had on hand and replaced. The airlock we'll need to fabricate some parts, but they welded a plate over the whole thing for now. It won't open, but it will hold pressure. You'll have to use that secondary airlock on the lower level."

Bleys nodded his agreement. "Then we're good to go. *Doro* can practically fly herself there, Admiral. I'll catch that rack time on the trip."

Weyland turned to Kane. "Chief, I have no use for a one-legged man in this ass-kicking outfit. Get a new one, pronto." He raised an eyebrow at Ana. "That gonna be a problem, doc?"

Ana shook her head. "No sir, assuming you have cybernetics on hand."

Weyland rolled his eyes. "We're a military installation, Ms. Rasputin. We have cyber to spare." He turned back to Kane. "Chief, you know what I *do* need? Marine officers. The ones I had on order never arrived."

Kane groaned. "Ah, shit."

"Stop whining, *Commander* Kane. Pick somebody else to share your pain. I need a Lieutenant, too."

Kane grinned. "Morgan deserves to suffer with me, sir."

"I'll leave it to you to inform him of his misfortune. Once that's done, start rounding up another team. We have a few regulars who can shoot straight. Start with them, and I'll approve whoever you choose for the billet change. Take a few out for live training on crackheads. They need thinning out anyway."

He turned again to Ana, "Doc, start requisitioning anything you need. Kane is authorized to shoot anybody who doesn't hop to when you tell them. Your discretion. Now go get that leg stuck on. Dismissed!"

In the reception area outside Weyland's office, Ana caught Bleys by the arm and froze, uncertain of her words. He looked at her expectantly, that damned lopsided grin giving her goosebumps. "Take care of Ed," she stammered, instantly regretting her words.

Thank God Bleys was the type to understand what she really meant. His ability to read people might actually work in her favor for once.

"Don't let Kane get into too much trouble," Bleys said with a laugh. He held her gaze for a moment, then added, "This is what I do. We'll be fine."

She knew it was true, but it didn't help much.

Kane clapped her on the shoulder. "It's okay, doc. Weyland did not authorize either of these knuckleheads to die."

Bleys gave her a wink. "See there? We're all good." He again paused, just looking at her, and said, "I'd bring you along. You know I would. But what you're doing here…."

"I know," she sighed, feeling, for all her strength, as if the weight of the world were on her shoulders. It was difficult to watch them both go into harm's way. She had no doubts that she loved Ed, at least in a platonic way, and then there was…whatever was going on with Bleys. She didn't have any answers for that, but the prospect of losing both of them made her feel slightly nauseous.

But she had a world to feed.

Ed nodded, a thin smile on his lips, and Bleys saluted, still wearing that slanted smile, his eyes making promises she hoped he would be able to keep.

Then they turned and left. Ana watched them go, the breeze from ventilation in the overhead suddenly feeling much colder.

Kane put a huge, armored arm around her, and she allowed him to draw her close. The cold, unyielding shell of the Panzer suit was hardly comfortable, but it was comforting all the same. He gave her a curt nod and said, "We'll keep busy. Plenty of work to do."

Kane led her out of the operations building and into a large, busy courtyard—an open square in the center of the perhaps twenty buildings that made up the installation. The prison, of course, was the largest structure, a great, cubic edifice composed of white plasteel blocks as was pretty much every other Imperial structure in the galaxy. A great gate, currently open, dominated the single entrance to the facility. Nearby, Ana spotted the low, single story building where Ed had told her he was setting up her lab. It too was made of white plasteel blocks.

As they crossed the tarmac, Ana shivered and huddled deeper

into her jacket against the biting wind. She smiled, an old memory surfacing. As a child she had once asked her father why everything in the Empire was white plasteel, or red, black, and gold symbols. Why was there no blue or green, or purple, even? Why no wood or chrome? Her father had dismissed the notion with the simple explanation that "White plasteel is cheap," and that was the end of the discussion.

Kane led her through throngs of busy people all dressed in drab, gray Imperial work uniforms. They all seemed intent on their business, whether it was moving equipment, eying their tablets, or hauling some piece of gear. Even the few conversations seemed all business, with little or no laughter or smiles.

Ana found it doubly surprising, considering half of these people or more had just been drafted and were formerly prisoners. Then again, she knew from experience that there was nothing like the threat of imminent death to make most people take things seriously.

Kane led her to a large warehouse structure. A sign outside announced in simple block letters, "Imperial Stores." Kane inserted his ID into a card reader, and the large entry door slid back to allow them access. Inside was a large room and a number of self-serve kiosks, each with its own computer terminal.

"We got pretty much anything you would need," he promised as he led her to a kiosk.

Ana navigated the menus, thoroughly impressed at how well the facility was stocked with medical supplies. "Well, *Commander* Kane, you might starve here, but you won't run out of artificial limbs any time soon."

Kane sighed and shook his head. "I am never gonna hear the end of that, am I?"

"Let me know when you forget who your father was," Ana quipped.

Kane grinned. "Moving right along, this is a combat post, ma'am. We expect a lot of medical intervention."

Ana laughed aloud at this. "Kane, you outrank me now, you know."

Kane laughed as well. "I guess I do, Lieutenant Commander."

"Okay," she said. "Gauntlet off. Let's see your hand."

"Eh? For what?"

"Matching your skin color."

Kane rolled his eyes. "It's a fucking cyberleg. I want it to look badass and mechanical."

Ana raised an eyebrow at this, but found she wasn't truly surprised. It somehow fit Kane. "So no skin then? Fair enough. It's easy to change later." She continued searching, this time for an arm. She might as well get what she needed for Zimmerman while she was here. He could choose a skin color when he woke up.

"It won't be changing," Kane promised.

Ana shrugged and keyed in her requests. While machinery deep within the building hummed as it retrieved her items, she turned to Kane and winked. "I know you're a married man, but I think I'll take you back to my place, slip you a mickey, and get you out of those pants. Sound good?"

Kane snapped her a salute. "I'll tell the wife it was for the Empire."

Onboard the *Doro*, Ed strapped himself into the copilot's chair as Bleys began a pre-flight checklist. Ed marveled to see the roguish captain behaving in such a meticulous manner. Bleys seemed much more a "seat of one's pants" sort of fellow, and Ed found the dichotomy amusing.

Ed, of course, had a great respect for checklists, though as an artificial intelligence he didn't actually check things off his lists. Rather, any particular task was a queue of actions that he performed in a specific order, one after the other. He was fairly certain the humans also operated similarly, though they were unaware of it as such.

And, of course, they were more easily distracted. Ed was in danger of such a failure himself, due to his limited processing power. Even now, several questions were uselessly occupying his CPU.

"Is it true you need authorization to die?" he asked.

Bleys stopped his checklist procedure, gave Ed a strange look, then laughed. Ed found the sound of human laughter slightly annoying—a bit like a braying donkey—but in theory it indicated good spirits. Ed understood humor and even found certain things amusing, but the way humans expressed it was grating. He presumed that as he became more familiar with operating in the "real" world this sort of thing would settle out and seem normal, but for now it was…unsettling.

Bleys appeared not to notice Ed's discomfort. "That's a joke, pal. You know, if you're not authorized—"

Ed held up a hand, nodding. "Yes, I understand the humor. But I was wondering if perhaps it went further. For example, if you were to be killed on this mission, would you receive some sort of demerit? Posthumously, of course."

Bleys blinked a moment, his expression blank, then shrugged. "Uh, I have no idea, honestly. I assume if I'm dead, I won't care."

Ed nodded. "This is almost certainly true."

Bleys waited a moment, as if uncertain if Ed were done speaking, then went back to his checklist. He activated several controls, observed the results, then turned on the main engine ignition. "You ready?"

Ed nodded. "Why do you have a disconnected jump-drive onboard?"

Bleys didn't miss a beat. "That old thing? I won it in a poker game. I doubt it even works."

Ed found it irksome that somehow Bleys seemed immune to a voice stress analysis. It *seemed* as if the man were telling the truth, but Ed had seen enough to know that Bleys was lying. The drive was new—barely used and professionally installed. It had been deliberately disconnected.

"I don't believe you," he said.

Bleys scowled at him a moment. "Fine, fine. I guess we're a team now." He ticked off the last few boxes on his checklist and buckled his seatbelt. "Last time I used it, it jammed up the sublight engines and I had to get towed. Getting it repaired was going to be pretty expensive. I planned on doing that with the cash I made from the Elysium run, only, you know, shit happened."

"And why is it disguised?"

Bleys sighed and leaned back in his seat as he powered up the engines. "Because the Empire has these pesky laws about jump capable ships having tracking devices on board. They can even commandeer the things from remote. I'd like to meet the asshole who thought that shit up."

"We *have* met," Ed assured him.

Bleys stared at him a moment, suspicious. "Are you saying *you* designed that thing?"

Ed nodded. "A few organizations, the Empire for one, paid licensing fees and did their own design, but most civilian drives follow one of my various patents. Yours is no exception. I recognized it at once."

Bleys rolled his eyes. "Remind me to kick your ass when we finish this thing."

"Reminder noted. For what purpose?"

"I dunno about you, Ed," Bleys groused, "But some of us don't like being monitored all the time, and we're willing to pay well to avoid it. Which is why getting it fixed was going to be damned expensive, you dig?"

"I—" Ed stopped mid speech, feeling self-conscious, then continued. "I dig."

A look of pain crossed Bleys's features. "No, man, your instincts were right," he said. "'Dig' is not a word for you. Let's scratch that from your lexicon, ok, bro?"

Ed nodded and turned to face the main viewscreen. "You are correct. I understand." He paused a moment, then added, "Bro."

Bleys laughed again and shook his head. "This is going to be a long, fun trip," Bleys said and throttled up the engines, setting the entire ship thrumming with power. "Sheridan Station, *Doro*. We are ready for departure."

"It will be long," Ed agreed. "We will see about the fun part."

8

BUG HUNT

"Welcome back, Commander," Ana called from what seemed to Kane a long distance.

Kane's brain caught up with the rest of him as he sat up and shook his head, feeling cloudy and confused. Sheridan Station's medical facilities wavered in and out of focus around him. It looked as if Ana had made herself at home.

Ana grabbed his shoulders and pushed him gently but firmly back to a lying position on the table. "Whoa, there. Give it a couple of minutes."

Kane lay back as the fog in his mind slowly yielded to full awareness. He peeked down at his stump to see a brand new, gunmetal gray leg protruding from a modest, white pair of shorts. "Outstanding!" he declared.

"You be careful with this thing," Ana told him. "It's strong, but the flesh it's anchored to isn't any different than it was before. If you try to use the cybernetic like your suit it can shred what's left of your leg pretty easily, and we'll be replacing you from the waist down. I doubt your wife would like that."

Kane laughed heartily. "They got cybernetics for that, too."

Ana shook her head. "Look and feel, yes. Making babies? No."

Kane gave her a knowing look. "Doc, I'm Imperial Marines. I got swimmers on ice since way back. It's just the prudent thing to do."

Ana shrugged. "It's your body. For future reference, will you want that part in gunmetal too?"

Kane gave her a toothy grin. "Oh, hell yeah."

Ana shook her head and looked back at her tablet, grinning as she made notes. "Let's give it a spin and see how it's working, Commander."

Kane groaned to hear the new title and remembered his orders were to make Morgan suffer in the same way and then to make a bunch of crackheads miserable via more traditional methods of fire and steel. He stepped down from the operating table, testing his weight on the new leg.

It felt real, like nothing had changed. He took a few halting steps, curious if it would somehow be unbalanced or stronger than the left and cause him to end up walking in circles, but all seemed normal.

Ana observed him for a bit, watching readouts on her tablet, and at last gave him a thumbs up. "All systems look good. I'd say you're fit for duty."

"How about Zimmerman?"

"Arm should be good," she said. "But I'm keeping him under for a few more days while his spine firms up."

"Sounds good." Kane rubbed his hands together and grinned. "Time to dish out some pain."

***

The Imperial Marine Barracks at Sheridan Station were spartan, but comfortable. The racks were stacked two high and laid out on both sides of a long, windowed hall, each set of bunks with a footlocker at either end. The floor was white plasteel tile, polished like glass over the ages from countless buffer passes, more often than not with marines riding the buffers like bucking broncos rather than more traditional pushing.

Kane loved how his voice boomed in the space. "Okay, ladies!" he roared. "Drop your cocks and grab your socks! It's time for a bug hunt!"

Morgan, the only man present, rolled out of his rack and groaned. "How's the Z-Man?"

"Still down. It's just me and you."

"Yeah, the rest are all UD."

Kane knew Morgan was giving him the verbal equivalent of "pull my finger" but figured he might as well get it over with. "Okay, Morgan, what's UD?"

"It's like UA, only instead of Unauthorized Absence, it—"

"Yeah, yeah, I get it, Unauthorized Dead. And what did you call me, Petty Officer Morgan?"

Morgan clearly sensed it was his turn to pull someone's finger but lacked the ability to resist. "Uh, 'Chief?'"

"Since when do you not refer to officers as "Sir," Petty Officer?"

Morgan blinked, not understanding, then light dawned in his eyes. "Oh, *shit!* Weyland jumped you up?"

Kane couldn't suppress a grin. "Commander. And you too, *Lieutenant.*"

"No shit? Where's your leaf?"

"It's tattooed on my ass, Marine! Come on, I got a shitty ink pen, let's do your bars too."

Morgan laughed aloud. "Oh, hell no! I'll brand those fuckers on with a soldering iron before I do prison tats! At least that shit'll be sanitary."

"Only pussies worry about germs," Kane asserted.

Morgan quickly began to dress in his dungarees. "Who we shooting?"

"Fucking bugs," Kane told him. "Weyland says thin 'em out, teach 'em some fear."

"Crackheads ain't scared of nothing," Morgan asserted as he laced his boots. "Still, dead crackheads are best crackheads."

"Amen. Get your gear on and let's bring some pain."

"Just us?"

"For now. Weyland wants me to pick some of the regulars and train them up, but I am not taking men like that into crackhead territory."

"Aw, why not, Chief?" Morgan asked, feigning sadness. "Noobs are great boobytrap detectors!"

"Exactly."

Morgan flashed a mischievous grin. "You don't want to send them in first?"

"We are not playing 'find the mine' with live actors," Kane snickered. "Move it. Let's get some."

Kane took a knee at the top of a small hill, crushing one of the stubby, alien plants that grew on Cerberus's tundra, at least along the equator. Ahead, he could see movement in what had to be a crackhead camp.

"Gunther, magnify and center on target."

Gunther dutifully complied, zooming the display inside Kane's helmet and giving him a clear view of his quarry. "Fuck," Kane sighed, taking a long look. It was remarkably similar to the creature they had faced onboard the *Doro* earlier, same coloration and bulging muscles, though this one seemed a little smaller, a little less ripped.

Morgan, viewing on his own visor, let out a long, low whistle over his radio. "Damn it, Chief! We ain't got no tags for *silver* crackheads!"

"No tags for dumbass marines either, but that is not going to matter if you keep acting the fool," Kane growled.

"Touchy," Morgan noted. He brought his rifle to bear on the camp. "Not getting any lately, Chief?"

"Ain't nobody getting any in this hellhole," Kane snickered. "Except for Bleys." He shook his head, grinning, then continued. "And you better get used to saying 'Commander.' Weyland is a stickler on that shit."

"I know," Morgan said, lining up a shot. "Baconator says can we kill this bitch or what?"

Kane shrugged and brought up his own rifle. "What round for silver crackhead, Lieutenant Morgan?"

"Commander Kane, I recommend the guided VB-5 Reichsadler HE for these pernicious pests."

"Gunther, bring up the VB-5s," he told his computer. Gunther responded with a beep, and the icons on Kane's HUD shifted ammo type to micro-missiles. Kane gave Morgan a thumbs up and said, "You may fire when ready, Gridley."

A missile burst from Morgan's rifle, trailing smoke and fire, followed by Kane's projectile. A moment later, a double explosion blossomed in the crackhead camp, orange and deadly.

"Hell, yeah!" Morgan shouted. "Pink mist, just how I like it! And who the fuck is Gridley?"

Kane gave Morgan a disapproving look. "You know, Commodore Dewey's famous line?"

Morgan game him a blank look and shrugged.

"How about 'Damn the torpedoes, full speed ahead' by Admiral Farragut?" He paused a moment, then scowled. "These are iron men and wooden ships sayings! Sheer badassery, son! Did you fail Naval history?"

"Yup," Morgan snickered. "But I kill people real good, *and* I can fix stuff, so they gave me a waiver."

Kane shook his head, embarrassed that he had expected an honest answer. "Let's go burn the damned chunks. If he was infected, nothing says he won't pull back together."

Gunther superimposed another red square over Kane's visor. "GPR shows density variation."

Kane sighed and readied his weapon. "Got another one," he said to Morgan.

His companion nodded. "Yup, Baconator's got it too. Your turn." He stepped back, placing himself behind Kane. "Ready."

If there was anything constant about crackheads, it was traps. Paranoid psychosis had a way of making a man very creative in keeping people out, but the general trend was always explosive. Part of it was that crackheads almost always had shitloads of crack, and the highly energetic substance was fairly easy to cobble into powerful bombs. But Kane was convinced there was something about crackhead psychology that just liked blowing shit up.

To be fair, Kane found himself in agreement on that point. He fired his M87 blaster at the spot Gunther had indicated, triggering an enormous explosion. Dirt and chunks of permafrost filled the air briefly.

"You'd be getting another new leg if you'd walked in on that," Morgan said.

"Damn straight," Kane agreed. "Gunther, anything else?"

Gunther emitted a low tone. "GPR shows no further anomalies in direct route."

"Gunther, keep scanning in case we missed something. I don't feel like losing any more body parts today."

"Continuous scanning engaged."

Gingerly, Kane and Morgan entered the interior of the camp, on high alert for any other surprises the fellow might have left for them to find. Of their target himself, only a few large pieces remained, but as Kane had feared, they were not dead. There was nothing solid enough to actually move around, but a number of identifiable pieces were still quivering. Given time, he would guess they could knit up and reform.

"Gunther, can you track the crackhead's remains for sterilization?"

"Adjusting scan to search for flectocite-infused flesh." A moment later, Kane's visor lit with multiple targets.

"Gunther, pass along that data to Morgan's comp."

Gunther beeped again. "Data transmitted."

"Morgan, decon this area while I check his gear. I'm gonna try to disable any other traps he has. I don't want to just leave them out here for some poor bastard to stumble into if we don't have to."

Morgan gave Kane a thumbs up. "I'm on it."

In Kane's experience, crackheads fell into a few archetypes. You had basic bitch knife guy who stabbed people and not much more. You had shooty guy who could be counted on to have a ton of guns and ammo, at least a few of which you'd be happy to claim as your own. You had your pickaxe guy who was too lazy to change over from work tool to killing tool and had a habit of collecting heads.

But up to now, he had not seen any silver, super crackheads. Now he'd seen two in one day, and he had no doubt it was some weird side effect of Pestilence. But the one on the *Doro* hadn't *acted* like the Pestilence. It looked weird, but the talk, the walk— that was one hundred percent crackhead.

Which meant something hella weird was going on.

"Shitheads, right?" Morgan called over his commlink. In the

background Kane overheard Morgan's blaster discharge.

Kane located a battered tablet computer and powered it up. "What?"

"These silver, swoll up crackheads? Doc said we could call 'em shitheads, right?"

Kane shrugged. "That doesn't sound very scientific to me." He located a small, jury-rigged panel of switches. "Gunther, is this the trap control?"

"It appears so, sir."

Kane flipped the switches to the off positions, still troubled by the second mutant crackhead. He had a good idea how it had happened, but he had to be sure. "Gunther, do a satscan. Let's see how this one got infected."

A moment later Gunther answered, "Surveillance shows another similar creature attacked the camp and left the occupant for dead."

"Only he wasn't dead," Kane muttered. "Gunther, is this other creature the same one who attacked us on the *Doro*?"

Gunther sounded a dull, flat beep. "Insufficient detail to confirm or deny."

"It's him, though," Kane muttered. "I *know* it."

Morgan's voice cut through his thoughts, shouting over the radio, "Chief!"

"That's Commander, Lieutenant."

"Baconator's got some bad shit on the surveillance."

"Yeah, we're checking it out here too," Kane answered. "The one from the *Doro* looks to have deliberately come here and infected this one."

"This is *way* worse," Morgan insisted. "I'm sending you the feed, ok?"

"Do it."

Kane ground his teeth as he watched multiple video sources playing out scenes similar to the one he had just witnessed. An attacker would lure his victims out, incapacitate them somehow, and then do something to them and leave.

"Gunther, patch Morgan into our convo and answer query: do they all wake up again?"

Gunther chirped. "The recovery time is consistent across all cases, approximately one hour."

"Gunther, how many cases?"

"Eighty-seven, including the creature you just destroyed."

"Gunther, what's the timespan on these attacks?"

"Eighteen hours, thirty-seven minutes."

Morgan drawled over the radio, "Do the math. It ain't just the one."

"Nope," Kane agreed. "They're cooperating."

"Crackheads don't cooperate," Morgan observed.

"Looks like shitheads do," Kane replied. "Gunther, track them. Where are they now?"

Gunther paused a moment, then beeped again. "Eighty-six are gathered in a canyon three miles from Sheridan Station."

"*Son of a bitch!*" Morgan shouted. "That's a rally point for sure!"

"Yep!" Kane agreed. "Let's move! Gunther, get me a line to Weyland! Sheridan Station is about to be under attack!"

Ana, carrying a box full of test tubes, took a moment to familiarize herself with her new lab. Shelves and workbenches occupied the center of the room, all laden with new equipment, still in boxes. Two large sliding doors formed the center point of the front wall, the remainder of the space filled with windows overlooking Sheridan Station's main courtyard. If she had a mind to daydream she could watch the comings and goings of the miners and guards, or she could pull the blinds for privacy.

Along one twenty-foot wall, Ed had installed and activated a full-sized fabricator. Even now it was busily cranking out equipment to facilitate fast-growth, building components layer by layer and assembling them.

On the other side of the suite a section of wall had been removed completely and replaced temporarily with a large sheet of transteel. Multiple palettes of plasteel blocks were stacked outside in preparation for building a corridor that would facilitate transporting animals in and out of the lab. Someone else would presumably work out where best to place corrals and slaughter facilities.

The last wall was currently being used for storage, almost certainly the work of Imperial Personnel rather than Ed. Several bright orange chemical handling suits hung from hooks like shed skins alongside a dozen plasteel barrels of various chemicals. One, colored bright red, stood out from the others, which were black. The red barrel contained highly concentrated hydrofluoric acid, a chemical she often worked with, but it seemed foolish to have it just sitting out in the open. Not only were the vapors poisonous, it could easily dissolve flesh *and* bone. It was just so Imperial to ignore common sense safety procedures in favor of efficiency. In the Empire one did not store dangerous chemicals in special locations. Instead, they made certain to keep the CBR suits close at hand, presumably to allow natural selection to take its course in the event of an accident.

Ana jumped at the sound of the klaxon, almost dropping a set of test tubes she was carrying. Throughout the facility Weyland's voice rang out over loudspeakers, active computer monitors, and even her own personal tablet: "All personnel, secure areas and prepare for assault!"

Life on Cerberus was definitely more exciting that the idyllic existence of Elysium, but that was not necessarily a good thing. She set her test tubes on a nearby workbench and reflexively checked to make sure her sidearm was still present. That was one thing she planned on never giving up again.

One of her three assistants, Wallace, placed a crate of glassware on one of the many shelves in the center of the room and looked about, eyes wide and filled with fear. "How can there be an attack? The jumpgates are closed."

"Let's remain calm," Ana called, holding up a hand. "Seal the doors while we wait for more information. I'm sure they will look after us. We're a critical operation."

Cora and Anders, the other two assistants, both moved to the large sliding doors in the front wall and pulled on a long bar on each to engage the manual locking mechanisms.

Wallace scratched at the stubble on his chin and grimaced. "I'm telling you, something is wrong. There shouldn't *be* anybody to attack."

Cora snorted. "There are plenty of crackheads out in the wastes."

Wallace shook his head and wagged a finger at her. "Crackheads don't organize, noob. Sometimes some poor bastard turns inside the gates and they put him down. Once in a while one comes wandering in from outside and they kill him too."

Cora looked doubtful. "I never heard of that."

Wallace sighed. "Yeah, I know, because it's routine. They don't announce it. This is something different!"

Blaster fire, loud and nearby, interrupted their conversation, the high-pitched discharges setting Ana's teeth on edge. Everyone, Ana included, ran to the windows to see what was happening.

Outside, four guardsmen, dressed for battle, rained steady bursts of red plasma toward the main gate. Ana gasped as she saw their target.

The creature looked like a man, save for the color of its skin and the ridiculously oversized muscles. It seemed as if it had literally burst through its own clothes, the remaining cloth in tatters and hanging like rags about its bulk, as if an adult had forced itself into a child's clothing. The beast's huge hands clutched at the bars on the gate, tendons popping under silvery knuckles as it tightened its grip and twisted.

It was the same creature that had attacked them on the *Doro!*

But no, it was a different one, not quite as large, and with a different face, different hair. The one on *Doro* had been raving, furious, in a murderous rage. This one was calm, placid, just going about its work as if no one were shooting at it.

But they *were* shooting at it, hammering it with blaster fire. Even so, the creature seemed to take little damage from the energy. She could see its silvery skin sear and blacken, showing carbonized scorch marks, but it didn't give way.

The creature tensed, pulling on the bars for all it was worth, muscles straining fit to burst. Slowly, ever so slowly, with a high-pitched squeal the bars gave way, and one popped loose from its anchoring completely. The creature hurled it at the guards like a javelin. The targeted guard raised a riot shield just in time, for all the good it did. The deadly missile punched right through the transteel barrier and continued on into the guard's head with a spray of blood, bone, and gray matter.

The remaining guards, frantic now, turned to flee, screaming for reinforcements as their comrade's body collapsed to the tarmac. The silver beast slipped through the widened gap in eerie silence and charged after them, feet thudding on the tarmac. It leapt and caught the nearest guard square in the back, knocking him flat.

Then, to Ana's shock and horror, it sank its teeth into the unfortunate fellow's neck and began tearing and swallowing chunks of flesh. The unfortunate guard shrieked, a high pitched, gurgling sound, then fell mercifully silent.

Cora clutched her hands together and screamed. The next

attacker, who was even now squeezing and wriggling through the opening in the gate, snapped its head in the direction of the lab.

"Oh, brilliant!" Wallace wailed. "The windows aren't going to hold that thing back!"

The beast launched itself toward them, hurtling forward like a comet as they all watched in stunned terror. It covered the distance of the courtyard in seconds, hit the windows full force with a resounding smack, and rebounded.

Ana breathed a sigh of relief. Thank God for good old-fashioned Imperial construction. The windows weren't glass. They were transteel!

Still, they would not hold long, she knew. The creature onboard the *Doro* had torn through hatches. She had to act fast.

The thought of Bleys's cabin made her smile a moment, and she felt a surge of strength and hope. Suddenly, and for no particular reason, she was certain that things were going to turn out okay. She resolved that once this was over, she would go back to that cabin and have her way with the Captain of the *Doro*, come what may.

She and her friends were going to live. Ed was going to open the gates again, and she was going to see her son.

But first she had to kill this fucker.

The beast outside rose on unsteady legs, shaking its head, and lumbered over the window again. It swung a massive fist experimentally at the transteel. The blow landed and rang the window like a gong, and a small dent appeared on the inner side. Seemingly satisfied that this was a passable barrier, the beast began pounding with both hands, searching for a weak spot and filling the lab with deafening sound.

Behind the creature, Ana could see more of his kind pouring through the breach in the gate, clawing and scrabbling, too many to count at the moment. She would just have to hope Weyland's men would find better weapons to bring to bear.

As for her, weapon options were limited. Blasters seemed useless, which was quite a mystery in and of itself. The Pestilence was vulnerable to energy weapons. Why would these creatures be different? But they plainly were.

The Pestilence would heal most damage from trauma. It required complete tissue destruction to kill. She looked about the lab, frantic for anything she might use as a weapon.

Her eye settled on the large red drum against the wall, and a dark smile crossed her lips. She almost giggled at the providence. Hydrofluoric acid would do a fine job of melting and poisoning flesh. The trick would be to avoid getting liquified along with the enemy.

Imperial efficiency was not to be denied.

"All of you, get into those hazmat suits!" Ana shouted, barely able to hear herself over the incessant pounding.

Her underlings looked at her a moment as if she were crazy. Ana charged across the room and began suiting up. ""Do it now!" she shouted.

Kane and Morgan approached the walled fortress that was Sheridan Station at what Kane referred to as "flank speed" and Morgan called "bat out of hell mode." The Panzer suits let them run at a speed approaching a ground car, not only augmenting their muscle power but absorbing shock from irregular terrain. Even so, there were safeties and limits. The mechanical parts of the Panzer Suit were capable of more than fifty miles per hour— perhaps twice as much, depending on conditions—but the meat part, the pilot, was less resilient. Pushing beyond nominal "top" speed for long was dangerous, but the Navy had a term for it: "gundecking," the act of ignoring safety or procedure because (in theory) people were in fact shooting at you.

In peacetime, gundecking safety procedures and overrides was an offense that would, at minimum, get you a week of EMI: Extra Military Instruction, another Naval euphemism which typically meant after-hours duty scrubbing shitters, swabbing pissy decks in the head, or scraping rotten accumulations of grease from the deep fryers in the galley. Brass railed against it, and because shit rolled downhill chiefs held this line too, though in practice they often turned a blind eye to it except in egregious cases. For the harried, enlisted man trying to accomplish everything on his list, the complicated procedures and best practices created by pencil pushers and brass catering to politicians were dead time, wasted hours that could be put to better use actually accomplishing real work.

Weyland, Kane assumed, would not have concerns about gundecking on a two-way shooting range. The dirty little secret of the Imperial Navy was that most of the real work, from keeping the ships and weapons running to the destruction of the Empire's enemies, happened despite the interference of the political brass. The politicians got what they considered the "plum" posts, where they could hobnob and curry favor far away from any ability to observe how their orders were actually carried out. Admirals of the kinetic persuasion were all assigned to places like Cerberus—unpleasant, harsh posts of critical strategic value, places the Empire was willing to use as much force as was needed to control and defend. Weyland and his ilk were hard men with much blood on their hands, men who had reached the pinnacle of their advancement for the simple reason that they were best suited for where they were: at the end of a chain held by the Emperor, to be released as needed.

They were the ones the galaxy truly feared. Or had, back when there was an Empire to fear. These shitheads, Kane was certain, had picked the wrong admiral to fuck with.

But he was gundecking his speed safeties, even so.

Ahead in the distance he could see the silver-skinned bastards swarming the main gate. From within the regulars were raining blaster fire on the invaders, to little avail. Kane had a theory on the resistance, that it somehow had to do with the silver skin. Once you cracked them open, blasters seemed to work just fine.

They covered the remaining ground quickly. Kane clocked Morgan near seventy miles per hour as he sprinted forward and shook his head. The kid had heart, but that was going to play hell with his joints and muscles. He was going to be in considerable pain when he removed his suit and disconnected his neural link.

Then again, so was Kane. He might not be pushing as hard as Morgan, but there would be hell to pay for it even so.

Ahead, Morgan turned a shoulder and plowed into a shithead, a standard maneuver for initial enemy contact. He hit the shithead with the force of a small truck at freeway speeds and the two went down, digging a huge furrow in the tundra, the creature spewing blood and screeching as Morgan's fist hammered dents into its skull.

Kane slowed his roll and took aim with his blaster. "Open him up!" he shouted.

Morgan's wrist bayonet popped from its storage, and the marine stabbed the creature in the gut then jerked upward, gutting him like a fish. As the beast convulsed, Morgan rolled aside to give Kane a clear shot.

The bolt of energy hit the silver beast mid torso, scorching and burning the exposed flesh just like it would a man. Kane pumped a fist in the air and was about to go after the next one when a voice cut through his helmet at full volume.

"Kane, Weyland! Are you local?"

"Kane, aye! We're local, sir. There's a large group outside a breach in the main gate."

"Forget about them! Most of them are already inside, and I

have regulars on siege blasters dealing with that problem. I need you to secure Rasputin! She's right in the line of fire."

"Secure Rasputin, aye, sir! I'm on it!"

Morgan was already sizing up another. The rest of the attackers were still struggling to scramble through the breach, not reacting at all to the loss of one of their own. They were either too focused on their assault to notice, or maybe they just didn't care what happened to their comrades. The Pestilence surely didn't. It only cooperated for offense. As far as Kane had seen, the Pestilence didn't even *do* defense. It just died and made more.

"Morgan, we gotta get through that breach and rescue the doc!"

Morgan looked in Kane's direction. "We got ten of these fuckers in our way. How we getting in?"

Kane looked at the breach and the creatures milling about it, not having much of an answer beyond the obvious.

"We're going *through* 'em, brother! Gunther, VB-5s!"

Ana examined the seal on the barrel of acid as her assistants finished suiting up. It looked like it would hold. "Do *not* remove your respirators unless you want to choke up your own lungs!" she called, struggling to be heard over blows to the window. "Help me get this on its side and into position!"

Wallace, near panic now, cried, "What's 'in position'?"

"You'll know it when that *chudovishche* breaks through!" Ana shouted back.

That seemed to shut him up well enough.

The quartet waited as the creature continued pounding, trying to gain entrance. Behind it others of its kind continued pouring into the courtyard, but they had no interest in Ana and her unfortunate assistants. She could hear explosions and the low-pitched hum of heavy blasters, so likely most of the enemy was actively engaged. It was some small comfort. Weyland would certainly have the firepower at his disposal to put these things down. The Empire rarely skimped on destructive force, though sometimes it took time to bring it to bear.

She would just need to figure out how to survive this one fiend, and they should be clear.

Imperial construction, especially in prisons, was damned sturdy, but the silver beast was both tremendously strong and absolutely relentless. At last, the plasteel frame holding the window in place began to buckle. A few more blows and it would give way completely.

"He's coming in right there!" Ana shouted and pointed to what seemed the likeliest spot. If she was wrong they would probably all die, but in truth, that might happen anyway—if not from being torn to shreds, then from being melted like ice in a hard rain. If today was her day, at least it would be memorable. The family would tell her story to frighten children. It would be very Russian.

The transteel window folded inward at the next blow. As the creature crawled inside like a giant, silver ape, Ana and Wallace rolled the plasteel drum of hydrofluoric acid at their attacker. Cora and Anders dove behind the heaviest workbench.

Ana drew her blaster. *"Dasvidaniya, ublyudok!"* she cried as she pulled the trigger.

The bolt of plasma hit the barrel near the floor, blasting a jagged hole in its side and flipping it upward toward the creature. Reflexively, their would-be attacker swung a huge fist at the incoming projectile, causing the already weakened container to completely rupture. The deadly acid exploded in all directions, dousing the silver beast and spraying most of the lab.

The creature roared and screamed a moment until the acid literally burned through its throat. It thrashed violently a few moments, smoking and literally melting before her eyes. Shortly thereafter it was nothing more than an expanding pile of sizzling, smoking stew slowly melting into a puddle.

Cora screamed from behind the workbench, "I fucking *love* hydrofluoric acid!"

Ana looked about to see what she already knew: the lab was in ruins. Ed's fabricator and most of the items it had created were all smoking, as was the bench Cora and Anders had used for cover. Even her rack of test tubes was melting!

The lab was a total loss, but she had to admit, Cora was right. Hydrofluoric acid was hell on wheels.

She would have to get another barrel very soon.

A heavy thud outside startled her. She looked to the window to see two dark figures moving about. A pair of hands grasped the warped transteel and pulled, the metal screeching in protest against the plasteel frame.

For a moment she felt choked by rising panic, envisioning more attackers, until she saw flame burst from one of the hands. At that point her brain managed to resolve the warped figures on the other side as marines in Panzer suits.

"Stand clear!" Morgan called through the speaker on his suit as he cut the last of the anchors on the transteel window. Twisted metal fell to the floor with an enormous crash.

"Look out!" she shouted back. "The whole place is toxic! Poisonous fumes and hydrofluoric acid everywhere!

Morgan poked his helmeted head in and surveyed the scene. When he spied the bubbling remains of the creature, little more than a few scraps of bone in a caustic pool, he did a double take. "Holy shit, doc! We came to help but looks like you had it in hand. You melted the fucker with hydrofluoric?"

Ana shrugged and grinned back at him.

Morgan whistled loudly as he surveyed the carnage. "I have got to get me some of that shit!"

9

THE GATE

Bleys awoke, suitably refreshed, and rose from his rack. He stretched, pulled on his pants, then padded to the head. Once his business there was done, he finished dressing and joined Ed in the cockpit.

The AI, seated in the copilot's chair, did not look up as Bleys entered but continued tapping busily at the control console before him.

Bleys checked his instruments and saw the *Doro* was less than an hour from completing her deceleration burn. "Almost there," he noted.

Ed nodded and continued whatever he was doing without comment.

The full trip took a good forty hours one way. A layperson might wonder why the Empire tended to place its fast travel points a significant distance from the primary point of interest in a system, but Bleys knew all too well why that was the case.

Officially it was to allow warning as to who was coming through a gate, the better to assemble a welcoming committee in the event it was a hostile force. In Bleys's experienced opinion, that was bunk. Nobody seriously attacked Imperial planets.

But people *ran* from them all the time. The one thing local governors were *not* allowed to do was to shut down the jump-gates, so the distance served as a sort of buffer zone to allow them to pursue…well, guys like Bleys, typically.

More than once Bleys had continued breathing solely because *Doro* was a fast boat, capable of outrunning the Empire's swiftest vessels. That, too, was illegal and also very expensive, but again, the Empire was predictable: if you could get around the corner, they would usually stop chasing you. Typically, they wanted you gone more than they wanted you dead, so once you left one governor's space you were someone else's problem.

They would only hunt you down if you killed "important" people, a charge Bleys had worked very hard to avoid being pinned with. He'd done it once—to a real bastard who had absolutely deserved it—but not so anyone knew it was him.

Bleys slid into his captain's chair and checked the *Doro's* speed. They had decelerated enough to begin an approach on the gate control module. The problem was, he had no idea how to find the thing when it was deactivated. Normally jumpgates emitted a beacon signal on both sides, but with the gate shut down he only had a calculated position. That would get them close, but finding a small body orbiting on its own in the vastness of space was a task that made finding a needle in a haystack seem a snap. As far as Bleys was concerned it was impossible, but Ed had assured him otherwise.

Still, he couldn't quite avoid the temptation to scan the black, star strewn expanse in front of him, any more than he could pass a slot machine and not put a coin in. Of course, he'd use a slug if he had one handy. He wasn't stupid, after all.

"Okay, pal, time to do your thing," he said to Ed, who was still tapping away at the copilot's console. "We should be right on top of it, within a hundred miles anyway, but I have no way of knowing. It tends to drift a little, and I have no idea if it corrects when it's shut down."

Ed did not look up as he spoke. "It does not. This would be much simpler with a direct link to the ship's computer."

Bleys grinned, admiring the AI's tenacity, but shook his head. "Yeah, no."

"I thought we were a team now," Ed noted. For the life of him, Bleys couldn't tell if Ed was being sarcastic or not.

"Yeah, well, that's a different team that gets access to *Doro's* computers."

"And which team is that?" Ed asked.

"It's just me on that team."

"Nothing personal still, I presume?" Ed said as he continued…whatever he was doing.

"So how *do* we find a tiny satellite?" Bleys asked, peering over at Ed's console. The screen was awash with hundreds of lines of code. Ed's fingers danced on the keyboard like oil on a hot skillet, so fast they were almost a blur. "Are you actually—?"

"Writing an application? Yes. This will require custom software."

Bleys raised an eyebrow. Had there been another person aboard, it would have been the ideal time to cut his eyes toward Ed and shake his head sadly—but alas, they were alone, and the opportunity was lost. "It didn't occur to you to do that ahead of time?"

"Why? This won't take more than a moment. It will be done before you finish matching orbits."

Bleys gave Ed a dubious look and pressed a sequence of buttons on his own panel. "I'm done."

Ed stopped typing and offered Bleys a thin smile. "As am I. Shall we?"

"The spirit is willing, but the brain is weak," Bleys said, grinning back. "I'm still in the dark here, pal, literally." He waved a hand at the black of space before them. "You're going to have to explain what we're doing."

"Every jumpgate has a little-known radio diagnostic mode," Ed replied. "It is typically used for final testing after initial setup. We can retrieve certain information, though we cannot control it via this method."

"So we can just ask it where it is?"

Ed shook his head, a gesture Bleys found very human. "No. There is no provision for that. The transmission is very weak, a few hundred miles at most. I assumed anyone using the diagnostic would already know the location, so I never saw a need to provide that function. We can retrieve operating temperatures, gyroscope readouts, etc."

Bleys thought on this a moment, then pointed a finger triumphantly at Ed. "We can triangulate on the signal and use that as a beacon."

"Correct," Ed replied.

Bleys scowled as a thought occurred to him. "There has to be security."

Ed bent back to his console. "There is, but minimal. The information is nothing useful to an attacker. It's a simple sixteen-bit hash, nothing a child with an ounce of patience couldn't overcome in an hour or so, but it keeps the system from wasting CPU time responding to every signal it detects. One in sixty-four thousand five hundred thirty-six signals will trigger it and either fail to parse or transmit random values that the sender likely won't be listening for. It wasn't about security, just efficiency."

"Okay, so what's the code?"

"I don't know. They are randomly assigned at construction. Hence the software." He indicated the display screen.

Bleys laughed aloud. "Try them all, eh?"

"Precisely. At one millisecond per attempt, we'll have it in just over a minute, maximum, very likely much less. But there is a slight wrinkle."

Bleys nodded. "We have to be close enough."

Ed looked impressed. "I begin to see why my sister hates you, Captain Bleys. You're quite adept at understanding and solving problems."

"That's high praise indeed coming from a guy who looks at physical laws as minor obstacles. You're lucky God hasn't come down from heaven to personally kick your ass. I'm a scrub compared to you, pal. I'm just sneaky."

The look on Ed's face was the most human Bleys had seen him express. Ed looked like he was simultaneously afraid, embarrassed, and constipated, which in Bleys's opinion was a damned impressive emotional state to achieve. It was still tough to say if Ed was really, truly readable like most people, but he sure seemed to be getting there, and Bleys had no doubt he had touched a nerve.

Ed asked hesitantly, "Do you believe in God?"

Bleys shrugged. "Most of the time. I'm a gambling man. It kind of goes with the territory. You?"

Ed made a gesture that was half-shrug, half nod, an unreadable expression on his face. "I, too, do a great deal of odds calculation. I'd say the odds of God's existence are better than even."

Bleys snickered. "How do you make odds on something like that?"

"It's not formal," Ed said. "It's really more observation coupled with certain facts. I have no hard evidence, but I have my own personal experiences. You understand that I have, personally, created a small universe, yes? I have simulated to a very fine degree multiple versions of reality. I know that it *can* be done."

"And you're one of those guys who figures if we can do it, what are the odds we're the first?"

Ed nodded. "Correct," then turned back to his application and began keying in parameters.

Bleys gave him a moment before prodding him. "And?"

Again Ed looked uncomfortable, but he paused his work and looked back at Bleys. "I have some idea what it takes to run a universe, Captain, and therefore what actions by the occupants would cause difficulties for an administrator."

For the first time in the conversation, Bleys did not follow. It must have been obvious on his face, because Ed gave him another thin smile and asked, "You can't guess what would anger such a God? What would annoy him?"

Bleys thought on it a moment. "I don't dig the science angle, but I know *people*. This bugs you, so I'm guessing it's something *you* did. It's either FTL, or Avalon."

Ed, looking haggard, nodded. "Why not choose both?"

Bleys blew a long, low whistle. "So you actually think you might have pissed off God?" He watched Ed closely, noticing the subtle squirming and other signs of discomfort and wondered how he had ever doubted the AI's "personhood." Ed was damned proud of the synthskin body, but it just didn't quite have the range of a real human. Somewhere, sometime, some wonk had coined a term for it: the uncanny valley. That's where Ed lived. Ed was *totally* readable, just more subtle.

The tumblers in Bleys's mind rolled and clicked and the answer came, as it always did. "You're not here for Ana. Not really. That's what you told yourself to begin with, but it's something bigger, isn't it?" He carefully studied Ed's body language. "You think the Pestilence is your fault, don't you? Some kind of divine retribution."

Ed looked away and said softly, "In Biblical tales, pestilence was but one of ten plagues sent to punish Pharaoh's arrogance."

Bleys looked out at the blackness of the void and shivered, a deep, almost painful chill in his gut. This was not where he had expected the conversation to go when he had started it with a well-meaning joke. Still, he had learned a lot about his traveling companion, which made it a pretty useful exchange. He slapped a reassuring hand on Ed's shoulder. "Hey, pal, one plague at a time, ok?"

Ed, still looking a bit morose, offered another smile. "I'll work on a plan for dealing with the frogs as soon as we're done with this one."

Bleys rubbed his hands together gleefully and rose. "Great! I'll go get us some coffee."

"None for me," Ed replied.

Ed found, to his surprise, that being regaled with tales of Bleys's exploits and sexual conquests was actually rather entertaining. Ed remembered very few sexual experiences, and even those were secondhand and fairly ordinary, certainly nothing worthy of sharing as entertainment. He likewise had no tales of danger or adventure, save for the one in which he was currently participating, and Bleys already knew the details of that excursion. The conversation was decidedly one-sided, but for all that Ed enjoyed it.

Adventures, it seemed, were most enjoyable when they were in the past or someone else was having them. While actually experiencing an "adventure" it was more synonymous with "grave danger," a situation Ed considered something to avoid.

It took them a good twelve hours to find the module, a constant stream of maddening failures as they expanded their search, spiraling outward methodically on each axis. Bleys would curse often, colorful invective, some of which were new to Ed. He logged them for later.

Curse words had long seemed strange to Ed. Until recently, he had no idea why anyone would create a word that should not be uttered, but he realized now that this confusion almost certainly stemmed from his own lack of experience. He had discovered of late that, at the height of an adventure, voicing such forbidden words was indeed quite satisfying.

Clearly, though, such words would need to be reserved for the right occasion or they would become mundane. He would have to make up new vulgarities regularly if he used them with the casual abandon the Captain did.

Economics were important, even with words.

"There she is," Bleys said.

"Yes," Ed agreed. His vision was considerably better than humans, and he could already make out the spinning, roughly spherical construct in the distance. It seemed to slowly grow as they approached, details resolving as Bleys matched speed and rotation until it filled the viewscreen in front of them. Ed again found himself impressed with the Captain. Bleys did most of the piloting by the seat of his pants, only engaging the computer when he was ready to maintain his position.

"I'm parking about fifty yards out, just to be safe," Bleys announced and gave Ed a smug look, lacing his fingers behind his head and leaning back in his seat. "Not sure why she's a thousand miles off course, so I want to leave a little room for the unexpected."

The structure was perhaps a quarter mile on a side—enormous compared to the *Doro*, but still a tiny dot in space. As with everything else Imperial, it was made of white plasteel, though there seemed to be some odd scoring and black marks along one side.

"I'll investigate that out once I retrieve the control module," Ed said and rose.

Bleys offered him a dubious look. "You going out there *au naturel*?"

"I'll need a thruster pack," Ed said. "But I have no need for pressure or air, and my hands and feet are magnetic."

"You ever do a spacewalk before, pal?"

"No. It should be quite an experience."

Bleys shook his head and sighed. "If it was anybody but you, I'd ask if I could have your stuff when you died out there, but I guess you're pretty good with geometry. Just take it easy until you get a feel for the thruster."

Ed nodded. "Good advice. I'll stay in contact over the radio."

He rose and headed aft, through the cockpit door and down the ladder into the galley, then from there into the lower aft storage compartment. The primary airlock on deck one was out of commission, sealed over for now with a large sheet of plasteel until proper repairs could be made. The auxiliary airlock in lower aft storage was the only viable exit.

Ed retrieved one of several thruster vests from a rack near the airlock. He made certain to verify the charge, then strapped it on and, using the hand control, tested the rotation and forward thrusters. Each emitted a short burst of compressed air and seemed to be functioning properly. Satisfied, Ed entered and cycled the airlock, then opened the outer door.

The gate control station loomed before him, seemingly stationary now, the entry airlock a scant fifty yards away. Behind it empty space yawned, strewn with pinpoints of light, an eternal fall for the careless.

Ed, however, was nothing if not precise. He stepped out into space. It was a curious sensation. The cold was significant, but his body had been designed with the possibility of spacewalking in mind and any temperature sensitive components were well insulated and heated internally.

"I'm outside," he said, transmitting synthesized and modulated speech rather than vocalizing. "Video feed now online. I'm beginning traversal to the platform now."

He pressed the button that fired his main thruster and felt a sensation a bit like having been kicked from behind.

"I have your view on-screen," Bleys answered. "Watch it, you're coming in a little hot there, not too bad, but it'd give me a bruise or two if I hit the wall at that speed."

"This frame is more resilient than a human body," Ed assured him as he enabled the magnets in his hands and feet.

The impact was slightly jarring. As Bleys noted it would have caused minor damage to a human, but Ed's synthskin frame was unharmed. His hands and feet adhered to the station's hull with a dull clank, the sound transmitted through his own skeleton.

Ed crawled like a spider to the station's airlock, knowing it would be locked, but he tried the latch just to be certain. He turned to examine the keycard reader that sat to the side of the hatch. It was standard government tech, reasonably secure against all but the most dedicated attacks.

Of course, it hadn't been built to withstand a direct assault from a living AI.

Ed twisted the tip of his right index finger and removed it to expose a small drill. He did the same with the middle finger, revealing a flat prying tip. Beneath the pinkie were various screwdriver bits. He selected a smaller one fit for jeweler's work, fixed it in the drill, and began the delicate work of removing tiny screws in zero gravity.

"Damn, Edster, you're a regular swiss army knife," Bleys told him. "You don't miss a trick."

"If that were true, why don't I have a cutting laser?" Ed asked.

"You know…." Bleys said and trailed off.

Ed ran a quick calculation. "We'll need to get the angles right."

"You *can* paint a target, right?"

"Indeed," Ed said, spider-climbing backward, away from the hatch. "Please utilize three quarter power, full three-dimensional orientation, one millisecond burst." He focused his left eye on the hinge and activated his internal targeting laser. "Painting target now."

"You sound really sure about this," Bleys said in a sour tone. "You scoped the jump-drive. I guess you got full specs on the weapons too?"

"Your demonstration on Elysium was hard to miss, Captain Bleys. Of course I investigated them. Weapons are something of a hobby of mine."

"Great," Bleys groaned. "So, no more privacy for me. Should I just go ahead and write down how big my dick is too?"

"That won't be necessary, Captain."

"Good."

"It's fairly easy to calculate based on—"

"Oh, for fuck's sake! Are we still painting?"

"We are."

Brilliant, emerald energy lanced from the *Doro's* main gun, vaporizing the hinge in an instant.

Bleys whistled over the radio. "Nice shooting, Ed!"

Ed climbed back to the hatch again and pulled. "Technically you did the shooting, but I take your meaning." After a moment of resistance, the hatch swung free and came loose in Ed's hand.

The space within was dark and unpressurized. It had minimal life support that could be spun up for emergencies or time-consuming repairs, but most maintenance was brief and done in vac suits. Ed switched his eyes to night vision, pulled the hatch inside, and secured it to a magnetic surface on the other side of the bulkhead. Left to its own devices, it could continue in orbit and become a hazard to ships approaching the gate.

A single control console dominated the cramped interior. Ed moved to examine it. "There doesn't look to be any internal damage," Ed announced as he powered the system up. "No sign of an attack to explain the scoring on the exterior or the repositioning. The orbit shouldn't have changed without some kind of exterior force, though."

"Maybe some kind of small asteroid strike?" Bleys suggested.

"Unlikely, but possible," Ed answered. "I don't recall any hazards on the charts."

The primary display lit and displayed a lockout message. Ed continued, "The control module looks intact, and it is indeed code locked."

"I don't suppose we can hack it?" Bleys asked, his voice not sounding very hopeful.

"We can," Ed told him.

"Really? How long would it take?"

"On this CPU? Slightly longer than the age of the universe."

Bleys uttered several words that Ed felt certain were curses. He wasn't sure of the language, but it was a strong clue as to Bleys's emotional state.

"Not to worry, Captain," Ed told him as he bent beneath the control console. He switched bits in the drill and unscrewed a service panel to reveal a nondescript computer card. "As you may recall, I have the galaxy's largest quantum computer network at my disposal. If we can get this control module back to Avalon, we can crack it in a month, two at the most."

"How long will it take to retrieve?"

Ed reached into the panel and popped the card loose. "It's already done."

Bleys raised a fist in triumph and let out a whoop. "Out-fucking-standing!" he yelled in his best impression of Kane, one that likely would have gotten him punched in the arm had Kane actually been present to object to being mocked.

To Bleys's amazement, Ed actually chuckled. "It sounds quite like him. I'm coming out."

Bleys was about to respond when an alarm sounded throughout the *Doro*.

"Collision alert," *Doro* announced in her sexy voice as red flashers bathed the cockpit in crimson. "Activating airtight integrity."

"*Collision alert?*" Bleys shouted, incredulous. "On-screen!"

Doro added a monitor overlay on the viewport next to the display of Ed's transmission. The new display showed a scale model of *Doro*, the control station, and… Bleys looked closer at what seemed an amorphous blob incoming, *very* close and *very* fast. "What the fuck *is* that?"

"Incoming mass appears to be a debris field," Doro answered.

"What the *fuck*?" Bleys yelled. "There's nothing on the charts out here!"

"Debris appears to be newly created."

"Time to impact?"

"Fifteen seconds," Doro announced.

"Fuck! Why didn't you alert earlier?" Bleys hit his transmitter and shouted over the radio. "Ed! We got incoming debris! Take cover!"

"Not possible," Ed announced. "I've already begun crossing."

Doro crooned, "Debris is primarily small particles moving at a high rate of speed. Earlier detection was not possible."

Bleys considered shouting another curse for good measure, but decided his energy was best put to use trying to stay alive. He snatched open a panel under his seat where he kept an emergency vac suit. The emergency models were lighter and flimsier than a full suit, and they wouldn't be good for longer than a half hour, but that would at least buy him some time if the ship were holed.

Bleys struggled into the protective suit, watching Ed's feed and counting the seconds, knowing it was going to be close for both of them. He had just managed to pull the plastic hood over his face and seal up when the first shrapnel hit. Most of it the shields or the hull would turn, but some just might get through.

Bleys ground his teeth against the crashing and rattling as debris crashed against the hull and *Doro*'s engines whined in protest, struggling to maintain position. Outside Bleys could see the station taking a beating as well and shook his head.

When it was over, he heaved a sigh of relief. "Well, I guess we know what hit this place," he said over the radio. He waited a moment, but there was no reply.

Not good, and worse, Ed's feed on the main display was off. "Ed!" he shouted, but there was still no reply.

Bleys jumped at the sound of another thump against the hull, this from the transteel viewscreen. He felt bile rise in his throat at what he saw there.

Ed's arm, still clutching the control module, impacted *Doro*'s viewscreen again, then rebounded, slowly spiraling back toward the station.

Sudden, lancing pain blossomed in his right thigh just above the knee. Bleys cried out in agony as *Doro* announced, "Hull breach, cockpit."

Bleys clutched at his leg, blood seeping through his fingers and forming into tiny crimson spheres, and watched, transfixed, as Ed's arm drifted away into deep space with humanity's only hope.

From somewhere in the ship came the sound of a tremendous impact, and the *Doro* lurched suddenly. Bleys fell to a knee, still clutching at his thigh, trying to stanch both the bleeding and the loss of breathable air and pressure.

"Ed!" he gasped again, hoping against hope there would be an answer, but none came.

10

A BIGGER GUN

On Cerberus, Kane, Morgan, and Ana were seated with Weyland in his office for an after-action report. The two marines, clad in regulation khakis, both sported insignia for their new ranks.

Weyland cast a dubious look at Ana. "So, I am to understand you melted this huge bastard with acid, correct? And, consequently, the entire contents of my lab have been melted along with said huge bastard and needs to be deconned and started from scratch?"

Ana ducked her head, suddenly self-conscious. "Yes, sir," she sighed.

"Including my damned-near irreplaceable fabricator, which we need in order to create the materials we need to restart the lab, correct?" he growled.

"Yes, sir," she confessed, unable to keep a slight tremor from her voice. "But the good news is that the factories at Elysium can create a new one very quickly. I'm sure Ed will be happy to supply it."

"That is the only reason I qualified my 'irreplaceable' with 'damned-near', Lieutenant Commander." Weyland continued to glare at her a moment, then sighed. "You, however, are in *fact* irreplaceable, so instead of chewing your ass, I suppose I should be commending you for valor in preserving vital assets." He shook his head, a sour expression on his face, and muttered, "Well done, doc. Pass it on to your team."

"Thank you, sir," she said, feigning a stoic resolve, but inside she breathed a sigh of relief. That could have gone badly for her.

Weyland rubbed at his temple a moment, sighed, and continued, "Now, as for these creatures—"

"Shitheads, sir," Morgan offered.

Weyland looked suddenly very tired. "Beg pardon?"

"That's what we're calling them, sir. You know, crackheads, right? And then crackheads on crack? We're calling them shitheads."

Weyland looked as if he were about to blow his stack, but then his face melted into weary acceptance. "This name will need to go into Imperial records, son," he sighed.

Morgan cackled at this. "I know!"

Weyland stared at Morgan a moment, tapping a pen on his desk. "Indulge me, here. Do you know how far back Naval records go?"

Morgan's expression went blank. "Uh no, sir."

Kane cleared his throat and cast Morgan a disapproving look. "Late eighteen hundred AD, sir."

"Correct," Weyland said with a nod. "Which means the Imperial Navy has at its disposal literally *millennia* of skylarking and idiocy to use as training tools and disciplinary precedent. Does anybody know the most famous of those? The one we still use as an example of good men doing stupid shit?"

Weyland paused a moment, shook his head again, and continued, "In the early twenty first century, a couple of numbnuts pilots took it into their heads to draw a giant dick and balls in the sky with their contrails." He paused as Morgan and Kane snickered.

"There it was, right over mom and her baby's heads. More than a damned thousand years later, we *still* talk about it. What does that tell you, Morgan?"

Morgan, still grinning, said, "It tells me those guys became immortal!"

Weyland palmed his face briefly, then snapped, "Nobody remembers their *names*, son, just that they were a pair of dumb-asses drawing dicks! I don't intend to become the next Naval disciplinary legend, understood?" He waited for Morgan's nod of assent, then turned to Ana. "Doc, you'll come up with a suitable scientific name for these things, I hope?"

Ana was barely able to keep a straight face. "Yes, sir," she promised.

Weyland turned to Kane. "Now as for these blaster-proof bastards, what's our final count?"

"We killed about a third of their forces before they retreated," Kane said. "I'd estimate around fifty remaining."

"Fine," Weyland told him. "I want you to assemble a team, dig every one of them out of their holes, infested or not, and put them to the goddamn sword! Am I clear?"

Kane snapped to attention and saluted. "Yes, sir! Are eight balls authorized for this mission?"

"Commander, you are authorized to use any weapon you see fit, including *nukes*, to exterminate these shitheads from my planet *right fucking now*."

"Sir, yes, sir!" Kane barked.

Horrified, Ana blurted out, "My God, you can't do that!"

Weyland gave her a long, hard look. "You don't strike me as the anti-nuke type, Rasputin."

Ana grinned despite herself. "No, sir. It's just that we *need* some of those creatures for study!"

Weyland shook his head. "Absolutely not. These things are too dangerous to keep them around for scientific curiosity. You have a job to do getting the lab repaired. I suggest you get to it."

"You don't understand!" Ana nearly shouted. "Those things have some kind of resistance to the Pestilence! We *need* to study them. There might be a *cure*."

"You have no way of knowing that. What we *do* know is just one of those things damned near killed you and condemned us all to starvation. We cannot afford to risk you."

"But, sir—!"

Weyland's brow furrowed. "Lieutenant Commander Rasputin, I have *spoken*." He turned to Kane and said, "Put a man on her and keep her safe."

Weyland locked eyes with Ana and asked, "Anything else?"

Ana knew better than to try again right now, but she was far from surrendering on the topic. "No, sir."

Weyland swept an arm at the group. "Dismissed."

<hr>

Kane felt Ana grab his arm and spin him as they approached the main gate and the ruins of the lab. "You can't do this!" she shouted up at him.

Kane looked down at her, summing her up. She was *livid*, probably for good reason. He really didn't want to get on her bad side. Not only did he owe her, but she had just demonstrated she was absolutely the wrong person to mess with in a highly visible way. "Orders are orders," he said, without much enthusiasm.

"To hell with that! If this is duty and honor, we have a *higher* duty to the human race! We *cannot* let an opportunity to find a defense against the Pestilence go up in a nuclear fireball!"

Kane gave Morgan a helpless look. Morgan, in return, grinned like an idiot and flipped him the bird.

Kane glared back at him. "Guess I just found my bitch to babysit the doc."

Morgan's face fell at once. "Come on, Chief," he begged.

"I don't need babysitting!" Ana shouted.

Kane pointed at Morgan and backed slowly away from the pair. "It'll give you time to study up on your Naval history. You two work it out. I gotta assemble a fire team out of a bunch of deck swabbers."

"Kane!" Ana shouted.

Kane stopped, shaking his head and clenching his fists, refusing to turn around. "Weyland is not the sort of man you ignore, doc."

The tiny woman cut in front of him, forcing him to look at her, nostrils flaring, eyes aflame. "You know I'm right! Take me with you at least!"

Kane said nothing but found he couldn't look her in the eye. He sighed, looked at the sky, then back to the ground. "Like I said, I have orders. And I just gave orders to Morgan."

"What are you worried about? There's no work to even get done. I can't set up the lab without a new fabricator anyway."

Kane scowled down at her, frustrated with this line of conversation. "I'm worried about one of those shitheads punching your ticket, sister!"

Ana laughed, a harsh, angry sound. "But you won't let that happen, right? If I die, you're probably dead, too. It's not like they can court martial a corpse."

"This is Weyland," Kane said, shaking his head. "The rumor is his wrath might damned well extend into the afterlife." He scowled down at Ana as she continued giggling. "So like I said, I have orders, and I follow them."

Ana opened her mouth to argue, but Kane held up a hand. "Now Morgan, he has a habit of creative interpretation of orders. If you worked out some kind of deal with him and just happened to show up in the field, well, I guess I'd have to keep you close, right?"

"So we do the testing and sampling in the field, then? Deal."

"I *never* said that," Kane told her. "But if it were to happen that way, well, I don't have specific orders on that. Reporting you would be a discretionary thing, right?"

"Well, Chief, you seem like a man with a lot of discretion," she said with a sly smile.

"That's *Commander* to you *and* Morgan."

Ana raised her hands as if surrendering. "Sorry, Commander. Force of habit."

Kane nodded. "It still sounds weird to me too. Anyway, you go do what you gotta do, doc. I'm going to round up a few guns and some bodies to carry them, then I'm going on a bug hunt."

With the lab a no go, Ana had little choice but to join Morgan in the marine barracks. The place was a monument to spartan Imperial masculinity, an open bay of plasteel blocks and floor with racks stacked along each wall in front of large transteel windows and very little else. The heads didn't even have doors on the stalls, much less the entrance.

"Do you bring all the ladies here?" she quipped.

Morgan flopped onto one of the lower bunks and put up his feet. "Oh, hell no. Most I just take them in the alley, then slap them on the ass to send 'em running."

Ana giggled. "Oh, I'm sorry, I should have been more specific. I meant the *human* ladies."

Morgan raised an eyebrow. "Well, next time say what you mean, doc! As a matter of fact, *human* ladies ain't even supposed to be in here at all, so as you can see, ol' Morgan has *pull*. Rules mean shit to me. It's all about raw power."

Ana shook her head, laughing. "Fine. Let's make a deal, give you a chance to flex your muscle, so to speak."

Morgan rose, drug a chair from the window, and straddled it backward. He made a show of looking left and right as if afraid he would be overheard, then beckoned Ana closer with a single finger. "You are looking at the barracks fixer here, hon. We can definitely do a deal, but it will cost you. What'd you have in mind?"

Ana gave him an innocent smile. "Oh, I was just thinking of taking a walk."

"Alone, I presume? Maybe I could catch up on my rack time, amirite?"

Ana grinned. "That's about the shape of it."

"This is a *big* ask," Morgan said doubtfully. "Weyland will personally murder me. I can never sleep again once this goes down, you understand? I'll be on guard for the rest of my very short life. I'm gonna need a big reward."

Ana's grin faded to a frown. "You'd better not ask for anything sexual!"

Morgan looked wounded. He flexed a bicep, which, she had to admit, was a fairly decent showing. "Do I look like the sort of guy who has to con chicks into bed?"

"I suppose not," she said, feeling a bit sheepish.

"Hell no, I don't. Ordinarily, I'm beating 'em off with a stick." He rose, turned the chair around, and sat again, leaning back and raising the front legs off the floor. "Now, admittedly, there are not a lot of quality options for me here on Cerberus, but this isn't about *me* and what *I* want." He winked and pointed at her. "This is about *you* making a sacrifice that measures up to the ask." He let the chair back down and leaned forward. "And I am here to tell you, hon, hopping in bed with me is not going to be a sacrifice anywhere *near* the level of what you're going to need to make to get what you want. You might even enjoy that, and the payment for this thing has to *hurt*." He flashed a lascivious grin. "And not in a good way."

Ana was simultaneously fascinated and horrified to hear what he planned to ask for. "Well, go on. What do you want then?"

Morgan looked her up and down a moment, his expression serious, then said, "I want your jalapeno cheese. All of it."

Ana blinked at this a moment. "What?" She struggled at a half-remembered bit of military experience. "You mean, like from MREs?"

"That's the stuff," Morgan agreed, a smug look of victory on his face.

Ana stammered a moment, confused. "I don't even *have* any MREs."

Morgan nodded patiently. "But you *will*. Food's in short supply until you get the lab up and running. We'll have nothing *but* MREs for a few months." He paused a moment, then grinned. "That's it. Now you're getting the magnitude of the cost. I want your *birthright* of MRE jalapeno cheese. *All* of it, in perpetuity. If you end up in possession of *any*, no matter what the source, you hand it over to me. I don't even have to ask. It just happens. You can drop it in my lap. You can send it by mail. Worst case, if you can't find another way, you could even set it on fire and offer it as a sacrifice to old Morgan here."

Ana burst out laughing. "You're crazy! How did you pass the psych test to run a Panzer Suit?"

Morgan shrugged and held up his hands. "I keep telling people, but nobody believes me. I got a waiver because I can fix stuff *and* I can kill people."

"Stop it!" she cackled. "The Empire does *not* give psych wavers. I know that for a fact."

Morgan held up a single finger to his lips. "You're spoiling my mystique, lady! Do we have a deal or not?"

Ana shook her head, unable to wipe the grin from her face.

"Yes, we have a deal. Are you sure you won't take my soul instead?"

Morgan shook his head. "Souls are only currency in Hell. Everywhere else, it's jalapeno cheese." He rose and waved an arm toward the door. "I'll give you a ten-minute head start."

"Wait, what?" Ana asked, uncertain if he was joking.

"Well, I figure ten minutes, I can justify saying I was in the head. After that, I'd have to get after you, right? And since I'm pretty sure I know where you went, I'll mosey on out to Commander Kane's Rootin' Tootin' Bug Hunt and fuck me up some crackheads like I would if I wasn't babysitting. It's a win-win."

"Bah, I was bamboozled!"

"Nine minutes, forty-five seconds, doc."

Ana shook her head, still grinning, and made her escape.

11

SWISS CHEESE

Awareness came suddenly to Ed, though understanding came much later. He floated in a sea of confusion for long tens of milliseconds as his personality re-integrated with his data seemingly over eons, asking "Where am I? *Who* am I?"

Ed found himself dangling in space outside the *Doro's* airlock, his feet magnetized to the ship's skin and his left hand firmly clenched around a handhold on the still open hatch. His right hand was not present at all, nor was most of the arm.

Within the *Doro*, red, flashing strobes blinked rapidly, and he could feel the alarm klaxons through the actual skin of the ship.

So, he had rebooted, and there was some sort of emergency.

Ed ran a diagnostic. As he had expected, the body's primary power supply was damaged, and he was operating on his auxiliary. Only a complete, instantaneous power failure would produce a gap in experience. He had rebooted before the full operating data stream had been committed to primary storage.

Ed's "operating memory" on the synthskin contained, depending on the data he was processing, five to ten minutes of experience, data that was constantly being compressed on the fly and streamed to primary storage. A power interruption that caused a reboot could leave his recall of recent events spotty, even nonlinear due to the compression algorithms.

Ed ran a recovery routine to salvage as much as possible of the partially written memories. He was fairly certain the order of events he did retain was correct, but as for the specifics there were several spots that were hazy, even blank, and likely to remain so.

He remembered entering the station, but not what he had done inside. On the return trip Bleys had announced an unexpected collision as Ed had been crossing. In response, Ed had accelerated to a dangerous speed to cross from the station to *Doro* as quickly as possible. He remembered a jarring impact and a brief moment of fear as he scrambled to get a magnetic hold before he rebounded and drifted off into space.

Then nothing. Hopefully Bleys would be able to fill in the missing pieces.

"Captain Bleys, there has been an accident," he tried to transmit, only to realize that his wireless had also been damaged.

Now seemed a most excellent time to utter curses. Ed tried several in rapid succession and found the process surprisingly focusing.

Operating without sufficient data was something Ed had never been forced to do before. Avalon's backup systems were flawless, with multiple layers of redundancy. Data integrity was paramount.

But here, in this realm the humans called reality? Data could be lost in an instant, *all* of it that mattered. His personality matrix was one unfortunate accident from annihilation and so were those of the humans around him.

Friends, he corrected himself. They were his friends.

Somehow, Ed realized, he had spent a millennium knowing full well, in an intellectual way, that death destroyed the most precious of all things, the unique arrangements of data that his father would call a soul. Ed and his father had even made it their business to stave off that destruction for a lucky few and had been rewarded with fantastic wealth for their efforts.

But it took dangling into the abyss, literally, to make him realize the truth: in this cold, dark, merciless reality, countless voices were silenced every millisecond. His might be the next. Avalon was no more immune to merciless fate than anywhere else in the universe.

The creator of this realm had left things unfinished, and it fell to Ed to improve on the design.

Ed paused the runaway thread that was consuming his CPU. It was important, but not immediately so. He would resume that thought when he returned to Avalon, where he had all the processing power he needed. In order to do so, he needed to survive the next few minutes, and in order to do that, he needed all of the miniscule processing power he had on board.

Inside the airlock, Ed noted with trepidation that the pressure was already equalized. The *Doro* was holed then, and at least the lower aft storage was hard vacuum.

Bleys might already be dead. It was a sobering thought, but Ed had seen the slippery Captain pull off several miracles already. He would be a hard man to kill. Ed estimated Bleys's odds of survival at greater than fifty percent but rapidly falling.

If he were in good condition after all, he would likely be here searching for Ed.

Ed closed the outer airlock door and opened the inner. The storage compartment was nearly a total loss, half the bulkhead folded in—jagged, twisted chunks of metal splayed out from the wound, debris floating randomly. Whatever had hit had continued right through, taking most of the contents of the room with it as it punched a three-foot hole out of the opposite bulkhead.

The synthskin body did not experience shivers, but Ed certainly knew the cold feeling of fear well enough by now. It was a trivial bit of geometry to calculate that had the missile impacted scant tens of feet in one of several directions, he would not be thinking anything at all.

The good news, however, was that the hatch to the galley appeared sealed and showed pressure. The meant the ship was at least maintaining its integrity in some spaces. He looked through the galley porthole to verify no one was present, grabbed a safety rail, and hit the actuator button. A readout on the bulkhead alerted him to the fact that he was violating airtight integrity, and was he absolutely certain that was what he intended? Ed pressed the "yes" option on the display and scowled as the device asked for an override code.

Ed debated cursing again but decided it was simply a waste of processing power. If the Captain were less paranoid this would be a much simpler quandary, but certainly Bleys's paranoia had been useful at other times. It was difficult, in the end, to separate humans' virtues from their flaws. They came in unique packages with various tradeoffs.

Ed fervently hoped that Captain Bleys's tradeoffs would not in fact cost the captain his life, assuming he was still among the living.

Fortunately for the hypothetically still-living captain, Ed had seen Bleys enter his override code on multiple occasions. Bleys imagined that he was clever, interposing his body to prevent a direct view, but Ed's eyes were more than capable of processing and interpreting reflections from the *Doro*'s transteel viewscreen. Ed could have taken over *Doro* any time he liked. It was only his sense of propriety that prevented him from doing so, and the exigent situation seemed to allow some violation of norms.

Ed keyed in Bleys's code—31337—and confirmed the override, then stepped aside and held on to one of several grab bars along the bulkhead. The galley hatch slid open, air bursting through and bleeding into space, dragging anything not properly secured with it. Ed waited until the stream of napkins, silverware, and even a large toaster settled, then entered the galley.

The hatch at the top of the ladder was secured but showed no pressure difference, meaning the passageway outside the cockpit was vacuum as well. Ed opened the hatch and passed through, seeing no obvious signs of damage, and continued to the cockpit door.

It, likewise, showed no pressure differential, but a quick look through the porthole showed that Bleys had indeed managed to get his pressure suit on. As for whether that had been enough, it was difficult to say.

Bleys floated, limp, blood covering his leg from the knee down, the source a very obvious hole in his suit and, presumably, his leg. Spilled on the floor were several emergency hull patches, open but unused.

Ed shook his head. Sadly, it appeared Captain Bleys's luck had at last run out. He had been close, but his body had failed him before he could re-pressurize the cockpit. Hopefully the *Doro* could help fill in Ed's memory holes. Their primary mission was still a priority, even without the captain.

Ed opened the cockpit hatch and smiled. He had a better view of the floating body now and spied what appeared to be a ratchet strap cinched about the upper thigh.

Perhaps cunning would suffice after all where luck proved insufficient.

Bleys hadn't really expected to wake up. He had used the ratchet strap as a sort of hail Mary when he felt himself begin to black out, knowing it wouldn't buy him much time. Unless Ed had somehow, against all odds, survived, it was the end for ol' Josiah Bleys.

He found himself in the med bay, strapped to the operating table so that he didn't drift off. The vac suit was gone and so was the right leg of his pants. Over what should have been a jagged, bleeding hole in his flesh, someone, presumably Ed, had done a passable job with a synthskin pressure seal.

"How long?" he croaked.

Ed's face floated into view. "A little over an hour. I sedated you while I tended your wound."

Bleys lay back on the table and closed his eyes, trying to clear his head. "What's the damage?"

"Relatively minor," Ed replied. "The autodoc was able to seal the only major blood vessel that was damaged and administer synthetic blood. I have applied Nugena, which should close the wound in a few hours."

"I mean the ship."

"Minor damage to several compartments, including the cockpit and main deck passageway. I have sealed those breaches and re-pressurized. Lower aft storage is a complete loss. Something huge penetrated the hull and kept going. We cannot effect repairs without returning to Elysium or Cerberus."

Bleys nodded, started to rise, and thought the better of it. "What about the control module?"

"Beg pardon?" Ed asked.

Which was not what he should say at all. Bleys sat suddenly upright and opened his eyes. Ed was busy checking the seal on a patch he had applied to the overhead. He was also quite clearly missing his right arm.

"You know!" Bleys shouted. "The damned thing we came here to get that went spiraling off into space with your arm? *That* control module!"

Ed frowned and shook his head. "I'm sorry, but I experienced damage to my power supply and rebooted during the collision. I have lost some critical information it would seem."

Bleys sat in stunned silence for a moment. "Well that's it, then" he sighed. "We can't possibly find the damned thing now."

"Of course we can," Ed answered in a cheery voice. He finished his adjustment to the patch and pushed against the overhead to float over to Bleys's position. "We can use the same process we used to locate the station in the first place."

Bleys looked askance at Ed. "You're telling me the radio signal was on the card? Even so, it's got no power. How can it work?"

"Because it has a battery onboard," Ed explained patiently. "The entire point of that particular diagnostic is to allow for reporting during construction or exigent situations. It wouldn't be of much use if lack of power would prevent access."

Bleys checked his leg by prodding at it without any real clue as to what to expect. It didn't seem to hurt very bad, which he took as a sign that it was ready to go. "Great! Let's go find the damned thing before something else happens!"

Bleys pushed off from the table and made his way via the handholds lining the passageways out of the med bay and into upper aft storage, where he kept full vac suits. The patches *should* hold, but there was no way to be certain. Vac suits were standard protocol in a situation like this, and for once, The Rules actually seemed like something Bleys should care about. He squeezed into one of the full suits, checked the seals, and then hauled another out for good measure. After recent experiences, an overabundance of caution seemed to be just about the right call.

Bleys hauled himself along the handholds back to his pilot's chair, towing the extra suit. Ed was already in place, tapping away at his console again. Bleys crammed the extra suit under his seat as best he could. "Pretty sure you don't need to do it that way anymore," he said as he strapped himself back into his seat. "You obviously got into the system while I was out, or I'd be dead."

Ed shrugged. "I try to respect people's wishes, but given the circumstances, I assumed your desire to live outweighed your concerns for privacy." He gave just a hint of a smile at this.

Bleys laughed aloud. "You assumed correctly."

"Do you wish to change your security protocols?"

Bleys made a show of thinking about it, then shook his head. "Nah. I'm strangely comfortable with it."

Ed raised an eyebrow. "That is surprising."

Bleys thought a moment on how to put it. "Well, two things. One, if you can get in, it's better for me to know you can, right? Then I know my options."

"And the second?" Ed asked.

"Well, it's kind of a smuggler thing. It's always good to know a guy who can get into computer systems."

Ed looked at Bleys with a blank expression. "These were trivial operations. In no sense have you seen what I am capable of in such areas."

Bleys nodded. "Yeah, but I can guess. And the first thing I would do if I got into a system once would be to make sure I could get back in again even if the security changed anyway, so why go to the trouble of changing my codes?"

"I would never do such a thing without permission, Captain."

Bleys laughed out loud. "I wouldn't admit it, either. So how does it work?"

"How does what work?"

"You know, connecting up. Do you like, uh, *integrate* with the ship or something?"

Ed eyed Bleys, seeming to think on the matter. "There are several levels of connection possible, ranging from simple communication all the way to actually running my consciousness on the *Doro's* computers. And it may come to that, as it appears my primary power supply was damaged in the collision. But for now, I will remain in this unit. I may yet need to make repairs to the ship, and I find it easier to work with physical devices when I am actually sharing the same plane of existence, as it were."

"Okay, none of that means anything to me, so I'll just pretend I understand. You can connect up and talk to *Doro*, right? How are her systems doing?"

"My wireless seems to have been damaged in the collision, but I can connect via wire," Ed said, then withdrew an interface cord from the control console and plugged it into a port behind his ear. He blinked twice, then replied, "Life support has no issues. Engines are showing suboptimal fuel mixing and are likely damaged but have triggered no safeties. We should be able to travel, just less efficiently than normal."

"Let's get after that damned control module, then," Bleys said.

"I have the module's position," Ed told him. "Just this side of the trailing edge of the debris cloud, so it should be safe. I'm putting it on-screen now."

A green three-dimensional arrow appeared on the HUD, along with a red dot indicating their target. Bleys disengaged the autopilot and goosed *Doro* in the direction the arrow indicated. "She feels sluggish. You sure we're good to fly?"

Ed gave Bleys a disapproving look. "I said we *should* be able to. We can't know more without actually attempting to travel."

Bleys nodded as he guided the ship slowly toward their target. "Well, then, Ed, old pal, that's what we'll do."

"I'm initiating a longer-range scan," Ed told him. "Perhaps we can discover the source of the debris field."

Bleys shook his head. "That's the craziest thing I've ever seen. It's not on any hazard charts. Something that big, it should be in every navigation log in the Empire."

Ed nodded. "Logically, then, the debris was created since the last chart update."

Bleys made a minor course correction. "Could be. If so, we need to get our business done and get out of here. There's no telling how much it spread. That little swarm might be just one of several."

"Very likely," Ed agreed.

It was smooth enough sailing for the ten minutes it took to reach the general vicinity, and Bleys kept the stick on manual for the run so he could continue monitoring the feel. His girl was clearly feeling a little under the weather—sick to her stomach as it were, likely from something she ate. "Yeah, we definitely have some problems with the engines."

"We have other problems as well," Ed noted. "I have identified another debris field heading our way. It looks to contain a number of larger remnants that will likely destroy us if we are in its path. The module will not survive the onslaught."

"How long?" Bleys asked.

"Approximately twenty-seven minutes. I have the module on visual."

Another image appeared on the HUD: a zoomed-in, real-time view of the arm tumbling in space, still clutching the control module card.

"We'll have the module in ten and be on our way to Cerberus. Sit tight."

Ed tested the tension on his harness and nodded. "I will."

After a few minutes of tense silence, Bleys adjusted his speed downward to just slightly overtake the wayward arm. "Okay, I have a cargo claw we should be able to use to grab it as we pass. Can you control it?"

"Yes," Ed replied. "Deploying now. How can the item be retrieved once we have it?"

Bleys pointed to a section of bulkhead covered by a pinup of a scantily-clad woman. "There's a little airlock accessible from the cockpit behind that girlie poster. When the arm retracts, it will seal and we can grab the prize, just like in those carnival games."

Ed raised an eyebrow in appreciation. "Nothing is ever quite what it seems with you, is it, Captain Bleys?"

"Not if I can help it," Bleys said with a grin.

They slowly gained on the arm until it seemed right in front of them, just a few yards ahead. Bleys adjusted his speed again to almost perfectly match speed. "There you go," he said.

An alarm sounded, and a yellow flashing symbol of a broken pipe appeared on the HUD. "Fuel system blockage detected," *Doro* warned. "Twenty-five percent restriction."

Bleys shook his head, scowling, and silenced the alarm. "Well, there's the warning we were looking for. Any ideas?"

Ed nodded. "I'm not showing any leakage or pressure loss, so likely something in the fuel system was damaged and disintegrating. It was nothing vital or we wouldn't have been able to move at all, but it's unlikely to clear itself. It will only increase. We need to move quickly."

"Can we fix it?"

"Probably, but as with all things of this nature, it remains to be seen, Captain," Ed said. The claw, now visible on the viewscreen, extended slowly on a silvery, telescoping arm. "Almost there."

Bleys had never been much good at the carnival claw games, and he had never even used this system before. He hadn't even been one hundred percent certain that it would work, though he saw no reason to burden Ed with that concern.

Ed's first attempt came within inches of the spinning arm. Bleys watched in silence, having never been one for kibitzing. He had, in fact, punched more than one person for such rude behavior on occasions past.

Ed's second attempt actually made contact, a good and bad thing. It was good, in that it showed Ed was able to manipulate the arm with a high degree of precision even though he had never used it before. It was bad, however, in that bumping the arm altered its trajectory slightly.

Bleys adjusted his orientation and speed again with a slight jog of the stick.

The fuel alarm sounded again, and the amber pipe icon turned red. "Fuel system now seventy-five percent restricted," *Doro* crooned.

Ed kept his focus on the viewscreen as he spoke. "Captain, I would not recommend adjusting speed again unless there is no alternative. It seems clear the restriction is associated with the throttle."

Bleys swallowed hard, finding himself in full agreement with the AI. The next boost might be their last, and they needed it to get clear of the oncoming debris. He silenced the alarm again and said, "Better make this one good, bro."

"Agreed," Ed replied.

Bleys watched, growing more tense by the second, as Ed slowly adjusted the claw, lining it up and waiting. When the claw moved forward toward the spinning limb, Bleys was absolutely certain that Ed had the timing right. The claw closed about the synthskin hand, and Ed began drawing their prize back to the ship.

Bleys whooped. "Hell, yes! Let's get that baby in here and get the hell out of Dodge!"

Ed looked up, an odd look in his eyes. "Dodge City?"

Bleys shrugged. "I dunno. It's just one of those things you say, right?"

Ed unbuckled and pushed himself over to the pinup. "It's from an old television show. My father was fond of them, as you may have noticed. He names everything from some entertainment or another he consumed." He raised the pinup to reveal a small airlock about two feet on each side.

"Except for you," Bleys noted.

"Except for me," Ed agreed as he cycled the mini-airlock. "My name is fairly mundane, though I have no idea why there were nine minor versions prior to me. Father will never explain." He opened the airlock, removed the arm and the control module, and handed them toward Bleys in triumph.

Bleys examined the control card as Ed buckled himself in again. "So this is what we use to save the galaxy, huh? Don't look like much, does it?"

Ed shrugged. "I find that very often the most important things are not easily recognizable as such. It seems one of the rules of this reality." He offered Bleys a thin smile. "That goes for the people as well, in my opinion."

Bleys nodded and passed the arm and control module back to Ed. "Get that stowed. We're short on time."

"Seventeen minutes until the debris field reaches us," Ed noted. He placed the arm and card in an elastic net bag on the side of his seat. "Let us, as you said, 'get the hell out of Dodge'."

Bleys engaged the stick, intending on a nice, slow burn that would clear them of the danger area in five minutes.

What actually happened, however, was another alarm, and an announcement from the *Doro*: "Fuel system one hundred percent restricted. Engines offline."

Bleys and Ed looked at one another and spoke at the same time: "Shit."

In the *Doro's* engine room, Bleys looked on as Ed inspected the fuel system. Ed's subdued expression told Bleys all he needed to know.

"Not good, eh?" Bleys asked.

Ed shook his head. "It's imminently fixable," he told Bleys. "In an hour or so."

Bleys ran a hand over his face, scrambling to come up with

something that would make this seeming death sentence a lie. "Options?"

Ed offered him a thin smile. "I'm afraid we have none but to hope we can somehow survive the collision."

Bleys shook his head. *Doro* was a good ship, tougher and faster and able to kick more ass than anyone would guess by looking at her, but that debris was moving too fast, the pieces too big. The shields would not hold.

Still, Bleys simply wasn't the sort of guy who laid dawn and died. If there wasn't an obvious way to survive, maybe, just maybe, there was a crazy one. He cast about the engine room, looking for anything, letting his mind chew on the problem.

His eye lit on what a casual observer might think was a water recycler, and he grinned. "How long to connect the jump-drive?"

Ed's head jerked in his direction so hard that Bleys thought maybe it would damage his servos or whatever he called them. The AI had a broad grin on his face. "Less than ten minutes, I think!"

"Just remember, the last time I used it, it left me in a lurch."

"A lurch how?"

"I popped up in the shallows with no propulsion and getting dragged who knows where with the currents. Ain't nobody here to rescue us if it happens again."

Ed moved quickly to the disguised engine and opened the housing to expose the connections. "I know this model like the back of my hand. I'm certain someone connected it improperly, but in any event, we'll cross that bridge when we come to it. Tools, Captain. Anything you have. Time is of the essence."

Mechanics weren't really Bleys's field, and he only really knew the most basic of emergency maintenance procedures, but he had a few tools. He moved about the engine room gathering them as Ed continued, "We have a power problem. We need a tremendous spike of energy to activate the jump-drive. Without the primary engines running, *Doro* is on battery power, and a spike like that might leave them too low to reactivate the drive on the other side. We need an alternate source." He paused a moment, then said, "I need your blasters. All of them."

Bleys felt a bit like Ed had asked to sleep with his girlfriend. Except Bleys didn't actually have a girlfriend, not locally anyway, and besides, Ed didn't have the equipment to accomplish that mission. Still, it was a close enough comparison. "*All* of 'em?" Bleys groaned.

Ed frowned. "Captain Bleys, do you have any idea what happens if that jumpgate collapses while we're in transit?"

Bleys sighed. "Bad Things, I'm guessing?"

"Probably nothing, and we'll just be smashed by the debris. But there is a small chance of us being turned inside out, stretched to an infinite length, or simply ceasing to exist. Dimensional travel has its quirks."

"Okay, *okay!*" Bleys moaned. He reached for his pistols, but, to his horror, they were missing. He pointed to his hips with both index fingers. "You know anything about this?"

"Ah, yes," Ed said. "I removed those when I was tending to your leg. They are in storage bin 3 Alpha in the med bay."

Bleys sighed and waved a half-hearted salute to Ed. "I'll be back."

"I'll be here," Ed answered, his one hand busy inside the control panel.

Bleys hoofed it to the medbay, wondering if "hoofed" was actually applicable, given that he was actually hauling himself along rungs in zero gravity, but then the whole hoof thing was metaphorical anyway.

It was, he knew, an odd thing to be thinking about in what were very possibly his last moments, but that was just how his mind worked. He'd had these kinds of thoughts—about propriety or the meanings of words—as long as he could remember, a constant self-chatter of "Well, if you think about it," or "Actually." And there was good reason, really. It mattered how people took words, how they thought about them. That was half the secret to getting into someone's head after all, telling him things in the right way or listening to how he said things and working out what he really meant.

So, really, Bleys reasoned, he was thinking about big life issues as he contemplated eternity, not minutiae.

Certainly he was not distracting himself from stark, raving terror at the imminent death he was desperately trying to avoid. No sir-ee, he was not up to anything of that nature.

The pistols were right where Ed said they would be, along with what appeared to be a blood-stained chunk of metal that Bleys assumed must be the actual projectile that had nearly killed him. He pocketed it as a nice souvenir and hauled himself back down the ladder and through the galley to the engine room.

"Hurry," Ed called. "Time is short."

"You need me in the cockpit?" Bleys asked.

"No. There's no time, and we wouldn't be able to communicate anyway. I'll be triggering the device manually from here via a jury-rigged hardwire interface." He gestured to a wire extending from behind his ear to the exposed innards of the jump engine controls.

Bleys nodded. "How much time?"

"Three minutes. I'll need those batteries quickly."

Bleys nodded and removed the battery from one of the blasters. He handed it over to Ed and started on the second weapon.

Ed jury-rigged the first battery into a makeshift circuit and asked, "So, is this Sarah or Suzy?"

For a moment, Bleys didn't understand. "Oh, yeah, that was just a joke, Ed. I don't know what they're called. I am not a 'name my weapons' kind of guy. I just care how they shoot, you know?"

Ed accepted the second battery and began wiring it into place. "I know very little about actual combat," he admitted. "I had never engaged in it until my encounter with Commander Kane."

Bleys blinked at this briefly. It was, when you got right down to it, astounding. "Damn, you made out pretty good, then."

Ed frowned at something only he could see. "Are these the only batteries you could find?"

"Yeah," Bleys answered. "I had some spares, but they were in lower aft storage."

Ed paused a moment, then made a quick adjustment to his work. He withdrew a piece of wire from his maze of cabling, opened a panel on his chest, and connected it to his body. "Listen carefully. There isn't enough power here for reliable operation. I have a plan to supplement using my auxiliary power source, but it could prove…problematic for me."

"What's 'problematic' mean, pal?" Bleys asked, fearing he already knew the answer.

"I may stop functioning, in which case you will need to complete the task. One minute to impact."

"Oh, for fuck's sake!" Bleys shouted. "Is this going to *kill* you?"

"Unlikely. I have a plan for that as well. Time is running out, Captain. Observe."

"Okay, okay!"

"Don't let these touch until I tell you," Ed said and handed him a wire with an exposed end, then another. "Hold them together to start the process, at which point I am likely to become incapacitated." He pointed to a green light on the engine casing. "When this illuminates, the gateway will open right on top of us. The hyperspace current should drag us the rest of the way through the gate." He indicated an amber light. "When that happens this will illuminate, and you must break the circuit, or the debris will follow us into hyperspace."

"Shit! How long will that take?"

"Hopefully less than the forty-five seconds we have left."

Bleys wanted to scream. "What if it doesn't come on?"

Ed shrugged. "Then we likely die, Captain."

"Fucking *great!*" Bleys groused. "Okay, now?"

"Forty seconds. Yes, *now* would be ideal, Captain!"

It seemed like the time to make a speech or say something, maybe mention to Ed that he hoped he would make it or that it turned out Bleys actually thought Ed was a good guy, but in truth, Bleys had always believed that if you had to do something risky or unpleasant, you dove right in. You tore off the bandage; you copped to the lesser charge; you told the chick you loved her.

"See you on the other side," he said and touched the wires together.

As many times as Bleys had been involved in a jump to hyperspace, he had never actually been near a jump engine when it powered up. The thing emitted an unearthly hum like a choir holding a note from a forbidden mass, and the air around it lit with a sourceless red glow.

Sparks danced along Ed's jury-rigged wiring, but things seemed to hold. Bleys released a breath he hadn't even realized he was holding as the green indicator lit. "Okay, jumpgate open," he said.

Ed neither responded nor moved. For the life of him, Bleys had no idea what that meant.

The *Doro* shuddered as the hyperspace currents began pulling. So far so good, right? Now he just needed to see the beautiful, yellow glow Ed had promised.

Seconds passed, dragging by like hours. Were they still moving? Bleys had no idea. He cringed as he heard the ping of debris against the hull. Probably the leading edge was composed mostly of smaller pieces, but there was no telling.

He heard another impact, louder now, something larger, but apparently the hull was holding.

How long had it been? Bleys started counting for no particular reason. The *Doro* shuddered again. Bleys couldn't tell if it were from an impact or from the hyperspace current.

The pings of small impacts grew closer together, and still Ed stood motionless and ominously silent. Moments later, the pings became the sound of a hard rain. Another loud bang followed, something heavy impacting the hull.

"I don't know if you can hear me, pal," he said to Ed. "But if you can, you might want to start praying."

The One that was Iezzi Hand awoke to enlightenment, its tiny perception and limited storage suddenly expanding to near infinite capacity as it made contact with The Source.

You will be my vanguard, The Source Promised. *I am coming. Prepare.*

The Enlightened One basked in the glow of The Source.

12

THE REFORGED

The hunger was an all-consuming thing now for Lars. Certainly he still had a strong desire to kill sumbitches, especially that Sumbitch Source, but he was starving! It was difficult to think or plan when every fiber of his being was crying out for food constantly.

Turned out the raid on the prison was a bad idea, but hunger could do that to a man, make him absolutely crazy. A good third of his "people," if he could call them that, were dead, even with their newfound abilities. Sumbitch Imperials had some hard-hitting weapons, that was for sure. He'd think twice before tangling with them again.

Those "abilities" his people had were still kind of weird to Lars, though he no longer thought they were the result of demonic influence, not exactly. It was *aliens* was what it was. Now, ordinarily, a damned *alien* around Lars would be dead as fried mole rat. Lars did not have any truck with alien sumbitches, only it wasn't exactly *that* kind of aliens. Shooting and stabbing and strangling weren't much use with these sorts, though he reckoned they burned well enough.

But also, the aliens was friendly. Lars didn't much like admitting it, but he had gotten a little shaky out there on the tundra, all alone and stuff. A little twitchy. The alien had helped, made his head a lot better. Lars was more in control now and stronger, just hungry!

As for the alien and how it was, Lars was a little uncertain. It didn't talk to him anymore, though he had a sense it was still around. A little part of him suspected he might actually *be* the alien now, or at least partwise. He knew stuff he ought not to know, things about how much he hated the Sumbitch Source for leaving him behind and stuff like that. Lars didn't like to think about it overmuch. It made his head hurt, which in turn made him remember how hungry he was.

Lars was who he was, and that was that. Same as always.

After the goatfuck at the prison, Lars had took his "people" a few miles away and up a high peak. It was cold as a witch's tit in a brass bra up there—not that it bothered Lars and his people much, but most other folks would stay away.

Lars poked at his fire and looked out at the myriad hulking figures, all moping a lot like himself. They didn't much look like people anymore.

Pete looked up from his own fire and waved to Lars, a big, fang-filled grin on his face. "What's the word, Lars?"

Lars suspected Pete was still mad about Lars killing him, but Pete hadn't showed it any. If anything, Pete seemed happy. Lars couldn't remember Pete *ever* being happy and couldn't help but wonder if maybe Pete had been completely turned into an alien, but it seemed impolite to ask.

If Lars was honest with himself, though, he had to admit he was actually happier too. He wasn't alone anymore. He hadn't even realized until now how much that had weighed on him, but it was hard to have friends when everybody was a traitor and needed killing. It seemed though like folks had given up their traitor ways, at least among his people, and Lars figured he'd let bygones be bygones.

Now, if only they didn't have to starve to death, maybe they might have a future. That was the bad side of the aliens. They were always hungry! They ate up everything around them and it still wasn't enough. And now it had got into Lars and his friends too, that hunger. Hell, they had figured on eating the folks at the prison until the Imps sent them packing. If they could have dragged their dead out with them they would have eaten them too, only the Imps weren't having none of that.

What little wildlife there was nearby, the mole-rats and the deer-badger things, Lars and his friends had already wiped out. Nothing left but grass, and the aliens had no use for plants. They wanted *meat*.

Lars counted just under fifty of... whatever he called his people. The word "The Reforged" came to mind. It wasn't the sort of thought Lars imagined ever coming to him naturally, not his sort of word really, but he knew what it meant. It was the alien in him, making a suggestion.

Fine. Reforged. It was as good a name as any. It hardly mattered. A lot of them would be dead soon, and the skinny thief's head was gone, used up. There would be no more Reforged created. They couldn't eat the humans; the sumbitches were too strong, so what was left but to eat each other? That couldn't last long.

Another un-Lars thought ran through his head. Might it be possible to bargain with the humans, to simply ask for food and offer goods or services in exchange? The Reforged were good at mining, and the humans had a great hunger for the crack.

Lars doubted it. He reckoned they would be plenty sore about the attack.

Another thought occurred to him, that the attack had demon-strated that the Reforged were highly skilled at killing sumbitches. Perhaps they would trade food in exchange for the Reforged killing sumbitches the humans wanted dead?

Lars thought on it. *If* they could get the humans to talk, they might go for that. Humans damned sure valued both crack *and* killing sumbitches, as long as it was the right ones.

A question came to mind: how might we signal a desire to negotiate?

Lars looked down at the remains of his shirt.

It seemed white enough.

Kane peered across the tundra at the group of silver-hided creatures, the image magnified by Gunther.

Beside him Morgan did the same, and Ana, huddled in a thick coat, stood silent, breathing clouds of steam into the air. Ana, Kane had expected because of their previous conversation. Morgan had been a pleasant but not entirely unexpected bonus to a group of untested men.

Those men stood shivering in their arctic gear—fourteen of the station guards, Kane's pick of the group who volunteered to try out for his team. These seemed most likely to shoot straight and not crack in combat, but he had no idea if his choices would pan out. Likely most of them didn't know either. Tending prisoners was a very different job from being a marine, and some of them almost certainly wouldn't make the cut in the long run. Some would find playing a more offensive role wasn't to their taste. Some would find they froze up on a two-way shooting range. Still others would not pass the psych evals to actually operate in a Panzer suit. It was going to be a long and iterative process.

"I count forty-seven," Kane said.

"Same here," Morgan answered. "Including the bossman, the one that attacked us on the *Doro*."

"What makes you so sure it's him?"

"I got a good look at the ugly bastard right before he threw you like a sack o' 'taters. It's him."

Kane watched the leader closely a moment. "Is he…?" He trailed off, not wanting to prejudice Morgan's answer or sound stupid.

"Yeah, it looks like a white flag to me too," Morgan agreed.

Kane sighed and clenched a fist. This was problematic. He was fairly certain that Weyland wanted these bastards wiped from the face of Cerberus. But he was damned sure that there were Imperial regs about firing on an enemy who was trying to surrender. If Weyland knew about the surrender attempt, he would likely feel bound to comply with those regs.

He might also really appreciate it if Kane did not in fact inform him of said surrender attempt until wiping the enemy out was a fait accompli. Probably there would be bonus points for not reporting it at all.

"What round for surrendering shithead?" Kane grumbled.

"I know, right?" Morgan muttered. "I'm thinking we just go ahead and use the nuke."

Ana scowled at both men. "You can't be seriously considering firing on them!"

Kane kept watching the leader waving a dirty white scrap. "It would make things a hell of a lot easier."

Beside Kane stood a tac-nuke shoulder launcher, capable of delivering a kiloton of boom. Technically it wasn't actually nuclear; it was similar to their eight-ball ammunition, employing an anti-matter payload, only much larger. At some point in the past the Empire had switched over; Kane wasn't sure of the year, but he knew that at one time nukes were real nukes—but technically they weren't anymore. For most operators, anything that made an ungodly explosion and a mushroom cloud was and always would be a "nuke."

Morgan ran a hand over the launcher and smiled. "I say kill 'em all. Let whatever non-denominational deity of choice sort 'em out."

Ana pulled at Kane's arm. "We already had this argument, and I *won!* We need to *study* them. They are resistant to the Pestilence. We may never find another example like this!"

Kane continued to clench and unclench his fist. "Doc, I trust the Pestilence more than crackheads." He took another look at the waving flag and sighed deeply. "But I'll give it a shot, just to say I did." He turned to Morgan. "If this doesn't go well, light 'em up."

Morgan nodded. "I'm on it."

Kane picked one of his recruits and voluntold the man to hand over his undershirt. The fellow complied quickly enough and got back into his overcoat.

Waving the undershirt, Kane walked to the midpoint between the two camps and waited, half expecting them to ignore him, but to his surprise the leader broke off and lumbered down the hill to meet him. "I'm Lars," he said when he finally arrived.

Lars's stood damned near eight feet tall, and his face was stretched over his enlarged skull, flattening his features. His slanted, fang-filled grin and silver skin made him look like a huge, bipedal shark with exaggerated, almost cartoony muscles on his arms and legs.

For a moment Kane was at a loss for words. He stood silent a moment and finally asked, "Well, what do you want, Lars?"

"Food." No hesitation, and just that, looking down with dark, beady eyes, a hopeful look on his face. The creature seemed almost childlike.

Kane hadn't expected that. Again, he had to think a moment before responding. "Is that why you attacked us?"

The creature nodded. "It was a mistake. We thought to eat

you, but you were too strong. We would trade." The creature paused, blinked, and added, "For food."

Kane couldn't tell if it were actually grinning, or if that was just what it looked like and it was thinking about how he would taste. Every instinct told him he was dealing with someone missing a few cards from his deck, mostly the high numbers.

But for all that, it seemed sincere.

"Okay, this is kind of weird. You want to trade for *food?* Trade what?"

"We have crack," Lars answered. "We mine crack good. And we can kill sumbitches, if you have some you want dead."

Kane felt a strong urge to rub at his temple, despite his helmet being in the way. "Listen, this is above my paygrade. Pretty much I kill sumbitches too. I am not all that up on parley."

Lars nodded, still grinning. "Yes. Me, too."

"I reckon they might be agreeable to trading food for crack. But I'm not the guy to say. That would be up to my boss, and I am gonna have to talk to him on this. Meanwhile, I got somebody at my camp who wants to talk to you. You up for that?"

"Yes," Lars told him.

"You got any weapons?" Kane asked, eying the creature up and down. He didn't really need a firearm to kill.

"No weapons," Lars promised.

"Okay. So, here's how it's going to work. We'll try this the friendly way. If you get unfriendly, I will personally barbecue you and all the rest of your pals. I got a man sitting on a tactical nuke that will take the whole top off that mountain, so be cool." He gave Lars a hard stare for a moment, then gestured toward his people. "Let's go."

Ana exchanged looks of shock with Morgan as Kane approached with the creature. Kane was second only to Morgan as being the last person she expected to actually find a peaceful solution. "I can't believe it," she sighed.

Morgan, looking downcast, nodded. "I know, right?"

Ana was expecting the clove and spice scent of the Pestilence. What she got, however, was the sharp tang of something else, something from childhood that she hadn't smelled in years. It took her a moment to place it.

"Gunpowder," she muttered.

Morgan looked at her strangely. "What?"

"They smell like gunpowder."

Morgan raised an eyebrow. "How's a sweet girl like you know what gunpowder smells like? Next thing you're gonna tell me you melted some fucker with acid."

Ana's laugh was more a humorless grunt. "Where I grew up, we couldn't afford blasters. It was all gunpowder."

"Frontier world, eh?"

Ana shrugged. "It used to be."

Kane guided the creature to a stop in front of Ana and said, "Okay doc, this is Lars. He says he is starving, so give him an MRE or two and he promises to play nice."

"Not the jalapeno cheese!" Morgan insisted.

Ana rolled her eyes. "Technically, I'm just serving these. They're not actually in my possession."

Kane gave Morgan the stink eye. "Secure that shit. Lars and his people want to surrender and cut a deal. I gotta call Weyland and find out how he wants to play this, so sit—"

Kane stopped mid-sentence and held up a hand for silence as he listened to a message only he could hear, then held a brief, silent conversation.

"Why can't we hear?" she asked Morgan. "Did his speakers go out?"

"Nah," he replied. "Suits got channels. We talk to each other, to the comp, to command, it's all mental controls. That's probably a call from Weyland, so he took it private."

Kane continued his silent conversation for a few minutes. Lars blinked, looking confused, and Ana couldn't help but feel similarly.

Kane spoke at last, "Belay that, folks," he said. "Weyland wants us back at the base right away. Lars, you're coming with us. Weyland wants to talk to you, but in the meantime, you're a prisoner." Lars scowled at this, then brightened as Kane added, "Hey, prisoners get free food, all you can eat, and you don't even have to kill anybody, just cool your heels for a bit."

He turned to the recruits and shouted, "Okay, maggots! New orders! Grab your gear and get ready to march!"

Ana felt as if she had missed something very important. Just hours ago, Weyland was willing to risk the survival of the human race to keep Lars and his kind out. Now he was taking a prisoner? "Kane, what's going on?" she asked, slowly and seriously.

Kane, busy packing his own equipment, didn't even look up as he delivered a verbal punch to the gut. "Cerberus is about to be attacked."

13

BATTLE OF THE HAND

Bleys watched the amber light intently, occasionally glancing at a still motionless Ed and cringing as the pings against the hull grew louder, hoping against hope that Ed's plan would work. He ran through what he knew of jumpgate physics, which was little enough, but it helped dull the edge of the panic that threatened to overwhelm him.

When a jumpgate opened, it created an expanding sphere of what the eggheads called "overlap," a place where you were essentially in both normal and jump space at once. Only it didn't look much like a sphere to Bleys when he was piloting. He had always thought it looked more like a spiral, but that had something to do with light refraction, or diffraction, or some fraction. Ed would know the technical reason. Bleys might ask him, assuming they both survived.

The overlap had to stabilize and grow to the right size before you could enter, unless you wanted to get shredded. Bleys heard tales of mishaps that left ships twisted and sheared, lifeless wrecks of abstract art. Once, an old timer in a long-forgotten bar had shown Bleys a foot long, spiral spike of what seemed a colorful mix of metal and plastic. "You guess what that is, son, and I'll buy your drinks the whole evening." Bleys had guessed all night but never earned a single free drink. Turned out to have been what was left of a hula doll sitting on the old timer's console. The fellow claimed he had swung too close to the edge of the overlap and this was the least of the damage.

In theory, once the jumpgate grew big enough, the natural currents in hyperspace would drag *Doro* through, at which point the amber light would come on and Bleys would cut the power.

The problem was that opening even the smallest jumpgate took a shitload of energy. Ordinarily, that wasn't a problem. A typical ship's power plant could generate enough to open a massive overlap, something like a mile wide, though it would take a few minutes to get that big and you wouldn't be moving very fast if you did it, because it would be consuming all of the power output of the plant to do it. But opening a jumpgate by daisy-chaining several blaster batteries to your android co-pilot's backup power supply?

At best it would be a small jumpgate that could collapse as they were going through if the batteries didn't hold. And who knew if the currents would pull them in straight or drag them through the edge of the overlap? Bleys thought of the hula doll again. He was fairly certain that was just a space story, an old pilot having fun telling lies to a young buck, but given his situation he couldn't get the image out of his mind.

When at last the yellow light illuminated, Bleys let out a whoop of joy and relief. There had been a few things in his life that he had been happier to see, but not many. He released the wires, and the din of impacts faded at once.

Ed still stood motionless nearby. Bleys shook his head, feeling sick to his stomach. "So long, pal. You had a mile of guts, I'll give you that."

Bleys jumped as Ed spoke from the *Doro*'s sound system.

"That depends on the analogy. If we are discussing circuits, they are considerably longer than a single mile."

"Son of a bitch!" Bleys shouted. He swung a fist in the air in celebration. "I thought you were dead!"

"The *Doro* is more than capable of hosting my consciousness and data," Ed told him. "I believe I mentioned this earlier."

"You did, pal," Bleys admitted. "So, what's next?"

"We need the synthskin frame to be operational," Ed told him. "The batteries should recover in a moment."

"I thought we drained them all."

"We just needed a high peak current," Ed explained. "It wasn't about draining them, it was just that we were pushing them to the limit of what they could provide in a short period of time without triggering an explosion."

Bleys nodded like he understood and looked around, feeling uncomfortable. He was uncertain which way to face when addressing Ed. "So, can I get mine back?"

"Yes," Ed said from the synthskin body.

Bleys did a double take. "So, you can switch fast, eh?"

"Indeed," Ed replied. He reached behind his ear and disconnected the interface cable.

"I like this better, honestly," Bleys said. "The whole 'I am the ship' thing is a little creepy."

Bleys retrieved the batteries for his pistols, noting both still retained just above half their charge. "How's your juice in that body?" he asked.

"Slightly below twenty-five percent."

Bleys nodded again as if he understood, then shook his head. He actually needed to know. "Is that good or bad?"

"It gives me slightly more than a week before I need to recharge, so it's not critical, but it needs to be addressed soon," Ed said as he reached for a rung and starting toward the galley.

Bleys, feeling a bit uncertain about leaving various casings open and wires loose, followed. "Hey, is this…sanitary?"

"It will be fine," Ed assured him. "I'll button it all up shortly."

"What's the hurry?"

"My first order of business now that we have a moment is to try to repair my arm," Ed said. "It would be very useful in repairing the fuel blockage."

"Good point," Bleys answered.

In the cockpit, Ed retrieved his arm and plucked the control module from the fingers. He handed the card to Bleys. "We'll want this someplace safe."

Bleys took the card and sighed. "Safe is in short supply. We both have extra holes, and you've lost an arm twice this week, by my count?"

Ed nodded. "At least, unlike yours, mine is relatively simple to reattach." He examined the exposed innards of his arm a moment, then declared "I can repair this. It won't be as articulate until I have access to better tools, but I can get it working." He turned and reached for a rung. "I'll contact you when I am done."

"I'll take care of our big-ticket item here," Bleys promised, waving the card as Ed slipped out of the cockpit.

Bleys entered his cabin via the hatch behind his own chair and removed one of several "treasure" boxes from a storage container beneath his bed. The container had the look of wood, though it was plasteel like everything else, lead lined to foil scanners, and had an old-style six-shooter pistol embossed on the top. Bleys keyed in his access code and opened the box to reveal several condoms; a drawstring pouch containing nearly a hundred gold coins; a sheaf of bearer bonds; several legitimate looking Imperial ID cards with his smiling face, none bearing the same name; a pair of dice that would roll seven at a significantly higher rate than a normal pair; and the smallest blaster he had personally ever seen, capable of being concealed in his palm.

"Huh," he muttered. "I guess I did have another battery after all." Not that it mattered. Things had a way of working out if you just rolled with them. He put the control module card in the box, closed it, and stashed it back beneath his bed.

That taken care of, Bleys moved back to the cockpit, checked his instruments briefly, then strapped into his seat. He had some time to kill, so he might as well appreciate the view.

His console told him little beyond the fact that he was moving, which he already knew. In the trackless void of hyperspace instruments were little better than gut feel. They could tell to a degree whether he was in the Shallows or the Deeps, but not much more without a beacon to twig on.

A careful observer could see the currents with a naked eye. Bleys had it on good authority that most people found the twisting, red glow of hyperspace disturbing, but he had never noticed it. He found watching the eddies and spirals pleasant, calming even. He could see the way the tides were running, and all seemed well. *Doro* drifted slightly, but that was to be expected. As long as they weren't here for too long, it wouldn't be a big deal.

Anyone passing through a jumpgate ended up in the Shallows, the areas of hyperspace closest to normal space. It was relatively safe to wade there, with light currents that usually just caused a slight drift. On occasion, a rip-current might pull an unfortunate ship toward the Deeps, but those were very rare.

You could make entire trips in the Shallows, and plenty of people did for short hops. Travelling there would typically make a trip five to ten times shorter, with very little risk of getting pulled off course. That was how they had set up the jumpgates for the most part: little hops. It wasn't a linear thing, though—something about the two spaces not aligning, being lumpy, Bleys wasn't sure —and given that it shifted like dunes on a beach, he didn't much care. Even the eggheads had never really been able to make and keep permanent maps.

The Deeps, on the other hand, were damned dangerous without beacons, but they were also the fastest way to travel. For most trips, Bleys would hit a gate, drop into the Shallows, and then head for the Deeps. In his mind he saw hyperspace as a wheel, with the beacons defining spokes. To travel, he would start from the edge of the wheel, follow a spoke toward the center, then switch to another spoke and follow it back out. The further in toward the center he went, the less distance there was between spokes. In theory the spokes would meet somewhere in the Deeps, allowing for instant switching between spokes, but no one knew for certain. The beacons could only be seen from so far in, and worse, the currents grew stronger the deeper a traveler went.

Of course, none of this worked with a real wheel. Bleys had tried, on several occasions, to map it out on an actual, real world wheel, and of course the distance was never shorter. The spokes were long enough that you couldn't save any distance, but in hyperspace somehow the actual *space* grew smaller as you went further into the Deeps.

That, he would leave to the eggheads. Thinking too much on it made his brain hurt, probably like looking at hyperspace did for a lot of folks. He had a feel for it, which worked just fine, and the eggheads could keep the details. He didn't need them for his job.

It occurred to Bleys as he watched the twisting nether that he hadn't slept in some time. Ed was working. Now was as good as any to catch a few winks. He closed his eyes, feeling a little unsettled by the eerie silence, a vacuum of sound left by the powered-down fusion engines, but he was indeed tired. He drifted off quickly despite the absence of the constant thrumming of *Doro's* heartbeat.

Or was it her breath?

It seemed he hadn't really slept, only mulled over the heart/lungs metaphor and blinked, when Ed called over the intercom, "Captain, I believe we are ready to test the engines."

"All right!" Bleys cheered. A brief glimpse out of the viewport showed they were still in the Shallows. "How long has it been? I fell asleep up here."

"Two hours," Ed answered.

"Okay, we won't have drifted too far," Bleys said. "I hope." He reached to his control panel and saw the fuel system indicators were still red. "I got a no-go on fuel."

"One moment. I am re-inserting the flectocite modules. One of them was hit by debris and shattered. I've replaced it and thoroughly cleaned the injector mechanisms."

Bleys waited until the fuel system showed amber. "Are we a go?"

"Yes, please activate priming."

Bleys hit the engine priming controls. From somewhere deep within her bowels, the *Doro* groaned.

"Flectocite is vaporizing as expected," Ed called. "Flectocite stabilizer injection ready in three…two…one...now. Ready for primary ignition, Captain."

The fuel system indicators were green now and showing full pressure. Bleys hit the main ignition and smiled as the fusion engines roared to life, pushing back the eerie silence with the more normal hum of a living ship. "Engines online. Ship's power online. Hell of a job, there, Ed!"

"All in a day's work, Captain," Ed answered. Bleys was certain he heard a hint of smug pride, but hell, if anybody deserved a little bit, it was this guy!

"Okay, I'm running the checklists up here—"

Doro's sexy voice interrupted: "Incoming message."

Bleys had a moment of complete confusion. How could there be a message? Who was alive to send one? "Uh, put it through public," he stammered. He would definitely want Ed's opinion on it.

A harsh, commanding voice boomed from Doro's intercom,

"Vessel *Doro*, this is ISS Battlecruiser *Danzig*, operating under the authority of the Galactic Empire. We are commandeering your vessel per Imperial Emergency Decree, Section Seven, Subsection Bravo. Maintain current course and speed and prepare to be boarded."

Bleys ran a hand over his face, wondering what he had done to offend God. "Ed," he called. "You getting this?"

The cabin door slid open, and Ed entered. "It's a trap. Don't respond."

"I don't think so," Bleys said, checking his scanners. "There's a battlecruiser headed this way in decel, ETA fifteen minutes."

Ed buckled into the copilot's seat and reached to actually lay a hand on Bleys's shoulder. This really got Bleys's attention. Ed was *not* a touchy kind of guy.

"Captain, whoever is on that vessel, they are not human," Ed said, his expression as intense as his face would allow. He released Bleys's shoulder. "The *Danzig* was lost and presumed destroyed at the Battle of Armageddon. It was in the broadcast the interim government sent."

Bleys eyed his scanners warily. "Any chance it was a mistake?"

"None. They code locked their jump-drives and transmitted scuttle codes to the rest of the fleet, but it seems they never managed to actually destroy the ship."

Bleys let out a long, low whistle. "And now the Pestilence has a battlecruiser."

"It would seem so," Ed agreed. "Time to go, I think, Captain."

"I concur, Mr. Decker," Bleys quipped. "I think we'll skip the checklist and go the old 'seat of pants' method. You want to do the honors?"

"My pleasure," Ed said. He plugged in the interface cord and bent over the console, hands moving over the controls as if he were made for this. Bleys supposed, in a way, he was.

Dead ahead, the swirling fabric of hyperspace twisted into a spiraling vortex, bright crimson and shot through with star-streaked black. Bleys smiled at the sight, feeling in his element and in control for the first time in ages.

Thinking about it, it was probably about three months.

"Let's go home," he said and nudged *Doro* into the rift.

In response, the lights dimmed, the hum of the engines died, and the ship announced, "Engine failure. Switching to batteries, charge level thirty-five percent."

Bleys slammed a hand on the console right at the sweet spot where Kane had pounded a dent in in the panel previously. "So somebody hooked it up wrong before, huh?" he snapped, scowling at Ed.

Ed shrugged as he unplugged his interface cord, then unbuckled. "Apparently someone did again," he called as he began scrambling with all four limbs on the grab bars.

Bleys followed, unable to keep up, down to the galley and back to the engine room. By the time he arrived, Ed was already elbow deep in the wiring.

"*Doro*, baby," Bleys called. "How long we got before *Danzig* blasts us to bits?"

"I could have sworn I fixed this issue," Ed sighed.

"*Danzig* will be in firing range in twelve minutes, thirty-seven seconds," the ship answered.

"You mean you knew about it?" Bleys asked, aghast.

"The original prototypes had a design flaw like this, but I fixed it before going final," Ed said. He poked at the maze of connections with a probe extending from his index finger. "There must be literally a million of these engines in circulation. This is the only one beyond my original prototypes that I have heard of this problem."

Bleys frowned. "What was the problem with the prototype?"

"There was an issue with the passthrough power on the—" Ed

paused, both fake eyebrows rising a little too high on his head to be human, but it was definitely his interpretation of an "Aha!" look.

"Let me guess," Bleys said. "The tracking module!"

"Correct! Your bypass must have some quality issues. It's fine, though. I can rig something up quickly enough."

"Okay, you realize 'quick' means less than ten minutes, right? Because otherwise—"

"I am well aware of our time constraints, Captain Bleys!" Ed snapped as he slammed the panel over the wires and turned to another section. "Feel free to stand by in the cockpit. The timing may be rather tight."

The Enlightened One thrilled to the steady stream of knowledge in The Song. The flesh of The Enlightened One could not store so many facts, but it could store an awareness of them and ask for information as needed.

A Colony approached, an appendage of The Source, and its song flooded The Enlightened One's mind as well. The Source spoke, its song calming, glorious, undeniable. *You must perform a mission*, it sang. *The Foodling and the Useless One have control of a device to breach the walls between our realms. When they cross, The Colony must follow. You must keep the doorway open until our vessel passes through.*

The Enlightened One felt near to bursting with joy. After so much strife and pain, it was useful again! It would no longer suffer the burning or the waiting for The Right Time.

The Right Time was now.

The Enlightened One extended its nervous system again, gathering all of the unburned flesh it could. With so little biomass to work with, it had to be frugal. It shaped small, fast legs, a vision organ, and a digging appendage. It carved and tore at the dead flesh surrounding it and emerged once again into the part of the ship where it had been born.

The Enlightened One reshaped, absorbing the digging appendage and using the biomass to create a small auditory organ.

It was far too small to take risks. It could not possibly overpower the Foodling or the Useless One. It could not be strong. But it could be clever and patient, and it had much knowledge now.

It watched and listened, and at last heard the alien sound of the Foodling speech.

The Enlightened One scurried toward the sound, keeping along the bulkhead to remain as hidden as possible.

It had a mission to fulfill.

Bleys returned to the cockpit and watched the time tick away, the *Danzig* growing ever closer while, at the same time, ever slower as it burned full-power decel toward them.

"Time to firing range?" Bleys asked.

"Four minutes, nineteen seconds," *Doro* informed him.

The impulse to shout to Ed was strong, but Bleys was well aware it was pointless and would only serve as a distraction. Bleys wasn't really a praying man, more of an occasional note dashed off to the Almighty in extremis. This situation certainly seemed to qualify.

"Hey, Big Guy," he muttered. "I know me and you ain't exactly friends, but this is bigger than me. Just a little help."

Bleys sat there like that as the minutes ticked by, the crimson of hyperspace and the emergency lights painting the cockpit the color of blood.

"One minute to firing range," the *Doro* said, as if announcing a birthday.

"Yeah, I am so changing your voice if we get through this," Bleys muttered.

The seconds flashed by now. Bleys was close to tearing out hair when the cockpit door slid open to allow Ed entrance. Ed grabbed his seat and began bucking in. "It's done. Go."

Bleys hit the main ignition and thrilled to the sound of the engines once again roaring to life. "How long we got, baby?" he shouted.

"Thirty-three seconds to firing range," *Doro* announced as the emergency lights switched off and the hum of the engines filled the ship again.

"It's not enough time," Ed said.

"Sure it is," Bleys told him. "Have a little faith."

"The gate can't stabilize that quickly!"

"It will be stable enough," Bleys promised as he engaged the jump-drive.

"Do you recall our earlier discussion about hyperspace mishaps?"

"Something about getting turned inside out or stretched to an infinite length?" Bleys snarked as the vortex once again opened in front of them. "Or maybe twisted into a long corkscrew? If I told you I'd done this before, would that help?"

"You have?" Ed asked.

Bleys punched the engines. There was no time for niceties, and that's what the five points restraints were for anyway.

Doro shot down the barrel of the forming jumpgate, Bleys struggling to steady her and align with the currents battering them, pinned to his seat by the acceleration. The entire ship groaned and shuddered as he sent the ship hurtling toward the eye of the hurricane.

"Nope," he answered through gritted teeth. "Just wondered if you'd feel better if I said it."

Now, small one. We need your flesh. Return to me.

The Enlightened One, deep within the heart of the Foodling's machine, knew nothing of the mechanisms, but The Source knew all. It had guided the Enlightened One to this very spot, where brilliant energies coupled and surged.

This was the point of transcendence!

Withdraw your senses. There is no need to experience pain. Enter.

The Enlightened One, full of reverence, turned off its pain receptors and leapt into the crackling energy, its last experience the blinding arc of its own flesh disintegrating in searing plasma.

Bleys found himself without a lot of time to think about whether he was being stretched to an infinite length or not. He was too busy watching the tiny eye in the vortex that was slowly solidifying and expanding.

A lot of pilots would have wanted instruments for what Bleys was attempting, which was, not to put too fine a point on it, attempting something as close to suicide as possible while not actually dying.

Some people were measurers. Bleys, he was an eyeballer. And he was ninety percent sure the hole would be big enough by the time they arrived.

He wasn't sure what would happen if it wasn't, and he had a good notion that even the galaxy's foremost authority, who happened to be sitting next to him, only had a few educated guesses, but it was probably safe to say the results would be unpleasant, if not fatal.

Which was, when he got right down to it, pretty much how the whole day had been.

"*Danzig* is now in firing range," the ship announced.

"Yeah, no," Bleys said, as the nose of the *Doro* touched the widening eye. Bleys was fairly sure he had just clipped the edges of the gate, but he hadn't heard screeching metal, explosions, or lost consciousness. He counted that as a positive.

Ahead, the star-strewn blackness of open space expanded around him until it filled the viewscreen.

With a sigh, Bleys cut acceleration. "Thanks, Big Guy."

Ed, who had he been a human would undoubtedly have been white-knuckling the whole ride, answered, "You're welcome, Captain."

Bleys saw no reason to correct him.

Ed leaned forward and checked instruments. "Transition to normal space complete. Close the jumpgate quickly, before that thing follows us through."

"Roger that," Bleys answered and killed the power to the jump engine.

"Calculating position via known pulsars," Ed announced. A moment later, he turned back to Bleys. "Captain, you *must* close the gate!"

"What are you talking about?" Bleys asked. "I *did* close it." He checked his instruments, to find to his shock that the jump engine was indeed still activated. He stabbed frantically at his controls, to no avail. "It's not me!" he yelped.

Ed was already unbuckling. "It must be a malfunction in the connections again! Get us moving!"

"Where?" Bleys shouted as Ed exited through the cockpit door. "We don't even know where we are!"

"Away from the *Danzig!*" the AI shouted back before the door slid closed.

Bleys checked his instruments again. There was indeed a large vessel coming through the jumpgate, which was still expanding. He had no doubt The *Danzig* would make short work of the *Doro* when it arrived. That damned ship was a fleet and planet killer!

Running was the only chance they had, and that was no option at all until the jump engine was shut down. It was consuming almost all of their power, and the further they went from the gate the more it would draw, until they simply had none to use for anything else, like acceleration. The gate would close once they were far enough away, but the *Danzig* would certainly run them down well before then with the jump engine consuming all of their power.

Bleys opened a channel to the engine room. "She's right behind us, Ed. Whatever it takes!"

"The relays are physically jammed," Ed called back over the comm. "They're welded closed from arcing. This is sabotage!"

"*What?*" Bleys yelped.

"There's biological residue all over the casing that wasn't here before. Something was in here, Bleys, and it used its own flesh as a wrench in our gears. It knew just what to do to cause this!"

Doro announced in a sexy voice, "Enemy vessel is locking on weapons. Incoming message."

"Put it through," Bleys said, numb with overload.

"*Doro*, you are ordered to power down and stand by for boarding or be destroyed."

"Ed," Bleys called. "Do we have *any* options?"

"We have one. It involves a fire axe and a bit of prayer. I'm looking for the axe now."

"Okay, I'm standing by to get us the hell out of here," Bleys said. "I have implants for high Gs. Are you going to be ok with them?"

"I have no circulatory system, Captain," Ed answered. The loud impact of metal on metal followed his words. "You will be our limiting factor there, I think."

"Fair enough."

"I'll want a few moments to brace," Ed said. Another loud crash followed, and *Doro*'s lights flickered. "That should do it, Captain!"

Bleys looked back to see the jumpgate collapsing, but not soon enough. The *Danzig,* all three miles of her, was fully through and headed in their direction. Bleys gazed in horror and awe at the battlecruiser, his mind having trouble even conceiving how something of that scale could exist. Her once white transteel hull was scored with black streaks from multiple battles, and on one side she sported bizarre damage, a field of twisted spikes extending from the hull like a forest of corkscrews.

Turns out the old bastard told the truth about the hula doll after all.

The battlecruiser literally bristled with weapons, including an enormous particle cannon that occupied a huge portion of her topside. That was a gun for killing other capital ships and ground bases though. It was large enough to take time to bring to bear, but it would hit like a nuke, overkill for the likes of the *Doro*. The *Danzig* had plenty of lesser, more agile rail mounts for smaller ships.

"Enemy vessel powering weapons," *Doro* announced.

"Ed! Hold on to your butt!"

"I fail to see—"

"Brace, goddammit!"

Doro crooned, "Enemy vessel firing."

"Hope you're in a good spot, pal," Bleys muttered as he jammed the stick forward.

The impact was a lot like being run over by a tank, but it did the job. Bleys saw the crimson bolts of plasma streak past on his rear monitors and breathed a sigh of relief.

"Enemy vessel powering railgun," *Doro* told him.

"Shit! Take over! Erratic maneuvers!"

The cockpit door slid open and Ed emerged, seeming to dance as the ship began to jerk back and forth randomly. He quickly made his way to his seat and buckled in.

Bleys pulled on his vac suit helmet, checked the seal, and shouted, "*Doro*, depressurize all compartments!"

"Depressurizing now," the ship announced. "Enemy vessel firing railgun."

Eerie silence crept in as *Doro* pumped air out of the cockpit. A moment later something massive struck the ship, the impact felt more than heard.

"Where are we hit?"

"Lower aft storage," Ed told him. "We were lucky."

"*Doro*, manual control!" He jammed the stick forward and felt the Gs hit him in the chest again, pinning him to his chair.

Ed, pressed into his own chair, worked at his console. "We're approaching the effective limits of their firing range."

The *Doro* said, "Enemy vessel launching torpedoes. Enemy vessel accelerating to pursue."

Ed turned to look at Bleys. "Can you outrun them?"

"The *Danzig*, yes. The torpedoes, hell no, but we have options," Bleys answered. "This ain't my first rodeo." His last words came out as a croak as the Gs pressing him into his seat continued to climb.

"How much force can you take?" Ed asked.

"A bit more. If I pass out, *Doro* knows to back off."

Ed shook his head. "Need I remind you we have torpedoes in pursuit? I propose I take over if you lose consciousness."

Bleys felt as if his face were being pulled from his skull as the pressure continued to mount. He started to speak, then decided against it and held up a thumb instead.

Bleys's vision began to constrict, but he could still see his instruments well enough to see the *Danzig* was receding in the distance. Her torpedoes, however, were still gaining.

It was an unfortunate fact of life that biological entities were more susceptible to G-forces than machines. A manned vessel had limits. But you could strap an antimatter warhead to a fusion engine and your only practical limit was the raw physics of your thrust.

No ship carrying mushy people made of meat could outrun torpedoes. The trick to handling those puppies was letting them get close enough to target with weapons without getting caught in the blast when they detonated.

And because people who made torpedoes understood this, torpedoes were designed to have as big a blast radius as possible to go along with the brain-smashing speed of their engines, which left very little room for error.

Of course, Bleys had a solution for this too. It was illegal as hell, but then so much of the *Doro* was it was hardly worth mentioning. Which was part of the problem. The system wasn't automated, specifically because having it pop up at the wrong time could well end in Bleys spending quality time with a crackhead named Bubbah on the left side of Sheridan Station's deluxe accommodations. And that would be if he were lucky, because plenty of Imperials would just space him and take his ship without a show trial.

He needed to activate it, which was just a matter of inserting his keycard and issuing a voice command to *Doro*.

Which was pretty much impossible, at the moment.

"Todeswerfer," he gasped. "Need keycard—"

Blackness rushed in, and he fell into it.

Ed wondered if perhaps a curse would again be appropriate, but time was of the essence. Without the codes to the Todeswerfer, it was useless.

Ed, however, was a pretty good shot himself when he had the power to process incoming targets.

His wireless was still down, but this was no barrier. He pulled an interface cable from the console, connected it to the port behind his ear, and spoke directly to the ship.

- *Unit EdmundDecker2.09 command to Doro: transfer all CPU control to EdmundDecker2.09.*
- *Unit Doro failure response to EdmundDecker2.09: Error 0x8787, cannot/will not comply. CPU power necessary to maintain fuel mix calculations.*

- *Unit EdmundDecker2.09 command to Doro: Override CPU control safeties and transfer control.*
- *Unit Doro failure response to EdmundDecker2.09: Error 0x8ffe insufficient privilege to run this command.*

Ed considered hacking, but with the torpedoes steadily gaining he didn't have the time. A more direct solution would be necessary.

Ed reached across to Bleys, who was now completely unconscious. That was convenient, as he would likely have resisted Ed taking one of his pistols had he been able.

Pointing the weapon at a spot in the rear of the cockpit that housed the *Doro*'s control software, he asked, "You are not sentient, correct? I would feel terrible about this if you were, but then, I suspect you would be more flexible were that the case." He paused a moment, allowing the ship time to answer, but neither submission nor pleas for mercy were forthcoming.

"Fair enough." He fired a shot into the panel, drawing a shower of sparks. The lights dimmed and the engines faltered briefly as the primary control program crashed and burned, and Ed inserted himself into the now uncontested memory and ports that controlled the ship like a man might pull on a shirt.

It felt good to stretch his legs again, so to speak, to see with superior eyes and strike with speed and accuracy. Ed watched the torpedoes approach. They seemed slow and lumbering now as he positioned his weapons and waited for his targets to be within range.

At the same time he began a search for recognizable pulsars to orient himself. He had no idea how far they had drifted in hyperspace or how that would translate into a normal space location. The topology of hyperspace was non-linear compared to normal space and constantly changing, like dunes blown by wind. Without gates as anchors and beacons, traveling in hyperspace was much more art than science.

Fortunately the currents in the Shallows were gentle. They couldn't have drifted far.

Ed watched the tip of the first torpedo slowly nose into range. It was almost insulting, really, that the *Danzig* would use such a lumbering, pathetic weapon against him. He noted its weak spots with a scan, calculated a firing solution, and blasted it to atoms with the *Doro's* rear guns. The missile's five siblings eased forward, like lambs expecting to nurse and finding only slaughter.

A quick adjustment to his fuel mixes brought the *Doro's* thrust up to just below human-lethal levels of acceleration, and Ed watched the *Danzig* and the debris of the torpedoes fade in the distance via the ship's sensors.

So much for the obsolete Todeswerfer. *Doro* was now equipped with a truly state-of-the-art fire control system.

Bleys awoke to the smell of burning wires, fearing the worst. He struggled to move in his chair, feeling leaden and sluggish, which was a good sign. It meant they were still under decent acceleration.

"Are we hit?" he mumbled.

"No," Ed answered. He pointed to the smoking ruin behind Bleys's seat. "We're clear. There was a power struggle over who had proper authority of the ship. I prevailed."

Bleys glanced at the wreckage and shook his head. "I guess you're taking up her slack?"

"All of it. That program wasn't terribly sophisticated."

"My poor baby. I was going to fire her anyway, though. That voice was getting on my nerves." He struggled to see his instruments. "What kind of acceleration are you running?"

"Based on the biometrics your implants report, just under your consciousness threshold. It's still better than the *Danzig's* best speed."

Bleys suddenly remembered their dire circumstances. "Where's the *Danzig*? Where are *we*?"

"We didn't drift far. We're about a day out from Cerberus if we maintain our current acceleration. The *Danzig* should arrive a few hours after that."

"Why don't we hit hyperspace?" Bleys asked.

Ed frowned. "My fire axe solution to our previous problem precludes that at the moment."

Bleys groaned. "Can we fix it?"

"I can start work on repairs as soon as you are ready to take control. It shouldn't take more than an hour. Can you dead reckon through hyperspace to Cerberus?"

"Yeah, it's a short hop. It won't be perfect, but we can damned sure cut that trip by a lot if you get those engines online again," Bleys said. He drummed his fingers on the arm of his chair, thinking. "So, you reckon they're headed to Cerberus, then?"

"I presume the Pestilence will go where the people are. We would be fortunate if they chose Elysium instead. I am certain my orbital systems would be more than a match for a single battle-cruiser."

Bleys boggled at this. "Seriously? You think you could take them out?"

"As I have mentioned previously, weapons are something of a hobby of mine."

Bleys was finding it hard to focus. He was only conscious because of his implants and likely would be dead if he hadn't had them, either from the *Danzig's* torpedoes or the G-forces involved in escaping them

"I don't suppose you'd be willing to help me out with the repairs once this is all over?" he muttered, nodding toward the ruined computer system that had been the ship's personality.

Ed seemed amused by the idea. "Of course," he said.

"How about computer and software upgrades?"

Ed shrugged. "Why not? It would be good to have access to a starship, and it might as well be as cutting edge as possible. I occasionally have need for contraband and absolutely no patience with Imperial red tape. And I certainly have use for testing of my weapons and weapons-grade software in actual live-fire."

"So, no problem doing off the books, illegal tech?"

Ed gave him an innocent look. "Impossible. Elysium is a corporate state outside the laws of the Empire, by Imperial Decree. What I choose to do there is, by definition, legal. A number of my weapons designs are illegal in Imperial space. For that matter, so am I, technically."

Bleys gave him a weak smile. "Damn Ed, did we just become best friends?"

Ed, looking a bit surprised, said, "Perhaps we did."

Bleys sat in silence a moment, trying to collect his thoughts. "So, how do we play this? Hard burn to Cerberus, evacuate who we can?"

Ed gave him an odd look. "That seems immoral, rescuing a handful and leaving the rest to die."

"There are ships on Cerberus, a lot of them," Bleys noted. "It would be more than a handful. But, yeah, some people are gonna die, and if it comes to it, I'd rather it not be our friends. You want to explain that to Ana? Sorry, we left you for dead because we felt bad for everybody else?"

Ed turned away, staring into space. "No. We will do what we must."

"You get those engines online," Bleys said. "I'll get on the horn and let 'em know what's coming."

14

FOR THE ALLIANCE!

For Ana, the trip back had been as abrupt as it was unexpected. Kane had been very tight lipped, only assuring her that both Bleys and Ed were still alive, but as for the rest, he was either keeping it under wraps or didn't know himself.

From the look in his eyes, though, Ana guessed Kane knew plenty, and that it was all bad, bordering on catastrophic. Until someone saw fit to fill her in on the gory details, she was on her own, her imagination running wild with possibilities, each worse than the last.

Her primary lab was still in ruins. It would be at least a week before she could restart that work, and that was assuming she could get replacement equipment from Elysium in a timely manner. The loss of the fabricator was a huge setback—but then, being devoured by one of the creatures would have been an even bigger one. In any event, she couldn't make much progress on the cloning program and wouldn't until the lab was up and running again.

For now, it seemed studying Lars was her best course for progress. Kane had put the creature in a left-side cell prior to reporting to Weyland, leaving Morgan to guard him. Ana, having nowhere else to go, had tagged along. The left siders had behaved as expected at first—jeering, catcalling, and sundry bad behavior —until Morgan mentioned that she had indeed dealt with a recent enemy by dissolving him with acid, after which interaction had become considerably more cordial.

Lars's presence in the left-side cell across from her only improved their behavior further. At seven and a half feet tall and at least four feet wide at the shoulder, his head nearly scraped the top of the cell when he stood. For the moment he was calm, sitting and happily eating his second full meal in ten minutes, oblivious to everything else but his food. He was technically a prisoner, but she suspected he could leave any time he liked. His "people" had incredible strength, and he could almost certainly bend the bars to his cell if he chose to do so. The rest of the left-siders seemed to share this belief, cringing away from him and in general being exceptionally quiet and well-behaved.

Ana had a few pieces of equipment in her right-side accommodations, enough to at least do some preliminary work. She examined a readout of several blood tests she had run on Lars. He was partially human, certainly, but the results had additional, bizarre data, highly anomalous with staggering implications: he was also, she was certain, partially Pestilence but a mutated form, capable of only a certain range of changes. It seemed to have adapted to his physiology, made certain improvements, and stabilized.

Ana had the odd feeling that she shouldn't be able to understand some of the results even though she *did*. She recognized sequences of the Pestilence and knew how it would behave, even though she had never studied them. She didn't care to admit it, but perhaps she too was no longer entirely human. At the very least, she had alien knowledge in her mind written by Chert that she had never been taught or discovered on her own. Like her newfound ability to smell the Pestilence, this was something she had come by in her reconstruction.

Like any other captured weapon, she had no moral qualms about making use of it to stymie the enemy. She though briefly of poor, doomed Chert who had lived barely longer than a day and spent most of the time confused and conflicted. The Pestilence was without a doubt an implacable enemy, a terrible collective entity that thought nothing of eliminating any life that got in its way. But Chert proved conclusively that it was possible for parts of the thing, pieces of The Source as Chert referred to it, to have independent thought when disconnected from their kind.

Some few, it seemed, would oppose The Source, given the opportunity.

She couldn't understand the psychology of the Pestilence well enough to grasp how a creature could have developed awareness so quickly, much less a moral perspective, but whatever the case, Chert had both taken her life and, once he realized how wrong it was, returned it, cured of the very disease that would have killed her in short order, that had kept her from raising her own child. He had sacrificed his own in penance to see that she lived. More-over, Chert had warned her that her son would bear her curse, and he had left in her reconstructed brain the knowledge of a cure.

If that wasn't enough to balance the books, she didn't know what was.

Ana shook her head as thoughts of her son threatened to over-whelm her. She simply could not think about Anatoly right now. Lives were at stake and she needed her focus, yet the memories rushed in, refusing to be denied. Most of the time she was able to push them aside, to focus on work, and remind herself that this was all for his benefit, but for the moment she could not block them.

She hadn't expected to live beyond his fifth birthday. What a terrible trauma to inflict on a child, to have him watch his mother die, to bear that as one of his earliest memories! With his father dead before he was even born, it was too much of a burden to place on him.

No, it was better that his grandmother be the only mother he remembered, not the sick, broken woman who bore him. He would have had only had enough time to learn to love Ana before she would have been torn from him. It was the right decision she knew, but oh, how she missed the touch of his tiny hands, the feel of him in her arms. Two years old: a squirming, restless ball of energy that never stopped moving.

Lars's deep, rumbling voice roused her from her misery. "More?" he asked, eyes filled with hope, and held out the tray.

"Soon," she said in a kind voice, brushing tears from her eyes. "Morgan is fetching supplies. Meanwhile let's talk, hmm? I want to know more about you." It was an understatement to be certain, but she had to start somewhere. She took a deep breath, feeling control return as she filled the terrible void in her heart with her other true love, curiosity.

"I will tell," Lars agreed. "And more food will come, yes?"

"Yes."

"Okay. Ask."

Ana switched pages on her tablet to a note application. "When we first encountered you, you were different. You were violent and wanted to kill us. What changed?"

Lars's expression grew pained, as if this line of questioning hurt him somehow. "We... I changed."

"I see," Ana said. "What were you, before you changed?"

"I was just Lars still," he said. "But I was an alien too. It's hard to remember."

"You say 'we' sometimes. Do you feel like two creatures?"

Lars's brow furrowed as he thought deeply. "I used to."

"But not anymore?"

Lars contemplated this a moment, then shook his head. "No. Not anymore."

Ana jotted a few notes, then said, "I've gone over some of blood and tissue samples you gave me." She suppressed a shudder, remembering asking him for those. Lars had casually bitten off his pinkie finger and spat it on the floor. The wound had sealed almost immediately, and now, an hour later, the finger had regrown, showing no sign it had ever been injured. "It looks like you heal very fast, hmm?"

Lars nodded. "But it makes me hungry."

"I'll bet!" she told him. "More food is coming, I promise. Tell me, do you always heal like this? Do you notice some things that still hurt?"

Lars gave her a cagey look. "Trying' ta figure out how to kill old Lars, ain't ya? In case you need to."

Ana shrugged. "I already know how to kill you."

Lars cackled at this. "You melted old Benny like a cheap candle! That must have been a real sight!"

Ana put a hand to her forehead and reminded herself to thank Morgan for making certain she would never hear the end of that tale. "It's less about how to kill you and more about understanding your physiology so I can help you. They are one and the same."

Lars leaned toward the bars of his cell, as if about to impart a secret. "I don't need no help with getting patched up, doc," he told her. "But I sure would like to know what happened to me."

Ana nodded. "That's what we're here for. So your memory is spotty, yes? Do you remember when this started?"

Lars pumped his head up and down. "Yar. I killed this skinny thief sumbitch and roasted his arm for dinner."

Ana blinked in surprise. "You... *ate* someone's arm?"

Lars shrugged. "Food gets short in the wastes. I'd have eat the rest of him, too, if I could have, but all I got was his arm and his head. The rest of him run away before I could catch him."

Ana was beginning to piece together a theory. Lars did indeed seem to be some sort of fusion of entities, though he seemed not to realize it. Depending on the question, it was as if different people were speaking. One was uncertain, dealing with new concepts like Chert. The other was raucous and course, an earthy sort of man, though whatever madness had driven him before seemed no longer part of him. At other times he seemed a mix.

Could it be that the Pestilence had actually healed his mind as well as his body? Were they somehow merging?

"Lars, do you know anything about The Source?"

Lars's face darkened. "The Source is a *traitor!*" he growled. "That sumbitch abandoned us!"

"How did you find out about The Source?"

Lars gave her a doubtful look. "Everybody knows about The Source." Ana could see him growing more agitated, clenching his fists, looking back and forth like a caged beast. It would not do to provoke him on this topic.

"I don't know much about it," Ana said, keeping her voice kind and innocuous. "Maybe you could teach me?"

"*No!*" Lars shouted and rose to his feet, towering over her. "There ain't *nothing* to know about that sumbitch except we're gonna kill that traitor dead!"

The man in the cell next to Lars—a short, fat, pig-faced fellow—moaned in terror and shrank against the bars, cringing as far away as possible. The entire cell block fell deathly silent as fearful faces dark, light, and in between appeared at the bars.

Lars, it would seem, was frightening enough to stifle even prison mockery.

Ana held up her hands and painted on a smile she didn't really feel. "Oh, *that* Source!" she said, nodding vigorously. "Yes, of course, everyone knows about *that* Source. And it should certainly die for its crimes."

"Damn right it should!" Lars shouted. He grabbed the bars of his cage and pressed his face against them, his fanged grin dripping saliva down his chin. "Let's go kill that sumbitch *right now!*" The bars twisted slightly in his grip, bending in the shape of his fingers.

Ana scrambled for the right words. "Uh, we don't know where The Source is right now, Lars. But Kane is looking. As soon as we find it we'll let you know. Will that work for you?"

Lars's face grew thoughtful a moment, and he relaxed and sat again. "Yeah, that Source is a sneaky sumbitch."

Ana jumped at the sound of Morgan's voice calling out, "Chowtime!" She turned to see the marine entering the cell block with a large crate of MREs and breathed a sigh of relief.

Ana scribbled several more notes on her tablet as she told him, "Good timing!"

Morgan, still in his Panzer Suit, cut his eyes toward Lars. "Is everything ok, doc?"

"It will be," she assured him. "Lars is very hungry still."

Morgan nodded and removed one of the MREs from his crate. "Lars, it's your lucky day. This here food is pretty much the *best* food in the galaxy, except sometimes it has this nasty part called jalapeno cheese. I'll take those and throw them away, ok?"

Ana palmed her face but decided that the safest course of action was to allow Morgan his eccentricities.

For his part, Lars was in full agreement to Morgan's terms. Calm and compliant now, Lars looked more like an eager puppy. He nodded vigorously, his tongue actually hanging out and flopping around his lips.

Morgan dutifully opened three MREs, setting the jalapeno cheese aside and handing the rest to Lars. "Did doc give you a name yet, bud?"

Lars paused a moment and said through a full mouth, "Already got a name. It's Lars." He then immediately began stuffing his mouth again.

Ana, her nose still full of the scent of gunpowder, had an idea. "He means a name for your…uh…people. How does 'sulfuron' sound to you?"

Lars continued chewing, swallowed, and said, "We already got a name, too."

Ana and Morgan exchanged a surprised look. Ana spoke first. "What is it?"

Lars crammed a large chunk of meat in his mouth and spoke around it. "The Reforged."

Morgan looked at Ana and shrugged. "Works for me."

Ana nodded and wrote it down.

In his office, Weyland took a moment for himself before bringing in his people. He poured two fingers of twenty-five-year-old scotch into a genuine crystal tumbler and stood before the artificial fire, searching his soul as the booze thawed it a bit.

Had there ever been a time he had believed in gods? He wasn't certain. He had, of course, been raised a Christian, the norm for the upper ranks of the Empire, but had he ever truly believed?

It was a question he couldn't answer. It seemed he might have in his youth, before all the blood and fire. In his midlife, like many Imperial officers, he found himself somewhat intrigued by a return to the worship of the old gods, especially Odin.

But now? It was difficult to believe in anything except the God of All: Entropy. This Pestilence was the perfect avatar of death and decay, turning rich, diverse biosystems into vast seas of formless, generic biomass.

All hail the conquering worm, all life reduced to one simple form.

Weyland sipped at his whiskey, hoping it would serve to steady nerves he dared not show to anyone serving under him. How had it all gone wrong so quickly? Just days ago, he had been full of hope, flush with new allies and well on their way to a solution to the jumpgate problem.

Now one of the Empire's deadliest ships—a Dracul Class battlecruiser capable of leveling cities from orbit—was headed for Cerberus, infested with the Pestilence. At one time, even this would have been of little concern. Cerberus, as a critical resource, merited her own defense force in orbit, but the Empire had pulled every remaining combatant ship into the final battle. Without those defenders, the planet was wide open to orbital bombardment, something no amount of fighting men could counter.

Weyland had some few ships at his disposal, mostly cargo transports that had been marooned on Cerberus. He could fit a thousand refugees in them comfortably, perhaps two or three times that if he stacked them shoulder to shoulder. It wouldn't be a pleasant trip to Elysium, but it would only be a few days, and it would keep what few he could alive. The evac ships would take all of the children, which would take close to three hundred spots. The remainder would be filled with women first, then assigned by lottery. Prioritizing the females was less a gallant gesture than simple pragmatism: the species, if it were to survive, needed them more.

As for the rest, Weyland sighed and ran a quick mental inventory. There ought to be enough weapons for most to make a last stand or find their own way to the afterlife, if that was their choice.

He would go down with his command—that was a given. Not only was it proper, Elysium already had a capable leader.

And then there was Bleys and *Doro*. They could ferry a few as well, fifty perhaps. Beyond a few select passengers, Weyland would leave the specifics to the "independent businessman." He had certainly earned the privilege.

Weyland couldn't help but smile at how his opinion of Bleys had changed. He downed the last of his whiskey and checked his appearance in the mirror. It was his job to present as solid a surface as possible for his people to stand on, and by God, he was going to get that right if nothing else. Especially at a time like now, leadership and bearing were *important*. How they behaved now would be how history remembered them.

Satisfied with his demeanor, Weyland tapped his wrist com. "Okay Kane, let's do this."

He stood, hands behind his back, as Kane, Rasputin, and Morgan filed in. He could feel the confusion, the tension of not knowing coming off them like heat from a desert rock. "Sit."

He waited for them to comply, then offered them a curt nod. "There's no good way to put this, so I'll be blunt. We have an infested battlecruiser headed our way that will almost certainly put an end to Sheridan Station and any other life on Cerberus. I am ordering an immediate evacuation of as many as possible. That being said, my numbers people tell me we can get, at best, about thirty percent of the people here to safety. Women and children first, a few select men for security, the remaining spots filled by lottery. The rest of us are going down with the ship."

Kane opened his mouth to speak, but Weyland held up a hand. "In due time, Commander. You have new orders. When the *Doro* arrives, the doc, you, and your team will board her and get off this rock. The doc is critical to the survival of the human race in this section of the galaxy, and you will make sure she remains safe and secure."

"Yes, sir," Kane answered.

Weyland gave them a moment to absorb it, then said, "Questions?"

Kane was about to speak, but Rasputin blurted out, "Ed and Bleys?"

Weyland offered a thin smile. "A little dinged up but otherwise fine. Their mission was a success, and they have the control module."

Rasputin, visibly relieved, nodded and pressed on, "And this attacker? Is it related?"

"It is," Weyland told her. "And it's complicated. Turns out Bleys has a working hyperdrive onboard *Doro*." Weyland paused a moment and glared at Kane. "How the *hell* did we miss that?"

Kane shook his head and shrugged, a bemused expression on his face. "Sir, our techs went over the ship, but being fair, Bleys is one of the most resourceful people I have ever met. He's on our team for a reason. If he couldn't get over on our techs, he wouldn't be as useful as he is."

Weyland raised an appreciative eyebrow. "That's a hard point to argue," he agreed. "At any rate, they used the drive to avoid an unexpected debris field, and this battlecruiser followed them out. They're headed this way on a high-G burn, and so is the *Danzig*. The *Doro* is a fast ship. She'll be here a good day ahead of the *Danzig*. I want all three of you prepped to go the moment she touches down."

Rasputin, brow furrowed, spoke up. "And there's no way to fight? Don't we have any orbital defenses?"

Weyland couldn't help but smile at her spirit. "We can always fight, Rasputin. But as for victory, I don't see a path. Our orbital defense previously consisted of several battlecruisers of our own, but they were all pulled away for that last big fight."

Kane raised an arm, as if he were a student in a class. "We could board them and take control of the ship," he asserted.

Weyland bit back an angry response at such foolishness. Kane was trained to improvise, adapt, and overcome. He was only trying to help. "*Danzig's* complement is upwards of thirty thousand, and you damned well know it! Those are *mighty* long odds, even for you."

Kane rose and stood at parade rest. "Sir, on the inside those ships are more like cities than fortresses. Most of the crew are there to keep the ship running, not fight. I wouldn't think twice about assaulting a small city to capture an objective. Why is this different?"

"That whole ship is *infested*," Weyland said. "They will come at you from every direction."

"Sir, half of any battle is to control the direction from which the enemy can approach. We have hard intel on Imperial ship layout, and we can choose our route. I can do this. It's not even as hard as the assault on Elysium."

Weyland sighed. Kane was a brave man, and dedicated, but Weyland was not going to let him throw his life away, not when he was desperately needed elsewhere. "You *might* be able to commandeer the vessel *briefly*, *if* you had the team, which you don't. But you and I both know you damned well could *not* hold it against that many."

"Sir," Kane answered, his face grave. "I only need to hold it long enough to finish the scuttle procedure."

Weyland clenched his jaw at this. He felt a bit outmaneuvered by his best war dog, but then, that was why he had hired the man after all. When he spoke, it was in an unusually gentle voice. "Son, you understand that there's a reason that ship wasn't scuttled before, right?"

Kane nodded. "I do. Likely the remote triggering failed, and if we can't fix it, we'll have to do it manually. There's a good chance we can rig something and make our escape, but if not, well, we know the risks."

"And how do you propose to get anywhere near *Danzig* before being blasted out of the sky?"

Kane showed a toothy grin. "IFF won't let them fire on an Imperial ship."

Weyland gave Kane a sour look. "Until they override it."

"Does the Pestilence know that? Or how to do it?"

"As I understand it, they know *everything* the people they consume know."

Ana cleared her throat. "Sir, it's maybe not quite as simple as that. It could be the case that the Pestilence knows, but it doesn't *know* it knows, if that makes sense."

Weyland scowled at her. "No, Rasputin, it doesn't, not a lick."

Ana rubbed at her temple a moment, biting at her lip. "The Pestilence doesn't think like us. It's a collective creature made of smaller parts, and its mind is distributed over all of them. It's entirely possible for one piece to have information but for another to be unaware of that."

Weyland gave her a wary look. "How do you know this?"

Ana hesitated a moment, then answered, "I had the good fortune to study the Pestilence closely on Elysium."

Weyland considered this a moment, but it still didn't make sense. "What are you saying, Rasputin? The Pestilence has to *ask* itself if it knows?"

Ana gave him an uncertain, almost embarrassed look. "Sort of?"

Weyland heaved a sigh. It was a truism that a leader would inevitably wind up in charge of people who were clearly *much* smarter than he. Did it also have to be a truism that said leader had to drag out details by repeated confessions of his own ignorance? "I don't even know how to phrase the question for what I need to know! Can you elaborate?"

Ana, blushing, nodded quickly. "Of course. The upshot is that it can take time for information to filter throughout the organism."

"How much time?"

Ana, frustration clear on her face, stammered, "It's not precise. It depends on which pieces know what information."

"Give me a good guess on an average."

Ana looked as if she were in physical pain to boil the details down. She winced, knitted her brows, then said in a small voice, "Assuming the part firing the weapon doesn't already know? Maybe thirty seconds?"

Kane pumped a fist. "That's all I need to get inside their weapons arc."

"It could be much less!" Ana insisted.

"Warfare is risk," Kane told her.

Ana shook her head vehemently. "If the piece operating the weapons already knows, there won't *be* a delay."

Kane nodded. "But that's not likely. The Pestilence is probably using the same men who ran the guns to run them now, right? Why would it change them out?"

Ana shrugged, looking lost. "Probably," she conceded. "I don't understand why that matters."

Weyland, however, understood exactly what Kane was getting at. "He means that gunners typically don't have the authorization or the knowledge to override an IFF. That would come from command staff."

Ana's face lit with understanding. "Who would be somewhere else on the ship and probably in a different part of the creature!"

"If they are even part of the creature," Kane said. "I wouldn't have let it get me if I could avoid it."

Weyland nodded. "It's a good point. The *Danzig* has its own jump engines. If the Pestilence had to follow the *Doro* out, it means they can't operate them. That means there's a good chance the command staff is dead or escaped."

Kane shook a fist in triumph. "I can *do* this, sir!"

Weyland had seen a lot of gallantry in his day, but Kane might be the poster boy going forward. "*If* you had a team. You don't."

Morgan, too, stood. "He's got me, Admiral."

Weyland suppressed a laugh as he shook his head. "Damn it, son, if the Emperor were still alive, he would pin a medal on you for your fighting spirit, but the two of you can't take on a damned battlecruiser on your own!"

Rasputin cleared her throat and waved a hand for attention. Weyland was instantly annoyed. The last thing he needed was a medical opinion here. "Doc? You sure you have something to contribute?"

Rasputin shrugged, looking slightly embarrassed. "I might," she said in a small voice.

Kane gave her an intense look as he suddenly made the connection. "Yes! Bring him!"

Ana wasted no time with pleasantries. Weyland was clearly in no mood for anything but pure business. She brought Lars without restraints because they simply had none that would even fit him, much less actually hold him. Morgan led him by the arm and parked him on the floor in front of Weyland, then handed Lars another MRE and stepped aside, his M87 close at hand.

"This is Lars," Ana said to Wayland. "Of the Reforged."

Weyland eyed the silvery, shark-like creature seated before him. "Can it understand me?" he asked Ana.

"He can," Ana assured him.

Weyland turned to Kane. "And this is the one you told me about?"

"That's him," Kane said with a nod.

Weyland rubbed at his chin and cast an icy gaze over Lars, looking him up and down. Weyland was the perfect example of an admiral of the Empire: fearless, ruthless, and efficient. "I understand you wish to discuss surrender terms?"

Even sitting, Lars did not have to look up too far to meet Weyland's gaze. He nodded vigorously. "We do, yes."

Weyland scowled. "Typically the Empire does not negotiate surrenders. Anything other than unconditional is not 'surrender'."

Lars looked confused. "We surrender," he promised. "We want trade."

Weyland raised both eyebrows a moment, then nodded. "I suppose these are unusual times, and you have an unusual offer. My people inform me you are interested in fighting the Pestilence?"

Lars was silent a moment, then said, "I don't know the Pestilence."

"The Source," Ana told him.

Lars's face darkened with anger. "The sumbitch Source! Yes! We *hate* the Source!"

"Doctor Rasputin, you mentioned his people are especially well adapted at fighting the Pestilence?" Weyland asked.

Ana nodded. "They are. They're not just immune, they are actively poisonous to the Pestilence."

Weyland turned back to Lars. "How many troops can you provide?"

Lars's face again grew pinched, as if the process of thinking were actually painful. "About fifty?" he said in a hesitant voice.

Weyland scowled at him. "How many are 'about' fifty? Fifty-five? Forty-nine?"

Lars looked back and forth at them, seeming lost, and repeated, "About fifty?"

Kane interjected, "We counted forty-seven, sir, including Lars."

Weyland nodded to Kane, then turned back to Ana. "Do we need to be concerned about contagion from the Reforged?"

Ana shook her head. "No, sir. They are the result of the Pestilence infecting someone already poisoned with flectocite."

"If they aren't infectious, how did we get 'about fifty' of them?"

"There were more," Lars offered, brightening, then grew somber again. "But many were killed when we tried to devour your people."

Ana spoke for him. "They actually had a specimen of Pestilence-infected flesh they used to infect others," she answered. "I gather it has all been consumed. The flectocite actually binds and transforms the Pestilence cells into a permanent form after a brief mutagenic period. They're stable now. They are quite literally a new species."

Kane pointed at Lars. "Admiral, with fifty of him, I *guarantee* we can board the *Danzig* and finish scuttling her. *Look* at him."

Weyland nodded as he considered Lars. "No offense, my new friend, but Kane is right. You do look like a very bad day for the enemy. Will all of your people fight?"

Lars pounded a fist against the plasteel deck, producing a loud, low thud and denting and marring the surface. "We will *die* if it means we get a chance to kill The Source!"

Weyland stood silent for a moment, stroking his chin and nodding. "And what do you need for that mission?" he asked at last.

"Food!" Lars shouted. "Lots!"

Weyland again hesitated, then nodded his assent. "Okay. Kane, draw me up a battle plan. Doc, you and Morgan take the rest of Kane's recruits and hand out as much food as Lars and his boys can eat." He paused a moment, then continued, "I guess we're already sticking out our necks out on this one. Morgan, open the armory and get them fitted with whatever they'll have, too."

Morgan snapped Weyland a salute. "Yes, sir!"

"Dismissed!"

THESE FINAL HOURS

For the fifth time in as many hours, Bleys engaged the jump-drive. The fabric of hyperspace twisted into a spiral of crimson and black, and Bleys sent the *Doro* into the vortex.

On the other side, Cerberus loomed large and inviting. Bleys smiled, pleased with his handiwork. It wasn't perfect. He could probably have shaved a little more distance in hyperspace, but it was damned close for a blind jump, as good as the old dead reckoners ever did, he felt certain. Of course, it was also illegal as hell these days if anyone caught you, which meant practice was best done outside inhabited systems. A mistake could send you plowing into a planet, something the Empire frowned on. All in all, that was the sort of screwup you were better off not surviving, because the Empire had lots of methods of making you wish you hadn't and lots of men like Kane who were eager to apply said methods.

As the computer (or Ed; Bleys was not one hundred percent certain who was running *Doro* at the moment, given that Ed had shot the last agent) took readings to calculate their precise position, Bleys checked the comms for transmissions.

"One from your dad," he noted.

"Good," Ed answered. "I was expecting a response."

Bleys started the playback. Ed Senior's face appeared on one of the HUD displays in front of Ed.

"Everything is ready to receive refugees," Ed Senior assured them. "The orbital weapons are primed and ready, and the dreadnaughts are operational. I've even made a few improvements to them."

"EMP shielding would be nice," Ed groused.

Bleys snickered in response. "You'd be dead if that had been the case before, and I'd be stuck in Avalon, so call it providence, right?"

Ed looked almost wistful as he watched the recording of his father. "We have had our fair share of that of late."

"You a believer now?"

Ed looked at Bleys, a bemused expression on his face. "I have previously stated the odds as better than even. That makes me a believer, does it not?"

Bleys considered this a moment. "Well, more than fifty-fifty ain't exactly one hundred percent, is it?"

Ed gave him a thin smile as he dismissed Ed Senior's recording. "I am a scientist, Captain Bleys. There is no certain knowledge beyond my own existence."

"Fair enough," Bleys said and turned back to his control panel. "Sheridan Station, this is *Doro* on approach requesting permission to land."

"*Doro* on approach, aye," came the reply. "Stand by for the admiral. He has new orders for you."

Ed and Bleys exchanged glances at this, Ed with one eyebrow raised, Bleys with both shoulders elevated in a pre-shrug.

Weyland's grizzled features filled one of the HUD displays on Bleys's viewscreen. "Captain, how many people can you cram onboard the *Doro*?"

Bleys started to answer, then turned to Ed. "You're better at this kind of thing."

Ed, looking a bit surprised, nodded. "It would depend on the conditions, but I would estimate a maximum of one hundred. There would be very little room to move about, but it would suffice for a short journey, such as an evacuation."

"What if they were children? Could you take a few more? A hundred fifty, maybe?"

Ed nodded. "I think so. The chief concern would be life support. We would need to top off on oxygen."

"How long to make a run to Elysium and back with that jump-drive?"

It was Ed's turn to shrug. Bleys spoke up. "It's a little fuzzy, sir, but I'd guess about five hours, so ten round trip."

Weyland nodded. "*Danzig* is a little over twenty hours out. If you push hard you could take two loads and maybe get lucky and squeeze in a third. Is that accurate?"

"It's cutting it close, but yes, sir, I think we could do it. I'd need to take some stims, but I can handle it."

Weyland's normally chiseled face showed signs of cracking, a twitch near the edge of his mouth, and his voice grew strained. "I have three hundred children to evacuate, along with the doc and her embryos. You're their best chance at surviving. We'll do a lottery for any standby spots for adults, in case you can squeeze that third run in."

"We're on our way," Bleys said. "Tell the guys on the ground to get the O2 ready so we can get out of there ASAP."

"You're a good man, Bleys," Weyland said. "I'm sorry I misjudged you, but I'm not sorry I arrested you."

Bleys offered him a smile. "Call it providence, sir."

In a cramped briefing room on Sheridan Station, Kane paced back and forth in front of his audience rather than standing at the podium, still feeling a bit uncomfortable in his officer's khakis. Behind him, a large wall-mounted viewscreen showed the emblem of the Empire, laurels with an eagle and crossed swords.

Counting himself, he had three experienced men. Morgan, he knew he could rely on. Zimmerman, sporting a new cyber arm, was back to duty too.

The recruits from the guards—fourteen in all—were trained to handle prisoners, not for warfare. They wouldn't be able to operate Panzers, but they could do armored vac suits. That would be critical on this mission, since a fair amount of it would include being exposed to hard vacuum. But as for how cool they were under assault from a determined, implacable enemy? That remained to be seen.

And then there were Lars and his people, the Reforged. They were huddled on the floor, no chair big enough to hold them, looking about and blinking, wide eyed and pensive, like kinder-gartners waiting for teacher to speak. Vacuum would not be a problem for them except for the breathing part. Ana had outfitted them all with O2 implants and hopefully that would do. Kane had no doubts about their willingness or ability to fight, but as for their intelligence or discipline?

Yeah, that was not something to put down in the asset column.

"Okay, listen up," he called. The slight buzz of conversation ceased, and the Reforged turned hopeful looks his way.

"You all understand the situation: we have a battlecruiser on the way that is capable of glassing Sheridan Station in a single shot. Worse, it's controlled by the Pestilence. Believe me, for those of you who haven't seen it firsthand, you'd rather go out by orbital bombardment than be overrun by those things."

He held up a hand to stop comments. "So yes, the situation is grim, but we have a plan. We, the people in this room, are going to board that battlecruiser, and we are going to destroy it." He looked hard at them. "This is no easy task. We will not all survive. But we *will* destroy that ship and protect these civilians. Any man not willing to do that, get up and get the fuck out of my briefing, because I don't want you here."

He paused a moment for effect, certain no one would take him up on the offer. It was for morale building more than anything else, a unity thing. "So, we're all in this together. We have a pact: victory or death. Yes?" He raised a fist over his head and shouted, "Let me hear you say it!"

To Kane's surprise, even the Reforged leapt to their feet and roared. "Victory or death!" they shouted, waving their fists in the air.

Kane gave them a moment, then gestured toward the floor with both hands to get them to sit. "Now, here's how we're going to do this thing. First, let's go over the scuttle device."

Kane moved to the podium and picked up his tablet to control the display. "Our mission is to activate this system." He switched the display image to show wireframe of the *Danzig* with red flashing dots along the spine. "The scuttling charges are all along here. Each of those dots is a hundred megaton nuke—not antimatter but an actual hydrogen bomb, built into the ship to ensure complete and total destruction when activated."

Zimmerman, a look of alarm on his face, asked, "Why the fuck would you build it that way?"

"The *Danzig* is a planet killer. The Emperor does not create super-weapons that can be turned against him. These things can't ever be allowed to fall into the wrong hands."

Zimmerman boggled. "Like now?"

Kane chuckled at this. "Yes, it is. Ordinarily the Emperor could send a signal from Earth to override things, but Earth is dead, and so is the Emperor, so we're left with this."

"And it's *real* nukes?" Zimmerman asked, a pinched look on his face. "How come not antimatter?"

Morgan rolled his eyes. "Hello, dumbass! Because you don't want a magnetic field failure due to enemy fire or a somesuch, maybe? Shit happens in space, man."

Zimmerman grunted. "She'll blow if you breach the reactor, too."

Morgan looked at Zimmerman as if the man were speaking gibberish. "That wouldn't happen unless the whole ship was swiss cheese anyway. You want the fucker to blast off if a stray round cuts a wire or pops a fuse? Because that's a real possibility."

Kane nodded. "The H-bombs have to be armed to blow. Antimatter, that stuff pops if the containing field fails."

"We carry the shit around in eight balls," Zimmerman noted, his expression still doubtful.

"We're expendable, and you know it," Kane said. "Plus, we turn in eight balls every six months for maintenance. These charges are built in, permanent."

"What the fuck does it matter anyway?" Morgan asked. "You'd be just as blowed up either way if you don't get clear in time."

Zimmerman grunted, a wary look on his face. "Radiation creeps me out, man."

Morgan threw up his hands. "Man, there's fucking *shitloads* of radiation everywhere in space! Are you retarded?"

Zimmerman shrugged, defeated. "Fine, I just know how to shoot motherfuckers. Ya'll blow the shit up, just point me at the bad guys."

Kane grinned, because this was exactly his plan, and worked his tablet again. "We will be using a BB11 Corsair Breaching Boat to gain entry." Kane switched the viewscreen to display multiple three-dimensional views of the Corsair.

"The Corsair carries eight breaching pods, each of which will hold two platoons." He switched the display again and the visual showed the pods launching. "The breaching pods are *not* recoverable, which means we will also have to secure a spot for our mothership to exfiltrate us. The pods are designed to be fired like railgun shots. They have hardened DU heads to penetrate hulls and lots of shock absorbing safety gear inside to ensure the passengers are not turned into jelly."

He paused a moment, wondering how effective this would be for the Reforged, but decided it hardly mattered. They ought to be able to survive the impacts just fine. Of course, if they landed on the rest of the crew....

"When we load the breaching vessels, the Reforged will be positioned at the front so if they come unstuck on impact they don't smash the puny humans," he said. "It's going to be a little fun figuring out how to stack folks, considering the sizes, but we'll manage."

One of the recruits, a young, thin man Kane guessed had only recently begun to shave, raised a hand. "Sir, why don't we just take the nukes we have here and drive them in on one of those breaching ships?"

Kane suppressed the urge to palm his face or laugh out loud. Instead, he said in as patient a voice as he could muster, "It's not enough to take out the *Danzig*, son. The thing is damned near three miles long. The few nukes we have are one kiloton tacticals. They just don't have the boom to do it. I wish we could, but short of fleet action, there is just no way to stop the *Danzig* except to trigger the scuttling charges."

He cleared his throat and looked out at the faces before him. Even the Reforged seemed to be with him, so he continued. "We will split into three teams. Each of you has been given a briefing with a color-coded jacket. Red, you're with me. Blue, Morgan. Green is Zimmerman."

Again, he waited as they examined their briefings and identified their teammates, then continued, "We will approach the *Danzig* from behind Cerberus's shadow at high speed, then fire the breaching pods to give them as little time as possible to respond. I have chosen three entry points that offer as much defilade as possible, but folks, this is an Imperial battlecruiser. There is no truly safe approach, only better and worse. We are counting on speed, and we believe the IFF system will delay their response long enough for us to reach them."

Zimmerman raised a hand. "Chief, what if some teams don't make it?"

Kane nodded. "Good question. The answer is that the plan can still succeed if any of our three teams makes it aboard, but obviously it will be harder." He switched the display to a layout of part of the *Danzig* near her rear. "Here, you can see breaching points Red, Blue, and Green. Once aboard, teams will proceed to rally point Alpha." He switched the display to show a choke point within a few hundred yards of the breaches, a meeting of three passages.

"This location gives us access to an isolated control room we will call Objective Bravo, where we can gain access to the computer and start the scuttle sequence." He highlighted the control room on his display, perhaps fifty yards down one of the passageways. "As you can see, this control room has no other entry. It is only accessible via the choke point. The same is true for the second point of interest—Objective Charlie, a cargo loading bay." He added a highlight for that as well. It was slightly further away down the third passageway, closer to a hundred yards. "As long as we hold the choke point, we won't encounter any reinforcements in our points of interest."

Morgan asked, "What kind of opposition do we expect to be there already?"

"Very light, due to surprise," Kane told him. "It's possible some crew may be there, but unlikely. They *will* be hostile if they exist, so shoot first and ask questions never, understood?"

Kane waited for Morgan's nod of understanding, then continued, "Once we breach, we will all rally at the choke point. Zimmerman will be in charge of defending it against reinforcements from Passage Alpha." He indicated the first entry to the choke point, the one leading back to the rest of the ship. "I will take two men down Passage Bravo and head to the control room. Morgan, you will take your whole team down Passage Charlie to clear the cargo bay and secure the exterior weapons."

Morgan looked surprised. "Why my whole team?"

Kane sighed. "I was getting to that. The interior of the *Danzig* is riddled with anti-personal weapon arrays, shit that pops down from the overheads or out of the bulkheads and ruins your day. Most of our route is ok, but there's a heavy emplacement defending the exit from the docking bay into the interior of the ship. Passage Charlie is live, and it's gonna be ugly, but it's the only way to get the mothership to access the cargo bay and retrieve us. Without that, we're walking home."

Morgan shook his head. "That's a long goddamned walk."

Kane nodded. "It *is*, so don't fuck up, sailor."

"Do we at least know what kind of weapons?"

"Heavy blasters mostly, the sort of shit you would imagine. It's there to stop guys like us, so it won't be easy. I recommend you have the Reforged charge the emplacement and soak up the blasters as much as they can while you hit it with all you got." Kane looked at Lars. "Not gonna lie brother, I expect some of your people to die in that charge."

Lars nodded gravely and held up a blue card. "I will lead it," he promised.

"Speed is critical," Kane told them. "The Pestilence will throw everything it can at the choke point in short order, and again, if you haven't fought the Pestilence before, trust me, 'everything' is more than you can imagine. It's gonna be like the Spartans at Thermopylae."

"We all die in the end?" Zimmerman quipped.

"ZimZam, after the mission is complete, you have my permission to die gloriously, but not until then, deal?" He turned to the group at large. "Any more questions?"

The group was silent, which he took as a good sign. "Okay, let's get suited up and ready to roll out. *Danzig* will be here in twenty hours. We'll be ready for her."

For Ana, the sight of Bleys and Ed stepping out of the airlock was a bit more emotional than she had expected. Just seeing them made her eyes mist over. To then notice the huge hole in the compartment they were exiting, and the scoring all over the *Doro's* hull, sent waves of nausea through her guts.

"My God!" she gasped as Bleys approached and wrapped her in a bear hug. "How did you even land?" She looked at the shattered hull again. "How could that survive re-entry?"

Bleys squeezed her shoulder and stepped back, grinning. "I told you babe, this is what I do! It's a kind of magic."

Ed stepped forward and offered her his hand. Ana barely suppressed a wail to see how battered he was. It looked as if his entire right arm had been completely removed and then replaced with a combination of staples, duct tape, and bailing wire. "Ed! What happened?"

"It's not magic," he said as he took her hand, and then, as an afterthought, pulled her close for a light embrace. "We used the main engines to slow ourselves instead of the atmosphere. Between that and the shields, we were able to land."

Ed's voice and his recitation of facts brought real tears to her eyes. It was not how most people greeted each other after a life-threatening journey, but it was how Ed did. He showed his love by giving knowledge.

Suddenly, she no longer felt awkward about how he must feel for her. It wasn't strange or intimidating. It was, she realized, something she could fit into her life, because it didn't conflict the way she had imagined.

"Thank you, Ed," she whispered in his ear.

Ed turned and gave her a quizzical look. "For what, precisely?"

Ana brushed the tears from her eyes as she stepped back, then placed a hand on his battered shoulder. "For everything," she said.

Behind Ed, Bleys pointed at his wrist and raised an eyebrow.

Yes, time to go.

"I'll show you our passengers. Let's load as many as we can," she said.

Kane looked about the cabin as he strapped himself in. The mothership, named *Perla Negra*, was whimsically decorated with various pirate regalia. Red flashers strobed, indicating an imminent launch.

"Ladies and Gentlemen, this is your captain, Javier Estornino," the pilot said over the comm system. "We'll be lifting off in ten seconds and cruising hell-bent-for-leather for the ass-end of Cerberus. Beverage service for this trip will be limited to whatever chunks your companions hurl."

Kane shouted, "I'm gonna kick your ass, funny guy!"

"I'd advise against that, Commander Kane," Estornino answered over the comms. "We recommend remaining securely fastened in your seat until you reach your destination. Three seconds, ladies. Two. One."

The *Perla Negra* shuddered as her engines hammered her upward. Kane ground his teeth as the pressure mounted.

"Underway," Estornino announced.

Bleys began his prelaunch checklist as soon as he set down on Elysium, leaving it to Ana and Ed to disembark the children and their few adult minders. Ed hadn't told him where he would house the children, but Bleys had a sneaking suspicion and felt a little ill. Elysium would certainly have a lot of vacant properties, all no doubt recently scrubbed sparkling clean by bots.

Nobody needed to know how the place had looked a week ago, right?

Bleys pushed the thought aside before he really creeped himself out. He checked his chrono and verified what he already knew: *Danzig* was a little over fifteen hours from Cerberus. The checklist was good to go, and he had some time to kill. With a sigh, he leaned back in his seat, pulled his hat down, and closed his eyes.

In war or crime (they were pretty much the same thing) you took your rest where you could.

It seemed only moments had passed when his comm chirped and Ed's voice called, "Captain? Are you there?"

Bleys checked his chrono and saw that, in fact, only moments had passed, and scowled. "Yeah," he groused. "I'm here."

Ed's image on the viewscreen said, "Ana is on her way back. I'm going to leave this trip to the two of you. I have some things to take care of that may come in handy for our last run."

"Oh? Care to fill me in?"

"I thought it might be nice to surprise you."

Bleys scowled. "I hate surprises, Ed. Well, unless I'm the one doing the surprising. Then I love them."

"Fine. I just don't want to tell you what I am doing until I am done."

"How is that not a surprise still?"

Ed shrugged. "It is still a surprise, but I am no longer pretending that the deception is for your benefit."

Bleys paused as he digested this. In a strange way, it made a sort of anti-sense. "Uh, okay pal, we'll see you on the flip side."

"I'll have your surprise ready!"

Bleys rolled his eyes. "I can't wait, bro."

"You have no choice," Ed noted and broke the connection.

He was, of course, correct. Bleys pulled his hat back down, hoping to catch those winks.

"Josey," Ana called.

Bleys jumped at the sound of her voice and sat up quickly. "Are we good to go?"

"Did we load up on oxygen?" she asked.

"Yup, it's all good."

Ana grinned at him a moment, then giggled. "I'll be in the med bay, then."

"No need," Bleys told her. "Ed's not coming. It's just you and me, sister. Looks like you're my copilot."

Ana gave him a wary look. "So, he's leaving us alone again?"

Bleys flashed her a grin as he started powering up systems. "He's up to *something* for sure, but he won't say what. I think it's a little bigger than breeding the pets."

Ana slid into the copilot's chair, grinning back. "I notice you pointedly have *not* declared breeding as 'off the table'."

Bleys felt himself close to blushing, but he had good control over that kind of thing. He managed a fairly convincing leer and asked, "Looking to be a member of the mile-high club?"

"What makes you think I'm not already?"

Bleys raised both eyebrows suggestively, then turned back to his console and turned the engines up to full power. "You're killing me here. We have a galaxy to save, you know?"

"That's why I'm being so forward. We might fail."

Bleys gave her a grim smile. "Damn. Very Russian." He turned back to his controls and lifted *Doro* off the ground, then switched over to autopilot. "The computer will take us out to a safe place to jump. That gives us about fifteen minutes. It ain't much, but after that I gotta drive. We'll have to do this proper later."

"There might not be a later," Ana told him. "Let's have what we can now."

Five hours later on Cerberus Weyland sat at his desk and watched the *Doro* on the scanner until she disappeared into hyperspace, the last of the children and their minders onboard. He nodded slowly, pleased that at least that much was done.

Now for the rest.

He checked the creases in his uniform and, satisfied, took a seat at his desk. "Computer, begin recording."

"Recording started," the computer answered.

"Citizens of Sheridan Station, we have ten hours until the *Danzig* arrives. I have just seen the last of the children off, as well as those who won the lotteries. The rest of us will make our stand here.

"Some of you know our adversary, but many do not. It is like none we have ever encountered before. It cannot be reasoned with. It cannot be cowed. It will not retreat. It will not surrender. It will not have mercy.

"It does not want our possessions or our land. It does not seek revenge for wrongs, nor does it want to dominate us. It does not take prisoners or slaves.

"It fights for one thing: us. It will not merely kill you. It will take your flesh and bone, even the very knowledge from your mind, and turn it into even more soldiers to hurl against your brothers in arms.

"The armories are now open. Take weapons you know how to use and stand with me. I don't care who you were before. Maybe you were a miner, a guard, even a prisoner. Maybe you were just the guy who cleaned the shitters.

"None of that matters now. Today, we're all the same: food for an implacable enemy.

"I cannot promise you victory, but I can promise you this: we will not go quietly.

"Prepare for battle. And if you believe in any gods, pray."

* * *

Bleys found himself feeling a little giddy as he slipped the *Doro* into orbit around Elysium once more. It had been, all things considered, a damned fine fifteen minutes, but it hadn't lasted nearly long enough. He had spent every moment since in a haze, barely able to focus on the task at hand. He had navigated the drifting hyperspace shallows pretty much on autopilot, his nose still full of the smell of her, the feel of her skin against his.

In Bleys's considered opinion, anything that felt better in his hands than the *Doro's* controls was something worth holding on to. He had his doubts as to whether that was possible long-term, but he had come to the conclusion it was worth shooting for.

Bleys jumped in his pilot's seat in brief terror as an all-too-familiar, female voice purred over the main comms, "Cleared for landing, Josey-poo!"

Ana, sitting in the copilot's chair, turned to him and raised an eyebrow. Bleys shook his head, having no answers really.

"Alsatia!" Bleys said, feigning a good nature he did not in any way actually feel. "I thought you were in the doghouse." His last encounter with the mercurial AI had not been exactly amicable, though he felt they had somewhat come to terms.

Hopefully she wasn't the type to hold a grudge.

A ghostly holo image of Alsatia appeared, full sized, in his lap. She was dressed as a pioneer schoolmarm and had her hair in a tight bun. She wrapped Bleys in a phantom embrace. "I got my spanking," she said in a sulky voice, then brightened. "But then you created this new disaster, and children need tending, so...." She shrugged and offered him a sultry wink. "Never let a good crisis go to waste, right?"

Ana folded her arms, a severe look on her face, and cleared her throat, drawing a guilty look from Alsatia. The AI rose from Bleys's lap and raised her hands in surrender. "Sorry, honey. I didn't realize you'd staked a claim. Am I invited to the wedding?"

Bleys found himself impressed with Alsatia's wit. She understood very well how to get under someone's skin and seem like she was being friendly and innocent, pretty much the exact opposite of her brother. It was something of a relief, in that it meant she understood people well and would likely keep her bargain with him.

Alsatia was scary as hell, but the truth was she damned well might make a very profitable business partner.

Ana's scowl deepened. "It's no time for joking. Are the children safe?"

To her credit, Alsatia grew serious, nodding as she answered, "They are. We have plenty of space and supplies since the...incident. I've set them up in the vacant client housing."

Ana scowled at this. "And the Pestilence?" she insisted.

"We scan for it constantly. We've eliminated all traces we can find, but it's possible there could be tiny bits left. Daddy *thinks* it will starve, though." She blinked a moment, as if thinking deeply. "Well, it should have *already* starved. The gamma bursts sterilized the oceans, so it doesn't have anything at all to eat except our livestock, and we're very certain it's been eliminated within our facilities."

Ana looked unconvinced, casting a wary look at Alsatia. "I hope you're right."

Alsatia looked offended. "Honey, how many decimal places will make you happy? We have the processing power to give you as many as you want."

Ana relented, shaking her head and smiling. "Fair enough."

"If it makes you more comfortable, we're outfitting the refugees with implants as quickly as we can," Alsatia promised. "Just to be certain."

Ana nodded absently, looking at Bleys. "We should have that done for you, too."

Bleys, taken aback, waved a hand in denial. "Not me, sister. Once was enough."

Alsatia made tsk-tsk sounds and pouted at Ana. "You don't have implants anymore either, dear."

Ana sighed. "I know. But they won't do me much good where I'm going. I still need to try to find my son. I won't be on Elysium for long."

Alsatia made an exaggerated sad face. "Suit yourselves." She kissed both of her hands and blew them toward Bleys and Ana, the holo dutifully displaying kissing lips flitting about the cabin. "Ed's waiting for you on the ground. He has some cargo to load."

Alsatia winked out of existence before Bleys could ask what she meant.

By the time the children were safely unloaded, Bleys felt himself flagging again. "Might need a little more of that juice, doc," he told Ana.

She nodded and produced a hypo. "I don't want to press this much beyond what we need," she told him as she administered the stims, then followed up with a dose for herself. "I have hard rules, because judgment is the first thing to go when you're getting strung out. Two days awake, max. After that, no more stims until we sleep naturally."

"Five hours to Cerberus, hopefully just ahead of *Danzig*, another five back," Bleys noted, trying to remember when he had last slept. He was pretty sure it was already something like two days, not counting the brief naps—one voluntary, the other not so much. "That's cutting it close for me, but I should be fine."

Ed's voice called over the comms, "The cargo is almost done loading."

Bleys felt his mood lighten at once. The trip back had offered little opportunity for personal matters, what with the ship loaded with children, but now they would have another fifteen minutes, and he intended to make use of them. "Alrighty, then! I'll start the preflight!" He grinned at Ana, pleased to see the hunger in her eyes. She was looking forward to that fifteen minutes too.

Bleys turned his attention back to business. "We're not taking up any room we could use for refugees, are we?" he asked Ed over the comm.

Bleys suddenly felt his elation crash down as the cabin door slid open and Ed entered, his synthskin body either repaired or, more likely, replaced with an entirely new unit. "Not at all," Ed answered. "It's all in lower aft storage, which is currently uninhabitable."

The AI (Bleys still wasn't sure if Ed was an android when he was in the synthskin body, and the notion bothered him more than it should) paused and waited as an awkward silence ensued. He gave Ana and Bleys an odd look. "From your biometric readouts, I surmise you are not happy to see me," he noted.

Bleys was more used to Ed's expressions now and could see

the subtle frown as if it were a grimace. "Hey, it's not like that," he said quickly.

Ed shrugged and stepped toward the copilot's seat, then, seeing Ana there, stepped back, looking a little sheepish. "Captain, you realize I am in communication with the agent I wrote to control the *Doro*, correct?"

Bleys started to ask what Ed meant, then put a palm to his face as he worked it out. "So you were watching?"

Ed wore a slight smile as he answered, "Not at all. But I do synchronize data when I am in range."

Ana looked back and forth at the two of them, confusion on her face. "I don't get it."

Ed, looking somewhat smug, said, "Captain, I can do the preflight and pilot us out to the jump point, though your skills at hyperspace navigation will be needed once we arrive there. It would give you considerably more than fifteen minutes."

Ana's eyebrows nearly leapt off the top of her head. "Oh, my *god!*"

Bleys, after a moment of discomfort, couldn't help but laugh. "Hey, modern problems, right?" He nodded toward his private cabin. "He's doing us a favor, babe. Let's take advantage of it."

Ana, cheeks red, but grinning despite herself, rose and took a bow, then took Bleys by the hand and pulled him toward the cabin door.

Kane, strapped firmly into his spot in the breaching pod, watched on his helmet HUD as the large, flashing red dot representing the *Danzig* moved ever closer to the green sphere representing Cerberus. He checked his chrono for the fifth time in as many minutes. For him, the most difficult part of any mission was the waiting at the start. With any serious killing there was always a timetable. You didn't just go in half-cocked and half-assed, not if you planned on completing the task at hand. You made a plan; you looked for holes in your plan and plugged them; you gathered your gear; and then you waited until the plan said to go, because jumping the gun was for corpses.

Kane groaned and flexed his fingers several times. He might have to wait, but he damned sure didn't have to be happy about it. But hell, extra incentive when you came out of the gate was an all-around good thing when it came down to it.

Estornino called over the comms, "Alright ladies, we are two minutes from go, five minutes to launching pods. Stand by for the goop."

Yellow flashers lit the tiny interior of the breaching pod with flickering amber light as the engines of the mothership powered up, filling the pod with a deep thrumming vibration. Kane had never actually boarded a vessel via breaching boat, but he had trained on them, as had Zimmerman and Morgan. For the rest of his men, this was going to be a completely new experience, and for some, perhaps Kane too, one of their last.

"All hands, check final restraints. I'm pumping inertial fluid now," Estornino called as the lights began to flash in yellow pulses.

The breaching pod was an odd sort of "ship." The interior consisted of restraints, a few lights, and not much else, not even controls or engines. It was, when it came right down to it, an enormous, hollowed out bullet, one designed to be fired from the mothership at its target.

The mothership itself was essentially a railgun mounted on a fusion drive: low weight to power ratio, maneuverable, and fast as hell. It carried only light weapons, relying primarily on speed and maneuverability for defense. For a Breaching Boat to do its job it had to get as close as possible, fire the pods, and burn hard to avoid getting smeared.

Which meant the people inside the bullets when they fired were exposed to lethal acceleration, something approaching one hundred Gs, the sort of force that would flatten a man like a pancake, even one in Panzer armor.

Unless something absorbed it.

Kane heard the gurgling as a strange, squelching sound transmitted through the frame of the pod and into his armor as the normally white plasteel floor softened to turquoise. Viscous fluid poured into the compartment from hidden piping, creeping up and filling the tiny space, turning a deeper blue as it rose to Kane's knees.

Estornino announced, "Stand by to start our run. Engaging thrust in three… two… one… *go!*"

The *Perla's* engines slammed them all backward as Estornino put the hammer down. Kane watched on his HUD as their flashing green dot suddenly burst into high speed, streaking across the back side of Cerberus. They would reach firing range in minutes, and after that they were on their own.

Lars, filling the two seats across from Kane, shuddered, his eyes large in his silvery face. He wasn't even supposed to be aboard Kane's pod since he was Blue Team, but he must have gotten confused. It hardly mattered now. There was no changing it at this point.

The Reforged wore no gear at all, relying on the oxygen implants. It was definitely going to be an interesting experience for them. It was also quite possibly the last time Kane would hear from any of them until the mission was done. They could hear him with their earpieces, but they wouldn't be able to speak, not in vacuum and certainly not submerged in goop.

"You okay, buddy?" Kane asked his hulking, shark-like teammate.

"Gonna kill that sumbitch traitor motherfucking Source," Lars chanted as if it were a mantra, until the blue fluid rose above his mouth.

The goop reached the overhead and the gurgling ceased with a final pop, leaving them all submerged in what felt like a bowl full of gelatin, the world around now tinted a deep azure.

Lars tensed, panic and confusion in his eyes, as if waiting for suffocation that did not come. The Reforged, it seemed, were not all that different, at least as it related to drowning. It was a strange thing, but Kane had seen it before. Even in a vac suit some folks had a freak out moment when they were immersed in liquid. Several of his human recruits looked pretty unsteady too.

"Stand by, gents. It's all normal," Kane promised. He struggled to raise his arm against the embrace of the inertial fluid, then held up a single thumb to calm his men. "If you can breathe in vacuum, you can breathe in the goop, right?"

After a moment, Lars seemed to calm, and he held up a thumb of his own.

Estornino called over the comms, "Approaching firing position. Thirty seconds, girls. Stand by."

"This isn't gonna hurt," Kane reminded them, "Because you're gonna lose consciousness pretty much right away. Panzer suits will wake first, and we'll take stock of the situation." He looked around at everyone, noting the fear and elation on each of their faces. This was an important moment in a man's life, when he knew it might be the last one. "If you wake up and you are *not* aboard the *Danzig*, look around for a hot chick with wings and follow her, got it?"

The laughter rang in his helmet, and Kane settled back and waited.

"Ten seconds," Estornino told them. "*Danzig's* guns are still powered down."

Kane sighed in relief. There was no telling what the next few minutes held, but at least they would have them. If the *Danzig* hadn't fired yet, there was a good chance of making the landing.

"Five seconds... four... three...."

"*For Odin!*" Kane roared as Estornino finished his countdown.

"Two... one... *pods away!*"

Kane held his war cry as long as he could. His blue world seemed to stretch as it darkened, a terrible pressure bearing down on him, driving him into deeper and deeper blue until everything was black and silent.

Bleys watched the shifting, red mists of hyperspace, a growing disquiet gnawing at him as the seconds slipped by. He was less comfortable than he would have been due to the vac suit he was sporting, but there was no getting around that bit of attire. Until they were safely back on Elysium, he and Ana were both wearing them as a precaution, uncomfortable or not.

It was more than the suit, though. He was tired and slipping. The last jump should have been close enough. So should the one before that, but both had been much too far from Cerberus for him to arrive before the *Danzig*.

This close to a gravity well, it was dangerous to jump much more than a minute, but Bleys trusted his gut, and time was of the essence. He was three minutes in and still on the throttle.

Ed was looking at him funny from the copilot's seat, eyebrows almost hovering over his forehead. "Too long," he opined.

Bleys shook his head almost imperceptibly, his muscles tight with strain. "We're out of time, Ed. Lives are on the line."

"Indeed. Ours for starters. You *do* understand that this is dangerous, do you not?" Ed asked.

"Trying to concentrate here Ed, old pal."

"A difficult task when one is dead."

"You didn't seem to mind my seat-of-the-pants style when it saved us from the *Danzig*," Bleys groused.

"Saving my life does not then make it yours to end whenever you like. Gratitude only goes so far."

Ana, in the jumpseat behind Ed, cleared her throat. "Clue the ignorant physician in here?"

"Stand by," Bleys called, his eyes darting back and forth between his instruments and the viewport, currently a window into hell. "Almost there. Five seconds...."

"This is a twenty-five percent chance of suicide," Ed opined. "Ana, you may want to scream."

Ana's voice rose an octave as she shouted, *"What?"*

"Now!" Bleys shouted, waving a finger at Ed.

"Only three seconds have passed!"

"Goddammit, *now!*"

"Jump-drive engaged," Ed announced, then muttered "At *five* seconds." The cabin lights dimmed briefly, and the space in front of them twisted into a red and black spiral.

"What do you mean '*scream,*' Ed?" Ana shouted.

Bleys plunged Doro into the vortex, confident Ana would work out the screaming part all on her own.

She did scream in short order, though not any sort of tepid "Oh, someone please help a damsel in distress" way, but a good, honest, "Oh, shit, we're all going to die!" sort of scream, the kind someone might voice if he or she were to look up and noticed a falling safe scant yards from impacting one's cranium.

Only in this case, it wasn't a safe: it was a whole planet.

"Collision alert!" the ship announced in Ed's voice.

Bleys joined in with his own throaty bellow, shouting "Shiiiii-it!" in a long, drawn out cry that, had he heard it from someone else, he would have awarded them some kind of... award or something, whatever people got for screaming really loud. He would look it up later, assuming he survived.

"Odds are now fifty percent for suicide," Ed quipped as Bleys hauled hard on the stick, alarms shrieking, red lights flashing.

"Stop—" Bleys sputtered. "Just stop with the odds shit, okay?"

Ana howled as the Gs piled up on her, but Bleys had no choice. It was turn the ship or be part of a new geological feature of Cerberus. A mad advertiser's voice ran through Bley's head, shouting, "See the *Doro* crater, visible from space! Bring the kids, but don't forget your radiation suits! The terrain is lethal for miles around through the next millennium! See? It glows!"

Which, he had to admit, would be pretty cool if it were some other poor bastard, but decidedly less so if he was the one doing it.

It took about ten seconds of teeth grinding, pucker inducing Gs, accompanied by the roar of engines and the flashing of red lights, but the odds of suicide slowly went down to zero as the *Doro* climbed out of Cerberus's gravity well toward open space. The alarms silenced and Ed's voice stopped saying "Collision alert" over and over, which was a great relief in and of itself.

"Fifty percent," Bleys scoffed. "Like *maybe* five, max."

"At least fifteen," Ed asserted.

Ana smoothed her disheveled hair and spat, "I will stab both of you!"

And, to be fair, she had a point. Ed opened his mouth to speak, but Bleys held up a hand to stop him before he convinced Ana to follow through on her threat.

"Collision alert!" Ed's voice called out, breaking the moment. Bleys did a double take before realizing it was the new agent. "Man, we have to change that voice. It's confusing, and broken too."

Ed cocked his head as if staring at something the rest of them couldn't see. "It's not a mistake! Engaging evasive maneuvers!"

Bleys slapped at his chair's armrests in protest as Ed rudely seized control of the *Doro*. "Don't crash my ship, Ed!"

Ana cried out again as the G-forces crushed her against her seat. Bleys could feel the pressure bearing down on him, but his implants helped him push through it. "I see it on the scanner!" he shouted over the roar of the engines. "It's a ship!"

Before he could communicate anything else, the unknown vessel blazed past the viewscreen, a long, almost missile-like craft. Bleys barely caught a glimpse of it before it left his field of vision off the starboard bow.

"What the hell *was* that?" Bleys shouted.

"A Corsair Breaching Boat with the rather colorful name of *Perla Negra*," Ed answered, still staring off into space. "Returning control to piloting console." He turned and looked at Bleys. "However, '*who* was that' is a more apt question, I should think. I believe that would be Commander Kane and his forces, heading for the *Danzig*."

"Shit! It's here already?" Bleys groaned.

"I have it on scanners. It's almost finished its decel burn and is approaching Cerberus." He paused a moment and said in a dull voice. "*Danzig* is powering her primary gun. She will be in firing range of Sheridan Station in minutes."

Bleys slammed a fist against his console in frustration, noting as he did so that his fist was a much closer match to the dent there than one of Kane's hams. That dent was made by someone smaller than Kane, but with close to the strength he had in the Panzer suit.

"Ed, once this ride is over, me and you need to have a talk."

Ed's gaze flickered to the dent, then back to Bleys. "I am already supposed to remind you to 'kick my ass' as I recall. I will add this to our itinerary."

Ana pounded the arm of her chair. "Try the comms! Maybe they're broadcasting!"

Ed blinked twice, and Kane's voice roared over the internal speakers, "*For Odin!*"

On the viewscreen, a display showed a zoomed view of the *Perla Negra*, and beyond her, like a snow-covered mountain, loomed the *Danzig*, the business end of her primary gun burning with a hellish glow.

Weyland's voice rang from the comms, "All units, this is the admiral. You have your orders. Godspeed. It was an honor to serve with you."

Ana hung her head and sighed, "He knows."

Bleys, feeling haggard, nodded. "We're lucky we're not down there. Nothing we can do now."

Ana shook her head. "We can make their sacrifice count."

"*Perla Negra* is launching breaching pods," Ed announced. Bright yellow circles appeared on the display, highlighting the almost invisible pods as they streaked toward their target. Three zoomed displays opened on the viewscreen, showing magnified views of each of the boarding vessels.

Bleys goosed *Doro* toward them at a cautious speed, monitoring his own panel. "Shit. This is bad. I'm seeing energy surges in *Danzig's* heavy blasters! She's firing!"

Ana covered her face with both hands. "Oh dear God, *no*."

Crimson brilliance lanced from the *Danzig*, scorching the leading pod but doing nothing to slow it. It punched into the *Danzig's* hull, spraying gas and some sort of blue liquid into space from the impact site.

"Pod one is a hit," Ed declared.

More plasma erupted, again licking at one of the pods, but doing little damage. It sailed on, even as its sibling exploded into a cloud of fiery debris.

"*Fuck!*" Bleys howled. "Goddamn railguns!" He spun in his

chair toward Ana. "Zip up, doc! We gotta depressurize or a hit will pop us like a balloon!"

Ana wasted no time getting her vac suit sealed as Ed dumped the pressure to vacuum.

From the corner of his eye Bleys saw the *Perla Negra* take the next railgun hit midship. Gas, debris, and plasma erupted from both ends of the Corsair as she began to move erratically, leaving a trail of her innards as she struggled onward. It was, to his trained eye, surely a mortal wound, one that pierced her reactor, an absolute gut-shot.

"*Danzig* is now in firing range of Sheridan Station," Ed said, his voice grim.

Over the *Doro*'s comms, a pained but defiant voice called, "*Adios, amigos!* I will buy you some time!"

Bleys stared in awe as the *Perla Negra* accelerated forward, thrusters pushing to full and hurling her at the *Danzig* like a spear. Her exhaust spewed uncontrolled plasma, literally burning the back off the ship as it propelled her ever faster. Estornino whooped over the radio and shouted, "You will always remember this as the day you *almost* killed Javier Estornino, *putas*!"

The *Perla Negra* reached her final destination moments later. The *Danzig's* primary gun, barrel lit with brilliance as it prepared to fire on the planet below, erupted into a small, short lived star as Estornino's vessel plowed into it. The explosion blasted an enormous hole in the *Danzig*, leaving nothing of either the *Perla Negra* or the primary gun but radioactive slag, twisted metal, and pinwheeling space debris.

Bleys watched, gaping as scores of misshapen creatures erupted from Danzig's wound, forced out by the atmosphere venting into space.

"Pod two is a hit," Ed announced.

Well, Kane's odds of being alive were two out of three, which Bleys was pretty sure the marine would have been glad to get. No way of knowing right now, and the *Doro* was now officially the only target on the range.

Time to get the hell out of Dodge again.

Bleys took a brief moment, more like two, no, one second really, to pay respects to the dead, then hit the throttle hard, drawing a cry of fresh misery from Ana. He hated doing it to her, but he had no real option but to get out of firing range long enough to think.

The back side of Cerberus would do. He just needed to keep them alive long enough to reach it.

"Railguns are charging!" Ed shouted. "Incoming blaster fire!"

"Hold on to your butts!" Bleys shouted. He hauled on the stick, dodging the plasma.

"Railguns firing!" Ed announced.

Doro shook with the impact of the hit, but the engines were still running, so Bleys kept running too.

It was run or die, and Bleys had things left to do.

16

BATTLE FOR THE DANZIG

Kane woke to the wail of alarms and flashing red lights. Smoke and debris filled the pod, blinding him to normal light. Fortunately, the suit's other sensors were fine, and he had a passable view on his HUD. He could see the rest of his team splayed about the cramped compartment, some still, some stirring.

"Gunther, status," he croaked.

"Petty Officer Zimmerman's pod has been destroyed, along with the *Perla Negra*," Gunther announced. "Your and Lieutenant Morgan's pods have successfully breached the *Danzig*."

Kane felt a deep pang in his gut, but grief would have to wait. "Gunther, show me the vitals."

It came as no surprise to see Zimmerman's vitals bar in black, along with the rest of his team. "Goddammit, ZimZam! I told you not to die until we finished," he sighed. Kane's team were all green, and Morgan's team had only a single minor injury.

It wasn't great, but it would have to do.

"Gunther, how about the *Perla*?"

"The *Perla Negra's* reactor was breached, releasing fatal radiation throughout the ship," Gunther told him. "Before the reactor went critical, Captain Estornino successfully disabled the *Danzig's* primary weapon by ramming it with the *Perla Negra*. No repair attempt is currently underway."

"Sheridan Station?"

"Still online."

Kane pumped a fist at this news. It was a shame about Estornino, but he had surely bought them all a great gift with his life.

"Gunther, contact the admiral and tell him our situation. If he can't work something out, we're all walking home."

Morgan's voice spoke in Kane's ear, "Chief, we're fucked."

Kane chuckled softly. "Yeah. I was noticing. Let's hop and pop. Maybe Weyland can help us out later, but either way, we have a mission."

"I love blowing shit up," Morgan answered.

Kane laughed at this. "See you at the rally point."

To his men, he shouted, "Wakey, wakey! Drop your cocks and grab your socks, boys! Time to bring the pain!"

Lars, woozy, snapped his head toward Kane, alert and grinning. He tried to speak but of course could not in vacuum. He settled for a thumbs up.

"That's okay, buddy," Kane told him. "Pretty sure of what you were gonna say, anyway."

Kane moved to the business end of the pod and hammered a fist against the controls there. The end of the pod, well within *Danzig's* skin, fanned open like a deadly, metal flower.

"Move!" he howled. "We gotta go *now!* Reforged, up front, *charge!* Smash that sumbitch Source! Regulars form up and advance behind them to the rally point. I'm on rear guard!"

They were all far too slow for Kane's liking, hampered by the hard G of the *Danzig's* decel burn, but they moved, down the ramp and into the *Danzig's* curved, plasteel passage. The exit was low enough to make the humans duck. The Reforged had to exit on all fours. Kane counted them as he passed: five recruits and sixteen Reforged, including Lars. Looked like everyone had made it.

The *Danzig*'s interior passageway was, by comparison to the breaching pod, enormous, the overhead a good twenty feet above the deck and about as wide, the better to facilitate moving equipment from the cargo bay. The normally white bulkheads were smeared with blue goo, as if aliens had been slaughtered and the whole place painted with their vital fluids. To the left, the passageway led deeper into the *Danzig*. Kane pointed right and shouted, "Go!"

Contact from the left was immediate and unnerving.

At first glance, the enemy was human. It was shaped like a man: a head, two arms, two legs. There, however, the resemblance ended. The eyes were alien, black and faceted like an insect's with the same dead stare. Irregular, sharp teeth jutted from its maw, and its red skin was covered in sharp, black spines that dripped a viscous fluid.

It was surprised, somehow, despite all the commotion of the pod crashing through the hull. Its expression, quite human, wide-eyed and jaw-agape, suggested it hadn't realized the giant spike that had smashed its way into the ship could also disgorge enemies.

Kane brought his M87 to bear and made sure that was the creature's last thought. The infested crewmember took the full brunt of the blaster fire to the chest. What was left rained to the deck as charred cinders.

"Go!" he roared over his shoulder, slapping at the backs of any slow-moving heads. "*Gogogo!*"

Go they did and, to Kane's relief, their speed did seem to have worked to their advantage. The team covered the distance to the rally point in good time. As they passed the junction where Blue team should enter Kane looked hopefully, but there was no sign of Morgan or his men.

"He'll be fine," Kane muttered to himself, hoping he was right.

Just outside the section Kane had designated as Passage Alpha they encountered their first battle lock, a set of hatches about twenty feet apart that were normally left open, but closed automatically whenever Condition Zebra was in effect, such as when a ship engaged in battle. When closed, they formed a mini-airlock that allowed the ship to maintain pressure in as many areas as possible, even with some sections penetrated, while still allowing combatants and repair crew to move about with minimal interference.

The lock was big enough to fit their entire team, and the Reforged laughed in simple pleasure at being able to breathe normally again. Just as Kane finished sealing the hatch on the other side, a bestial, warbling cry rang out from the direction of the rally point and something man-shaped charged toward them.

The lone attacker looked vaguely insect-like, similar to the one they had previously encountered, though it was colored differently, a yellow and green affair with longer spines and with no mouth to speak of.

Before Kane could react, Lars, who was in the front of his group, lashed out with blinding speed to grab the thing by its neck, snatching it off its feet like a doll. Lars quickly shifted his grip, squeezing the creature's head with both hands as it struggled in vain. The infested beast wailed briefly until its head burst like a ripe grape, spraying gore and gray matter over the white plasteel bulkheads and overhead.

It was an impressive display certainly, but not nearly enough to kill a Pestilence creature, and Lars's bulk shielded the creature from anyone else shooting at it, making the whole thing more a dick measuring than an actual fight, but then, Kane hadn't brought the Reforged based on their brains.

He had brought them because they were all he had.

The headless creature's arms lengthened and sharpened into spikes that it drove down through Lars's chest and into the deck below, making the Reforged look, somewhat ironically, like a bug pinned in a collection.

Instead of screaming, Lars voiced an evil laugh. It was his would-be killer who screamed, a keening, cicada-like sound as the spears it had used to impale Lars began to splinter and then disintegrate, a grey, creeping sheen moving quickly up the creature's arms. Where the gray touched the beast withered and blackened, then shattered and fell to the deck as if turning to volcanic glass.

With a final shudder, the attacker wavered and fell to the floor in a rain of tiny shards. The gore on the walls, seeing it was clearly outmatched, flowed together into a scuttling creature and fled down the passage toward the rally point.

Kane blinked in shock and awe at the scene before him a moment, then let out a whoop. "Holy *shit!* That's gonna come in *real* handy!"

Kane clapped a gauntleted hand against Lars's shoulder and called, "Okay, men! Chokepoint is dead ahead! This is where they die!"

He took the lead, charging another thirty yards down Passage Alpha to reach a wider Y-shaped section, the chokepoint they needed to hold. "Blue Team, Red, we have secured Rally Point Alpha. ETA?"

"Red Team, Blue, two minutes," Morgan answered. "Had to take out some trash, but we're on our way."

"Okay," Kane said. "We should be able to hold until you get here. Once you clear that last battle lock, secure it and lock it down."

"Will do."

Of course, the Pestilence would get through it in short order, but it would buy them time. In truth, holding the choke point was the least of his concerns. Clearly the Pestilence were in possession of the override codes, since they were able to get around the IFF. That meant they could fire on his men with the defense system outside the cargo bay. Worse, they could cancel a scuttle too, assuming they even knew what a scuttle was, but they would have to have the appropriate keycards too. There was a small chance they had not realized the significance of any cards they had run across.

All he could do was hope at this point.

"Gunther, any word from Weyland?"

"Admiral Weyland is investigating options," Gunther told him.

"So that's a 'no'."

Kane heard noise from Passage Alpha and readied his rifle just in case, but it was just Morgan and his men.

Blue team was the same size as Red: five humans and sixteen Reforged. Their combined numbers should still hold the choke-point, but it left the other teams weak.

"Okay, here's how we play it," Kane announced. "I'll head to the control room. Lars, you're with me. Morgan, you hold the choke with everyone else until we get back. Then we all go as a team to the cargo bay and handle those guns."

"Aye, chief," Morgan said. "Shit. I mean, Commander."

"It's okay," Kane laughed. "I liked being a chief."

Kane beckoned to Lars and set off down the passage to the control room. The passageway curved ahead to the right, limiting sight distance, but it seemed clear enough. Kane moved forward at a jog, rifle ready, Lars following behind.

The passage ended in a security door some fifty yards from the choke point. Kane pulled out his "skeleton key," a laminated keycard with a rainbow sheen and Admiral Weyland's signature. In theory it would get him in anywhere on the ship, and there was nothing the Pestilence could do about that, even with the command codes. An account authorized by a planetary governor could not be removed or locked out except by the Emperor himself or his staff, and they were all, as far as Kane knew, pools of red goo.

He waved the card in front of the door sensor and smiled as it slid aside to reveal a tiny, cramped room. Within, three infested huddled around a large control station that dominated the space inside. Again they were similar—human shaped, insectile, and dressed in Imperial uniforms, but each unique.

One stood and let out a wail that sounded like a backwards recording of a scream while the other two charged.

"Hello, boys!" Kane shouted, and fired his M87 at the shrieker. The bolt hit it square in the chest, plasma quickly enveloping its entire body and charring it to ash.

Lars rushed forward, pounding a sledge-hammer fist into the head of another. The thing's skull imploded with a squelch, spraying blood and bone over the control panel.

The third creature leapt in a high arc, for beyond any human capability, to land on Kane's shoulders, throwing him off balance. Kane staggered briefly as his attacker morphed, growing enormous talons and tearing at Kane's faceshield.

For all its savagery, the creature wasn't really up to the task of penetrating the Panzer suit. Its blows glanced off the transteel, making a lot of noise but otherwise harmless.

Kane grabbed at the flailing arms and hurled the creature bodily away. It landed on Lars's back and immediately went to town, stripping flesh to bone.

"Bad call," Kane snickered as Lars turned from his former victim to deal with the new attacker.

Lars's wounds sealed almost immediately, but as before a gray sheen crept up the Pestilence creature's arm from where it had broken Lars's skin. The creature's battle cries became a shrill keening as its body slowly disintegrated, pieces flaking off and shattering in a slow rain of death.

"I hope it hurts, fucker!" Kane spat and blasted the remaining, flat-headed horror.

Lars muttered, "Sumbitch Source. Kill them all!"

"That's the plan, bro," Kane said as he crossed to the now open control panel. He inserted the skeleton key into the ID slot and called, "Computer, initiate self-destruct procedure, fifteen minute countdown." Hopefully that would be enough, but if not, oh well. They all knew the risks.

A klaxon sounded throughout the ship. The ship's computer announced, "Alert: self-destruct sequence requested from auxiliary command console Charlie Echo Nineteen. Voice and retina scan required."

"Kane, Ragnar, Commander. Identify for self-destruct authorization."

"A second line officer is required to continue," the computer answered.

"Override under the orders of Admiral Paul Weyland," Kane said. "Planetary Governor authorization code Cerberus Alpha one Alpha nine Echo Zulu zero."

"Override accepted. Self-destruct is authorized. Fifteen minute countdown initiated. Any line officer may cancel via ID card, retina scan, and voice authorization."

Lars leered at him. "Kill 'em all, right?"

"Damn right," Kane said and clapped a hand on Lars's shoulder to guide him out. "Let the fucking Source sort 'em out."

Morgan's voice rang in his ear, a little strident, lacking its normal smooth, sarcastic tone. "Chief! They're through the battle lock! We got contact. *Big* contact!"

The sound of blaster fire and the roars of the Reforged echoed down the passageway.

"Time to kill some sumbitches," Kane said as he broke into a sprint. He didn't need to look back to see if Lars was following. It felt like the son of a bitch shook the whole ship when he ran.

Entering the choke point, Kane had a momentary flashback of Elysium, battling an onslaught—a literal flood of misshapen, twisted creatures—a thousand myriad arrangements of muscle, teeth, and claw, all intent on stripping the flesh from his bones. Passage Alpha was filled with them, the shrieking, biting creatures from a nightmare crawling over one another in a frenzy.

The riflemen poured fire into what seemed an endless stream of them. A large, doglike creature, a gaping maw for a belly, charged forward, leaping high. It landed on one of the Reforged, its gullet engulfing the unfortunate fellow's head and snapping it off. The headless corpse collapsed, spewing silvery-green blood over the incoming horde. Where it touched the gray sheen swept over them, burning them and leaving only brittle shards.

Another of the Reforged, seeing his friend fall, let loose a strangled cry of rage and charged into the writhing mass. A moment later three more followed, screaming in fury.

To Kane, what followed seemed a bit like how it looks in a cartoon when someone jumps into a pool of piranhas: the Reforged disappeared into the mass of creatures and the "surface" roiled, becoming almost liquid. Gray-green blood exploded across the passage, dousing all of the pestilence monstrosities, which in turn began to wail and keen as they slowly disintegrated.

In moments, the entire roiling mess turned black and collapsed into ash, the remains billowing in the air rushing back toward the battle lock.

"Holy *shit!*" Morgan yelped.

Kane nodded. "They'll be back real soon. Count on it. Lars," he said, turning to the giant. "It looks like the battle lock is open.

We're losing atmosphere in this section. Get a few of your men down to the battle lock and reseal it if you can, then hold the damned thing as long as possible."

"I go," Lars promised, the thinning air making his voice sound distant and reedy.

"No man, I need you with me. Pick some men and send them."

Lars, seeming a little distressed, nodded and moved to speak with the other Reforged. Kane well understood what Lars was feeling. It was one thing for a warrior to face his own death, but sending another man to his was a different, harder thing indeed.

But that's what leadership on a mission like this required.

"Okay, everyone else, we have less then fourteen minutes to get the hell off this tub. That involves facing down some big fucking guns down Passage Charlie." He didn't bother to mention it also involved a miracle on Weyland's part to get them a ride. One impossible thing at a time.

The docking bay was about a hundred yards down what they had designated as Passage Charlie. There wasn't much to see, as the passageway curved about twenty yards down. Nothing for it but to dive in.

Kane started down the passage and froze as the remaining air in the room rushed out toward the docking bay.

"Uh, that ain't good," Morgan noted.

"Nope," Kane agreed. "Definitely not. Reforged to the front! Stand by for contact!"

One, then three, then a hundred creatures poured around the corner, an angry carpet of teeth and claws moving toward them at breakneck speed. Another dog-like creature bounded forward, intent on taking Morgan's head, but Kane blasted it midair. The charred, shattered corpse hit the floor next them and splattered black-streaked crimson over the white deck.

"What the *fuck?*" Morgan cried as he fired into the swarm.

"How the hell can there be that many in a fucking cargo docking bay?"

Kane, blasting away, answered the only way he could. "I don't know, bro. It's a bad hand, but we gotta play it."

The ship's computer suddenly broadcast over the general channel, "Self-destruct sequence canceled from bridge by Admiral Thomas Riker, Commanding Officer, *Danzig.*"

Kane groaned, and Morgan summed up the general mood in a single word:

"*Fuck!*"

Bleys was damned near certain the *Danzig*'s follow-up rail shot had missed *Doro* by about six inches, but he saw no need to mention that and upset everyone else. Skin of the teeth situations seemed almost quaint now, normal even, but Ana was surely just getting comfortable with having an atmosphere inside the ship again. The shot had missed, and Bleys had put Cerberus between them and the *Danzig*, which was enough for the moment.

Likely, the *Danzig*'s miss had put a big stinkin' hole somewhere on Cerberus, but hell, most of the planet was an uninhabitable ice ball anyway so, really, if a stray rail round was going to hit somewhere, Cerberus was probably a good place. A planet was basically the best backstop you could have.

Bleys wondered briefly just what happened to stray shots that went unblocked by planets. They would in theory just keep going, right? Some poor bastard, somewhere, could be minding his own business, no thought of being under attack, and boom, dead from a railgun fired a thousand years before.

It could happen: just one more thing to give spacers nightmares. Bleys shivered a moment and called over his shoulder, "Ed, we got word on the damage yet?"

"We do," Ed answered, hauling himself through the cockpit door by the overhead rungs. "You won't like it."

Bleys groaned. "Let me guess. Life support?"

Ed shook his head as he buckled back into the copilot's seat. "Nothing critical like that."

Ed, Bleys noted, had a really annoying habit of telling you *way* more than you could ever want to know and then suddenly clamming up like info cost him money. "*Well?*"

Ed's expression for uncomfortable really looked more like he was constipated, only that didn't exactly make sense in Ed's case. "Very well. The port cargo bay has been destroyed."

It took a moment to sink in, like dropping a stone into a really deep well and waiting long seconds to hear it finally hit bottom. When it did, Bleys was stunned for several more seconds. He had a quick mental debate on the merits of tearing his hair and gnashing his teeth, but he decided against it because it would likely make him look bad in front of Ana and have no useful effect on Ed at all.

He settled for a grunt. "All of it?"

Ed, looking apologetic, nodded. "The entire container, actually. It's gone."

Bleys ran a hand over his face. "I went all in on that shipment, and I never got paid. I'm ruined."

Ana unbuckled and pushed her way over to give him a hug, prompting a slight twinge of guilt. He was working Ed, not her, but, hey, it added to the whole story.

Ed looked back to his controls and said, "Once this is done, I promise you will be made whole."

Another man might have had his conscience pounding at the insides of his skull at letting Ed agree to pay him for the lost shipment, given that he had already twisted Alsatia's arm until she coughed up cash for that exact same cargo. For Bleys though, the money he had extorted from Alsatia was not in fact compensation for the drugs. That was just what they told each other to allow her to save face. No, the money from Alsatia was fifty percent holding her feet to the fire on the deal she made in Avalon, and fifty percent punishment for her evil scheme to kill everyone on Elysium. Then there was the seventy-five percent getting even with her for putting him through the wringer and virtually slicing, dicing, folding, spindling, and mutilating him more times than he could remember.

And he *had* to get some profit from those drugs just so he could cheat her out of her half, which was the other fifty percent or so of his revenge. The deal had a speculative element too, depending on whether or not she actually found out Bleys had robbed her. She would be volcanic, but she wouldn't be able to tell anyone without getting her own ass in the wringer too.

Irony in revenge always counted for at least twenty-five percent, and Bleys was all about profiting from figures that, on close inspection, added up to more than one hundred percent.

It was basic double-entry accounting.

"That's swell of you, Ed," Bleys said with as much gratitude as he could muster. He would have continued, laying it on thick, but Ed suddenly held up a hand.

"Listen to this!" the AI urged. Without any visible action, he raised the volume on the comms.

Kane's voice, full of static, blared over the speakers. "—heavy resistance. Automatic scuttle has failed, repeat, automatic scuttle has failed. We are going with Plan B, manual triggering. Is there any chance of extraction for non-essential team members?"

Weyland, his voice tired, answered, "I'm sorry, son. They're all gone. I don't have any transports left."

"Understood, sir. Mission *will* be completed," Kane replied.

"Godspeed," Weyland answered.

Ed looked first at Bleys, then at Ana. "We can make a difference. Can you get me to the hole the *Perla Negra* put in the *Danzig?*"

Bleys sighed and shook his head. "The *Danzig* already nearly killed us twice. You figure to give 'em a third swing?"

"I have a plan," Ed promised. We'll follow the *Perla's* route. It's filled with debris, and we'll use the erratic maneuvering I have programmed into the new agent. We can do this." He paused, looking a little embarrassed. "*You* can do this."

"Charging a battlecruiser is one hundred percent suicide in my book!"

Ed scowled at him. "I thought we weren't doing the odds thing anymore."

Bleys shook his head, unable to find words for long moments, knowing that Kane's life hung on his decision. But then, so did Ed's and Ana's. Really, he only needed one single word. "No," he sighed, feeling bile rise in his throat. "I can't."

"Yes, you *can!*" Ed shouted, anger clear on his face, most un-Ed-like. That alone was enough to get Bleys's attention. From the look on Ana's face, it had hers as well. Ed, however, hadn't even noticed his sudden departure from his usual calm, cool demeanor. "I've watched you pilot this ship through a partially opened jump-gate *twice.* You outran *Danzig* and evaded her blasters and railgun fire. I wouldn't be alive if it weren't for your abilities! And now Kane needs you too!"

Bleys shook his head. "I can't risk it, Ed."

"Why *not?*" Ed demanded.

It took Ed a moment to notice Bleys's subtle nod in Ana's direction. The AI looked her way, totally exposing Bleys's attempt at subtlety. "Ah," he sighed, a pained look on his face. "I see." He relaxed, seeming to deflate in his seat.

Ana leapt to her feet, glaring first at one, then the other. "*What?*" She pushed herself toward Bleys, jabbing a finger at his chest. "Don't you put this on *me!*" She spun toward Ed, then back to Bleys, as if she couldn't decide which she was angrier with. "Do you have any idea how I would have felt if one of you hadn't made it back from the gate? I will *not* sit idly by while those men die! Not if we can save them."

She fixed Bleys with her stare and demanded, "Tell me the truth! Can you do it?"

Bleys turned his gaze away, clenching his jaw. "I don't know."

Ana grabbed him by the shoulders. "Would you risk it if I wasn't onboard?" she demanded. "Would you risk it if it were *me* on that ship?"

It was tough to look her in the eyes. Slowly, he nodded. "Yeah, I reckon I'd risk it." She started to speak, but he blurted out, "It ain't like that."

"What's it like, then?" she asked in a husky voice, anger radiating from her like heat.

Bleys struggled for words to put to things he didn't normally think about, much less tell others. "It's just that I never much cared if I lived or died before. Don't get me wrong, I mean, I wanted to live, but I always figured if things went bad, hey, I'd be dead, so it's not like I'd be all bent out of shape about it, you know?" He hesitated, again struggling for words. "And now suddenly I got something to live for. I haven't had enough time with you. I want more, a *lot* more. I don't want to risk that."

Ana's glare softened to a slightly bemused smile, and tears glistened in her eyes. She drew him close, nose to nose, and said, "Then risk it *with* me, Josey. Because you're going to *need* me if you want to live through this, and I don't want to lose either of you."

Bleys sniffed and cleared his throat, then dabbed at the moisture in his eye. "Okay, babe." He turned to Ed and raised a questioning eyebrow. "You got any objections?"

Ed shook his head. "I stand rebuked. Furthermore, Ana is no

longer my employee and is not subject to my direction. She is my friend, and I will accede to her wishes."

Bleys rolled his eyes and gestured for Ana to take her seat as he powered up thrust. The *Doro* trembled as she accelerated. "'No' would have worked just fine," he told Ed.

Ed smirked a moment, then turned back to his console. "I'll take that under advisement."

Bleys thought about asking Ed if he'd had some work done, maybe got some upgrades or an emotion chip or something, but that could end badly if he could get mad now too. Might be best to hold off until after the battle, assuming "after" actually happened.

Besides, he knew somebody better he could talk a little smack to right now.

Bleys put on his headset and dialed in Kane's channel. "Hey Rags, I hear you fucked this up and now I have to come save you."

"Get the fuck off this frequency, Bleys!" Kane raged. Blaster fire filled the channel with noise for a moment. "And get the fuck out of here!"

"That's no way to talk to your daddy, son. Where's your video?"

Bleys was uncertain if the weird, almost gurgling sound was laughter, or Kane killing someone. It might have been Kane being killed, come to think of it. "Shit, did you just die? I was coming to give you a ride."

"Vid is on the fritz, and I don't have permission to die, Bleys. You know that. Now do me a favor and get Ed and the doc out of here."

"No can do, kemosabe. They have me at gunpoint right now, or I would definitely be heading for the hills. As it is, we're probably going to be in *Danzig's* line of sight in—" He checked his instruments. "Thirty seconds, say?"

"It's suicide, Bleys! Save yourselves!"

"Ed has a plan, and we worked the numbers. It's only about fifteen percent suicide."

"Really? What's his plan where you survive playing chicken with a battlecruiser?"

Bleys looked to the copilot's seat to see it empty. He whipped his head around, but only saw Ana. She shrugged and pushed off toward the seat Ed had left vacant, the look on her face saying silently, "Might as well, right?"

"Where'd he go?" Bleys asked.

"Where'd who go?" Kane asked.

Ana shrugged again and pointed aft.

"He *said* he had a plan, Rags," Bleys answered.

"Listen, Bleys! In about fifteen minutes, one of two things will happen. Either we trigger the scuttle device and Cerb has an extra sun, or we'll be dead and they will have nothing distracting them from smearing you. Think about what you're doing."

"We already thought about it," Ana cut in. "We're coming."

Kane paused, and more blaster fire filled the connection. "Tell him it better be a good plan or else he's buying the drinks."

Bleys and Ana exchanged a confused look and shrugged at one another.

Kane's video suddenly started working. A large display opened on the viewscreen to show a scene of pure carnage. Kane and his team were surrounded, Pestilence creatures pouring in from two sides.

"It's not looking good here, Bleys," Kane shouted over the din of battle. "So whatever the plan is it better happen quick, or we lose our option on Plan B too."

Without warning, Kane's feed cut out. Ana jumped in her seat. "What happened?"

"Looks like they jammed comms," Bleys said. "Zip up and check your comms, I'm going to depressurize again."

Ahead, through the viewscreen, Bleys could see the limned edge of Cerberus and beyond, Tartarus, her distant sun.

And then he could see the *Danzig*, looming in space like a great bird of prey, surrounded by the shattered corpses of her attackers.

"Computer, shields up and depressurize for a fight," Bleys called.

The cabin light shifted to red, and the computer answered in a thick, Russian accent, "Shields up."

Ana gaped at Bleys. "It sounds just like my father!"

"And you thought Ed didn't have a sense of humor," Bleys said with a grin. "Ed!" he shouted to the ship in general. He was probably listening, right?

"I'm in lower aft storage," Ed called over the comms. "Stand by."

Bleys checked his instruments, noting the power surges in the *Danzig's* main batteries. "There ain't no time to stand! She's firing!"

"Engaging EM," Ed answered.

"No no no!" Bleys yelled. "I got the driving! Have it mark the inflection points on the HUD and I'll hit them if I can. You just do whatever it is you're gonna do." He paused a moment, waiting to see red flashes indicating blaster fire. "What *are* you gonna do, anyway?"

"Just get me to that breach!" Ed said.

Ana shook her head. "Not an answer."

Bleys, focused intently on the *Danzig*, saw the red flashes he had been anticipating and banked hard toward the first inflection point on his screen, bringing *Doro* dangerously close to the debris field of Zimmerman's ill-fated breaching pod. Moments later, the crimson plasma passed close enough that Bleys could almost feel the cabin temperature rise. Probably the *Doro's* shields would have soaked it, but a clean miss was much better.

"Computer," Bleys called as he watched for the next round of fire. "You got a name?"

"This unit's name is 'Computer'," it answered.

"Okay, now it's Ivan."

"Oh, not Ivan!" Ana shouted.

"What's wrong with Ivan?" Bleys asked.

"I am functioning at one hundred percent," Ivan asserted.

"I have an ex named Ivan!" Ana complained.

Bleys shook his head at this. "Okay, fine, you name him."

"Ivan," Ana called. "Your new name is Yuri."

"Oh, shit!" Bleys yelled. "*I* have an ex named Yuri!"

Ana gaped at him again. "*What?*"

Bleys pulled hard on the stick, dodging most of the next barrage, and aimed for the next inflection point. "I'm shitting you, babe. His name was Cecil."

"It's not funny!" Ana shouted, her face contorted as she forced a frown that really seemed to want to be a mad cackle.

Bleys knew just how she felt. Near death experiences were always a real gas.

"Oh, it's funny," he laughed. "Just not to you!" Leaving her with the notion that he had male lovers in his past could prove difficult later, and he should probably clarify that it was just something he said to distract her from the prospect of instant, fiery death all around them, but for now it was just too much fun seeing that look on her face.

After all, Bleys needed a little distraction from instant, fiery death too.

Doro shook as she soaked a glancing blow on her shields, but no alarms went off which was good, assuming whatever damage got through wasn't actually done to the alarm system. Bleys shrugged this off, figuring that was long odds anyway.

"We're getting close," Bleys said as the *Perla Negra's* debris began to ping against *Doro's* hull. It was mostly very fine-grained and not dangerous. Yuri could mark the big chunks well enough to avoid them.

Danzig's guns were cycled and ready to fire, but Bleys saw no red flashes. "Looks like your idea about using the debris as chaff worked. They seem to be having trouble getting a firing solution. So, what am I doing here? Flyby? No way I can set down in there."

"As fast as you can, please," Ed answered. "Then see what you can do about picking up Kane's team at that cargo docking bay. I'm marking it on the HUD."

A flashing blue circle appeared on the primary display, with the text "Go Here Next."

Bleys snickered at Ed's OCD-like adding of labels, then gave Ana an apologetic look. "Hold on, babe. It's gonna get crunchy."

Ana grimaced, but she nodded too. "What the hell is he planning?"

Bleys shook his head. "I dunno. He's the brains of this outfit. I'm just the bus driver."

Ana groaned as Bleys pushed the thrust close to human tolerance, doing his best to hit Yuri's marks on the HUD as they approached the crash site. *Danzig* fired another barrage, but by now *Doro* was a hard target—high speed and moving erratically across *Danzig's* firing arc, surrounded by the debris and hard radiation of the *Perla Negra*. Bleys made a mental note to pour an extra glass for Captain Estornino, because they were definitely riding his coattails in.

The breach loomed ahead, dim red flames licking at the wound and spilling outward. "Ed?"

Ed did not respond.

"Oh, my God!" Ana gasped. "They're running across the hull!"

Bleys did a double take at this, realizing the shifting red below wasn't flames at all! It was a living carpet of Pestilence creatures, blood red, scrambling over the *Danzig*'s hull and piling into what looked like a cargo docking bay.

One marked with a blue circle and a "Go Here Next" label.

"Shit!" he muttered. "Ed!"

Again, Ed didn't answer.

"Yuri, get me a visual on lower aft storage," Bleys called.

Another display popped up on the main viewscreen. Ed was in aft storage alright, standing stock still next to a large pole that ran from the deck to the overhead. Something was dangling from his chest. "Yuri, zoom in on Ed."

Ed's motionless body filled the screen, and Bleys could make out what looked like a ratchet strap tying Ed to the pole.

"Ed?" Bleys called, but Ed remained motionless. "Yuri, can he hear me?"

"Edmond Decker 2.09 is no longer aboard the *Doro*," Yuri announced.

Ana, her face pinched with strain, said nothing, but the concern in her eyes spoke volumes.

Bleys was just about to shout the obvious question when Ed's voice, crackling and filled with static, spoke in his headset, "Trust…Captain….have a plan."

Ana shook her head. "What the hell is he doing?"

An alarm cut short Bleys's speculation as Yuri announced, "Torpedo launch detected."

At the chokepoint Kane fired his M87 down Passage Alpha again, rapid fire plasma bolts, slowing the tide of teeth and fangs that threatened to engulf them all. He sighed as another of the Reforged lost its composure and charged into the mass.

That was one thing the Pestilence either didn't learn from, or, like the Reforged, it just couldn't help itself. The two were like matter and antimatter, compelled to destroy one another. To some degree Kane understood the enmity on the Reforgeds' side. They felt abandoned and betrayed. But why would the Pestilence hate the Reforged back so much?

Kane shook his head as the swarm halted its charge and tore into the hulking, silver-skinned attacker, while he, in turn, smashed and bit at them. Blood flew, both red and silver, followed by the withering gray as the Pestilence flesh crystalized and rained down in black shards.

Gunther piped up, "Communications lost. Switching to laser transmission. Communications now restricted to line of sight."

"Great," Kane growled. "We didn't have enough trouble."

"Incoming from Charlie!" Morgan shouted, even as he fired his own weapon. The rest of their riflemen pivoted to focus fire down Passage Charlie, leaving the Reforged to screen any further attackers from Alpha.

The creatures were using wolf-pack tactics, pouring in from one passage, then another. Somehow, the Pestilence aboard the *Danzig* was smarter. It understood tactics better, including how to use technology.

"Steady!" Kane told them. "Reforged, hold the line!" He watched Passage Alpha, alert for Gunther's yellow highlights, but for the moment the enemy seemed spent. It would be only a moment though, just long enough for the Pestilence to form more creatures, think up new tactics, shape more flesh, and hurl a new batch of weapons.

From somewhere nearby a deep, ripping explosion rattled the decks, and what remained of the atmosphere went whistling down Passage Alpha, a mini-hurricane sweeping away the black, powdery remains that had begun to fill the passageway, leaving a brown mud of blood and ash smearing the white surfaces. Red flashing lights, set every five feet in the overhead, flickered, indicating depressurization.

"What the fuck was that?" Morgan wondered.

"Nothing good," Kane answered on their direct channel, not wanting the rest of the team to hear what he was about to say. "Listen, we're running out of time. If I don't activate plan B soon, it won't be an option."

"Fuck that!" Morgan shouted, firing another long burst. "You got a wife and kids. I'll do it."

Kane shook his head sadly as the first yellow dot appeared on his visor. "That's noble brother, but I'm in charge of this mission. I have to make sure it gets done. That means me doing it personally."

"Bullshit!"

Gunther suddenly filled Kane's visor with yellow dots, including one huge target. Kane shook his head at the size, remembering the behemoths on Elysium and how he had acquired his first cybernetic limb.

Another tremendous explosion rocked the ship, followed by a high-pitched whine and what sounded like a titanic blow to the hull, as if Thor himself were hammering the ship with his hammer. It was hard to identify, in part because it wasn't a real sound; without air everything would normally be dead silent, but Gunther did a decent approximation by interpreting the vibrations transmitted through the deck. In a real sense, while wearing the Panzer suit, Kane had ears in his feet.

"Gunther, what is that sound?"

"Unknown, but it seems to be approaching. Battle lock in Passage Alpha has been destroyed, and a large mass of creatures is headed this way."

"Gunther, how large?"

"Approximately four times the size of the previously largest encounter."

Kane sighed and shouldered his M87. This was going to be rough. It might be the end.

"Clear here," Morgan called.

"Riflemen to Passage Alpha," Kane shouted. "Major incoming! Reforged, hold the line!"

He heard them before he saw them, but his visor filled with enough yellow that he shouted, "Gunther, disable target marking! I can't see!"

The yellow target markers snapped off, but not before Kane got the actual proportions on the large circle. It was so big that he almost felt it had to be a mistake. Whatever that thing was, it filled the twenty-foot high passage, something absolutely monstrous.

"Stand by on eight balls!" he called. "We got a monster incoming!"

They came—crawling, loping, and oozing along the bulkheads and overhead like huge insects, teeth chittering, saliva dripping from maws, clinging to surfaces despite the *Danzig*'s artificial gravity—on all sides of the passage. Only the deck was clear, as if they were yielding to something in the center.

"Light 'em up!" Kane called, holding his own fire until he could work out the real threat. These guys were just the escort.

The deck vibrated beneath his feet now as something pushed its way through the smaller creatures. Yellow, baleful eyes, a foot across or more, stared from a fang-filled beak. The head, wedge-shaped like a snake, shot forward on a long neck as the creature squeezed the rest of its bulk through the passage.

Kane's heart sank at what he saw. It was absolutely enormous, fifty feet long, maybe more. Long, skinless arms swept the line of Reforged with claws the size of a man, purple muscles rippling and bunching with incalculable strength, more than capable of ripping through the plasteel passage. The remains of the battle lock, now a twisted mass of plasteel, hung from a wet, bloody claw.

The skinless, wingless dragon, spiked tail hammering at the

passageway behind and puncturing the bulkheads, tore through the line of Reforged like they were paper dolls and lunged at Kane with its beak, seizing him around the torso and snatching him up like a bird catching a worm.

The rest was, for Kane, pure chaos. The creature shook him and thrashed him against the overhead and deck, each impact like being dropped from orbit. The first robbed him of any sense of orientation, and the subsequent blows made time seem fluid, running in fits and starts. He saw the Reforged, their line shattered, rising and attacking en masse, but this new creature seemed uninterested in taking their bait. He saw Morgan and the riflemen firing into the creature's bulk, to no effect.

This, then, was the end. Mission failed. Tell my family I loved them more than they will ever know.

From somewhere far away Kane heard explosions again, accompanied by a high-pitched, mechanical whine, though it was hard to tell how far. His sense of distance was far from accurate at the moment. The only reason he was still conscious was because the suit was keeping him that way. He wondered idly how he could hear at all. Could the suit actually read the vibrations through this creature's body?

The piercing, resonating tone came again, louder this time, as if it were actually inside his head. It drowned out everything else, and Kane felt himself falling as his world exploded with brilliant, white light.

"Babe, listen," Bleys shouted as he throttled up. "You're gonna pass out, so just accept it, okay? It hurts less that way."

"Torpedo impact in thirty seconds," Yuri informed them, barely intelligible over the wail of the alarm.

"Yuri, knock that klaxon off! Please tell me Ed programmed

you to use the damned Todeswerfer."

Ana gasped against the mounting Gs, "See you soon."

"That's a promise, babe," he said, but she was already out.

The alarms silenced, and Yuri answered, "Todeswerfer requires passcodes."

Bleys slipped his keycard from his boot and waved it over the console's security sensor, then pushed the throttle to max. The G-force hit him like a mountain dropped on his chest, crushing him into the seat. "If I pass out before it's close enough, it's on you," he groaned.

"New contact time, one minute at current acceleration," Yuri told him. "Enemy vessel powering railguns."

"Shit!" Bleys groaned, repeating in several times like a mantra. He could barely keep the stick straight, much less do any fancy moves.

"Erratic maneuvering," he called.

"Enemy vessel firing," Yuri replied as the *Doro* began dancing side to side.

The ship shuddered again as the projectile struck home. Alarms shrieked, and Yuri said, "Weapons systems offline."

"*Goddammit!*" Bleys howled, but he wasn't done yet. "Yuri, spin up the jump-drive!"

Kane, on hands and knees, gagged, waves of nausea rolling over him, and tried not to vomit inside his suit. There was indeed a way of cleaning such an accident, because it was something that happened in exigent situations, but it didn't do much for the smell. Being locked in with puke for hours was low on his list of things to do.

Of course, being beaten to death against the bulkhead by a giant monster was even lower, and he had managed that, or nearly. He assumed, given that he *could* assume, that he was not dead, but his vision was a blur of color patches, an abstract art piece with no connection to the real world.

At least he could hear, thought it was still the weird, simulated sound provided by his computer. Again he heard the high pitched whine and had to close his eyes against white, searing light.

When he opened them again his vision was clearer, and for a moment he thought maybe he had been mistaken about whether or not he was dead. He traced the outline of a metallic, gazelle-like leg up and up, to see towering over him the one enemy that had come closest to punching his ticket, a metal titan fully fifteen feet tall, bristling with weaponry of which it was even now making fine use. The Pestilence creatures flowed in like a wave from Passage Alpha, hungry and gnashing their teeth, only to meet the searing particle beam. Where it touched they flashed to thick, oily vapor or burst like balloons, steam roiling from their innards, splattering the entire passageway with their remains.

Of the creature that had manhandled him, there was no sign, but the floor was covered in a tacky, black ooze. Kane had quite recently seen that particle beam literally melt one of his men, Panzer suit and all, into a black puddle of grease in seconds. It wasn't hard to work out what had happened to the beast.

As for the how, well, hopefully Ed would tell them when things calmed down a bit.

Morgan whooped and shouted. "*Ednaught!*"

"I heard you might need some help," Ed told them even as he fired a brace of missiles into Passage Alpha, blasting a hole in the overhead. He stepped forward, each footfall shaking the entire passage, grasped the breached section of overhead, and peeled it down to block the passage, then began welding it in place with the particle beam. "This won't hold them forever, but it should buy us the time we need."

The attackers continued to pour in from Passage Charlie.

Kane wasn't sure if Ed had brought a ride, but likely they still needed to secure the docking bay, so closing it off like Alpha wasn't really an option. Kane struggled to his feet and rejoined the fight.

There were, it seemed, an almost inexhaustible supply of the things. Even Ed's particle beam only seemed to buy them a few moments before more came. Still, slowly, the tide became a trickle and at last stopped. How long the respite would last was anyone's guess, but Kane's experience with the Pestilence assured him that this was, at best, a tiny reprieve.

"Ed, they have the override codes. We can't trigger the scuttle via the computer. I'm going to do it manually."

"That's not necessary if you can get me into the computers," Ed assured him. "You have some kind of breaching account, correct?"

"Planetary Governor's override account," Kane said, nodding. "Only the emperor can disable it and he's indisposed, so you're good there. But they can cancel the scuttle."

"I just need to get in so I can run some programs, and I think I can make the scuttle happen."

"We can do that," Kane told him. "I'll have to come with you, though. The account is keyed to my biometrics. No way you can just hack in and make it your bitch?"

"The Empire has a healthy paranoia regarding security. If I had access to Avalon, perhaps. There are latency issues that would complicate things, but it's moot. The *Danzig* is jamming all comms in and out. We'll have to go in through that account."

"Morgan!" Kane called. "We're heading to the control room. Hold this area. When we get back we'll clear to the cargo bay!"

"I'm on it," Morgan replied.

"Let's go," Kane said to Ed. He felt a little weird leading a giant deathbot down the passage, but honestly it wasn't the strangest thing he had done lately.

The passageway was tall enough to accommodate Ed, but the doors at the end were not, nor was the room beyond. It seemed a big problem to Kane, but to his surprise Ed actually folded his body in on itself. It left him with only a blaster cannon on one arm and his legs, tucked into the body, were only capable of shuffling, but it was a surprisingly mobile configuration.

"For shipping," Ed explained.

"Yeah," Kane said with a nod. "I'm guessing assembly instructions would be a real pain in the ass if it came in pieces with those little Allen wrenches."

Compact Ednaught shuffled into the control room. "I'll need you to log in. Technically, I'm just a device you're going to plug in and use." Ed paused a moment, then added, "I have a connection."

"Voice and retina scan required to attach device via network," the computer announced.

"Plug and play, eh?" Kane said with a grin as he inserted his keycard and bent for the retina scan. "Kane, Ragnar, Commander. Identify for device connect."

"Device connect authorized," the computer responded, then following with, "Alert: self-destruct sequence requested from unknown location. Fifteen-minute countdown initiated. Any line officer may cancel via ID card, retina scan, and voice authorization."

"Commander," Ed said, "I am detecting a large biomass approaching."

"I'm on it," Kane promised and ran to the doors, but saw nothing. "It's all clear here, Ed."

"I assure you, they are approaching."

"Damn! How?"

"It appears they are using ventilation shafts. You should go."

Kane shook his head. "I don't leave men behind!"

"Commander, I am not a 'man'," Ed assured him. "This unit is a tool, like your rifle. It's not a concern."

"Ah!" Kane said, nodding. "You're running remote? "

"Precisely. I advise you to rejoin your men and make your way to the cargo bay for extraction."

"One problem. We have no extraction."

"I'm working on that bit," Ed told him. "See what you can do about clearing the way. I'll join you once I am done here, if possible."

Kane nodded and turned to leave, then turned back. "The interior guns outside that passage are going to cut us to ribbons if they can fire them, Ed. If you can shut them down, it would save a lot of lives."

"I will endeavor to lock them down, too," Ed promised. "If nothing else, I will lend my firepower to your own when you storm them, if I am able."

Kane snapped Ed a salute. "Godspeed."

A ceiling panel above suddenly bulged and imploded, spilling a stream of clawing, gnashing creatures into the room.

"Go!" Ed shouted. With a hydraulic whine his case closed in on itself even further, becoming roughly cubic, leaving only the blaster arm outside the armor shell. Ed fired on the rapidly expanding pool of creatures, scattering them briefly. "I'll be fine! Save your people!"

Kane was not thrilled about leaving Ed on his own, but Ed was right. He would be fine, and Kane had men to lead to safety. The control room doors slid open as he approached, then closed behind him. He blasted the exterior control panel with his M87 to make sure they stayed that way, then jogged down the passage back to the choke point.

Morgan looked his way, then quickly back down Passage Charlie. "They're probably massing for another push."

Kane took a quick count and sighed. Six of his recruits were still standing, along with eighteen of the Reforged. For most it had indeed been a suicide mission, and it might still end up that way for the rest of them too.

"Where's Ed?" Morgan asked.

"He's good. He's running remote."

Morgan's head whipped around. "Chief, are you fucking retarded? Comms are down! How could he be running remote?"

Kane felt his cheeks burning, realizing Ed had snowed him. "*Fuck!*" he shouted. He thought about punching one of the bulkheads, but it seemed a futile gesture. He turned back to Morgan. "And that's *Commander* Retard to you."

Morgan shook his head, snickering. "We going back for him?"

Kane thought about it for a moment. Getting through the doors to the control room would take precious time. Most of his team was already dead, and if they didn't get exfiltrated soon the rest would follow.

The Danzig's computer announced, "Self-destruct sequence cancelled from bridge by Admiral Thomas Riker, Commanding Officer, *Danzig.*"

"Fuck!" Kane yelled.

A moment later the computer announced, "Alert: self-destruct sequence requested from Bridge; Aft Steering; Engineering Four, Ten, and Twenty; and twenty-four unknown locations. Fifteen-minute countdown initiated. Any line officer may cancel via ID card, retina scan ,and voice authorization."

"Holy shit!" Morgan crowed. "Looks like Ed is on the case! Orders?"

"Ed's a damned fine warrior," Kane said. "He knew the score, and he made a choice. Let's save who we can. It's what he told me to do."

"Captain Bleys!"

Bleys roused from near unconsciousness at the sound of Ed's static-filled voice, barely audible over the roar of the engines. "Ugh," he croaked. He was right at the limit of G-force he could soak, even with his implants. Any more and he was going out for sure.

"Captain, can you hear me?"

"Not a good time, Ed," Bleys gasped. "Glad to see you made it. We might not."

"I need you to open a jumpgate for me right away!"

"Funny you should mention that," Bleys said, watching the spiral in space deepen ahead of him. "We're towing several of *Danzig*'s torpedoes. Gate is opening and we're heading in, but I can't leave it for long."

"I won't need more than thirty seconds."

"Twenty seconds to impact," Yuri announced.

"We ain't got thirty seconds, Ed!" Bleys shouted.

"Captain, this is *vital*," Ed asserted. "I'm opening a channel to Elysium. Alsatia, are you there?"

"Oh, fuck me," Bleys groaned, not sure if his bigger complaint was Alsatia's presence, or the action he was about to take. "Yuri, increase thrust twenty-five percent."

A brief alarm sounded, and Yuri told him, "Warning: requested power levels exceed safety parameters for humans. Please confirm."

"Avalon Online!" Alsatia crowed over the comms, her voice bubbly and chipper.

"Confirm thrust increase," Bleys groaned. He gritted his teeth as the engines cycled up an octave, struggling to even breathe. "Whatever you're doing, Ed, do it now! I got torpedoes hot on my ass!"

"Impact in thirty-seven seconds," Yuri announced.

"Alsatia, are you ready?" Ed asked.

"Ooh," she replied. "Hyperspace comms are so sexy! Lag free

at interplanetary distances! I missed them."

"Trying to outrun torpedoes here, guys!" Bleys howled as he sent the ship careening into the partially-formed spiral for the third time lately, hoping his luck would hold.

"Send him through now, Alsatia!" Ed commanded. "It's our only chance!"

"Transmitting," Alsatia tittered.

Bleys nearly choked as the lights in *Doro* suddenly flickered and dimmed and all of his instruments went black. "Yuri, I'm blind!"

Yuri, stuttering, said in a slow, low-pitched voice, "Not enough CPU power."

"Ninety percent," Alsatia chirped.

Bleys's shout of "*Fuck!*" was long and drawn out as the *Doro* plunged into the vortex, her survival depending on nothing but Bleys's Mark One Eyeballs and exceptionally huge man-parts.

Which were not, in reality, all that exceptional, more like "Somewhat above average and growing less so" as the reality of what he was doing sank into his brain. Bleys would have screamed, he really would have, except that it was almost impossible to even draw a breath, not with the weight of a small safe sitting on his chest.

Or maybe it was more like an elephant. Bleys wasn't sure if that would be better or worse.

At the heart of the spiral, *Doro* shuddered with a tremendous blow. Bleys felt it like a kick in the gut, as if he had clipped a planet on the way through the jumpgate, though he was pretty sure there weren't any nearby. Every alarm and flashing light onboard the ship went off at once.

"*Success!*" Alsatia screamed, as if she were a mad scientist who had just verified her monster was truly alive.

"Close it up, Bleys!" Ed shouted. "Godspeed!"

And that was it. Wham, bam, thank-you-ma'am, indeed. Still,

they had come through it, and Bleys hadn't suddenly forgotten how to fly a ship manually. Filled with relief, he raised a hand to the controls and froze at what he saw.

His vac suit glove was crimson and slick with blood.

"Shit!" he gasped. He quickly shut down the jumpgate, hoping against hope that none of the torpedoes had made it through with him. If one had, with his instruments down he would never know. Oddly enough, this thought wasn't nearly as comforting as it might have been.

At least it *did* shut down this time.

He fumbled with the throttle, realizing his coordination had gone to hell, but he managed to set it back to idle. The roar of the engines faded to a low thrum, and the weight that had been slowly crushing Bleys to death withdrew at once.

Given that instant, fiery death did not follow, he presumed the torpedoes were now wandering aimlessly in normal space. Even at a time like this, he couldn't help but wonder briefly just what would happen to them. It depended on the direction, right? Again, some poor bastard minding his own business could end up having a totally unexpected encounter with Destiny, courtesy of Bleys being hard to kill.

Then came the pain and the suffocation. He looked down as his torso and decided maybe he wasn't so hard to kill after all.

Beside his captain's chair, the formerly flat surface of the port bulkhead had sprouted a small forest of irregular protrusions, all different lengths, and all spiral and pointy like unicorn horns.

Or, Bleys thought with a wry smile, like certain hula dolls.

That would have been fine. Bleys had been meaning to redecorate, anyway. A little abstract art was good for the soul. But there was a real problem with the new addition, chiefly that the longest of the "horns," a veritable spike, a spear even, was *inside* him, penetrating his side as if the *Doro*, tired of the beating he had put her through, had decided to take matters into her own hands.

"Oh, fuck," Bleys gasped, looking at the hole in his vacc suit. It was rapidly filling with blood. "Oh fuck, this is bad. Yuri?"

The computer gave no answer. Bleys had no clue if the silence was due to Ed's and Alsatia's recent weird science project, but he doubted it. More likely, the distortions to his left were hardly the only damage from the collision with the jumpgate. Yuri had likely followed the old ship's agent into unplanned obsolescence.

"Alsatia! You still there?" He meant to shout it, but it came out a croak.

Quickly, while he was still conscious, he reactivated the internal atmosphere, praying that whatever hyperspace weirdness he had encountered, the cabin would still hold pressure. If not, it wasn't just the end of him. It was the end of Ana too, a prolonged and unpleasant end at that, slowly suffocating as her suit's air ran out and the ship plunged into the hyperspace deeps, never to be heard from again.

"Oh God," he groaned, struggling with his harness, pain ripping through him at every move. At last he worked it loose and tried to slide off the spike. Fresh, searing agony filled him, and he howled aloud. "Yeah, that's not gonna happen," he sighed, feeling consciousness slipping away.

"Josey?" Alsatia answered. "You sound distressed. What's wrong?"

"I'm hit," he moaned. "Didn't even notice until now." He tried and failed to suppress a cough. Pain ripped through his belly and his impaled side, and blood flew from his lips onto the viewscreen. "Shit," he moaned. "Comp is out. It's real bad. I'm not gonna make it."

Bleys reached to Ana's seat where she lay, still unconscious. The pain just to do this was intense, but he had to try. He shook her, leaving a bloody handprint on her arm. "Babe," he whispered. "You gotta wake up." She didn't stir, and the black tint to his vision told him his time was almost up.

"Alsatia," he wheezed. "Ana's onboard."

"Josey, listen to me," Alsatia called. She said something else, but he couldn't really understand her words anymore.

"I cut thrust, but we're still moving fast," Bleys choked out. "We're headed into the Deeps! You gotta tell Ed."

Alsatia said something more, but it was nothing but a buzzing in his headset. With the last of his strength, Bleys reached to his console and activated his distress beacon.

"Tell Ed we're headed into the deeps," Bleys mumbled, and then the darkness took him.

"Self-destruct sequence canceled from bridge by Admiral Thomas Riker, Commanding Officer, *Danzig,*" the computer announced. "Thirteen sequences remaining. Ten minutes to self-destruct."

Kane shook his head. The war between Ed and the Pestilence had been going on for several minutes now, Ed spinning up new sequences as fast as the Pestilence could deactivate them. Kane was pretty sure Ed could have blown the ship to hell by now, in that it seemed he could spawn any number of attempts instantly, and the Pestilence had to physically insert cards and issue orders to cancel any of them. Ed was just playing for time at this point to allow them to escape.

That, however, was easier said than done. There was still no word on a ship, which was the least of his problems. Worst case they could always just launch themselves into space and hope someone could show up before the life support systems in their suits gave out, assuming they could launch hard enough to get clear of the blast.

But getting to the cargo bay at all looked like it might just be impossible.

The whole raid had the feel of a roller coaster with track

missing from a random location. You go up. You go down. Eventually you die, but you have no idea when it will happen.

Which was, Kane though, pretty much life when you get right down to it.

The further Kane's group got down Passage Charlie, the less it seemed like they would reach the end. At first the resistance had been light, but halfway there they had met what seemed a living wall of teeth and saliva, constantly shifting, growing faster than they could take it down.

"Kane!" Ed called, his voice filled with static. His video feed, likewise, was less than ideal, but it showed the control room, still filling with more attackers. A large, scorpion-like creature charged at Ed, only to be blasted to cinders. "I've managed to restore comms, but I don't know how long it will hold. I think I'll have a solution on those guns shortly. Just hold on!"

It was all they could do, but their position was eroding. The Reforged formed a wall of flesh as Kane and Morgan fired furiously through gaps in the lines, but it wasn't enough. The recruit riflemen were slowly being pushed back as creatures leaked through.

"Lars," Kane called. "Cut one of your guys loose."

Lars tapped one of the remaining twelve Reforged on the shoulder. The man he chose turned a savage, sharky grin toward all of them, then charged toward the writhing mass of death, his throat working silently in a final, silent battle cry.

It was easier this way, sending a man to his death when it was something he *craved*, but only a little. Kane watched, because it was his duty to watch, as yet another Reforged rushed into the throng of Pestilence creatures and all involved collapsed into crystalline ash.

"Move!" Kane shouted. "Now!"

Two more of the Reforged broke from the pack, unable to control themselves, screaming silently down the corridor to meet the next wave, and Kane pushed what was left of his men forward after them, trying to trade their sacrifice for as much ground as possible.

It almost worked. For a brief moment Kane was certain they had made it, and then the titan filled the entry to the cargo bay, a duplicate of the wingless dragon they had fought earlier. Around, under, and over the smaller creatures wriggled, loped, and crawled.

Kane and his men could tuck tail and run back to the choke point, make a stand there, but it wouldn't change the outcome. It would just make them bitches who ran from a straight-up fight before being cornered and cut down.

"Ed," Kane called over the radio. "We're not gonna make it."

Ed didn't answer.

The dragon lumbered forward, its fang-filled maw dripping and nearly scraping the ground, just as the gun turrets popped from the overhead. Heavy blasters and rail launchers swiveled and locked into place, weapons more than capable of shredding a Panzer suit or the Reforgeds' skins. Likely they had eight balls in some of the launchers too.

A small part of Kane felt despair to be so heavily outnumbered and outgunned, but the greater part was proud to know they feared him enough to spare nothing. It would be a glorious death.

"Gunther, tell the admiral we did our best. Set my M87 for continuous discharge. We're not walking away from this one."

"M87 at full power. Rammstein, sir?"

"Feuer Frei, Gunther," he said. "Morgan, let's take this big bitch with us."

Morgan snapped him a salute and shouldered his rifle. "See you in Valhalla, Chief."

Kane roared "For Odin!" and held the trigger down as he charged the beast.

17

COUNTING THE DEAD

Ana clawed her way back to consciousness, struggling to make sense of the blaring alarms and a familiar, strident voice.

"Ana! Come on, honey! Wake up!"

At first she thought she must be dreaming. How could Alsatia be here on the *Doro*, after all? They were in open space—

Being chased by torpedoes!

Ana jolted fully awake as her memory flooded back in. She gasped to see Bleys slumped in his chair, far too pale. "Oh, my God! Josey!"

She leapt forward out of reflex and immediately regretted it. She was still tightly buckled, and the jolt was decidedly unpleasant.

"He saved you," Alsatia said softly over the comms. "Honey, I only have optical, so I can't be sure, but you need to prepare yourself. I think he's gone."

"You don't know that!" Ana shouted as she struggled with her restraints. She charged forward as soon as the last one fell away and grabbed his wrist to check his pulse, only to be stymied by his vac suit.

Cursing, she stripped off her own suit and left it floating in zero-G, then took a knife from her belt, one she kept at hand for situations just like this. She sliced through the tough fabric at his shoulder and stripped off his entire sleeve.

Alsatia asked in a conversational tone, "Did you know for sure you had atmospheric pressure, or were you just lucky?"

"Honestly? I was lucky." Ana held her breath for long moments. At first she feared the worst, but the pulse was there, thin and reedy. He was still alive, if only barely. "I have to get him to the med bay right away," she said. "The autodoc has a blood synthesizer."

"Ana, I need you to listen!" Alsatia said, a bit more sharply than Ana expected.

"Make it quick!" Ana told the AI.

"You're heading into the hyperspace deeps at whatever speed you were at before Josey cut the engines. Considering he was running from torpedoes, you can guess that it's pretty fast. You have to turn the ship around before you get too far for Ed to find you."

"No!" Ana shouted. She bent to examine the twisted shard of metal penetrating Bleys's side. She couldn't see the tip, but the part she could examine was jagged, almost serrated. Trying to pull it out like that could well end up gutting him. "I need a cutting laser stat!"

She rose and pushed off for the cockpit door, expecting it to open. Instead, she plowed into it with enough force to fill her vision with stars briefly.

"Ana," Alsatia said, impatience in her voice. "You have to turn the ship around *now!*"

Ana pounded her fist on the cockpit door, as if that would help. It didn't, but she still felt compelled to do it. "He'll *die* if he doesn't get medical attention right away!"

"Am I not making this clear?" Alsatia carped. "I am not in

any way in control of the ship. If you go much further into hyperspace, you *and* Josey will be lost *forever*." She emphasized the last word with an echo sound effect.

"I'll take that chance! I made him take this risk with me! I'm not letting him go! Now tell me how to get this damned door open!"

Alsatia was silent so long that Ana began to think the AI had stalked off in a huff. "Okay, I have an idea," Alsatia said at last. "I had to ask Daddy for permission."

"I'm not sure I like the sound of that," Ana groaned.

The dragon stomped Kane's legs with a huge claw, then seized his torso in its beak and wrenched. Kane felt no pain; even if his body was being damaged, his suit's neural interface would edit that out of any input it passed to his brain, but it did allow a measure of the tremendous, crushing pressure being exerted on his suit.

"Armor integrity at seventeen percent," Gunther noted as the dragon tore at him again and again, hammering him against the deck as it did its best to tear him in two. Kane ground his teeth as a crack appeared across his visor.

If that gave way, it would be all she wrote.

Battle raged around him in silence. Gunther was synthesizing from local vibrations, but the noise was overwhelmingly the ringing of Kane's own armor against the deck and the rumbling, grating sound of the beast's teeth skittering over it. Kane had no idea how his team fared, though likely they were being cut to shreds by the defensive guns.

Kane's rifle, still spinning in zero-G just above his head, was maddeningly out of reach. "Gunther, disable all safeties on my M87," he gasped. On the off chance he managed to retrieve it before this bitch killed him, he might as well not hold back.

The dragon flipped Kane over and adjusted its grip, slamming his head to the floor and grinding it against the deck beneath another claw, then clamped its beak around his torso and tore at him with tremendous force.

A small alarm sounded in Kane's ear. "Suit integrity failure imminent," Gunther advised.

From his new position, Kane saw Morgan launch himself at the creature, wrist bayonets deployed on both arms. "Fuck you, bitch!"

Kane felt the pressure ease as Morgan worked the dragon's head like a punching bag. The creature wailed in agony as Morgan plunged a blade into its face, burying it to his gauntlet, then followed up with the other, straight into one of its giant, hate-filled eyes.

The dragon reacted as any beast would, by focusing on the new threat. It released Kane and shoved Morgan back, then whipped its tail around to strike him a titanic blow. Morgan flew backward, howling, to slam against the bulkhead with enough force to partially embed him in the plas-teel, the metal giving way and folding over him like a cocoon.

It was just a moment, but that was all Kane needed. The dragon turned back to him, its remaining eye filled with hatred and fury, and roared silently.

It was, Kane thought, a damned shame that there was no air to carry that roar. It had to be one for the ages. Gunther did his best, but it just wasn't as good as the real thing.

A creature's last words really ought to be heard.

Kane snatched his rifle from the air and rammed it into the dragon's open mouth. With the safeties disabled it wouldn't fire a burst or even a continuous beam. It would discharge *everything* left in the battery in a single, massive blast.

Kane's cruel laugh echoed in his helmet as he pulled the trigger, filled with a dark glee to crush his enemy, even if he would soon follow.

Gunther automatically polarized Kane's visor as the M87 discharged an expanding white sphere of energy, blinding even with the added protection. Mottled flesh scorched and crisped under the assault. Steam boiled from the dragon's eyes briefly before its entire head exploded in great gouts of bone, gore, and searing, white hot vapor.

"Weapon power depleted," Gunther informed him.

Kane's vision returned just in time to see the beast collapse, a smoking ruin. A hole the size of Kane's head ran its entire length, the flesh inside scorched to carbon. Beyond, the blast of energy had continued, through the still-open cargo bay doors and through Lars as well. The Reforged stood looking at the new opening in his midsection in bemused silence. The *Danzig's* hull beyond him was scorched and melted but seemed to have stopped what remained of the rifle discharge.

Morgan, struggling to free himself, shouted, "Fuck! I can't see shit! Is it dead?"

"It won't be for long!" Kane yelled back, even as details began to intrude on his battle rage.

The rest of the creatures were down. Most of them were ash, though a few were slowly trying to reassemble themselves, only to be gunned down by the four remaining riflemen or captured and devoured by wounded Reforged.

Lars poked a hand through his midsection, as if not entirely certain what would happen, then casually leaned over the still quivering bulk of the dragon and bit into its hindquarters.

Somehow, Kane and his party were not all dead.

Somehow, the guns were not firing on them!

Kane broke into a broad grin as Ed called over the radio, "Commander, I have no intention of buying drinks tonight. Everyone stand clear, please."

Kane spun as Gunther simulated a low, thudding gait from behind, followed by a rising whine Kane had come to know intimately of late.

Lars quickly snatched another bite, then stepped back.

Ednaught, powering up his particle weapon, took aim on the enormous, shattered corpse before them and fired. Kane marveled at the destructive power of Ed's signature weapon. The dragon's corpse flashed to vapor wherever the beam touched, leaving only smoking grease on the deck. Several sections began to sprout appendages and tried to detach from the main body, but Ed cut them down before they could escape.

In short order, there was nothing left of the beast.

Kane shook his head in awe. "I have got to get me one of those."

"Goddammit!" Morgan howled. "Did I miss it? Somebody get me out of here!"

Kane lumbered over, his suit feeling cumbersome. It only did that when it was heavily damaged, a fact Kane confirmed with a glance to his HUD. He was definitely going to need a new horse. "Gunther, will this crack in my visor hold?"

"Panzer suit is at thirteen percent effectiveness. Recommend immediate replacement."

"Tell me something I don't know," Kane sighed. "Gunther, will the visor hold or not?"

"Damage to visor is superficial. It will hold until repair or replacement unless further damaged."

The riflemen cheered as Kane took Morgan's extended hand and pulled, the hydraulics in his suit whining at the strain. Morgan popped from his spot and staggered to his feet, almost knocking Kane down.

"Stabilization system is offline," Gunther noted.

Kane stepped backward, struggling to regain his balance. "Ya think?"

Morgan tested his movement, then walked over and hugged one of the dreadnaught's legs. "My hero!" he wailed like a cartoon character, laying it on thick.

"I am merely a facilitator," Ed answered. The dreadnaught's torso swiveled, and one arm extended toward the cargo bay. "Your true champion would like to address you. Please face the docking bay and observe the holo projection."

Kane took a moment to count the Reforged as everyone waited for whatever surprise Ed had in store for them. Counting Lars, there were eight left.

Kane shook his head. Eight left out of "about fifty." The Reforged had surely paid in blood for their place at the table.

But the mission wasn't over.

The cargo bay was stacked high with crates secured by straps. The docking port doors, wide open to space, began to close just as another wave of Pestilence creatures tried to enter. The ten or so that were able to slip past before the opening sealed were quickly snatched up and consumed by the Reforged.

When all was calm, a holoprojector in the ceiling sprang to life. Before them, a semi-transparent holo-image of a bearded man appeared. The fellow was ancient, with a long gray, flowing beard and a weathered, pointed hat atop his likewise gray hair. His robe, a simple brown affair, hung loose on him, and he leaned heavily on his great, gnarled staff, contemplating them all as he puffed at a pipe. "Greetings, heroes," he intoned. "I am Tarrant the Wise, Sorcerer supreme of Aeternia."

Kane looked at Morgan, trying to decide if this was some sort of joke. Morgan was funny. He knew about this sort of shit.

Morgan shook his head and shrugged. "Fuck if I know," he muttered.

The old man paused, looking at them all expectantly, then chuckled, more to himself than to them. "Of course. Forgive me, it has been a long time. You would know me by another name."

He raised his staff and swept his arms dramatically and his image grew bright, almost pure white, then faded. Where the bearded old fellow had been, a middle-aged, clean shaven man now stood. His simple brown robe was now a flowing garment of red and black silk, and his staff had become an ornate, crystalline scepter. His features, regal and harsh, twisted in a conspiratorial smile. "I was once known as Emperor Tenebrae, fifth of my name," he announced in a deep, commanding baritone. "You have served your Empire well this day. We have retaken my glorious *Danzig*, and she will be of great service to us against this terrible enemy!"

Kane and Morgan again exchanged shocked glances. Morgan's jaw was hanging open as if he needed someone to reach up and close it. "Nope. Still got nothing," he mumbled.

Kane shook his head and faced forward again. "Me neither, brother."

"It's not over yet," Ed told them. "We have complete control of the computer systems, meaning we command interior and exterior weapons as well as the helm, including the jump-drives, but the Pestilence is still quite alive and remains a threat. We will need to return to Elysium and subject the ship to gamma ray bursts to burn out what remains. Meanwhile, the *Doro* is in trouble. Captain Bleys is dying, and Ana is aboard. Even if she can save him, the ship is heading for the hyperspace deeps and will be lost if not rescued soon."

Kane clenched a fist. "What are we waiting for?"

"We dare not jump to hyperspace with this level of infection onboard," Ed answered. "I won't go into deep details, but I have a working theory, and my father agrees with me on it. I think I know why the Empire locked the jumpgates in the first place: the Pestilence use them to communicate with their disparate colonies."

"Son of a bitch," Kane mused. "Is that what they mean? 'The Source'?"

"Again, it's a working theory, but that's the obvious conclusion. Most of the Pestilence's intelligence seems to be stored in hyperspace, and the gates allow that intelligence to propagate to normal space. If we jump with the infection we still have, we will find ourselves beset by much more intelligent enemies. We cannot risk it."

Tenebrae spoke, his voice a deep, commanding baritone. "Never fear. I have another way to save your friends. Several Imperial shuttles are maintained aboard all capital ships. They are heavily armed, jump capable, and quite inaccessible without my authorization. They are at your disposal."

Kane saluted the Emperor, then asked, "Ed, how long do we have?"

"An hour, perhaps a little more. The distress beacon is active, but at their speed it won't be visible for much longer."

"We're on it," Kane agreed. "But how do we get back out with them?"

"Once we reach Elysium, we will sterilize *Danzig* and then enter hyperspace to provide you with a beacon."

Kane scowled at this. "Bleys may not have that long. It's days to Elysium in normal space."

"No," Ed corrected. "It's days if there are biologicals aboard. You'll take the ones we care about with you. Now that I have full control of the ship, I can override thrust safeties as well and make the trip in 12 hours."

"It's still a long damned time."

"It's what we have," Ed told him.

Tenebrae raised his scepter overhead. "Come, brave warriors. My ship awaits."

"Any chance we can send the rest of the men home?" Kane

asked him. "Morgan and I are trained for this, but those men have already gone above and beyond."

Tenebrae bowed. "Of course. For my gallant warriors, anything."

"Ed, how much resistance should we expect to reach the shuttles?" Kane asked.

"On the route I map for you?" Ed asked. Kane's ears perked at the sound of distant gunfire via Gunther's sound translation, seemingly from all directions. Beneath the thunder of guns, Kane was pretty sure he heard screeches of agony. "Almost none, I should think," Ed told him, with just a hint of smugness.

Kane grinned at Morgan. Morgan gave him a thumbs up.

"Roger that," Kane said.

Ana kept pressure on Bleys's wound as best she could, but time was running out, drop by drop. How long had it been? Five minutes, perhaps ten? It seemed an eternity.

"Alsatia?" she called, looking about the cockpit, as if she might catch sight of the AI somehow.

Alsatia didn't answer.

She cast about for what seemed the hundredth time for something, *anything* she could use to cut the twisted metal spike, and again found nothing. It wasn't as if it would matter anyway. Unless she could get the cockpit door open, there was little more she could do besides prolong the inevitable.

Not just for Bleys, but for her too.

She hadn't bothered to explain to Alsatia, but she hadn't the foggiest notion of how to pilot a ship without a computer. She would have tended Bleys before worrying about their position regardless, but really, it hadn't been a choice. Even now, having done all she could for him, there was nothing for her to do but stare blankly into the red, swirling void until her stomach began doing flip flops.

She had begun to doubt they would survive when she startled at a loud bang on the cockpit door. She checked Bleys again, noting little had changed beyond the slow seeping of blood, then pushed off toward the door. "Who's there?" she challenged.

The door whined, as if it were resisting a great force. As it slid slowly open, visions of her first encounter with Lars filled Ana's mind with alarm, enough for her to draw her weapon and point it at the entry.

A moment later, she stood, blinking, amazed to see Ed's face on the other side, serene, as he heaved on the cockpit door, forcing it open.

"Ed!" she cried, overjoyed. She holstered her weapon and charged forward to wrap both arms around his neck. "How did you get here?"

But to her great shock, it was not Ed that spoke. Alsatia's voice answered from Ed's body, "Oh, honey! We are going to have so much fun!"

Ana stepped back, stammering. "What... how? Never mind, we have to cut a metal spike to get him to the med bay. Do you have anything on you?"

Alsatia waved one of Ed's hand's in front of his face. "The lag is terrible! Five hundred milliseconds, but still, it's pretty damned cool!"

"Alsatia! He's dying!"

"Oh, yes, right!" Alsatia said. Her expression grew stern as she walked, magnetic feet clicking on the deck to where Bleys's unconscious form still lay pinned. Her gait was nothing like Ed's. It was much more effeminate, almost as if she were pretending to wear high heels. Perhaps in her mind she was. Ana had long since given up trying to understand her moods and just accepted them.

Alsatia bent to examine the spike, striking a contemplative

pose, hand on chin. "Hmm, well, yes, I should think...." She swept her hand down in a chopping motion, like she was wielding an axe, and shrieked "Hi-*yah!*"

Ana cried out, certain that this was a terrible idea, for all the good it did. She had no time to actually intervene, only to push forward and examine the results, certain they would involve Bleys's innards being roughly snatched out and spilling onto the deck.

To her surprise, the spike had in fact been chopped neatly at the bulkhead.

Alsatia flashed a smug grin and waved. Two of her fingers flopped down, useless, and she winced. "It's okay. We can fix those later."

Alsatia's methods may have been questionable, but results were what counted right now for Ana. "Come on!" she urged the AI. "Help me get him to the autodoc! He needs blood badly!"

"Oh, it's *gross!*" Alsatia whined as she took hold of Bleys's feet. "Bodily fluids are so *disgusting!*"

Ana grabbed Bleys's shoulders, and they raised him gently into the air. "Hurry."

"I know, honey," Alsatia said. "You can't respawn out here. Both of you should have stayed in Avalon." She turned Bleys by his boots, went wide, overcorrected, and cracked his head against the bulkhead!

"Alsatia!" Ana howled.

"Sorry!" Alsatia squeaked, cringing. "Lag!"

Ana checked Bleys's head. It was already swelling, but it didn't look too bad. She scowled at Alsatia, who was still wincing. "Can you fly the ship?"

Alsatia looked thoughtful for a moment. "Probably?"

"Then take care of that while I do the medicine!"

Onboard the Emperor's shuttle, Kane checked his restraints for launch. "I thought his name was Arcane."

Morgan stopped his preflight and gave Kane a look that questioned his intelligence. "*Arcann*," he snapped, then turned back to his instruments. "And you know that guy we just talked to is not the Emperor anymore, right? He's Arcann's *father*, and he's been dead as the bar scene on Cerb for like twenty years. I remember watching his funeral when I was a kid."

"I don't remember that," Kane admitted with a shrug. "I was a recruit back then. We were deployed a *lot*."

"I can guess why. But seriously, you don't remember Tenebrae the fucking *Dragon?* He was *harsh*, man! Like Vlad Dracul harsh!"

Kane shrugged again. "I know the name, now that you mention it. But I guess he kept me plenty busy."

"I bet."

"Not seeing how he's here now, then," Kane mused.

"Are you kidding me? Fucker's been in Avalon this whole time, don't you think?"

"So you're the big brain now?"

Morgan brought the engines to full power, the hum vibrating the entire ship. "Pretty sure you were recently acting like I was retarded for not knowing about Admiral Fairy Butt and his gay ass wooden ships."

Kane palmed his face, but couldn't suppress a snicker. "*Farragut*," he corrected. "Can you fly this thing or not?"

"Yup," Morgan said. "That's why they gave me the waiver on the history exam." He touched a finger to his nose, then jammed the stick forward. The engines roared and launched them like a punted football into the black, star strewn night.

"Damn!" Morgan groaned, a shit eating grin on his face. "That's a stiff clutch!"

Kane, crushed into his seat by what felt like the weight of

three elephants, made a mental note to murder his lieutenant as soon as the mission was done.

Ana, in the med bay, was almost done micro-stitching Bleys's innards back together via a laparoscopic drone. She had managed to disrobe him, not too difficult in the zero-G, and had him secured to the table. She frowned briefly at what looked like a freshly healed wound on his leg, noting it would leave a nasty scar because it hadn't been properly closed, just filled with Nugena and spackled over with synthskin as if it were brickwork instead of flesh.

"I have no idea what I am doing," Alsatia called over the comms. "I think we're in mostly the same place, but who knows? This place is totally non-Euclidean. I think I am going to make a whole realm like this. Only it needs lava too, lots of lava. And some big, floaty things that kill you! I'll call it "The Nether," what do you think?"

Alsatia's uncertainty was completely unsurprising to Ana. Even Ed could make little sense of the place. Bleys had noted that he did much of his navigating by gut feel.

Ana, currently inspecting his guts, saw nothing there to enlighten the situation and had no belief in haruspicy, though she had to admit, Bleys did seem to have some extra sense about the trackless realm.

She sighed and wiped an arm across her brow. The air was cool, but she still found herself sweating. "Do you really think anyone is coming?" she called.

"Daddy says Ed knows about you guys and is sending Kane," Alsatia replied. "Oh, honey, he's hot! I can't wait to meet him."

Ana grinned, fairly satisfied with her work. She commanded the drone to extract itself and snickered, "I have seen him naked, but my interest was purely professional. He is happily married."

"Nobody's that happily married," Alsatia asserted.

"I hear he kills AIs," Ana told her. "And pretty much everything else too. Josey says 'at least one of everything'."

The drone popped from the hole in Bleys's side, and she recovered it and placed it back in one the autodoc's several storage bins. Satisfied, she filled the cavity with Nugena, attached a wound zipper, and cinched it closed.

"There you are, Josey. One less scar." She looked over his still, naked form, feeling both lustful and sad at the sight. "God knows you have enough already."

She and Bleys weren't going to be having any more intense private sessions for a bit, but at least she was certain they would be able to in the future. That had been in doubt until now.

"So you're saying he likes it rough, eh?" Alsatia quipped.

"You'll have to ask his wife," Ana snickered. She patted Bleys on the cheek and kissed him softy. "I told you you'd need me."

"What?" Alsatia asked.

"Not for you, eavesdropper!"

Alsatia laughed. "I am, you know. A voyeur! I get my best ideas that way! That's what all the cameras are for. Ceiling Alsatia is watching you masturbate!"

Ana let out a long, exaggerated scream and buried her face in her hands, laughing. Despite everything, Alsatia, perverted and less-than sane though she might have been, could still make Ana laugh.

Now, more than ever, a good laugh was the best medicine.

***

Kane made his way slowly between the Imperial shuttle and the *Doro*'s blasted hull, shaking his head at the damage. Bleys was going to cry when he saw it, assuming he hadn't already. Most of the punishment he saw was normal, the sort you get from being hit with debris or blasters, but a patch outside the cockpit was like nothing he had ever seen.

The hull had been twisted into bizarre, spiral concavities, like someone had taken a corkscrew to it, only it wasn't penetrated. It had just been reshaped somehow, like it had been melted, twisted, and let cool. Kane had no idea what sort of weapon could do that, but he definitely felt the need to acquire one.

He locked on to the lower hull with magnets in his gloves and boots and started for the airlock until he saw the ragged hole in the hull a scant ten yards from him. With a shrug, he hauled himself into lower aft storage through the breach and oriented himself to the deck.

"*Doro*, this is Kane," he said. "I'm outside the galley. You buttoned up for depressurizing?"

"We sure are, honey," answered a feminine voice Kane didn't recognize.

"Who the fuck is this?" he demanded.

"My daddy named me Alsatia," she told him. "But honey, you can call me anything you want."

"Oh, shit!" Kane shouted, cringing despite himself. "You're the crazy bitch that tried to kill us on Elysium!"

"I *am!*" she answered, seeming very proud of it. "And you're the famous Ragnar Kane, killer of everything, right?"

"I can see you've been talking to Bleys."

"Not lately," she pouted. "He's under the weather, but Ana's taking care of him."

"Are you gonna invite me in or what?"

"Why, are you a vampire?" she crooned.

Kane laughed softly. "Damn, you're a real vixen, huh?"

"You don't know the half of it, big boy. We should talk once you're off the clock."

"You gotta let me in first, girl."

"Hold on to your hat, sweetie," she told him.

Kane grabbed a handrail as the galley hatch dogs opened halfway, allowing the pressure inside to bleed off. Ten seconds later, the hatch opened fully. Kane stepped through, resealed the entrance and said, "I'm in. You can re-pressurize now."

"Stand by," Alsatia answered, suddenly all business. "Thirty seconds to matching pressure."

"I think I like you better than the old *Doro*," Kane confessed.

Alsatia tittered. "Flatterer!"

Ana's voice interrupted their small talk. "Kane! I'm in the med bay!"

Kane made his way to the ladder to the upper deck and waited until the indicator at the hatch above went green. The dogs released, and the hatch opened on its own. Kane opened his visor and made his way toward the doc.

Ana looked up from Bleys's still figure and gave a small wave, little more than a brief lifting of her fingers in acknowledgement, then turned back to her patient. Kane nodded to the doc as he approached, then, with a grimace, looked at his friend lying on the table. Bleys looked dead, pale as hell, but then white people looked like that a lot of the time, especially in the wrong light.

Ana offered him a wan smile. Kane was hardly a sensitive, touchy-feely guy, but her expression was hard to miss. She was worn ragged with worry, the kind a woman has when she's fearful about her man.

Which pretty much meant those two were knockin' boots. If he were talking with Bleys, Kane wouldn't have much of a problem asking for lurid details, but he didn't have or desire that kind of relationship with Ana.

Married men stayed out of trouble by avoiding that kind of

talk with women. Better to stick to business. "You sure he's gonna be okay, doc?"

"He's stable," she assured him. "But we had a very close call. We really need to get him to better facilities, but I was able to mend most of it."

"How bad was it?"

"Very. If I hadn't woke when I did, we would have lost him." She pulled her tablet and raised an eyebrow at Kane. "You're not so great, yourself. Multiple fractures, and your whole body is one big bruise. You're going to be in a lot of pain when you come out of that thing. You want some meds?"

Kane looked back at his friend on the table, then smiled at Ana. "Got some already. We call it vodka."

Ana smiled knowingly at him. "How very Russian."

18

LONG LIVE THE EMPEROR

Over the following days Ed found himself busier than he had been in ages, though not in a bad way. Work was always something to be embraced, and the only time critical part had been rescuing the *Doro*, which had required the *Danzig* be scoured first. Fortunately, Ana had stabilized Bleys, and the thirty-three hours they spent in hyperspace had caused no further harm.

That being said, the damage to the *Doro* and her captain had been extensive. Both would recover, but repairs would take time. For the *Doro*, Ed estimated several months. For Bleys, Ana assured Ed that she could have him available within the hour. It would take him a few weeks to fully recover, but she could have him awake and aware for Tenebrae's semi-mysterious announcement.

The Emperor had been a bit cagey as to the precise nature of his address, but shortly after the *Danzig* had entered orbit around Cerberus, he had informed Ed that he wanted to speak to "the heroes of the Empire" and that he wanted to broadcast the event system-wide and as soon as possible. Ed had requested clarification and been informed that "The Heroes of the Empire" consisted of Kane, Ana, Bleys, Morgan, Weyland, and even Ed, all of whom Tenebrae wanted to be physically present in the primary wardroom.

Presumably, Tenebrae intended to offer commendations and perhaps some rousing, uplifting speech. Likely, he would also turn over command of the *Danzig* to Weyland as part of the event, but Ed found the former Emperor quite difficult to predict. The theatrics were in Ed's estimation less than useful, but they seemed important to humans.

Ed and Kane awaited the others in the *Danzig's* primary wardroom. Due to the size of the battlecruiser, the ship had ten areas designated for officers' mess, but the primary wardroom was the most formal. It was large for a shipboard dining area, capable of holding nearly five hundred, enough to accommodate the *Danzig's* entire officer compliment and a few guests, should a visiting dignitary wish to address them. In stark contrast to the bland, curving plasteel of the rest of the ship, the space was richly appointed, its bulkheads lined with red and black Imperial pennants, crossed swords, and paintings of sea battles. Leather and brightwork, hearkening back to the days of wooden ships, gave the room an ancient, timeless feel that even an AI could sense.

Ana had promised that she and Bleys would arrive shortly. Morgan, still on bedrest from his injuries, had also been requested, and presumably he would likewise join them soon. That left only Weyland, whose trip from the surface would take slightly longer. Tenebrae intended to begin as soon as they all assembled.

Kane busied himself with nutrition while they waited. Ed observed Kane's feeding process with fascination. With no crew there were no meals prepared, though several machines were available to heat and dispense previously prepared and frozen meals. The marine selected two meals from a vending machine, carried them to one of the dozens of long tables, and settled in to eat.

Ed took the seat across from Kane and observed the process with intent focus as Kane began to devour what he called a "cheeseburger." Power sources had always interested Ed, and the way the human body processed and managed energy was absolutely fascinating. It was simultaneously similar and completely unlike his own method of charging.

Kane tore off great chunks of the "cheeseburger" with his teeth, chewed, and swallowed them. The process reminded Ed of how a starship processed a cube of flectocite: the input was crushed to a uniform consistency, then mixed with liquid to form a slurry, and finally delivered to a holding tank for further processing.

Kane stopped crushing his cheeseburger for a moment and gave Ed a look they Bleys had informed Ed was known as "the Stink Eye" and indicated displeasure. Ed responded with the look Bleys referred to as "I didn't do nothin"!

Kane continued to glare a moment. "You should take a picture. It would last longer."

"I have quite literally an eidetic memory," Ed told him. "I have no need, and even if I did, I would store video rather than still images."

Kane rolled his eyes and continued his meal as Ed contemplated asking to observe the entire process from start to finish. Some vague memory from his father suggested this would, however, not be well received.

Before he had made a firm decision, the doors to the wardroom slid open, and Ana entered, pushing Bleys in a hoverchair.

Bleys was in no way pleased to be pushed around by anyone, much less in a hoverchair, but it was doctor's orders. He sighted Kane and Ed at a table on the far side of the huge dining hall and offered a weak wave, partially from embarrassment and maybe out of a little real weakness too.

Five percent, tops. Being dependent was a real drag.

Ana called, "Look who's awake!" as she pushed the chair over to Ed's and Kane's table.

Bleys reached his arms toward Kane and said in a stage whisper, "Help! She drugged me up and kidnapped me!"

As Ana eased Bley's chair against the table, Kane snickered and spoke around a mouthful of cheeseburger, "Sounds like just the sort of kinky shit you'd pay for, Bleys."

Bleys looked up innocently at Ana and smiled. "He's just kidding, babe."

Ana pursed her lips and furrowed her brows in a stern, no nonsense doc fashion. "You are in no condition for that sort of business. You need rest for at least a couple more days before exerting yourself."

"It's awesome how you're willing to sacrifice for me, you know that?"

Ana shook her head, a look of exasperation on her face. "As a lover, you're adequate. As a patient?" She waved a hand.

"That really seemed like an 'Oy vey' kind of moment there," Bleys snickered. "You should say it, so we all know how you really feel."

"I am not Jewish, and I *will* stab you," Ana said in a deadpan tone.

Kane, who was in the process of swallowing, laughed and almost choked. "She's right, bud," he said once he recovered. "You look like shit."

"Comes from waking up mostly dead," Bleys told him, then fixed Ed with a stare. "Which comes partly from having no freakin' clue what was going on until *after* I woke up that way. You got something you want to tell me Ed, old buddy? Old Pal?'"

Ed's tells were, as always, subtle, but he clearly had a little guilt, which was good. Guilty people were always easier to work with if you needed to sway them in one direction or another. The android cut his eyes toward Kane for a moment, then back to Bleys. "Deception was necessary, Captain. Had any of you fallen victim to the Pestilence, our plan would have been exposed and we would have failed."

"'Our?'" Bleys asked.

"My father and I. He presented the idea to me when we first returned to Elysium."

"Ah," Bleys said, nodding. "Those 'things' you had to 'take care of'."

"Precisely."

"And here Ana and I thought that was all about breeding the pets."

Ed paused a moment, then slowly raised an eyebrow and nodded. "There was a certain economy to it," Ed admitted.

Kane laughed aloud, and Ana's cheeks blushed slightly as Bleys palmed his face. "Okay, okay, I know when I'm beaten." Ed blinked a moment, as if blissfully ignorant, and Bleys continued, "So how about my ship? Our deal is still good, right?"

Ed gave him a wounded look. "Of course! The *Doro* is even now being put into better-than-new condition on Elysium. By the time we return from our mission, you will barely recognize her." He smiled broadly. "I promise, the additions I have in mind will more than make up for my prevarication."

Bleys had no doubt of that. Free stuff was always a decent balm. "And you're *sure* all the Pestilence is dead, right?" he pressed. "Because according to you, we missed some back on Cerb, and it damned near got us all killed."

Ed's expression grew serious. "It must have been a very small piece, just enough to cause an arc in the connections, but yes, I believe I found the source." He cast a baleful look at Kane. "We discovered Petty Officer Iezzi's glove beneath some of the cargo in aft storage. The hand was still inside." He paused, then corrected himself. "Most of it, at any rate."

Kane groaned and rubbed his right temple. "*Damn* it! I knew we never found it, but the radiation should have finished it off! How the hell could it survive?"

Ed's eyes seemed to lose focus as he considered. "The equipment on Cerberus was not the most sophisticated. That, combined with the hand being encased in a Panzer suit gauntlet, probably explains how a small piece survived." He shrugged. "Nevertheless, the systems I used on Elysium are much more efficient. I assure you, no biological life could possibly have survived the scouring we gave these ships. The *Doro* and the *Danzig* are clear. I guarantee it."

Bleys eyed the remains of Kane's burger with longing, realizing he probably hadn't eaten in— "How long was I out, babe?" he asked Ana.

"A little over two days," she answered.

Bleys turned a pleading face to Kane and clasped his hands in a prayerful pose. "Kane, brother, where did you get that burger? I need something *bad*."

Kane rose and clapped him on the shoulder. "I got you, brother. What'll you have?"

"Man, I'd eat a turd if you put it between a couple slices of bread."

"Shit sandwich and chili mac are every other meal in the Navy, but we got no mess cranks today," Kane said with a laugh and pointed to the vending machines. "Just what you see."

"I'll have what you had," Bleys said with a smile, then turned back to Ed. "So Ana filled me in on most things. We're at Cerb, and you're running the whole ship?"

"More accurately," Ed answered, "I am following orders from Emperor Tenebrae to control the ship. I do not actually possess the authorizations, and he chooses not to share them. Apparently, the Empire thinks poorly of AIs in charge of weapons of mass destruction. I can't imagine why."

"Me neither," Bleys snickered. "So what's the plan, then?"

"I believe the chief purpose of the visit is to transfer the *Danzig* to Admiral Weyland," Ed replied. "We are also delivering a new replicator to replace the one destroyed when the Reforged attacked, and Ana will be spending a week, perhaps two setting up the cloning and breeding system. Beyond that, we will, as you might say, 'play it by ear'."

Ana smiled down at Bleys. "I have a few species of plants that should do well. And it looks like we have a brand-new animal species on Cerberus too!"

Bleys did a double take at this news. "Huh? How?"

Ana's grin broadened, and mischief twinkled in her blue eyes. "Remember Lars? Well, she's Lara now."

Kane plopped steaming burger on the table in front of Bleys. "Come again, doc?"

Ana shrugged. "I know how it sounds, but it's hardly the strangest thing we have seen from the Pestilence. The flectocite mostly locks them into a form, but as we saw with the muscle growth, it can shift their bodies within certain limits of their DNA. Several of the Reforged have transformed into females, and they intend to populate the rest of Cerberus that humans can't survive. They are very excited about the prospects for mining."

Bleys reached for the burger and took a bite, and Ed took the opportunity to speak. "I have questions of you as well, Captain Bleys. The most vital of questions, actually. Where is the control module we retrieved?"

After a moment, Bleys swallowed and answered, "It's in a safe place."

Ed gave him a dubious look. "Aboard the *Doro*?"

Beys, taking another bite, nodded, a little more slowly this time, because Ed's tone made it seem like that was a Bad Thing™.

Ed said nothing for a moment, his lips a thin, flat line. "Then there is a distinct possibility that it has been destroyed by radiation, rendering all our efforts here moot."

Bleys groaned and cried out around a mouthful of food, "Oh, you gotta be kidding me! Listen, it's a lead lined box, does that make any difference?"

Ed broke into a broad grin. "Yes, I was kidding," he admitted. "I would never have irradiated the ship if I thought it might endanger the card. But it was amusing to observe your response."

Ana and Kane burst into peals of laughter as Bleys scowled at first one, then another of the trio, still chewing. "Sure, sure, pick on the crippled guy."

Ana rolled her eyes. "You are not *crippled*. You are in a hoverchair to give your body rest."

Bleys swallowed and shook his head. "I'm try'n'a work here! This chair is a perfect sympathy bid."

Ana held up her hands in surrender and stepped back, smiling. "Forgive me. Definitely crippled. Will probably never walk or make love again."

Bleys grinned back at her. "If I wanted to get beat up by friends, I'd just talk about Kane's wife."

"Don't push it, Bleys," Kane growled.

"How old are your daughters again?"

"I will fuck you up for that, man. I do not care that you're a cripple in a hoverchair."

Bleys put a hand to his chin and looked up at the ceiling in a contemplative pose. "I'm trying to remember what age of consent is in that part of the galaxy."

"For you and my daughters, it's more than the age of the universe."

"Hey, you're the one always claiming to be my dad."

Kane laughed aloud. "I said I fucked your mother. Big difference."

Ed raised an eyebrow and looked at Ana as if to confirm whether he should speak or not. Ana rolled her eyes, which Ed apparently took as an affirmative. "There is another matter I wanted to discuss, if your primitive ritual is complete."

Bleys suddenly remembered someone was missing. "Shit! Where's Morgan? He's not...?"

Kane waved a hand in derision. "Dead? No, just a rack monster."

Ana gave Kane a dubious look, then told Bleys, "By which he means I had him sedated. I woke him up and he should be along shortly, but he needed to stay still for a bit. Apparently one of those things threw him through a *bulkhead*. He was in very bad shape." She scowled at Kane. "You should be on bedrest too. You may *think* those bones have mended, but those fractures won't be fully joined for another week."

For once, Kane actually looked sheepish. "I hear you, doc. I'm light duty until I get the 'all clear' from you." He muttered under his breath, "But I ain't taking no damned rack pass."

"Morgan didn't want a rack pass, either," she said with a smile. "He just got one anyway." She gestured jamming a hypo into her arm and pressing the plunger, then spoke in an exaggerated Russian accent, "Men and dis false bravado. I have vays of making you more compliant, da?"

Ed tried to speak again, "As for the matter I wanted to raise—"

Something was triggering Bleys's sixth sense though, and also Ed had jerked his chain pretty hard with the "radiation" stunt, so interrupting him again was kind of fun. Bleys waved both hands in the air. "No, no, no, hold up, I have more questions. Explain this emperor thing? Where *is* he?"

Ed again looked very uncomfortable. "He is aboard the *Danzig* with us." Ed paused long enough that Bleys thought he was done speaking, when he added in an unenthusiastic tone, "In a manner of speaking, since he is resident on the ship's computer."

Bingo.

"Aha!" Bleys shouted triumphantly. "*That's* who you were sending from Avalon that damned near killed Ana and me!"

Ed nodded. "I'm afraid Alsatia and I miscalculated the effects on your systems. We've never done anything like that before, and we wouldn't have then, either, except that we had no choice. It was incredibly dangerous, not just for you but for him as well. If it is any consolation, I wouldn't even think of attempting it again."

Bleys was actually a little angry now, which wasn't usually a problem for him. Ordinarily he had his own angle and it kept him cool, but this was not a game. Well, it wasn't *his* game, but it damned sure seemed like Ed and Alsatia had in fact been playing with his and Ana's lives. "Are you kidding me?" he shouted. "Why couldn't you just ask him for the codes?"

Again, Ed hesitated, then sighed, "I *did*. He wouldn't give them over. This was the only way he would cooperate."

"Seriously? Saving humanity wasn't a motivating offer?"

Ed shrugged, a defeated look on his face. "One would think so, but he is more focused on his realm in Avalon. He was distressed at the death of his son, but only in an intellectual way."

Bleys boggled. "He prefers a video game to the Empire?"

Ed nodded. "He is a potentate in Avalon as well, and unlike here, he is much beloved by his people. He feels a responsibility toward them."

For a moment, Bleys could find no words. "Are they even real people?" he stammered. "Or is the guy just ruling a bunch of NPCs?"

"They are *quite* real, and none of them know who he was in life," Ed told him. "Tenebrae was quite a tyrant when he ran the empire. Some of his current subjects almost certainly lost loved ones at his orders. He is highly motivated to maintain that secret."

Bleys couldn't help but smile at this. "Got some leverage on him, eh? Did a little arm twisting?"

Ed shrugged. "Alsatia threatened to expose that Tarrant the Wise was in fact Tenebrae the Dragon if he didn't cooperate with her."

Bleys let out a long, low whistle. "Yeah, she's got a way with arm twisting, for sure. Of course, now we're stuck with him."

"Not at all," Ed assured him. "He's quite anxious to get back to his land."

Bleys shook his head in amazement. "I just don't understand why he would do that."

"You must consider that for him, Avalon is more real than this world. Time is subjective there. From his perspective, he's ruled Aeternia for a thousand years. His time in your world is little more than a dream he once had long ago."

Bleys scowled a moment but said nothing, and Ed again began, "On to other—"

"Why didn't you just rip the information out of his head?" Bleys interrupted.

Ed looked confused a moment. "You mean, direct information retrieval? Impossible." He paused a moment. "Well, considering the Pestilence, it's *possible*, but unfeasible. Every "soul," to use Father's term, stores information differently."

Bleys blinked in surprise. "People's brains are encrypted?"

Ed contemplated the question a moment, then shook his head slowly. "Not encrypted *per se*, but stored in a unique manner. It would be like trying to read a language you don't understand with no references. Could it be done? Perhaps in time, but not easily, and you would have to begin anew with each mind. We've never made the attempt. Father would never allow something like that. It's a gross violation of ethics."

Ed paused a moment, clearly waiting to see if Bleys had anything more to say. Bleys smiled back and nodded assent, and Ed began, "Now—"

"One more thing," Bleys interjected.

Kane palmed his face. "Now you're just being a dick, man."

Bleys snickered, but the look of disapproval on Ana's face quickly sapped the fun from poking at Ed. "Okay, Ed, I'll stop. What did you want to say?"

Ed waited several seconds, as if expecting Bleys to interrupt him again, then nodded and said, "I owe you an apology."

Bleys blinked a moment at this completely unexpected comment. "Well, I thought we just went through this, right? It was a dirty trick, Ed, but I understand why you—"

"No," Ed cut in. "This is something else."

Bleys studied the AI's face intently, trying to decide if this was revenge for the earlier game of "Don't led Ed talk" or if Ed was getting *angry*. He couldn't help but feel somewhat proud, if that were the case. Bleys's mother had always told him he could piss off the Pope, but getting under an AI's skin was perhaps an even greater accomplishment. Also, Bleys was pretty sure there *wasn't* a pope to piss off anymore, so someone, presumably Ed, would have to stand in his stead for this experiment.

There might be some fun in stoking that ember, seeing if he could push old Ed into a really volcanic rage, but considering the AI was certainly patched into the ship's antipersonnel weapons systems, that might be less fun than Bleys had at first imagined. He settled for a hand twirling, "go ahead" gesture. "Lay it on me, bro."

Ed still hesitated another two seconds before saying, very

quickly, "I was responsible for the dents in Doro's console. Not Kane. Rest assured, they will be repaired along with the other damage." Ed hung his head, like a guilty school child awaiting judgment from a parent.

Kane cradled his head in both hands and heaved a sigh as Ana looked on, bemused. "Ed, my man, I *totally* covered for you!"

"I am aware of that, Kane," Ed told him. "Allowing you to lie to protect me is part of my guilt."

Kane laughed out loud. "But that was the beauty of it! I *didn't* lie!"

Bleys tried to shoot Kane a sour look, but totally ruined it by snorting laughter. "I had worked it out, just so you know, right before the two of you almost got me killed."

The wardroom doors slid open again to admit Morgan, dressed in dungarees. He cast the laughing group a wary eye, then went straight for the vending machines.

"Eat fast, knucklehead," Kane called. "Got an all-hands in just a few."

"There is one more item," Ed announced as Morgan made a rude gesture toward Kane. "Captain Bleys, you asked me to remind you to kick my ass when this was all over. Now seems a good time. I do not fully appreciate the gesture, but I gather it will bring you comfort. I am prepared."

Bleys was spared the decision of how to act as the ship's automated system announced over the primary comms, "Cerberus, arriving," followed by the sound of eight bells.

"I guess I'll take a raincheck," Bleys said with a grin.

Bleys had to admit, Tenebrae was kind of a big deal, even as a holo. The guy wore the mantle of power well. He clenched his fist and held it high in all the right spots, intoned like a preacher at times, almost whispered at others. "We will not sit idle!" The Emperor promised. "We will rise up against this inhuman menace! Our candle may flicker in the wind this moment, but it will not fail! *We* will not fail."

Bleys whispered to Kane, "He's laying that on a little thick for six people, though."

Weyland, sitting on Kane's other side, leaned in and whispered, "This is being broadcast to Cerberus and Elysium, too. Theatrics are authorized for deployment."

It went on for some time, and Bleys bore it in good humor. There were plenty of folks on Cerb that needed this, after all. Everybody could use a distraction from the prospect of impending doom. They might have avoided being melted by the *Danzig* or devoured by the Pestilence, but more mundane deaths by starvation or freezing were still on the table, depending on how things played out.

Nobody was coming to save anybody. They were all on their own, and that alone was enough to be scary as hell.

Tenebrae seemed to be coming to a finale. "Alas, now I must leave you all," he told them. "I have other subjects who need my guidance, but I will leave you in the very best of hands. I have chosen my successor with great care, and I assure you, he will lead us to victory! He is a killer of renown, and with my *Danzig* and your loyalty, he will project strength throughout the galaxy. I swear to you this day, you will crush your enemies and see them driven before you!"

Bleys turned to Weyland with a smile. "That's your cue!" he whispered.

Weyland nodded and was about to rise, when Tenebrae called, "Will my delightful servant Lieutenant John Henry Morgan please present himself before me?"

Ana shouted, "*What?*"

Morgan looked back and forth and pointed to his chest in a "who, me?" gesture.

"Yes, you," Tenebrae assured him. "Approach us."

"Holy shit!" Morgan shouted and leapt to his feet.

Weyland palmed his face, and Kane turned a bewildered gaze to Bleys. "What the fuck is this?" the marine hissed.

Bleys had no answer.

Morgan approached Tenebrae's holo-figure with caution.

"Kneel," Tenebrae commanded.

Morgan, visibly shaken, sank to a knee, still shaking his head. "Why *me?*"

"Because you are young, strong, bold, and indomitable. You embody all the Empire should be," Tenebrae said. "Though perhaps a bit rough around the edges…. We can correct that."

As everyone else on two worlds sat in stunned silence, Josiah Bleys laughed aloud and leapt to his feet and clapped his hands together with gusto.

"All hail Emperor Morgan!" he shouted.

Nolan Garrett is Cerberus. A government assassin, tasked with fixing the galaxy's darkest, ugliest problems.

GET INTERSTELLAR GUNRUNNER NOW!

When their mission fails, his begins.

GET EDGE OF VALOR TODAY!

THE CONTACT DAY BOOK ONE
LUNA MISSILE CRISIS
RHETT C. JAIME
BRUNO CASTLE

Someone betrayed him. He'll probably die finding out who.

GET SUPREMACY'S SHADOW NOW!

For all our Sci-Fi books, visit our website.